# Dangerous Battle of Wills

"If you want to see things no other woman has seen, I can show them to you," Luke breathed. He stopped mere inches away, letting her feel his nearness, not quite touching. "Is that what you want, Joey?"

Her eyes were hooded with deliberate allure. "What do *you* want, Luke?" She stretched her arms behind her, curving about the trunk, open and vulnerable. He gave up any pretense of circumspection.

"You know what I want, Joelle." He pressed against her, feeling the swell of her breasts. Then he set his hands to the rough bark on either side of her.

"I know you want me. I want you, too—but first I need you to help me get what I want."

The words cut through his potent hunger like a dash of water from a mountain stream. A tremor ran through him, a shudder of unexpected fury. For a long moment he wavered between taking her then and there, silencing her cold bargaining with the rage of his lust, and abandoning her to the uncertain mercy of the forest. But he drew into himself, allowing the anger to become cold and hard.

He looked her up and down. He shouldn't care. He wanted her, and it shouldn't matter how he got her. But it did matter—more than he cared to admit. . . .

# Prince of Wolves

Susan Krinard

 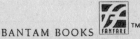

BANTAM BOOKS

New York • Toronto • London • Sydney • Auckland

Prince of Wolves
A Bantam Fanfare Book / September 1994

ISBN 0-553-56775-6

Published simultaneously in the United States and Canada

*Bantam Books are published by Bantam Books, a division of Bantam Doubleday
Dell Publishing Group, Inc. Its trademark, consisting of the words "Bantam Books"
and the portrayal of a rooster, is Registered in U.S. Patent and Trademark Office
and in other countries. Marca Registrada. Bantam Books, 1540 Broadway, New
York, New York 10036.*

PRINTED IN THE UNITED STATES OF AMERICA

RAD  0  9  8  7  6  5  4  3

*T*O JENNARA WENK
AND ROSEMARY EDGHILL,
WHO GOT ME STARTED
AND
TO SERGE,
MY REAL-LIFE
FRENCH-CANADIAN HERO.

# Chapter 1

There was a stranger in town.

His keen sight picked her out from his vantage atop one of the rocky cliffs that formed sentinels on either side of the narrow two-lane highway that led into town. From here he could see the main street with its clumps of buildings, a warren of human habitation surrounded by wilderness. There were people moving about as there always were, even in this isolated place—but she stood out. She was different. An outsider. The townsfolk of Lovell, British Columbia, might not care for strangers, but he occasionally had use for them. At least the women . . .

His long suntanned fingers stroked slowly through the dense fur of the wolf beside him. It had been a long time since he'd enjoyed the company of a woman, and the desires that had awakened with the coming of spring had not been satisfied. There were women in town who would share his bed, who would be more than willing to overlook his reputation. But he had long ago lost any appetite for the entanglements that came with local relationships. The few times he'd tried it hadn't been worth the trouble.

And he'd been alone so long. . . .

The wolf under his stroking hand shifted and whined softly. With a murmured apology, he released his grip on the heavy mane behind the animal's neck. He didn't care that the townsfolk regarded him with suspicion; they were not his kind. But their distrust limited his choices. When winter drifted into spring and the need came on him, there was only one way to meet it. Hikers and adventurers and tourists out to see their last chunk of real wilderness came year by year to Lovell's single lodge, and nearly always there were women among them willing to share his cabin and bed. But this year had been a lean one. Until yesterday.

And she was lovely. It hadn't been difficult to find her desirable.

It had been easy to observe her, to mark her out from the rest. She shone among the townsfolk, a flame among ashes, luring his senses with an undeniable attraction. She wasn't the most beautiful woman he'd seen, but there was a vitality about her that burned as brightly as the sun on her hair.

He smiled slowly, a slight upcurve of lips that seldom resorted to the expression. Yes, she would do very well.

The wolf interrupted his reverie with an impatient thrust of its muzzle under his hand. Intelligent eyes, pale and rimmed in black, met his questioningly. He drew his hand over the broad forehead and scratched between the triangular ears. The wolf closed its eyes and stretched with a yawn that revealed rows of sharp teeth. Then it straightened, yipped once, and turned in a tight circle.

The impatient gesture drew a rough chuckle from the man. "Yes, my friend. Don't let me keep you from important business." The wolf waved its tail once in answer and sat on its haunches, regarding him. "I won't be joining you now. I've got other game today." He turned again to gaze at the town, though the woman had long since disappeared. "I haven't done this kind of hunting in some time—and I think this one might prove to be a challenge. I'll have to be careful to stay downwind until I've caught her."

Anticipation tightened his muscles, and the wolf yipped again. "Go. I'll find you later. We'll have to plan this carefully—and keep an eye on her in the meantime." He pushed gently at the wolf, and the beast whirled and vanished like a gray phantom.

The sun rose higher, limning the serrated hillsides to the east with radiant yellow light against deep blue-green. The mountains beyond caught the illumination with the brilliance of a diamond. He breathed in the crisp air, savoring the myriad scents of a new day. Before it ended, he planned to know more about the stranger—and begin his hunt.

Joelle Randall didn't think she'd ever seen anything so beautiful.

The long slope, carpeted in wildflowers, released a heady perfume on the cool air of late summer. Conifers bordered the meadow like the watchful sentries of a vast army, marching up the slopes of surrounding mountains—sharp peaks streaked with the white of perpetual ice. Just out of sight were lakes of perfect crystal blue, fed by streams that cut their way over jumbled rocks and through forests almost as pristine as the day they were created.

Joey drew in a deep breath and closed her eyes. It was hard to believe so much beauty could conceal, somewhere among its secret corners, the tragedy that had left her alone in the world. Somewhere in these mountains and valleys lay the key to freeing her heart of its long-held burden.

Freedom. Joey took another deep breath of scented air. That was all she had left, the hope of resolving the old sorrow at last. It could never be finished—not until she found the place where her parents had died.

Even now, that word was hard to acknowledge. They'd left her, without a good-bye, without giving her a chance to tell them how much she loved them. She'd only been a kid then: sixteen, still at that vulnerable age, so close to her parents when they'd left on their final journey.

If it hadn't been for a freak storm, the kind of accident even the most experienced pilot couldn't always avoid—Joey clenched her fists, feeling the sudden sharp twist of painful memory. Her father had been careful, she knew that; he'd been flying for years, and the small plane had been meticulously kept up. Not his fault that they'd gone down in these mountains they'd loved, never to be found. . . .

Opening her eyes, Joey pushed back the sadness and focused on the resolve that had kept her going during the past months.

This was the turning point, the time that she would take back her life at last. She would find the place where they had been lost, confront that crippling sorrow, let the clear mountain winds carry her good-byes over the wilderness. There was nothing, now, to hold her back.

She looked down at the half-finished sketch in her lap. She knew she'd made the right decision to leave her architect's job in San Francisco, no matter how comfortable and lucrative. There'd been too much waiting, too much wasting of her life in a vain effort to find the security her parents' death had taken from her.

Even Richard—what she'd had with Richard had been a desperate grasp at replacing something of what had been lost, restoring some meaning to her life. She'd still been young, vulnerable, so full of need; he'd seemed strong, controlled, everything she thought she'd wanted then. But she'd grown up, found that security could be an illusion, control a trap. And all the empty places in her heart had not been filled. . . .

She tossed her head angrily. That was behind her, and well left behind. There could be no more dull security to cover the hurt. No, she wouldn't think of Richard. No regrets. From now on she'd be in control of her own life.

Absently she set down her sketchpad and caressed one of the vivid blossoms at her feet. It was a deep pink shooting star, one of many wildflowers that turned the mountain hillsides into brilliant canvases from late spring through early autumn. She'd had ample time to study just about every kind of wildflower from the very first blooms after the snowmelt; but now the summer was fading, and all the beauty of Nature couldn't change that unalterable fact.

When she'd come to these mountains in the spring, she'd been confident of finding what she sought before midsummer. But after searching several of the most likely areas in this stretch of the Rockies, she faced the very real possibility of failure. This was her last hope—this town, this valley, and the wild stretches of surrounding mountains. If they weren't here . . . She bit her lip, hard.

She had to find them. They had to be here. Time was running out. Here in the north, the time of blue skies and green growing things—and passable trails—was all too brief. City-bred she might be, but she understood that once the first snows fell, her quest would be over for the year. That was simply a thought she could not bear.

In an effort to clear her head, Joey focused on her breathing and steadied it until her pulse had slowed again. No smog here—no fumes, no constant racket of cars and human clamor. Here, away from the town, it was easy to pretend you were the last person on earth. Joey grimaced to herself. She might be savoring that feeling if it hadn't been for the constant worries that hung over her. She'd been waiting for her local guide now—one she'd hired in the last town—for over a week. If he didn't show up soon . . .

Her brooding thoughts were interrupted by a pale flash of movement among the trees at the foot of the slope below. It wasn't a deer—that much she was sure of—but it wasn't something immediately recognizable to her unpracticed eye. She reached down to the binoculars at her belt. Fixing the location of the elusive shape in her mind, Joey unhooked them and focused on the blue-green blur of trees that marked the lower boundary of the meadow.

Close up, the details leaped to life in her vision: individual Douglas fir, spruce, and pine with a scattered understory of shrubs and brush. She almost passed over the pale shape the first time she caught it in her sights, hurriedly readjusting until she had it in focus again. Her breath tangled in her throat.

A wolf—a great gray timber wolf—stood absolutely still in the half-concealment of a larchberry bush. Joey's hands tightened on the binoculars to steady them. Her first wolf. All this time in the mountains and she'd never seen one, though she'd heard them in the summer nights, shivering in spite of herself at their eerie chorus. She knew they were elusive, uncommon even in protected areas. But to see one here, alone, in broad daylight . . .

Joey studied the wolf intently. It was huge—even from this distance, she could tell that—and its coat was lush and heavy, pale on the belly and legs, shot with silver and gray and black across the back and masking the face. The triangular ears were alert, the bushy tail slightly raised. It seemed to be watching, or waiting. For prey, perhaps? Joey moved the binoculars to get a clearer look at the pale, tilted eyes. She nearly dropped them in astonishment. The wolf seemed to be staring straight at her.

Fascinated, Joey stared back. She knew it was impossible that the wolf could be looking directly at her through the binocular lenses, but the sensation persisted, all logic to the contrary. Perhaps it simply sensed her presence with the uncanny ability wild animals have. That seemed reasonable, but Joey wasn't feeling very reasonable at the moment. Those eyes—pale and slanted and oddly intelligent—had a very strange effect. She almost got the feeling that the wolf not only saw her but was studying her in turn. The longer she looked, the stronger the peculiar feeling grew. Those eyes . . .

It took a long moment for Joey to realize she had been lost in that wild stare for a frightening length of time. Unnerved, she dropped the binoculars. She blinked as her eyes adjusted, and without intending to, she found herself searching the forest edge again for the pale shape of the wolf. For an instant she caught sight of it, its head still raised as if to watch her. And then it moved, disappearing silently between one blink and the next.

Joey bit her lip and hooked the binoculars back to her belt. She realized her back and arms were taut with tension. True, it was the first time she'd ever seen a wild wolf, but that was no reason to get quite so worked up. She knew healthy wolves weren't dangerous to people, and that wolf had certainly kept its distance.

But she couldn't quite shake the weird intensity of the wolf's gaze, or the bizarre way she'd almost gotten lost in it. There was something in this mountain air and ancient wilderness that made a person feel . . . not quite earthbound. But such flights of fancy were useless to her and could only distract her from her purpose.

Joey flipped her braid over one shoulder with an irritated toss of her head. She'd just have to make doubly sure from now on that she didn't let this countryside hypnotize her into complacency—or turn on her with the treachery it had shown her parents.

Sighing deeply, Joey lay back and stretched out into the bed of grass and flowers, allowing the soft scent of crushed blossoms to soothe her. She concentrated on the distant chatter of birds from the trees at the meadow's edge, the soft soughing of a breeze through the fir and spruce, drifts of air idly teasing the pale hair that had escaped her braid. She smiled experimentally into the sun, eyes squeezed shut, and decided to live for the moment—at least for a few minutes.

Joey came to full, sudden wakefulness with an odd, distinctly unflowerlike odor assaulting her nose. In the moment it took her to realize she'd relaxed enough to fall asleep in the grass, she knew that something was different. As she rolled over, her body tingled with a primitive urge to run and hide. She froze instead. It was then that she saw the wolf.

Her fingers dug deeply into soft earth as she stared at the animal. It was the same wolf—the very same wolf, but this time considerably closer and much, much larger. It sat on its haunches no more than a few yards away, and its gaze was locked on hers. She could see every detail in the cool depth of its pale eyes, the dark round pupils, the black rims, and the masklike markings of its facial fur.

For a moment she distanced herself from fear by studying the wolf dispassionately, as if it were simply one of her architectural designs, a living construct to be classified and assigned its proper place. The coat was thick and heavy and woven of many subtle shades, ranging from nearly white to nearly black in the fur across the broad shoulders and back. The bushy tail rested half-curled behind the haunches, and the paws—each toe tipped with a thick black claw—were huge. The neat ears were cocked forward, and there was no doubt that the animal's attention was most definitely focused on her. She could hear the soft puff of its breath as it regarded her, glimpsed menacing white teeth and curled pink tongue as it panted. But it was the eyes—those strangely intense eyes—that caught and held her just as they had before. This time she didn't have the protection of binoculars and distance.

It seemed to be an impasse. Joey bit her lip and held herself very still. She was not quite prepared to test the theory that normal wild wolves would not attack human beings. Even if this one did seem rather friendly and not particularly threatening. She had the sudden, absurd desire to hold out her hand and say "Nice doggy," an image that immediately provoked a gasp of stifled laughter. She choked on it as the wolf stood up on all fours and moved a step closer. Its gaze never wavered.

Joey knew the wisest course would be to stay in place until the wolf got bored and went about its business; if it hadn't been for the cooling air and darkening sky, she would have been resigned to an indefinite wait. But the sun was setting—and if this wolf had friends likely to join it after dark, she wasn't particularly keen on being here to meet them.

There didn't seem to be much point in prolonging the confrontation. Joey drew in a deep breath, gathered her courage, and decided to risk it. "Look, wolf," she murmured as it regarded her in grave silence, "I don't know why you're here or why you're so interested in me—but it's getting late, and I really have to be going."

The sheer absurdity of the situation made her tremble and choke back another inappropriate giggle as the wolf tilted its head to one side. She moved experimentally, gathering herself to rise. The wolf went very still.

And then, almost as if it understood, the wolf looked off in the direction of the town. It was the first time it had broken eye contact, and Joey felt a profound sense of relief to be free of that unwavering stare. She rose cautiously to her knees. The relief was short-lived, for within a moment the wolf looked back and moved several steps closer, putting it within easy leaping distance. Joey braced herself.

But the wolf didn't leap or make any threatening move. Instead, it crept forward and pushed its nose toward her hand—almost trembling—and touched the backs of her fingers ever so gently. The contact was surprisingly warm, not cold and wet as she'd expected. She didn't have time to flinch or react in any way, for almost immediately the wolf retreated, barked once, trotted a few yards in the direction of the town, and looked back at her. Stunned by the oddly intelligent behavior, Joey watched as the wolf repeated its action with something unmistakably like impatience.

Joey shook her head, forcing her muscles to relax one by one. This had to be one of the strangest experiences of her life—but she was as sure as she was ever likely to be that the wolf would not attack. Eyes fixed on the animal, she got slowly to her feet.

With a soft yip that sounded strangely like approval, the wolf waved its plumed tail and opened its mouth in a toothy grin. As she began to move forward, the wolf kept its distance, always ahead, always turning to look back at her in encouragement. At last Joey gave up trying to figure it out and set off with a determination aided by her awareness of the fading sky. If she were lucky, she'd make it back to town by dark. Of course, she might be able to rely on the wolf for protection. . . . Her half-hysterical giggle turned into a gasp as she caught her foot on a rock hidden in the thick grass. Absurd amusement fled, and her mouth set in a grim line.

Perhaps she'd been too casual, too certain of her own competence. This was not her world, and it might send her warnings—but it would never defeat her or scare her away. She would win. She'd set a goal, and she always did what she set out to do.

She almost didn't notice when the wolf disappeared, just short of the light cast by the windows of Lovell's first outlying cabins.

The warm wooden paneling of the O'Briens' guest lodge was a welcoming sight as Joey pushed open the heavy door and entered the common room. It was deserted, but the rich smells of recent cooking hung in the air, and Joey felt her stomach rumble in response. She'd probably just missed dinner, but even after so short a time she knew Mrs. O'Brien well enough to expect that a sizable portion had been set aside for her return.

The O'Briens had been attentive hosts during the past week of her stay in Lovell; guests were sparse this late in the summer, and they'd taken a great deal of trouble to make her feel welcome. In turn Joey had spent the quiet evening hours regaling them with tales of city life, much to their amusement and fascination. Lovell, B.C., was a very long way from San Francisco, California.

As Joey shut the door behind her, Mrs. O'Brien swept into the room, her arms full of clean linen. Her faded gray eyes peered over the stack as she caught sight of Joey and hurried to put the neatly folded cloth on the nearest table.

"There you are!" she exclaimed. "We were wondering what happened to you."

Joey smiled and made her way across the room to a worn easy chair, settling into it with a sigh. It felt like heaven.

She looked up at Mrs. O'Brien. "Nothing too exciting by local standards, I suppose," she said, deliberately casual. "I was out on the hillside, and I managed to fall asleep. When I woke up, I had company." Her smile turned to a wry grimace. "I know I should have been a lot more careful, but I never thought a wild wolf would come right up to me and—"

"A wolf?" Mrs. O'Brien's friendly voice went strange, her expression drawing tight and closed.

"Yes," Joey affirmed, watching the older woman's face in puzzlement. "A lone wolf, a big gray one—it just sat there and stared at me. It didn't try to attack, or threaten me in any way. After a while I tried moving, and the wolf actually seemed to . . ." She broke off, embarrassed. Mrs. O'Brien's reaction was very odd, and Joey felt rather foolish. "I know it sounds pretty ridiculous, but I would almost swear the wolf was trying to lead me back to town."

Mrs. O'Brien shook her head. "That wolf," she muttered. "That damned wolf . . ." For a moment she seemed lost in her own troubled thoughts, and then she pursed her lips and turned back to Joey with a frown. "You want my advice, Joey? You watch out for those wolves. Can't trust 'em." Still muttering and shaking her head, the older woman retrieved her linens and bustled out of the room. "I'll go heat up your dinner. Those damned wolves . . ."

Staring after her, Joey shrugged and leaned back into the chair. Mrs. O'Brien clearly didn't like wolves, but this one hadn't done Joey any harm. In any case, she had more important things on her mind at the moment. A hot meal and a hot bath could do wonders at the end of a long and somewhat unsettling day; there were still a few of the benefits of civilization to be had here in the wilds of the north, and for that she was profoundly grateful.

But, she reminded herself, she'd learned an important lesson today. Face-to-face with a powerful timber wolf, she'd managed to keep her head. If nothing else, it proved she could do what she'd set out to do—she'd just have to be a little more careful from now on. If the wilderness had seduced her into forgetting her natural caution, she'd be sure not to let it happen again. Things were going to go her way. With the proper planning life was a lot less likely to deal nasty and unexpected blows. This had just been a reminder.

Mrs. O'Brien broke into her reverie with the concrete distraction of a hot home-cooked dinner. Joey started into the generous meal with enthusiasm. She was just finishing the last bit of bread and home-made jam when the local doctor, Allan Collier, emerged from the hallway.

"As I said, Martha, don't worry about Harry. Just give him a couple more days in bed, and he'll be good as new."

Joey politely turned her attention to the business of stacking her plates as the doctor spent several minutes reassuring Mrs. O'Brien that her husband's condition was not serious. She dropped off her dishes in the kitchen, and when she returned, Collier was alone in the common room, consulting a small appointment book with a pencil clenched in his teeth.

The doctor was a man of middle years, a little younger than Mrs. O'Brien, with a face still bearing the traces of a handsome youth. His eyes were generously marked with laugh lines, but there was a sadness about him that Joey had seen from the first, the day she'd been introduced to him by the O'Briens. Dr. Collier was the town's only doctor and one of the few serving the surrounding region, and so was a valued local figure; Joey had also seen immediately why he was also well-liked. In many ways he reminded her of her own father.

"Hello, Doctor," she said, leaning against the serving counter that ran between the dining area and the kitchen. Collier blinked, the pencil dropping from his mouth. He caught it in midfall and smiled at her warmly.

"Good evening, Miss Randall. Nice to see you again." Closing the notebook with a snap, he tucked it into the black bag resting on the counter. "How are your plans progressing?"

"A little slower than I'd like," Joey admitted. Collier cocked his head with an inquiring look that invited trust; he gestured her over to a cluster of chairs near the fireplace.

"I'm sorry to hear that," he murmured as they settled into a pair of mismatched armchairs. His gentle fingers stroked the worn leather of the doctor's bag in his lap. "Martha tells me you had a little encounter with a wolf today." He raised his arched brows and looked her over significantly. "Obviously it wasn't a fatal one, for all of Martha's dire pronouncements."

His conspiratorial smile seemed to release the last of Joey's remaining tension; she chuckled in spite of herself. "I guess I was a little careless," she admitted. "I always thought that wild animals were shy."

"Most of them are," Collier said. There was an odd, distant note to his voice. "Though there are times . . ." He fell silent, his gaze turning inward, and when it became clear he was drifting in his own thoughts, Joey leaned forward to interrupt.

"Then that wasn't normal behavior, was it?" she asked softly. Collier's attention came back to her with a snap. "The way the wolf seemed to want me to come back to town—brought me almost all the way to the lodge."

He gazed at her for a long moment. There was sudden tautness in the long fingers that closed about the handles of his black bag. "It's hard to predict the ways of Nature, even when you've lived with it all your life," he answered at last. Joey sensed evasion, though she could not have explained the feeling. Like Mrs. O'Brien's peculiar reaction . . .

"I was wondering if anyone else here in town had observed that kind of behavior," she remarked, watching his face. "Could it have been one of those semidomesticated wolves? Someone's pet?"

Collier's laugh almost startled her, breaking the odd moment of tension. "I seriously doubt that, Miss Randall. There are places where wolves are raised with people, and I've heard that wolf dogs are popular pets down South. But here—no, I very much fear that was a wild wolf you ran into, and the only explanation I can offer is that all wild animals are somewhat unpredictable."

In spite of the doctor's casual words, Joey knew he was holding something back. "What I don't understand, Doctor, is why that wolf got so close to me, as if it weren't afraid of humans at all. And I got the distinct impression that Mrs. O'Brien was upset when I mentioned it. Has there been some kind of trouble with wolves here before?"

Dr. Collier shifted in his chair, a restlessness he masked as a stretch. "There are quite a number of people in this part of the country who don't much care for wolves," he explained, looking away at the racks of antlers displayed above the hearth. "At one time they were hunted almost to extinction, and they still have a bad reputation with some folk. Old habits die hard." He sighed. "They're protected in many areas now, but it's still quite possible to find places where they are hunted down by human sportsmen."

His gray brows drew together as he spoke, the pleasant aspect of his expression slipping subtly into something darker. It was anger—a slow, hidden anger as inexplicable as Mrs. O'Brien's antipathy. "It's human nature for people to want to master, or destroy, what they can't control or understand."

For a beat the anger lay revealed in his face, and then the good-natured mask replaced it again. "In any case," he said briskly, "that probably accounts for Mrs. O'Brien's reaction. You'll find similar opinions in town. But in answer to your earlier question—no, there hasn't been any trouble for some time. Not with wolves." Gathering his long legs under him, Collier rose to his feet. "My advice is to stay alert and keep your eyes open whenever you're out in the wild."

Joey managed a distracted smile, still considering the doctor's vague explanations. "Don't worry, Dr. Collier. I won't let it happen again. It was definitely a learning experience—and I'm a pretty fast learner."

"I've no doubt of that," he murmured. Abruptly he looked directly into her eyes, searching them intently. "In many ways this is a world very different from what you're used to. If I can be of any help, Miss Randall—"

"Joey. Call me Joey," she interjected, extending her hand.

He took it in a strong, gentle grip. "Only if you'll call me Allan. And if I can ever be of assistance, Joey, please let me know." He held the clasp a moment longer and then let her go, gathered up his bag, and headed for the door. Pausing on the threshold, he gave her a nod and a smile before disappearing into the night.

Joey sighed. Her bones and muscles ached from the day's hiking; she was more than ready for that long hot bath. The lodge was silent now, and there was nothing left but to set aside her worries for one more day. Working the kinks out of her legs, Joey walked across the empty room and hoped for a peaceful span of untroubled sleep.

That night she dreamed of wolves.

When Joey came down to breakfast the next morning, it was with the sense that things were about to change.

She greeted Mrs. O'Brien with a quick stop by the kitchen and gazed around the small dining room. The lodge's two other guests were already getting up from their meal, and Joey was content to have the place to herself. As she settled down at a table, Mrs. O'Brien brought out a steaming mug of coffee and tipped her bifocals to regard Joey with raised brows.

"Looks like you're none the worse for wear. That's good." She bustled among the tables to clear the other places and added on her way out, "I hope flapjacks suit you this morning. You're the last one down." Joey choked on a mouthful of coffee in an attempt to answer, but the older woman had already disappeared into the kitchen.

The smell of pancakes and real maple syrup preceded her as she returned to set a full loaded plate in front of her guest. As Joey began to eat, Mrs. O'Brien fished in the wide pocket of her apron and drew out a slightly crumpled envelope.

"I forgot to give you this last night. Came for you in yesterday's mail." She set the envelope down on the table and swept out of the room again.

Chewing hastily and wiping her fingers, Joey studied the envelope eagerly. There was no return address. That was strange in itself, but as she tore it open and scanned the short, handwritten lines, its significance became all too clear. "Damn!" She crumpled the note into a tight ball and tossed it across the table. It was entirely too much. The pancake she'd consumed lay like a lead weight in her stomach.

For a moment she allowed herself to experience the full brunt of anger and despair. She dropped her head in her hands, uncaring that the end of her braid was close to trailing in sticky syrup.

She should have known better—better than to trust that so-called "guide" in East Fork. Some well-meaning soul had taken pity on her and anonymously written to let her know that her hired mountaineer had vanished two weeks ago with all his belongings, heading east. Away from Joey. With the money she'd already paid him to secure his services. And the anonymous note made clear that he'd left no forwarding address that a foolish city girl might use to track him.

Joey struggled to control her rage, pushing it back under the surface bit by bit until she was able to raise her head and present a placid face to the empty room. The angry tears never spilled from her eyes. She'd learned long ago to rein in her emotions, lest they destroy what peace of mind she'd been able to make for herself over the years.

She'd always prided herself on her practicality. Facts were facts. She had no guide, and she was going to have to have one to reach her goal. Time was running out. That meant she'd have to secure a replacement—a local replacement—and quickly. Lovell wasn't a big town, but surely she could find someone able to guide her into the nearby mountains, someone willing to take a little outsider money and indulge her eccentric desire.

After this last experience she'd have to be careful; but she couldn't afford to be overly selective, either. Nothing had really changed. She'd lost a little money, but that could be dealt with. There was only one important goal now, and that was to find her guide.

Night came altogether too quickly here in the north, Joey reflected grimly. Another day wasted, and no concrete leads on a replacement for her runaway mountaineer. She'd met with sympathy, indifference, and even ridicule among the townsfolk she'd questioned, but not a shred of real success. Someone knew somebody's cousin who might be willing to help—but that somebody was out of town for two weeks. Old Jack used to do that kind of thing, but he'd retired three years ago.

Joey didn't like butting up against a brick wall. Not when she was so damned close . . .

Well, it was too late to do anything more. She stood in Lovell's main street, hugging herself against the evening coolness. With the shorter days came colder nights, and the chill nipped at Joey through her light jacket. Townsfolk passed by silently, ignoring her. Across the road the neon lights of Red's Tavern came on, promising warmth and some measure of companionship. Joey knew she didn't want to spend another night alone poring over her maps, berating herself for past mistakes, or listening to Mrs. O'Brien's well-meant lectures. She needed more stimulating company tonight.

A blast of warm air swept over her as she entered the smoky room, carrying with it the unmistakable smell of alcohol and humanity. Joey made her way between the close-packed tables and over to the pock-marked wooden bar, where Maggie was busy mixing drinks for a boisterous group of drinkers in the corner. The blare of a sports program rose above laughter and loud conversation.

Joey leaned on the bar, loosening her jacket and scooting onto an empty stool. The redheaded barkeep looked up and grinned, tossing a mass of curly hair out of her eyes.

"Well, how are you, Joey? Glad you could drop by. Let me get this bunch taken care of, and I'll be right back."

With a graceful pivot Maggie pushed away from the bar balancing a fully laden tray of beer and liquor, and Joey watched her progress across the room, punctuated by well-intentioned ribaldry and the occasional rude remark. Maggie bore it all with far better grace than Joey could imagine herself doing. The rough comments of the largely male clientele did not appeal to her in the slightest.

Maggie dipped back behind the bar and pulled out

a chilled bottle of white wine, pouring a glass for Joey with a smooth, practiced motion. Her playful expression acknowledged Joey's last censorious glance at the racket behind them. "Their bark is a lot worse than their bite." The redhead shrugged, pulling her T-shirt tight against her bosom. "I'm used to it."

Joey found it impossible to maintain her grim mood in the face of Maggie's perpetual good cheer, and she grinned back. The wine was cool and soothing, even if it wasn't exactly top grade.

"You see, I made sure I had some of that wine for you. I know you're not the beer type!" Maggie winked and turned back to acknowledge the shouted request of another patron.

Joey sipped at her wine, drawing patterns through the condensation on the scratched wood surface of the bar with her finger. She looked up again as a stream of wine gurgled into her glass, replacing what she'd already drunk.

"You look like you need it tonight," Maggie explained. She leaned over comfortably and gave her full attention to Joey. "I can tell it hasn't been a great day. Want to talk about it?" The warmth of her flaming hair and the matching warmth of her eyes and voice invited complete trust, and Joey felt some of the tension slide out of her.

She found herself telling Maggie everything—about the wolf, the note she'd received about her errant guide, and her fruitless search for a replacement. Maggie listened with real sympathy, breaking her attention only to deliver an occasional beer to a rowdy customer. The wine and good company were conspiring to make Joey feel considerably better.

"So now I'm really stuck, Maggie. I haven't got that much time left." She sighed heavily and drained the last of the wine in her glass. "Any suggestions? I'm feeling a little desperate."

Maggie's cheerful face lengthened. "I can see you are. And you don't wear your heart on your sleeve the way I do, either." She chewed her full lower lip and studied her bright red nails. "Don't give up yet. Let me ask around a little—and you keep trying, too. Something may turn up. And you've still got a little time left." She hesitated, meeting Joey's eyes earnestly. "Did you ever consider maybe waiting until next year? You'd have plenty of time to prepare that way, and . . ."

"No." Joey kept her voice level, but her fist clenched on the countertop. "I can't. I've waited too long." With an effort she relaxed her hand. "I appreciate what you're saying, Maggie. But I've got to do it this way. If you can give me any help at all, I'll owe you."

Maggie reached across the bar and touched Joey's hand lightly. "I'll do what I can, I promise." A silence fell between them; Joey let the mild sedative of the wine calm her. Control. If she could just keep things under control . . .

She was too lost in her own musings to immediately notice the sudden hush that fell over the bar. The absence of human chatter caught her attention slowly, and she blinked as she looked around. The noisy clumps of men were still at their tables, but they seemed almost frozen in place. Only the television, nearly drowned out before, broke the quiet.

Maggie, too, was still, gazing fixedly in the direction of the door. Joey swung around, noting that every other face was turned the same way. There was a man standing just inside the doorway, as still as all the others, a silhouette in the dim light. It took Joey a moment to realize that he was the focus of this strange and vivid tableau.

Even as the thought registered, someone coughed. It broke the hush like the snap of a twig in a silent forest. The room suddenly swelled again with noise, a relieved blast of sound as things returned to normal. Joey shook her head and stared as the new arrival moved across to the single pay phone in the alcove near the entryway, turning his back to the room. She could just make out the man's height, a certain lean grace in his movements, a head of darkish hair; but nothing about him indicated a reason for the peculiar reaction his entrance had provoked. The stranger picked up the receiver and began dialing, seemingly as oblivious to her scrutiny as to what had just occurred. She turned back to Maggie and met the woman's distracted gaze.

"What was that all about?" she asked. Maggie was slow to answer, but the moment of gravity was short-lived, and the barkeep smiled again and shook her head.

"Sorry about that. Must have seemed pretty strange, I guess. But he tends to have that effect on people around here."

Joey leaned forward on her elbow, avoiding a wet puddle on the counter. "Who's 'he'?" she demanded, casting a quick glance over her shoulder.

Setting down the mug she'd been polishing, Maggie assumed an indifference Joey was certain she didn't feel. "His name is Luke Gévaudan. He lives some way out of town—up the slope of the valley. Owns a pretty big tract of land to the east."

Joey slewed the stool around to better watch the man, chin cupped in her hand. "I know you've said people here don't much care for outsiders," she remarked, "but you have to admit that was a pretty extreme reaction." She strained to hear the man's voice over the din but could make nothing out. He kept his back turned to her. "Gévaudan, you said. Isn't that a French name?"

"French-Canadian," Maggie corrected. "There are a few people living farther out on the slopes and in some of the more isolated valleys. Sometimes they'll come into town, though not so much over the past few years."

"So he's one of these . . . French-Canadians? Is that why the people here don't like him?" She studied Maggie over her shoulder.

"It's not like that," Maggie sighed. "It's hard to explain to someone from outside—I mean, he's strange. People don't trust him, that's all. And as a rule he doesn't make much of an attempt to change that. He keeps to himself."

Unexpectedly intrigued, Joey divided her attention between the object of her curiosity and the redhead. "Don't kid me, Maggie. He may be strange and he may be standoffish, but you can't tell me that wasn't more than just mild distrust a minute ago."

She pulled absently on her braid where it fell over her shoulder, examining what little she could see of Gévaudan. There was nothing particularly unusual about his appearance that she could see from here. He was tall and big and dressed in jeans and a green plaid shirt, like any number of the other men in town. She couldn't get a clear look at his face.

Maggie leaned against the bar and sagged there as if in defeat. "I said it's complicated. I didn't grow up here, so I don't know the whole story, but there are things about the guy that bother people. I hear he was a strange kid. And there's the matter of his lands—he owns a lot of prime timber up there that would make work for local folks. So I've been told." She hesitated. "He's also got a bit of a reputation as a—well, a lady-killer, I guess you could say." She grinned and tossed her red curls. "I'm not sure that's the right word. Let's put it this way—he's been known to attract the ladies, and it's caused a bit of a ruckus now and then."

"Interesting," Joey mused. "If he's so popular with the local women, I can see why the men around here wouldn't be overly amused." She couldn't help but consider the local men she'd met; some of them had been pleasant enough, but none had come close to attracting her interest. Not that that would have been likely in any case, after Richard . . .

"It's not just local women," Maggie broke in, falling naturally into her usual habit of cozy gossip. "Though there were a couple of incidents—before my time, you understand. But I know there've been a few outsiders who've, shall we say, taken up with him." She gave an insinuating leer. "They all left, every one of them, after a few months. And none of them ever talked."

Wondering when she'd get a clear look at his face, Joey cocked an eye at her friend. "I guess that could make for some resentment. He may be mysterious, but he doesn't sound like a very nice guy to me."

"There you go," Maggie said, pushing herself off the bar. "Consider yourself warned." She winked suggestively. "The way you're staring at him, I'd say you need the warning."

At Joey's start of protest, Maggie sashayed away to serve her customers. Joey was left to muse on what she'd been told. Not that it really mattered, in any case. She wasn't interested in men. There were times when she wondered if she ever would be again. But that just wasn't an issue now. She had far more important things on her mind. . . .

Her thoughts broke off abruptly as the man called Gévaudan turned. There was the briefest hush again, almost imperceptible; if Joey hadn't been so focused on him and what had happened, she might never have noticed. For the first time she could see him clearly as he stepped into the light.

The first impression was of power. It was as if she could see some kind of aura around the man—too strong a feeling to dismiss, as much as it went against the grain. Within a moment Joey had an instinctive grasp of why this Luke Gévaudan had such a peculiar effect on the townspeople. He seemed to be having a similar effect on her.

Her eyes slid up his lithe form, from the common-place boots and over the snug, faded jeans that molded long, muscular legs. She skipped quickly over his midtorso and took in the expanse of chest and broad shoulders, enhanced rather than hidden by the deep green plaid of his shirt. But it was when she reached his face that the full force of that first impression hit her.

He couldn't have been called handsome—not in that yuppified modern style represented by the clean-cut models in the ads back home. There was a roughness about him, but not quite the same unpolished coarse-ness that typified many of the local men. Instead, there was a difference—a uniqueness—that she couldn't quite compare to anyone she'd seen before.

Her unwillingly fascinated gaze traveled over the strong, sharply cut lines of his jaw, along lips that held a hint of reserved mobility in their stillness. His nose was straight and even, the cheekbones high and hard, hollowed underneath with shadow. The hair that fell in tousled shocks over his forehead was mainly dark but liberally shot with gray, especially at the temples. The age this might have suggested was visible nowhere in his face or body, though his bearing announced experi-ence. His stance was lightly poised, alert, almost coiled like some wary creature from the wilds.

But it wasn't until she reached his eyes that it all co-alesced into comprehension. They glowed. She shook her head, not sure what she was seeing. It wasn't a lit-eral glow, she reminded herself with a last grasp at logic, but those eyes shone with their own inner light. They burned—they burned on hers. Her breath caught in her throat. He was staring at her, and for the first time she realized he was returning her examination.

She met his gaze unflinchingly for a long moment. His eyes were pale—and though in the dim light she could not make out the color, she could sense the warm light of amber in their depths. Striking, unusual eyes.

Eyes that burned. Eyes that seemed never to blink but held hers in an unnerving, viselike grip. Eyes that seemed hauntingly familiar . . .

Joey realized she was shaking when she finally looked away. Her hands were clasped together in her lap, straining against each other with an internal struggle she was suddenly conscious of. Even now she could feel his gaze on her, intense and unwavering, but she resisted the urge to look up and meet it again. The loss of control she'd felt in those brief, endless moments of contact had been as unexpected and frightening as it was inexplicable. She wasn't eager to repeat the experience. But the small, stubborn core of her that demanded control over herself and her surroundings pricked at her without mercy. With a soft curse on an indrawn breath, Joey looked up.

He was gone.

The shock of it had little time to register. "You there, Joey? Anyone home?" Maggie's voice drew her attention reluctantly away from the place Gévaudan had been standing only seconds before. "I thought for a moment you might be having an out-of-body experience or something." The redhead lifted the half-empty wine bottle in invitation, but Joey shook her head with a sigh.

"Something like that, I guess. I'm just tired. I should probably turn in so I'll be fresh to start over in the morning."

She forced her body to move in accordance with her words, but she couldn't shake the disorientation the strange encounter with Gévaudan—or more precisely, with his eyes—had left her with. She slipped off the stool and immediately lost her balance; only a quick clutch at the edge of the bar saved her from a fall.

Maggie's voice floated down. "You all right? Are you going to need some help getting home?"

The concern in the redhead's voice was a welcome and familiar comfort Joey grasped at as she righted herself. "No, I'll be okay." She grinned wanly at Maggie as she searched her pocket for change. "Thanks for everything."

Maggie waved away the neatly folded bills Joey retrieved from her wallet with an answering grin. "It's on the house. You be damned careful heading home now, okay?" Joey nodded, starting across the room as Maggie's words chased after her. "Don't forget to watch out for strange men, you hear?"

For once Joey fully resolved to follow well-meant advice.

# Chapter Two

Luke stalked away from the tavern in a distinctly satisfied mood. It had been a very pleasant surprise to see just how receptive she'd been to his challenge. That had been an added bonus to the confirmation of his earlier observations; she was an attractive woman. The subtle curves of her body had not been disguised by the loose-fitting jeans and overlarge shirt she'd been wearing. Her long, pale hair was worn in a severe and practical braid, but it was not difficult to imagine it loose about her shoulders. Her face was stubborn and serious, but he was easily capable of bringing distinctly different expressions to those sensual lips and sternly arched brows.

As he walked, Luke ignored the occasional suspicious, vaguely hostile stares of the few people he passed. They were nothing. At the moment he was firmly focused on the woman, and what tactics he might use to catch her. Yes, she had faced him down with surprising courage, but she hadn't managed to hide her inner fire from him. And he was no ordinary man to be so easily turned aside.

She believed herself safe under that stern, no-nonsense facade. But there was wildness under that calm, collected exterior—a dichotomy that made the challenge infinitely more interesting. "Joelle Randall," he murmured to himself, tasting her name.

It seemed one more good sign among the others that her first name held the lilt of his mother's native tongue. The sensual sound of it suited her—that hidden part of her that he intended to awaken—though she might prefer the camouflage of her nickname. Before he ended his play with her, her control would be defeated by the passion he sensed rigidly concealed in her heart. And that passion would be entirely his.

Luke slowed as he left the outskirts of town, automatically searching the darkness beyond the reach of man-made light. His taut smile eased. It wouldn't do to become overconfident like a clumsy cub on its first hunt. He could still scare her away; his natural magnetism would not be complete proof against her practiced wariness. He couldn't expect her to fall as easily as the others. This would require more finesse, and he was more than willing to take the time. He had learned patience long ago.

The softest whisper of a footfall from behind caught him in midthought, and he turned on his heel to regard the man who had been trailing him.

"Allan," he acknowledged, making out familiar features in the waning light. "You know better than to sneak up on me like that."

The older man shrugged. "You have to admit I've gotten pretty good at it, if I was able to come this close before you noticed me." His smile hid an undercurrent of unease; he had good reason to know it was never wise to provoke Luke.

Sensing this, Luke kept his irritation in check. He

allowed himself a faint answering smile. "I was a little careless tonight," he admitted. Anticipation rose in him again. "You might say I have quite a bit on my mind."

Dr. Allan Collier gazed at him in a way few of the other townsfolk would have cared to risk. "Could this very engrossing subject possibly be Miss Joey Randall?"

Luke's full attention snapped back to his friend. Even Collier shifted under the weight of his stare. "You know her, then," he said softly. "That shouldn't be a surprise." He looked the doctor over with cold deliberation. "What I don't understand is what possible concern any thoughts I might have about Ms. Randall could be to you."

The edge in his voice should have warned Collier off, as it would have done with anyone else. But Collier knew him better than the others; he knew just how far he could push. Luke had had reason in the past to curse the fetters of his unique relationship with the doctor. It put restraints on him he did not always like.

As if fully aware of Luke's ambivalence, Collier took a cautious step forward. "I suppose it isn't my business, but I'd like to ask you this one time, Luke, to let her alone. She's got her own problems. . . ."

"What makes you think I would harm her in any way?" Luke growled. "If you know me as well as you think you do, you'll keep to your own affairs." He half turned away in dismissal, but Collier caught at his arm.

"Oh, I know you wouldn't harm her," Collier said. His hand trembled on Luke's rigid biceps, but he maintained his grip. "No more than you 'harmed' any of the others. You'll play your games and let her go free at the end, but while you do that, you'll disrupt her life and everything she cares about."

Luke controlled his instinctive response and forced himself to turn slowly. His eyes raked over the hand on his arm until it dropped away.

"What is your interest in this, Doctor? You never interfered before." His eyes narrowed to threatening slits, and his voice fell to a rasp. Collier flinched in spite of himself but stubbornly stood his ground.

"I don't want to see Miss Randall get hurt. She's not a plaything for you or anyone else." He held fast under Luke's glare. "Leave her alone, Luke. If I've ever done anything for you that mattered, then return the favor and do this for me." The strained emotion in Collier's voice reached Luke through his anger, and he shook his head in genuine puzzlement.

"I don't understand you, Allan. And I won't make you any promises. You know my requirements." At the doctor's attempt to interrupt, he raised his hand to forestall it. "I'll promise this much: I won't hurt her. She won't suffer in any way. Quite the contrary—she needs what I can give her."

He set his jaw and stared at Collier until the other man dropped his head in defeat. It seemed to Luke a hollow victory. Collier turned away, shoulders slumped, looking like a weary old man. Luke snarled a curse—at Collier, at himself, at what he was—and turned back for the welcome safety of the forest.

A shadow darted out from among shadows and flowed to his side. Luke's fingers found the rich fur and raked through it slowly. He could not maintain his anger for long; there was too much anticipation. The wolf raised yellow eyes to his.

"Yes, my friend. This will be a difficult hunt, but I think the prey is well worth it." The canopy of trees closed over him as he padded into the forest, the wolf ranging just ahead.

The day was half over by the time Joey was able to follow up on her latest lead. A small bell rang overhead as she entered the general store, and the resident Labrador retriever acknowledged her presence with a thump of his tail.

"Hi, there," she said with a grin, crouching down beside the dog and cupping her hand under the broad, moist muzzle. Tail-thumping became more enthusiastic; Joey obligingly scratched the dog's belly as he rolled over with a languid yawn.

"I see Gunnar has taken a liking to you," a musical, friendly voice called down from behind the counter.

With a final pat Joey pushed herself to her feet and transferred her smile to the storekeeper. Mr. Jackson supplied most of the essentials to the town and surrounding regions; what he didn't have, he boasted, he could find. Joey had been surprised at the variety his small store contained. Stuck out here, she mused, one would need a bit of variety to keep from going stir-crazy.

"I like Gunnar, too," she said with a glance at the animal, who had drifted off to sleep again. "I've always liked dogs."

Mr. Jackson leaned over the counter and scratched the back of his thinning hair. "Anyone who likes dogs is okay with me. Now what can I do for you today, Miss Randall? Need some special supplies? I know things aren't too fancy here, but I can order just about anything. I've got it down to a science by now. Anything you want, I can order." He straightened and beamed at her. Joey felt almost sorry to disappoint him.

"Actually, Mr. Jackson . . ."

"Everyone here calls me Bill," he interjected amiably.

"Bill, then. Bill, you've probably heard the reason I'm in town." At his nod she continued, "Right now I've got a bit of a problem. I lost my guide, and I need a new one to take me into the mountains. I have maps, money for supplies, and I'm willing to pay well for experienced service. But I need to find someone quickly, so I can beat the bad weather."

She watched as Jackson's mouth puckered into a thoughtful frown. Not quite disapproving, she thought—

though she'd seen that reaction plenty of times since coming here. But she had a sinking feeling this was another dead end. "At any rate," she continued, "Walter Everhard over at the garage told me that you might know someone I could hire. As I said, I can pay well, and I've done a lot of planning."

She broke off, waiting for some response, hoping against hope that her gut feeling was wrong.

Jackson plucked uneasily at the back of his collar, his eyes sliding away from hers. "Well, Miss Randall, I'd sure love to help you. And I'm really sorry to hear things haven't worked out. But the truth is, the person I know who used to do guide work isn't really active anymore. The work wasn't steady enough, so he went on to other things. I really wish . . ."

His voice trailed off as Joey set her wallet on the counter and calmly counted out several crisp bills. Jackson stared at the money. "That's just a down payment," Joey assured him. "Once the work was finished, my guide would get twice that much again." The practical, almost cynical part of her knew that hard cash was a strong argument, and it didn't seem to be going over Jackson's balding head. "Are you quite sure this person you know couldn't be persuaded to take on one last client?"

There was a long moment of silence. At last Jackson blew out a deep sigh and shook his head. Joey's heart sank. "I'd sure love to oblige you, as I said, Miss Randall. But I just don't think it's possible."

He glanced up at her and took in her reaction; by the softening of his expression, she knew her own face must be showing her despair. She bit her lip and raised her chin. With a helpless shrug, Jackson spread his hands out on the counter. "Listen, Miss Randall. I can't say there's any chance that I can persuade my friend, but I'll run it by him. I'll see if I can give you a definite answer in a day or two."

Joey could not conceal her sudden hope, for he shook his head again. "Don't count on anything, please, Miss Randall. As I said, I'll have to run it by him and . . ."

The jingle of the entrance bell brought him to a sudden stop. Jackson's mobile face, which had been fixed in an expression of reluctant apology, tensed into quite a different aspect. Something about it made Joey forget her arguments and turn around.

It was like a replay of last night's scene in the tavern, on a much more intimate scale. The imposing figure of Luke Gévaudan stood in the doorway, and once again Joey felt her attention inexplicably riveted on him. Jackson, too, remained very still. There was a beat of silence, and then Gunnar, forgotten in the corner, growled softly.

Joey glanced down at the dog in startlement. The animal was up on his feet, head and tail lowered and motionless, a ridge of hair raised along his spine. The growl rumbled again, an obvious warning. Aimed at the man in the doorway. Joey blinked and moved without thought to the dog's side, resting her hand on his head. She could feel the vibrations of his exhalation under her fingers. Again her gaze was pulled to the stranger; she opened her mouth to speak, but the sound seemed caught in her throat.

Gévaudan's pale eyes met hers for the briefest instant and then rested on the dog at her side. In the filtered light Joey could make out their color—a clear, unusual amber-green, ringed in black. Not hazel—those eyes were nothing as ordinary as mere hazel. She stared, but he ignored her. The intensity that seemed to flow from him, the same intensity she'd felt the night before, was focused on something else.

As if in response to her thoughts, Gunnar shivered under her hand. The low growl faded. She could feel the animal's head drop lower, sensed the subtle shift in his muscles. Her fingers tightened to prevent the coming attack; but as she looked down, the dog seemed to shrink in on himself, whining softly.

With slow and subtle grace Gévaudan stepped into the room and crouched before the dog. His gaze, still locked on the animal's, never wavered. The dog shivered again beneath Joey's nerveless fingers and crouched down, sliding forward until his dark head rested on the ground inches from Gévaudan's knee. Joey's fist clenched on empty air as Gévaudan extended a hand and held it just under the animal's nose.

Gunnar whined softly, thumping his tail; his pink tongue shot out to touch the man's knuckle. Gévaudan's hand slid over the side of the dog's head and lightly gripped the loose skin at the back of the neck. The dog collapsed into an amiable puddle and thrust all four legs into the air. With long, sun-browned fingers Gévaudan scratched the dog's belly, and then he looked up. The full intensity of his stare met Joey's, and the hard lines of his face shifted into a faint, unsettling smile.

"Hello, Ms. Randall," he said.

Luke stood up, watching the woman as she felt the brunt of his attention. Her eyes—brown eyes, lightly flecked with gold—widened as he spoke her name. Apparently, he thought with a wry inward smile, she hadn't expected him to be capable of speech. He allowed a little of the smile to reach his mouth, though it was a deliberate gesture designed to put her at ease, not one that came naturally. Her eyes traced over his face; she did not look particularly reassured.

He took a moment to look her over more carefully. His first impressions had all been accurate; the patent femininity of her body was enhanced, not disguised, by her practical mountain clothing. Soft silver-gold hair drawn back in a braid freed the delicate lines of her face. Her brows, darker than her hair, were lowered in a subtle frown; the soft lips were slightly parted. He gazed at those lips for a moment, reminding himself that a hunter never gave himself away by striking prematurely. As much as he might wish to throw caution to the winds and feel that sweet, supple body against his, explore the promise behind those parted lips, he would have to remain in control.

It amused him to consider that she, too, wanted control. Even now she struggled to gain dominance over her own response to him—a response he felt with absolute clarity. It told him he would not have to wait too long to have her in his bed. Not if he took the minimum precautions. Considering the strength of his need—and his increasing conviction that she would fill it perfectly—it was a very good thing that there would be no complications.

And as for who would be in control . . . His eyes narrowed and met hers again. This time she broke the gaze, and her tongue darted out to touch her upper lip. His belly tightened in response to the unconscious sensuality of the gesture. No, there could be no doubt as to who would be in control.

"I don't believe we've been introduced," he said, gliding forward a step. At his feet the dog Gunnar rolled out of his way and resumed its place in the corner. Joelle Randall started, apparently taken aback once again by his attempt at friendly conversation. He moved forward another step, and she compensated by inching backward until she came up against the unyielding counter.

Sensing that he had established his dominance with her, as he had done earlier with the dog, Luke paused. Like the dog, she shivered—but it generated a considerably different effect. Luke controlled his sudden arousal, extending his hand to her with the same care he'd used before. "My name is Luke—Luke Gévaudan."

For a moment his hand hung in midair while she

stared at it in fascination. Then her own came out to meet his, delicate fingers lightly touching his own. At first he thought she would drop his hand immediately, so powerful was the jolt of sheer attraction that passed through him at her touch. But though her eyes widened and her breath caught, she did not draw away. Instead, her hand suddenly tightened on his, hard.

"I've heard of you, Mr. Gévaudan," she said, voice throaty and cool. Her eyes narrowed again, and all traces of her nearly mesmerized reaction to him fell away. What must have been considerable pressure for her hardly registered on his hand as she gripped it; even as he savored the feel of her soft fingers nearly lost in his, he respected her attempt to assert her own dominance. With another man she might have succeeded.

As before, she was the first to finally break the subtle confrontation. The way she unobtrusively shook her cramped hand did not slip past him; his smile widened. She caught the expression and leaned back over the counter with studied casualness. The movement pushed her small, firm breasts against the fabric of her shirt, and it was with some effort that he kept his eyes on her face.

"Since you know who I am," he said with deliberate softness, "you probably know I don't live in town. I've been remiss in taking the opportunity to meet you. We don't get many Americans here."

She shifted under his gaze but continued to meet it stubbornly. "So I've been told. I've been told quite a few interesting things since I've been here, Mr. Gévaudan." Her lower lip jutted out and she tilted her head back, eyeing him in obvious challenge.

"I'm sure you have," he murmured. He moved experimentally, watching her shift again and then straighten. It delighted him to see that she was not easily intimidated. Long experience told him that her response was not typical; he was reminded of that every day he spent in town. "Life must be very different for you up here. I understand"—he came to a halt a little to her left—"you're from California. San Francisco." He noted her subtle movement that brought her around to face him once again.

"It seems that you've heard things too, Mr. Gévaudan." She looked away from him in sudden indifference, indifference he knew clearly was feigned. Her stance told him she was determined to end their brief acquaintance by refusing to offer any further conversation. But she wasn't going to escape quite that easily.

"Luke. My name's Luke. Up here we don't usually require formality."

She arched her brow and looked him up and down. "Do you speak for the town or just yourself, Mr. Gévaudan?" she queried with a faint, false smile. "I understood that you don't care much for local company." As if suddenly realizing she'd spoken too freely, she flushed and turned away, pretending interest in a row of canned goods on a nearby shelf.

"It depends on the company." Luke drifted closer to her, maintaining the same distance between them. He could smell her: the light perfume of the shampoo she'd used, the body-warmed cotton of her shirt, and the subtle odor of woman. He drew in the scents and savored them.

Her own nostrils flared like a deer scenting cougar. Warm brown eyes flecked with gold darted back to observe him. "I'm afraid I won't be good company right now, Mr. Gévaudan," she muttered. "I have business to attend to."

She turned her back full on him, muscles rigid with an anxiety she could not possibly understand. He admired that courage in her, even now. With one silent step he came up behind her, so close that his breath stirred the delicate hairs that had come loose from her braid. His eyes traced over the curve of her hips and rump, inward along the small waist and up the graceful line of her back and shoulders; his hands yearned to follow that path, and he clenched them with a soft intake of breath.

She jumped. She whirled about to glare at him, her face inches from his. He could see the throb of her pulse in the delicious column of her neck. It took every ounce of control he possessed to keep from seizing her there and then.

Before he could lose that control, she slipped to the side, out of the shadow of his body, and darted around the counter to pause in the apparent safety of the doorway to the storeroom. *Her* instincts, at least, had been the correct ones.

For a long moment he struggled with himself, fighting down the powerful urge to take the prey. Every shudder of her body, every indrawn breath, tempted him. But the moment passed. He willed his muscles to relax, one by one; by the time he felt capable of coherent and reasonable speech, he and Joey Randall were no longer alone.

Bill Jackson hovered just behind the woman, one hand hesitating just above her shoulder. She pressed back against him.

Luke's eyes narrowed, and his lip curled. They joined forces to face him down, with all the self-preservation instincts of herd animals facing a wolf pack. But she—she was no herd animal. Not like the others. That was something he would make her understand, when she was his.

They were talking together in hushed voices now, and the woman was pretending interest in discussing some item she needed to order. The hunt was up for the day.

Luke turned on his heel, pausing with his hand on the door latch. Silence had fallen over the room again.

He pivoted to face her and caught her eyes watching him when she didn't think he would notice.

"It was a pleasure meeting you, Joelle Randall," he said. "I hope we'll see each other again soon." With a final smile, he turned his back and left her staring after him.

*Heat. Everything was heat, burning within and without. Joey shuddered with it, her body writhing to escape it yet yearning to be consumed by it.*

*His breath was hot on the back of her neck, inches away from her skin, sensitized nearly to the point of madness. His touch scorched her; long, callused fingers traced over her neck and shoulders, moved with aching slowness down her back, and spread out to circle the flare of her hips. No sound escaped her as he pressed his hard length against her back, though she could feel his arousal with aching clarity. As if in response to her unvoiced cry, the moist warmth of his mouth descended to brush the hollow where neck flowed into shoulder; his tongue moved in slow, delicious circles over her skin. Still she found her gasps and moans of pleasure and passion locked in her throat, even when his hands left her hips to slide over her belly and capture her breasts.*

*Her nipples were already erect as he cupped her in his big hands, rough against silky, yielding softness. His mouth sought the other side of her neck, licking and sucking, while she arched in desperate, blazing silence against him. When he caught her nipples between his fingers, it was more than she could bear. She struggled in his grip, and he obeyed her unspoken desire, turning her in his arms. Before she could see his face, he lifted her, pressing his mouth between her breasts, his hands holding her in place. She could do nothing but fling back her head, unbound hair cascading behind her, as his tongue moved in circles over her heated skin, catching her nipple between her teeth. He moved from one breast to the other, claiming each thoroughly, ignoring her hands as* they clutched helplessly at his shoulders. The trapped cries in her throat were an exquisite torture.

When he withdrew at last, she pressed against him, cold in the absence of his scalding touch, but he let her slip down in his arms and took her mouth in a kiss that drew the sounds of passion from deep within her and set them free. Her own arms came about him, raking his back as his hands tangled in her hair. His arousal was a shaft of furnace heat against the inside of her thigh, rising to meet her flowing warmth.

In the instant before union, as he lifted her onto himself and she prepared to take him, she opened her eyes. His face was cast in shadow, taut with hunger, but she could see his eyes. They were the source of the burning heat; they radiated it, glowed with it. The full shock of those eyes drained all the desire from her body.

"No!" She pushed at him, repelled his immovable strength, pummeled his shoulders and chest in rage. He was hard, demanding, unyielding, staring at her with that hot, terrible gaze. Even as she struggled, she knew if she looked at him again, she would lose herself to him forever. His grip tightened, and he forced her against him; he compelled her—he compelled her to meet his eyes, to surrender, to submit to him now and for all time.

Her voice rose in a ragged cry of defiance, but her gaze was drawn irrevocably to his, and she was lost. Lost, burning and lost. . . .

"No!" Joey jerked to wakefulness, her body tangled amid the sheets and blankets of the bed. The only sound was the harshness of her breathing; there was no one with her, no burning eyes engulfing all the world. For a long moment she lay gasping, trapped in the clinging warmth of the covers and staring into the moon-laced darkness of her room.

She focused slowly on the homely furnishing of the guest chamber, the old oak bureau and the antique radio, the ancient pictures discolored by age and sunlight.

The light of the moon, cutting a brilliant, broken shaft across the floor, gave the illusion of midday and cast the corners of the room in deep shadow. Joey concentrated on the light until her breathing had slowed and she was able to think clearly again. A nightmare. She reassured herself with that thought over and over until its reality took firm hold.

With slow, deliberate movements she freed her arms and legs of the entangling covers. They were soaked with perspiration; the illusion of heat that had infused her dream had not been entirely a fantasy. It helped to remind her that the feeling of being trapped had also come from a very real condition.

But that was not entirely comforting. Joey could feel remnants of another kind of heat, coiling unfulfilled deep with her. There was moisture there, too; her mind and body had reacted to the nightmare with an enthusiasm that frightened her. In the nightmare she had lost control—completely and irrevocably. Her body had rejected the careful fetters that her mind had struggled to impose so many years ago. In dreams her mind lost its mastery.

Joey sat up, ignoring the hard edges of the wooden headboard at her back. The eyes in the dream. She had recognized those eyes. She wrapped her arms tightly about herself and suppressed a shudder. It had been *him*. The man she'd seen in the bar and the general store—Gévaudan. The man who had at once frightened and fascinated her. In her dream it had been Gévaudan who had caressed her and breached all her careful boundaries, who had taken control and dominated her—until that very last moment, when the sanity of her waking mind had freed her from a situation that had become unbearable. . . .

The images were burned into her mind, though she stared into the silence of the room until she had memorized every tiny detail of it. Rage welled up in her—

rage that Gévaudan had invaded her dreams, upsetting her careful equilibrium. Why? She pounded the damp mattress with her fist. Why was her own mind betraying her?

She remembered the incident in the general store— the way his mere presence had almost overwhelmed the room, quieted a threatening dog, and frightened Mr. Jackson into retreat.

She remembered fighting the powerful attraction of him, even as she struggled to understand it and tried without success to dismiss it. Every logical faculty denied that a total stranger should affect her that way. Her own anger at the irrationality of it all had helped her to reject it.

But that changed nothing. It was a fact that Gévaudan evoked peculiar and powerful reactions from those around him—and even she was not immune. That he could invade her dreams was more than she was prepared to accept. That he could make her feel this way, forget herself . . .

Unable to govern a flood of contradictory emotions and incapable of sleeping again that night, Joey scrambled out of bed. The floor was cold under her feet, though the room itself seemed far too warm. She began to pace across the short space from door to window, crossing and recrossing the shaft of moonlight, driven by her agitated thoughts.

She had one goal, and one goal alone. That goal did not allow for any ridiculous flights of fancy—or any side trips into unwanted relationships. The only way to deal with the situation was to acknowledge it.

Fact: Gévaudan existed, and he did seem to have a kind of charisma about him that even she had to accept.

Fact: Her dreams proved that she felt that charisma much more strongly than she cared to admit.

Fact: Gévaudan's behavior suggested he was interested in her, and it was likely she'd run into him again.

Fact: The only way to deal with this distraction was to confront it head-on.

And that meant facing up to Gévaudan, looking him in the eye and erasing his influence from her mind—conscious and unconscious.

The logical array of facts did much to comfort Joey, and having a plan of action, however vague, was a vast improvement over the uncertainty she'd felt moments before. She knew what she had to do; she simply had to keep thinking in terms of facts and reality. Given no encouragement and nothing but remote courtesy, Gévaudan would surely lose interest. And she, in turn, would be able to complete her goals without further distractions.

Stretching her arms behind her, Joey crossed to the window and turned her face to the silver moon. The cold light seemed like an embodiment of pure reason—a kind of mascot, she thought to herself with a smile, reminding her of her purpose. No more day-dreaming or wallowing in the beauty of Nature—and no more nightmares.

Below her, two stories down, the small manicured lawn flowed to the edge of the forest, dark and impenetrable even in the moonlight. The mountains formed a black silhouette against a carpet of stars. There was nothing romantic about the view. It represented something she had to overcome to reach her goal. Everything she did from now on had to be a means to an end.

As she turned away from the window, she heard it: the distant wail of a howling wolf.

She froze in place, compelled beyond reason to search the darkness for what she half-expected to find. A chorus rose to join the first cry, receding at first, then drawing nearer.

Joey clutched the edge of the windowsill. There was an endless time filled only by the eerie voices, and then she looked down and saw it.

Her wolf.

It stood alone in the grass, its heavy fur frosted with moonlight. It gazed up in silence, and though she could not see its eyes, she knew it saw her. For an instant it held its place, and then it flung back its head and howled. The sound was chillingly mournful, and Joey shivered in sympathy. As the echoes of its cry faded, it bounded away, flowing into the forest.

Luke paused by the outer glass wall of the coffee shop, knowing she would be there. He watched her for a moment as she sipped her coffee, cradling the mug between her hands, eyes closed to savor the aroma.

He envied her the ability to find solace in it. His sleep had been restless, filled with dreams of her, and nothing so simple as coffee could soothe his spirit or ease his need.

He knew the instant she felt his presence; her eyes snapped open and focused on him without the slightest hesitation. The coffee shop was almost deserted, and Luke was grateful for that. Collier's appeals still stung him more than he cared to acknowledge, and he wanted no further complications.

She watched him warily as he approached the table. It was clear she was trying to keep her expression as cool and severe as it had been the day before, but there was a subtle change in her—something he sensed but could not define.

Her eyes did not quite meet his as he leaned over her table. Steam from the coffee swirled up between them.

"Do you mind if I join you, Ms. Randall?" He kept his voice light, reining in the intensity that drove him; he saw her fingers tighten on the mug and then gradually relax.

"Mr. Gévaudan. I'm just finishing my coffee—but yes, by all means." Her tone was distant but lacked the bite of near hostility it had carried in the general store. Luke regarded that as an improvement, however small.

He favored her with a smile. "I think we may have gotten off to a bad start. It wasn't my intention to offend you in any way. The fact is, we don't see many strangers here. I guess I let my curiosity get the better of me."

Her expression wavered between an uneasy frown and a strained smile. "I wasn't very polite myself, Mr. Gévaudan. I apologize for that." For a moment she seemed about to continue, but she dropped her eyes and lapsed into silence.

"In that case, if it's all right with you, I suggest we start over. My name is Luke Gévaudan." He extended his hand again, and she freed her grip on the mug to take it. This time her hand barely grazed his, and she pulled it back almost as if she had been burned.

The contact, brief as it was, had an unexpected effect on Luke, and he covered his confusion by sliding into the seat opposite hers. She blinked but did not object; her gaze slid away.

"My name is Joey Randall. But you already knew that, didn't you?" The bite in her tone was astringent, but she seemed to catch herself and gave him a slight, apologetic smile. "Sorry. My name is Joelle, but I go by Joey. That's what I prefer."

Luke rested his arms on the table. "Joey. And please call me Luke. What I said yesterday about informality still applies." He sought her eyes, but she continued to avoid his gaze, looking everywhere else with a nonchalance he knew she didn't feel. "Now that we've met, I hope we can be friends."

Her face flushed again; with a visible effort she collected herself and finally met his eyes. "I'll be honest with you . . . Luke." The words were almost toneless. "I was telling you the truth yesterday. I've got some very important business to attend to in the next week or so—and it's really taking most of my time and energy. I don't think I'd be a very good friend just now."

"I heard about your meeting with the wolf the other day," Luke persisted softly. "Wolves won't hurt you—but if you wouldn't mind taking some advice, stay away from the high meadows and open woodlands from now on. The grizzlies are foraging for winter, and many of the sows have cubs with them. They can be extremely unpredictable. . . ."

"I appreciate your advice, Luke, but I'm not entirely without intelligence. I have no desire to be eaten by a bear, believe me." For a moment there was heat in her voice; she reached over her shoulder to run fingers along her braid, tidying it, and Luke watched her with a hunger he struggled to conceal.

"Good. Being smart and cautious can help you survive up here," he said, leaning back in a stretch. He saw her eyes brush over him. There was something there, something she could have hidden from anyone else. Anyone but him. "This isn't what you're used to, coming from down South."

"Believe me, I'll take your warnings under consideration." Her eyes dropped to regard the coffee before her; she raised it to her lips and grimaced in distaste. Luke could see that her hands were shaking. "It's cold."

Luke started to his feet. "I'll get you more."

"No, that won't be necessary. I was finished anyway." She made a move to get up, but he shifted slightly to block her way, careful not to alarm her. She sank back down into the seat, biting her lip. "I do have things to take care of, Luke. I'm sure you understand. Maybe later . . ." Her expression revealed her immediate chagrin at even so vague a suggestion.

Luke was not daunted by her reluctance. Every passing second in her presence convinced him that she was far from immune to him, though she seemed determined to reject her own response. And he was certain now that she would fulfill the promise of his dreams—those incredible, sensual dreams that had haunted his sleep from the moment he saw her.

"What about tonight?" he asked smoothly. "We don't have many fancy dining establishments in town, but I'd be very pleased if you would join me for dinner. This place serves a reasonable steak. . . ."

"Luke, I do thank you for your offer—but I'm under a great deal of pressure right now." She stared fixedly into her coffee. "I can't guarantee when I'll be free. I hope you understand." Her voice had become cool and distant again, polite and correct and without a shred of warmth. It provoked him unexpectedly.

"I hope you don't mind a blunt observation, Joey," he remarked with a casualness as false as her own. "I've heard something of your business in town, and I'll risk giving you a little more advice. The mountains become dangerous with the coming of winter, and there are some very isolated areas that very few people have explored. The wilderness is unpredictable at the best of times. It isn't a place for someone of limited experience. You may be disappointed in finding what you're looking for."

Within an instant all reserve dropped from Joey's face; the fire was back in force, though it burned with a savage chill. "And do you know just what I'm looking for, Mr. Gévaudan? Do you know me at all? I don't think so. And I'd greatly appreciate it if you'd just leave me alone."

Her eyes flashed on his, the gold flecks bright against deep brown, and Luke was startled to find that his gaze broke first. He hardly noticed when she stood up and pushed him aside.

"If you'll excuse me, I have things to do. Good-bye, Mr. Gévaudan." Her body brushed by him as she marched away, shoulders rigid with anger—and something less easily defined.

Luke watched her go, amazed at his own bemusement. She was the first who had ever managed to face him down.

The thought was not particularly pleasant, and Luke felt his hackles rise. One thing had become very clear; she most definitely reacted to him. Her attempts at cool indifference were a transparent mask for something she didn't care to acknowledge. And for all her will and determination, she had never faced his like before.

Luke smoothed the frown from his face, glancing around intently. If anyone had witnessed the episode, he was staying carefully out of sight. Luke straightened and stalked out of the coffee shop. So she was able to resist him in a way the others hadn't—but she had a weakness. There was something she wanted very much. Almost as much as he wanted her.

It was only a matter of time.

# Chapter 3

The week passed all too quickly.

Joey had met with nothing but frustration in her search for a replacement guide, and the fading summer fled before her. The first golden leaves were beginning to appear on aspen and cottonwood, and the bellowing of moose would soon herald the arrival of autumn. Already the air was touched with chill in the mornings and evenings. No one had to remind Joey that her time was running short.

To add insult to injury, Joey found herself haunted by Luke Gévaudan. Her best efforts at dissuading him, all her determination to give him not one shred of encouragement that might embolden him in his pursuit of her, went for nothing.

If she dropped in to exchange a friendly word with Dr. Collier, Luke was there. When she went by the general store for supplies, Luke just happened to be in the area.

He haunted her; and although he maintained a persistent presence and that same intense regard he had shown from the beginning, he never quite pushed beyond it. He might offer casual comments but never again pressed unwanted advice on her.

And because he stayed within the limits of propriety—and also, she admitted, because he was a very attractive and charismatic man—Joey simply could not ignore him. What frightened her more was the notion that soon she might not want to.

The dreams still came with distressing regularity. Each one seemed more vivid than the last; it was all she could do to prevent her chagrin from showing on her face in Gévaudan's presence. Even so, she had the uneasy feeling that he could see through her facade and knew what he was doing to her. Somehow, he knew.

Reflecting bleakly on her situation, Joey sought sanctuary in Red's Tavern. Maggie had been a constant source of support for her, and their friendship had grown so strong that it felt to Joey as if she'd known the other woman for years.

As usual, Maggie was busy waiting on her regulars; Red's was a haven for many local folk. They no longer looked up when Joey arrived, and Maggie had told her their indifference was a sign she'd been accepted. That, at least, was a welcome change.

But, Joey mused as she sat sipping her usual glass of wine, being accepted didn't solve her current problem. And of all the local people, only one seemed to fill her mind.

"A penny for your thoughts," Maggie said, grinning as Joey looked up with a blank, unfocused stare. At once the redhead's cheerful face grew serious. "I see you haven't had any more luck. Damned shame." She wiped the counter off with long strokes of a towel and talked as she worked. "I sure wish I knew how to help, Joey. But I've tried every lead I could think of, even outside of town. I just haven't come up with anything."

Joey nodded gloomily. "Bill Jackson wasn't able to help me, either. I'm getting to the end of my rope, Maggie." She sighed and dropped her chin into her hands. Her reflection in the spotted mirror behind the counter looked like a stranger's: grim, weary, and helpless.

Maggie frowned in sympathy. "Well, kid, try to get it off your mind for a while. Relax a bit—you don't look like you've slept well lately." She set down the towel and peered into Joey's face.

"As it happens, I haven't," Joey admitted. She took a sip of wine and experimented with a smile. "Sorry. I'll try to be better company."

"That's it. Just take it easy for a while. You've earned it." Maggie swept away to look after a patron and returned with a wink and a glance back over her shoulder. "Might interest you to know you're at the center of town gossip these days. You know how dull things are around here—doesn't take much to set tongues wagging."

Joey managed a wry grin. "Tell me about it. I suppose it's my silly city-girl attempts to conquer the wilderness—or maybe that I don't know when I'm licked?" She couldn't help but admit that the townsfolk had a point there, even though she had not retreated one step from her goal.

Maggie shook her mane of red curls. "People are getting used to that. No, it's the fact that Luke Gévaudan has spent more time in town over the past two weeks than he normally does in a year—and word is it's all because of you." She put her hands on her hips triumphantly and beamed at Joey. "Looks like you've made a conquest, like it or not."

Unable to control her instinctive response, Joey tried to relax her taut muscles and maintain an even expression. "Is that so? I'm glad to be a source of entertainment for people, but I'd just as soon Mr. Gévaudan went back to his old habits and stayed away." Her best efforts could not quite keep the bite from her tone, and Maggie's brows shot up in surprise.

"Sorry, kid. Didn't mean to offend. So he's making a pest of himself, is he?" She learned over the counter. "I told you before he's got kind of a reputation, but I'll be honest with you—in the past, he never went to much effort. The ladies just sort of fell into his arms." Her tone grew confidential. "He'd usually disappear with the lucky girl, and people wouldn't see much of them for a season or two. And then, eventually, the girl would leave. Every time."

"I hope you don't think I have any intention of 'falling into his arms' and disappearing anywhere with him," Joey said with some heat. "That's the last sort of complication I need."

"As I said, it's not the same with you. That's what has people talking," Maggie admitted. "People may not trust him, but he's different. And so are you. So it's got people a little curious."

"Just as long as they don't get their hopes up," Joey snapped. Closing her eyes and drawing in a deep breath, she smiled apologetically at Maggie. "All right. He's attractive. Maybe if things were different—but you've said yourself he has a reputation, and I am not about to become anyone's 'conquest.' In fact, if you happen to have any advice about how to discourage him, I'd sure appreciate it."

The redhead leaned back and folded her arms with a thoughtful tug on one earlobe. "Well, I wish I knew. He's always given me the impression of being very persistent—sort of like someone else I know." She took the sting out of her words with a wink. "Trouble is, no one here knows enough about him. Except maybe Dr. Collier . . . I hear he got as close to Gévaudan as anyone ever did."

Joey shook her head. "I like Dr. Collier," she murmured, "but I don't think I'm ready to ask him for advice about another man. Especially not one like Mr. Gévaudan." She fell into a brooding silence, vivid images of her dreams bringing an unwelcome flush to her skin.

There was a long stillness, and Joey was hardly aware of the constant din of the bar as she tried not to think of Luke Gévaudan. Maggie's return to conversation was a much-needed distraction. "You know, I've been thinking, Joey. You probably aren't going to like this, but something just occurred to me. . . ." She broke off, frowning in thought, and seemed to reach a decision. "You've been searching for a guide, and all this time there's been one overlooked possibility right under our noses."

Joey sat up. "What's that?" Gévaudan fled her mind at the sudden wash of hope that followed Maggie's pronouncement; but the redhead's next words chilled her.

"Luke Gévaudan." Maggie didn't wait for Joey's reaction. "I don't know why I didn't think of it before, except that he's such a forbidding character—and I've never known him to hire out before. But the fact is, I doubt there's another man around here who is likely to know more about the area you want to go into. Come to think of it, he owns a sizable parcel of the land out that way. You might even have to pass through it to get where you want to go." The redhead nodded to herself, falling silent as Joey sat back and absorbed the unexpected revelation.

Gévaudan as guide. It had simply never occurred to Joey, even with his near-constant presence; and though the idea dismayed her for a wealth of very complicated reasons, it was the first real chance she had. . . .

Her fingers were gripping the fragile stem of the wineglass hard enough to snap it. She relaxed them slowly and met Maggie's gaze. "Are you serious, Maggie? Do you think he could do it?"

"I'm sure he could do it," the redhead assured her. "He's lived up there in the woods too long not to be damned good at wilderness travel. No . . ." She paused to fill a pair of glasses with foaming beer and slide them down the bar to waiting customers. "It's not a matter of could he do it, but *would* he do it."

"He's never hired out before?" Joey frowned over the possibilities, defying her uncertainty. "How much do you think it would take to get him to do it? I still have money left, and I'm more than willing to pay whatever it takes."

Maggie chuckled, undaunted by Joey's implacable demeanor. "I have a feeling money wouldn't tempt him, kid. Fact is, he seems to have plenty of that already—I heard he inherited it from his old man." She hurried on before Joey could interrupt. "But you've got an advantage here. And I'm afraid this is the part you may not like."

Joey did not have to hear more. A shiver passed through her, beyond her physical control just as the dreams were beyond the authority of her rational mind.

"All I have to do," she said softly, "is play his game. Convince him I'll give him whatever he wants—in exchange for what I need."

There was a long silence.

"It sounds pretty awful, put that way," Maggie admitted at last. "I'm sorry I mentioned it. Bad idea." She hesitated. "Stringing him along like that—" She shook her head. "Frankly you don't strike me as the type. And I don't think I'd feel very safe trying that with him. . . ."

Lost in her own thoughts, Joey was hardly aware of Maggie's retreat. The idea had shocked her at first. But suddenly it seemed not only reasonable, but the answer to all her problems.

She could get Luke Gévaudan to guide her. She could use his pursuit of her and turn it around to get what she wanted. And in doing so, she could end this futile struggle against her own obsession with him. It all worked out very neatly.

Joey liked neat answers. The fact that playing this sort of game with Gévaudan might burn her didn't matter; her priorities were set. She was willing to use any reasonable means to reach her goal, and now that a real chance had been handed to her, she wasn't about to pass it up. Gévaudan wanted her; she would make him believe she was willing to give herself to him—for a price. He could stand to be taken down a peg or two, and in the end she'd repay him for his trouble, if not in the highly intimate way he expected.

Sometimes you had to play games to get what you wanted out of life. So she told herself, again and again until she began to believe it.

When she turned to Maggie once more, the redhead was busy rearranging bottles behind the bar. Joey slid off the stool and leaned over the counter. "Thanks, Maggie. I think you've solved my problems."

Brushing hair out of her eyes, Maggie straightened. "I did?" Her hazel eyes searched Joey's face and narrowed. "No. You're going to do it? I'm not so sure it was such a hot idea after all, Joey. Really. You know, there still may be another way. . . ."

"Maggie." Joey smiled with a calm she didn't feel. "I've already made up my mind. You were right—I should have thought of it before. It's going to take care of everything."

"Now wait a minute." Maggie nearly frowned. "You don't know anything about this guy. I don't, either. No one does, really. You'd be alone with him, Joey, and you don't know what you'd be getting into."

"Don't worry about me, Maggie. I know what I'm doing. And this is something I've just got to do—one way or another. And as for the mysterious, persistent Mr. Gévaudan . . ." She allowed herself a tight grin. "Maybe he doesn't know what *he's* getting into."

She slid off the stool and slapped two bills on the countertop. "I really can take care of myself, Maggie. Don't worry, all right?" She started for the door, pausing to smile over her shoulder at the other woman. "And thanks, for everything."

"Me and my bright ideas," Maggie muttered just loud enough for Joey to hear. "You'd damn well better take care of yourself, kid, or you'll have me to answer to. Okay?"

"Okay," Joey replied, brushing by a rowdy band of drinkers as she left the tavern. Maggie's woeful expression seemed to chase after her as the door closed. She banished it, along with her own lingering doubts. She knew what she had to do, and once she'd made a plan, she stuck to it.

Joey's heart was pounding with anticipation as she set about putting her new plan into action. She did not attempt to examine that anticipation too closely. As she crossed the street and made for the lodge, she glanced up at the mountain peaks basking in the late-afternoon sun.

*Soon,* she promised them. *Soon.*

As Joey Randall emerged from the lodge into the crisp morning air, Luke could see immediately that something had changed.

It wasn't simply a matter of her hair, which now hung loose in silver-gold strands that fell to her waist. Or the way she walked—with greater confidence, hips swaying seductively. The subtle alterations in her appearance bespoke a fundamental difference, but they alone did not earn Luke's full attention. No—there was a definite, deliberate allure there now that hadn't been present before.

Luke straightened from his easygoing slouch against a lamppost opposite the lodge and watched her. She didn't see him yet, but her eyes were scanning the area in expectation. She already knew he would be there. She'd become very efficient at spotting him, he had to give her that—even if it didn't keep him away. With all the persistence of a predator, he tracked her and kept her in sight. Her resistance to him had increasingly become a very powerful motivation for his desire. That she was worth the effort he never doubted for an instant.

He admired her long-legged stride and uptilted chin as she crossed the street and felt his muscles tense in anticipation of pursuit. Soon, now, she'd see him and hurry off in the opposite direction.

For the second time she caught him completely off guard. He had only a moment to adjust to the unaccustomed sensation as she closed the space between them and stopped, regarding him with a familiar, direct stare.

"Good morning, Luke," she said.

Luke felt rather like a wolverine whose choice of breakfast had suddenly turned and wished it good hunting. He caught himself quickly.

"Good morning, Joey." He took a moment to look her over, from sun-topped head to boot-shod feet. Yes, there was definitely something different. "I'm glad to see we're on a first-name basis now."

Her curved lips, so often set in a severe frown of concentration, relaxed into a remarkably pleasant smile. "I suppose we've—known—each other long enough to justify the informality." Her gold-flecked eyes met his steadily.

"I'm delighted to hear it," Luke murmured. She was wearing the same loose-fitting shirt and jeans, but he could not miss the fact that she had left a number of buttons undone that revealed a pleasing amount of cleavage. And she stood with her arms relaxed at her sides, not folded like a barricade across her chest or bent with clenched fists, as if she expected to repel attack.

Though her gaze was still cool and direct, and her chin was lifted in that proud way she had, the smile could not be mistaken. It almost came as something of a shock when Luke realized she was not only being civil—she was actually encouraging him.

This revelation kept him silent for a moment, as he considered various possibilities in rapid succession. Either she had finally broken down before his persistence and many charms—though something about his acquaintance with her urged a cynical inner laugh at the assumption—or she wanted something.

Though he had known that might be a very real possibility, the idea chafed unexpectedly. He concentrated on keeping a frown of annoyance from his face.

Joey broke the silence. "Well, the fact is, I may be here a while longer, and there's no reason not to be friendly." For a moment Luke had the bizarre notion that she'd actually batted her eyes at him. As if she read his thoughts, she gave a rueful shrug. "I've had a lot on my mind, and I probably haven't been as . . . neighborly . . . as I should have. Some of the people here"—her almost-coy glance included him—"have been very helpful, and I don't want to seem ungrateful."

Feeling unaccustomedly off balance, Luke cleared his throat. "Not at all, Joey." He pushed away distracting speculation about her motives. With a deceptive shift he moved closer to her; she didn't step back, though a flicker in her eyes told him she was aware of him—very much aware of him. Physical reaction quickly overcame the last of his skepticism. Her warm scent rose up in waves to engulf and mesmerize him.

"Good," she whispered.

He watched her eyes move away from his, stray to his shoulders, his chest and back up to scan his face; for the barest instant her smile lapsed as her teeth caught at her lower lip. Luke hardly noticed it; all his attention was for the heat of her body, the smell of her, the rich sensuality she no longer struggled to hide. Whatever her motivations, he felt it clearly—she wanted him. The knowledge washed over him with the heady arousal of victory.

"In that case," Joey continued, cutting through his dazed admiration, "let's do as you once suggested and start over, shall we?" Suddenly her smile was broad and bright and very far from sensual. Luke felt a wall rise up between them almost as daunting as her earlier coolness.

"By all means," he answered. So she *was* trying a different tack with him—or so it seemed. He managed to keep the grim edge from his smile as he fell into step beside her.

She chattered about something inconsequential with a false vivacity that nettled him as he nodded in time to her comments. Joey Randall thought she might hold him at bay, behind a wall built of light words and the charm she'd withheld from him in the past. She hoped to string him along, keeping him at a safe distance, encouraging but never quite issuing an invitation. Other women had done it before, but none with any hope of success. Unfortunately those women hadn't been Joelle Randall.

Luke grinned, and Joey didn't seem to notice the promise implicit in the expression. She was different, this one, but she was still a woman. He had felt something unmistakable. Joey was playing a dangerous game—with him and with her own desire.

And he would let the contest play out to its inevitable conclusion.

As she entered the post office, glancing a smile back over her shoulder, he held the door open for her with a mocking bow.

*Play your game, Joey,* he thought as he watched her hungrily. *You won't see the trap in time to escape it.*

* * *

Joey felt that things were going very well indeed. And, surprisingly, Luke Gévaudan's company had not been as disagreeable as she'd expected. He could be quite charming when he wasn't playing the wolf out to snare the newest babe in town.

The only difficult part was the uneasy feeling that she actually liked the intensity of his regard. He seemed to have taken her increased friendliness at face value. If his pursuit was less ferocious, it was no less determined.

They sat now on a bench outside the tiny bank, where Joey had completed arrangements to withdraw funds for the coming week. Her money was not going to hold out forever—but with any luck, it wouldn't have to. She smiled sideways at Luke and tried not to stare at the firm line of his jaw, the peculiar color of his eyes. She felt herself squirming on the polished wood of the bench as last night's dream came back to her.

The dreams hadn't gone away, either. They had only grown more powerful, and more undeniable. If she hadn't had her goals in mind . . .

But she did. "Tell me more about growing up here, Luke. It must have been pretty lonely, with so few children your own age. I understand they don't even have enough kids now to justify a school, and they have to send them by bus all the way over to East Fork."

She gave him her full attention, which wasn't difficult; even her conversation was not without purpose. To draw him out, yes—to get him to trust her as well as desire her, to use whatever means necessary to set him up for her request. But she also found herself wanting to know about him—and why faces always turned to him when he passed, and people whispered about his "differences."

His face seemed relaxed; his pose was that strange combination of utter ease and complete alertness that she couldn't remember seeing in any other man she'd ever met. But again and again she sensed some part of him closed off, even as he did his best to charm her into his bed.

"I doubt it's ever easy being a kid, no matter where you grow up," he answered with a casual stretch. His eyes grew hooded and drifted away from hers, as if he found the topic tedious.

"But you had some higher education," she persisted after a moment. "Where did you go to college? I understand the university system up here is quite good." She tried a flirtatious toss of her head. "If you'll forgive me for being blunt, it's pretty obvious you've had exposure to a lot more"—she coughed delicately—"diversity than Lovell might ordinarily provide."

Luke's lip curled in a smile that almost seemed self-mocking. "I'll take that as a compliment, coming from a sophisticated lady from San Francisco." He offered nothing further, his whole manner turning aside further inquiry as he had done consistently throughout the day—evading each of her probing questions about himself and his past with good-natured facility.

"I don't think past life here in Lovell would be of much interest to you, Joey," he drawled, his amber-green eyes sliding back to hers. "The present is much more interesting."

She waited for his usual round of questions about her—which he seemed to ask with genuine curiosity—but none were forthcoming. Instead, he allowed his gaze to sweep across her face and over her open shirt-front. She controlled a desire to clasp it closed about her throat and reminded herself that this was what she had aimed for. Even so, his open stare still felt like a searing blast of heat that burned through her clothing and left her as naked as she had been in her dreams. . . .

She hardly realized it when she slipped free of him just as his arm slid over her shoulder. She pretended not to see the brief narrowing of his eyes as he drew back again, making the movement part of a stretch and widening the space between them.

"It has certainly been a very enjoyable day, Joey," he said with sudden, scathing coldness. The abrupt withdrawal of his focused admiration was almost like a slap, though it saved Joey from a decision she was not yet prepared to face. Her body stiffened in reaction, and she nodded with an oblivious ease she was far from feeling.

"I've had a good time, too, Luke." She searched his shuttered eyes. "I'm glad we got a chance to talk, get to know each other a little better."

When he showed no signs of softening, she continued, "I was thinking—I don't have any plans for dinner tonight. Would you like to join me? Maybe you could tell me more about the upcoming moose migration." Her grin was as flirtatious and flattering as she could manage, but he merely gazed at her as if he saw through her unpracticed efforts.

His eyes were not on hers when he finally answered. "I have other plans." His gruff and unapologetic tone irked her, and she struggled to maintain her amiable demeanor. Damn the bastard! He couldn't have his way with her instantly, and he sulked!

"I'm sorry to hear that," she said with a softness that hid the sharp sarcasm she longed to hit him with. "What about tomorrow night? It's Thursday, and they always have a fancy meal at the lodge on Thursdays. I'd like you to be my guest." The insipid eagerness she gave the words almost made her choke, but at least she wasn't forced to simultaneously fend off his single-minded attentions.

She had become accustomed to the various expressions that played across his rough-hewn face: faint seductive smiles that never quite seemed to blossom into real warmth; a distant coolness when she asked a question he planned to evade; burning intensity when she knew she felt close to winning her. But she had seen this particular aspect only once or twice before: a truly cold and merciless ferocity, an intense and powerful satisfaction. It was the kind of expression she'd glimpsed when he observed the townsfolk who peered at him with silent suspicion and resentment. She shuddered.

But the strange ferocity vanished as quickly as it had come. "It so happens I will be free tomorrow night, Joey," he murmured. The familiar seductive smile was back, resting on her with a warmth she knew instinctively to be as false as her own attempts at vapid flirtatiousness. "I won't be seeing you earlier, but I look forward to a very . . . interesting . . . meal." As if to reinforce his words, he bared his even white teeth in a grin, and before she could respond with insincere thanks, he had risen and stalked away.

Joey stared after him. Damn the man. If she didn't need him so badly, she'd have great pleasure in showing him just how possible it was for a woman to resist him. Unfortunately, the only resistance she could permit herself was against the echo of her dreams.

Tomorrow night, he'd have to believe he'd well and truly caught her—but not before she'd caught him first.

"Hello, Dr. Collier. Nice to see you again." Joey took his hand and gripped it with real warmth as he turned away from the door. "You're here for the weekly feast?"

"Wouldn't miss it," he assured her with a wink. "I understand it's Mexican tonight—and Mrs. O'Brien never disappoints."

He looked over Joey's shoulder as others drifted into the common room and found seats at the tables set up for the occasion. "May I join you for dinner? I have to admit the prospect of a delicious meal in the company of a lovely young lady is most appealing." His faint English accent gave his words a very definite charm, and the hopeful expression on his face was very hard to resist.

Joey thought for a moment of the evening's purpose and reached a sudden decision. *He'd* been so damned arrogant yesterday—ever since she'd met him, in fact—that it would serve *him* right to find himself sharing her.

At least until she was ready to let him have her.

She consented graciously to the doctor's request and allowed him to seat her at the small table while the local girls who served as waitresses moved among the guests. The room was rapidly filling; Joey scanned the faces but did not see Luke's among them. Somehow that didn't surprise her. He'd turn up eventually—like a bad penny. *But a very, very valuable penny*, she reminded herself.

"How are you doing these days, Joey?" Dr. Collier asked as they unfolded their napkins. "Any more luck with finding a guide?"

"I'm still working on it—but I'd say things are definitely looking up," she replied, masking her unease with a smile.

"Delighted to hear it." With raised brows he made a great show of breathing in air suddenly redolent of the spicy aroma of Mexican cooking. Even Joey's mouth watered.

She caught the attention of a passing waitress. "Do you think you could add one more setting? I'm expecting another person." At the waitress's brisk nod she leaned back in her seat and tried to relax. It was not as easy as she would have wished, though Dr. Collier's presence certainly helped.

The doctor's inquisitive look required an explanation. "I hope you don't mind, Allan, but I had arranged to meet someone else here tonight as well. I believe you know him." Her gaze moved back to the door. Everyone had been seated, and service had begun. What kind of game was *he* playing with her?

She was hardly aware of Collier's reply. Just as one waitress finished setting a third place and another was serving up generous portions of enchiladas, tacos, refried beans, and rice, Luke arrived. He swept in on a breath of cool air and shut the door behind him in one smooth motion, turning to stand almost defiantly in the entryway. Joey rolled her eyes and stifled a groan. He never failed to make a dramatic entrance, and if he had planned to draw the castigating eyes of the town to him once again, he had certainly succeeded.

Dr. Collier paused in the act of raising a forkful of rice to his lips as he followed her gaze to the door. The clink of silverware and glasses faded to silence. Joey felt her own face flush with chagrin and something she didn't care to name.

Luke's attention was only for her. Like a hero out of an old western, he strode into the room, ignoring the stares, and stopped before the table. His green-gold eyes moved from hers to Dr. Collier's.

"I see there has been a change in plans. I hope I'm not intruding." His voice was silky and almost intimidating, but the force of his concentration was now on the doctor. Collier shifted in his seat but set his fork down calmly, giving Luke stare for stare. Fascinated in spite of herself, Joey twisted her hands in her napkin and watched.

"Ah, Luke. So nice to see you. It's not often we're graced with your company here." His mild blue eyes shifted from Luke to Joey and back again. "Joey was just telling me she was expecting another friend tonight. I can see I won't have to introduce the two of you."

There was a brief moment of perceptible tension between the two men, and Joey remembered what Maggie had told her. These two knew each other—and clearly knew each other well. Collier wasn't like the other townsfolk, who seemed reluctant to deal with Luke at all. And, unlike the others, Allan Collier stood his ground.

"Sit down, boy. Don't just stand there. The food'll get cold, and it's much too good to waste." Collier dropped his gaze back to his plate and began to eat. Joey watched Luke stiffen at the word "boy"—and suddenly succumb to the doctor's eminently unruffled good sense. He slipped into his chair noiselessly and pinned Joey with a stare that she interpreted as disapproval—and something more ambiguous. She smiled back sweetly.

Just as Joey began to resent the long silence, Luke seemed to relax. He leaned back in his chair; one of his booted feet touched Joey's under the table. "Sorry I'm late," he said softly, all the threatening tension gone in an instant. "I didn't realize you knew Allan. It's always a pleasure to see you too, Doctor."

His unnerving golden stare did not seem to break the older man's concentration on his food, which he consumed with every evidence of enjoyment. The doctor swallowed and took a sip of wine.

"Have you ever had Mexican food, Luke? Considering how seldom you usually come to town, you should take advantage of the opportunity." He seemed to emphasize certain words in a way Joey couldn't quite interpret; there was definitely an undercurrent here. She took an experimental mouthful of enchilada, hardly tasting it.

"It's very good," she put in quickly. Luke's gaze shifted back to her. She leveled her best and brightest grin at the doctor and caught Luke's reaction out of the corner of her eye. Surely that quickly suppressed frown couldn't suggest something as simple as jealousy?

"You were right about the food here, Allan," Joey said.

Luke's eyes narrowed. "I see Allan's been doing his best to make you comfortable in town, Joey," he murmured. His sudden smile was not particularly friendly. "Like most doctors, he's very handy with advice."

Collier looked up from his meal. "Alas that more

people don't recognize good advice when they hear it," he commented softly.

There was a long, humming moment of tension between the two men, but at last Collier dropped his eyes, and the moment passed. Luke lifted a fork and picked at his food in brooding silence. He examined the rice critically and let it fall back to the plate.

"If you won't eat it, I certainly will," Collier said jovially as he pushed away his empty plate. Luke scowled and gestured; the doctor took the proffered food with a nod of thanks.

The rest of the meal alternated between periods of silence, mild verbal sparring between Luke and the doctor, and long, significant looks between her and Luke. Joey had found herself with little appetite; her unease was suddenly back in full force. She'd been prepared to flirt outrageously with Luke at dinner, but Collier's presence seemed to inhibit both of them. Luke was subdued, more restrained with her than he'd ever been, no evidence of his predatory interest other than the intensity of his gaze.

However much Joey might have appreciated the temporary reprieve, it did not serve her purpose. She contented herself with encouraging glances at Luke, meeting his eyes as if she were delivering an unspoken promise. Had they been alone, she thought she might have touched him; she wanted to know if he would burn her.

Sooner or later she would have to find out.

When the meal ended and groups of sated diners scattered to gossip or leave for other activities, the three of them sat in subdued solitude. Luke's gaze came to rest more and more frequently on the doctor. *If looks could kill,* Joey thought absurdly. Collier seemed oblivious, sipping the last of his wine with many sighs of contentment As much as she enjoyed his company, it was clear she would make no progress with Luke in the doctor's hindering presence.

Even so, her heart began to pound with leaden thuds as she cleared her throat and straightened in her chair. "It's been a wonderful evening, Allan. I'm glad you were able to join us." She smiled, hoping he would take the hint graciously. At first she was certain he would ignore it, but he fixed her with a sudden, very knowing look that confirmed her earlier suspicions.

"Ah. You have plans for the evening." His lifted brows made it a question; he seemed to be studiously avoiding Luke as he gazed with real interest at Joey. She shifted uncomfortably.

"Yes. We have plans." Luke cut off her stammered reply and rose to his feet. The move was somehow ominous; in a single, almost imperceptible motion he shifted to stand behind the doctor's chair, leaning over it in a way that sent shivers up Joey's spine.

Collier slumped more deeply into his seat. He took one last lazy sip of wine and smiled at Joey. Luke's fingers tightened on the carved wood of the chair back. Collier's only acknowledgment of his presence was the barest tilt of his head; his eyes never left Joey's.

"Well, my dear, far be it for me to interfere in the plans of two young people." His tone was even, but the searching quality of his expression could not be mistaken. Joey shivered again at the unspoken message in his eyes. Was it because he knew Luke all too well that he seemed to be trying to warn her?

With deliberate confidence, Joey answered him. "I hope we'll be able to have dinner again soon, Allan."

The doctor nodded, all the laugh lines smoothed from his face, and rose. Luke had so effectively boxed him in that he could not leave the table, and he turned and looked the younger man up and down with a stare that came very close to scathing. Luke stepped back quickly and released the chair. Collier's gaze lingered on

Luke's face for a long moment, and then he turned back to Joey.

"I share that hope, Joey." He looked over his shoulder as he moved away. "Please do remember that if you ever need me—for anything—I'm easy to find." With one last significant glance at Luke he left them in silence.

Joey locked gazes with Luke across the table. There was an almost tangible potency in him, as if he had been restraining some wild passion and was on the verge of releasing it at last. She almost called after the doctor then. But even her uncertainty—yes, even her fear, she admitted—could not erase the memory of why she was here. What she wanted, what she needed and had fought so long to find.

His long fingers played across the worn wood of the chair back. "I find it very stuffy in here, don't you?" His tone was light, so unlike what she expected to hear that she nearly jerked in reaction. Her gaze broke from his to take in the empty room.

"Yes." She stared down at the table before her. "Yes, I find it very stuffy in here."

"Then why don't we find somewhere more pleasant to talk," he suggested, moving around the table to take her arm. She flinched and caught herself as he touched her, offense and excitement mingling uncomfortably. He didn't quite burn as she had feared, as her dreams had promised—but the casual possessiveness of his gesture, the subtle intimacy of it, almost made her tremble.

"Shall we go?" he said, seemingly unaware of the effect he had on her. Struggling for composure, she allowed Luke to guide her out the door and onto the porch, and then across the verge of neatly kept lawn. Beyond, the forest was darkening; the sky was still flushed with a patina of gold and pink. It was beautiful. Joey wished she were able to appreciate it. But her heart was in her throat, and it was all she could do to suppress a powerful desire to shake from head to toe. Even as they walked across the grass to the forest's edge, she was preparing herself for the next move in the game.

# Chapter 4

Luke felt her tension under his hand as he led her out of the lodge. He had learned enough of Joey—of her stubborn pride and determination—that he could not believe she was truly afraid of him. She had held up remarkably well, all things considered. Ordinarily he would have been happy to make use of any advantage in the hunt, but he found in himself a sudden—and surprising—realization that he didn't want her fear. He wanted very much to believe that her almost imperceptible shivers were the result of desire. The same desire he felt for her.

She did not resist as he crossed the lawn and into the trees. He was eager to get the smell of the lodge out of his nostrils—the smell of too many people, of tension and hostility. He had gone there tonight fully intending to take advantage of his reputation, to upset the narrow-minded townsfolk gathered there in a place where he seldom intruded. But somehow it had not left him with the usual satisfaction. And there'd been Allan with his damned interfering ways. . . .

Perhaps, he considered as the trees closed over them, he was simply too preoccupied. The clean odor of pine needles, rich earth, and growing things gradually washed away the stench of civilization, and he could smell *her* again—that unique scent that drew him so powerfully.

As he paused to look down at her, she tugged her arm free of his grip and rubbed it slowly, gazing about. He could sense no unease about the place he had chosen—nothing but restrained curiosity and that same fierce resolve that never left her eyes. She, too, was preoccupied.

"I'm sorry if I hurt you," he said. With a start she ceased the absentminded massage of her arm and disguised the movement, folding her arms across her chest.

"You didn't hurt me," she answered. Her eyes scanned over the trees again and finally met his. "Though it would be nice if you asked next time instead of grabbing me." She did not quite manage to hide a faint tone of irritation in her voice, though her expression remained smooth and unruffled. He sensed her nervousness clearly under the calm facade; she might have succeeded in deceiving another man.

"I'm glad to hear there will be a next time." He let his eyes wander over her as he had not felt free to do in Collier's presence, admiring the clean lines of her body, the lithe suppleness and delicacy. She was beautiful— but not merely beautiful. His pulse rose as she shifted, leaning back against a tree trunk with unconscious grace.

"You didn't eat much tonight," she offered at last, sidestepping his comment. She was not looking at him now; looking, in fact, everywhere but at him, and her fingers played idly with the rough bark at her back. Luke wanted to see her eyes again; he wanted to see the desire in them. "Allan was right, you know. That was pretty decent Mexican food."

He found it hard to concentrate on her attempts at conversation. "I'm sure it was. But I leave exotic cuisine to Allan; I have a taste for other things." He moved forward a step, willing her to acknowledge him. She turned her cheek against the bark, pale hair fanned out to catch in the serrated edges of the dark wood. The twilight calls of birds, the chattering of a squirrel above them filled the long silence. Her breathing was soft and rapid; he could feel her uncertainty as clearly as if she had spoken it aloud.

When she turned to him at last she had put on a smile, but her chin was tilted up, and her shoulders were squared with decision. "Shall we walk a bit?" she suggested. It was she who took the lead this time, pushing away from the tree and reaching up to tuck her arm through his.

The gesture startled him. A shock ran through his body as it had when he had touched her before; it overwhelmed any desire to examine her change in attitude. Her hip touched his thigh, and he could sense every inch of her in his imagination. He fought the rising compulsion to forget caution and feel her body against his in truth.

But she was talking again, with that lightness that seemed designed to hold him at bay. "I never quite get over how quiet it is here—how untouched. Where I'm from, it's hard to remember that any place like this exists."

She reached out with her free hand to brush fingers across the leaves of a mountain ash, pausing to examine the small applelike berries. "It would be nice sometime to come up here with no other purpose than simply to enjoy it. There's so much to see, and I feel as if I've only scratched the surface."

Luke looked down at the pale crown of her head,

breathing in the scent of her hair. "The forest has many mysteries," he murmured. "There are things here few human beings have ever seen."

"But you have?" She stopped to meet his eyes, the deep brown of her own catching the last of the light filtering through the trees. "Do you suppose you might be willing to show me some of these 'mysteries'?" Her voice had suddenly become throaty, her expression almost an invitation.

Luke shifted to face her, bringing his hand up to touch her shoulder in the lightest of caresses, deliberately keeping his craving in check. "That might be possible. Very possible."

He leaned forward slowly, and she did not draw back; his face hovered inches above her own. Parted and full of promise, her lips beckoned. . . .

Her deft retreat was so subtle it took him completely unaware. Somehow she slipped away, moving back until she stood once more against the anchor of a sturdy fir. A smile flickered on her face, almost teasing; he drew in his breath and forced it out again carefully.

"If you want to see things no other woman has seen, I can show them to you," he breathed, his footsteps soundless as they passed among the ferns and fallen needles. She was tall, but she had to look up at him as he advanced to trap her against the tree. He stopped mere inches away, letting her feel his nearness, not quite touching. "Is that what you want, Joey?"

Her eyes were hooded with deliberate allure. "What do *you* want, Luke?" She stretched her arms behind her, curving about the trunk, open and vulnerable. He gave up any pretense of circumspection.

"You know what I want, Joelle." He pressed against her, feeling the swell of her breasts, his arousal hard where she was soft. He set his hands to the rough bark on either side of her, leaning forward until the pale hair falling over her forehead stirred with his breath. Her palms came up flat against his chest, and his heart beat hard under her touch. Never, never had he wanted any woman this much. But soon, soon, he would have her. . . .

The pressure of her hands was firm and steady. "I know what you want, Luke. I'm flattered by your interest." Her eyes flickered down. "I've never been the impulsive type, but you're very . . . persuasive. If only I didn't have other commitments, things I have to do first . . ." Her voice was still throaty, but it quivered now, her body resisting his. The words cut through his potent hunger like a dash of water from a mountain stream.

He froze and stared into her eyes. She looked up, blinking but holding his gaze unwaveringly. "I know what you want, Luke. And maybe, if I can finish what I set out to do here, I might feel free to accept what we could both enjoy." She let out her breath slowly. "If you'll help me, Luke."

A tremor ran through Luke, a shudder of unexpected fury. For a long moment he wavered between taking her then and there, silencing her cold bargaining with the rage of his lust and abandoning her to the uncertain mercy of the forest. But he drew into himself, allowing the anger to become cold and hard, as it did when he caught the townsfolk glaring at him with their implacable bigotry.

He withdrew from her slowly, pulling his body away until he could no longer feel her compelling warmth.

"So."

He looked her up and down, and she set her jaw defiantly. Even now he could admire her for that. "You've been playing a nice little game with me, Joey. A dangerous game." He suppressed the desire to turn and pace furiously up and down before her. "I'm not in the mood for any more games. You want something from me. What is it?"

To her credit, she never hesitated. "I want you to

guide me up into the mountains to find the place where my parents died." She let the words fall into silence.

Luke stood very still, listening to the wind in the tops of the spruce and fir. "Of course. That *is* why you came to Lovell, isn't it?"

He remembered everything he'd learned of her and knew that his first guess had been right. He'd known she wanted something, had even acknowledged to himself that he would use that to further his own ends. It should come as no surprise that her change in attitude had been no more than a desire to get what she wanted. She had never fallen prey to his charms at all.

He shouldn't care. He wanted her. It shouldn't matter how she came to him, or for what reason. But it did matter. It mattered more than he cared to admit.

He laughed harshly at himself, and the laugh escaped him. "I see. You haven't been able to find anyone else, and you thought I would serve your purpose."

She was still staring at him, wide-eyed, biting her lip now. Luke felt some grim satisfaction. Even she wasn't quite as fearless as she wanted him to believe. Not so entirely unlike the others. For a moment he let her feel the force of his power and watched her react. It seemed cold comfort, even when her next words carried a stammer of distress.

"Yes." Sensitive lips trembled. "It's the only reason I'm here. It's something I have to do, and—I'll do it however I have to." Her low voice shook with emotions so tangled he could not tell which was dominant: fear, determination, anger, pride. "I know you can help me."

For the first time Luke turned away, gazing out into the welcoming dark of the forest. "What do you know about me, Joey?" In the wake of her silence he circled to face her again. "I don't hire out. I don't take city girls into the mountains, and I don't like being used."

"Neither do I." She stepped forward, abandoning the dubious security of the tree. "You'd use me the same way, for your own—gratification. I've heard all about you, Luke. Don't go lecturing me about using."

The edge in her voice challenged him, and for a long moment their gazes locked. "I can pay you, Luke. One way or another." Her voice softened, and lambent brown eyes drowned him like dark water. "It's not so much. All you have to do is take me where I need to go before the first snow falls."

Luke let his gaze drop first, curling his lip as he looked her up and down. He was not used to this strange war of emotions within himself; far less did he understand it. "What do you know about the mountains, Joey? Have you ever gone a day without food or a night without electricity?" The cold harshness of his tone was a deliberate blow. "Have you ever walked ten kilometers over rough uphill terrain and then spent an hour gathering wood for a fire? Have you ever, in your sheltered life, faced the possibility of a lonely, painful death?"

Joey froze a few steps away, her expression rigid. "Yes, I have." The gold embers in her eyes sparked into flame. "Damn it, Gévaudan, I've worked long and hard for this. I've trained and prepared, and I'm as fit as anyone could be."

She set her hands on her hips and bid him look at her; he could not have done otherwise, even now. Her body was taut with indignation, and for the first time, coldly, Luke evaluated her: not as a woman he wanted, but as he would an animal for health and fitness—as he would look for fatal weakness in potential prey.

Under the grace he had admired was strength, that much was certain; there was the firmness of muscle under soft skin, the erect posture that hinted of confidence, the flush of health that extended to the aura he had sensed about her from the beginning. There was a flush to her cheeks, too; even as she held herself for his inspection, she was aware of him. He could see it in her eyes, hear it in the hiss of her indrawn breath. And he—he could not look at her without feeling a return of overwhelming desire. With an angry curse, he rejected it.

"Impossible," he snapped. He watched her jerk at the outright rejection. Had she expected otherwise— expected him to agree because she had a fit body—a body he wanted? Oh, he wanted her, he still desired her, but he found within himself a stronger compulsion. She would not win her little game; she would not be the first to dominate *him*.

He began to turn away; the confusion of his feelings for her had become entirely too complex. This was not what he had wanted, not what he needed. The night called to him, urged him to leave her manipulations and compelling attraction far behind. He wanted nothing more now than to escape. . . .

The feather-light touch of her hand on his arm stopped him with the grip of a vise. He cursed himself again for being unable to shake her off, to leave her standing there; but he stayed.

"Luke, I need you." Her voice had grown soft, almost pleading. Her fingers moved against the flannel of his sleeve, and he felt them as if there were no barrier at all between. "I'm desperate. I *need* your help." The warmth of her body radiated against his back. "Nothing has ever been more important to me than this— nothing. Please . . ."

The raw note of despair in her voice was like pain, so unlike what he knew of her that it almost shocked him. It almost took him out of his anger, his pride and confusion. Almost.

He pulled away from her abruptly, freeing his arm from her grasping fingers. "I'm sorry, Joey." The coldness of his voice mocked his words. "I can't help you. It's too bad you wasted so much of your time." She made a soft, helpless sound, but he refused to look back. "I suggest you come back with me now, if you don't want to be left out here alone."

Without further words he started back for the lodge, his strides long and heedless. The crackle of brush sounded behind him as she struggled to keep up.

"Luke, please . . ."

He whirled so suddenly that she stopped herself only inches from colliding with him, her face frozen in startlement. "Don't push me, Joey. *Don't push me.*"

He knew from the slow alteration of her expression that she finally grasped what he said; that she saw the force he held in check, the savagery just under the surface. He willed her to feel it so she would never forget.

When he turned his back on her again, he hoped she did understand.

At the end of another nearly sleepless night, Joey sat in bed with the covers pulled up to her chin and contemplated utter failure.

How had things gone so wrong? She knew he'd wanted her—and she'd made doubly sure of that before attempting to strike her bargain. If only she'd had more time, more time to lead him on, make him believe he wouldn't be sacrificing anything—least of all his pride—to help her. . . .

The morning light gave a cheerful cast to the room that seemed to mock Joey's despair. She caught the blanket in both fists and pulled as if she might tear it apart. She had moved too quickly. She had been too impatient, too inept at making veiled promises she had no intention of keeping. Luke had seen through her. She'd ruined her last chance.

Joey seriously considered spending the entire day under the covers, refusing to face a world that seemed altogether hostile. She could not even face the prospect of turning to Maggie—not after what had happened. It was far too humiliating. Better to avoid people entirely, so that her defeat remained hidden from everyone but him.

In the few hours of the night when she had managed to sleep, *he* had been in her dreams. She could not even bar him from that last refuge.

Joey got out of bed and moved to the window. It was another of those crisp, flawless days when the sky was so blue, it almost hurt to look at it. The trees lay like a rich green carpet over the hills and valleys and mountains, up to the timberline where the peaks rose in stark, forbidding splendor. *He* had said there were many mysteries there few human beings had ever seen. The one mystery she needed most to solve was still beyond her reach.

With a groan of utter frustration, Joey grabbed her brush from the bureau and began to pull it through her tangled hair with punishing jerks. This room, this lodge, was too small to contain her equally tangled emotions; she knew she had to escape, to be alone and walk the woods and hills until she could walk no farther. Beyond that she refused to think.

She threw on jeans and a shirt and a light jacket, laced up her boots, and filled her water bottle in the communal bathroom down the hall. Food was the last thing on her mind; she slipped out the back way, avoiding the kitchen and dining room. It wasn't until she'd crossed into the woods that she felt some of the oppressive despondency lift.

For a long while she did nothing but wander aimlessly, making no attempt to choose one path over another, deliberately ignoring all the dictates of safety she had learned over the summer. Safety, security, caution— all those things seemed unimportant now.

She followed narrow deer trails that cut swaths through the ferns and shrubs and small trees under the canopy of the forest, found the places where moose had bedded among the willow thickets alongside meandering streams. She discovered late-summer fruit burgeoning on thickly crowded shrubs and shared the sweet ripeness of huckleberries with forest birds. Grouse and chipmunks scurried out of her way as they gorged on the season's final bounty; jays and squirrels scolded from above, contrasting with the sweeter songs of chickadee and warbler. She watched a black bear forage from the cover of a thicket of dogwood and narrowly avoided a pointed brush with a porcupine.

Her wandering led her out of the aspen groves, quaking leaves already gold with the touch of autumn, and up into the province of Douglas fir and spruce. Here the land rose, broken by meadows with the last of their summer wildflowers, reaching up to the elevations ruled by towering lodgepole pine. And beyond that, beyond her reach, the timberline marked the highest places, where only the hardiest wildlife flourished. All but a few of the animal species of the high slopes would move to the sheltered lowlands with the coming of winter; already the migrations had begun.

Joey settled on a large rock at the edge of a meadow and watched a wedge of geese move across the sky. Their mournful cries seemed to express her feelings more clearly than any sound a human voice could make; she observed them until they disappeared over a distant mountain range, tiny motes almost lost from sight, and did not give in to the urge to cry with that same wild longing.

She sat there as the day passed and saw the goshawks and red-tails as they passed overhead in search of prey; held so still that even the deer left the sanctuary of the woods' edge to browse in the meadow. It was hard to focus on the death of her dreams when so much life surrounded her. But always, always, there was the bleakness of that unresolved loss, the memory of what she might have had, of wholeness, that might forever be just beyond her reach. . . .

Had she not been so lost to any concern for her own safety, she might have felt surprise at the light touch on her shoulder. There was no warning, no footfall to alert her, but her heartbeat remained dull and steady as she turned to face him.

"Luke." The indifference in her voice seemed alien even to herself. She felt no anger, no humiliation—only a leaden acceptance. "I don't really want any company right now, if you don't mind."

Joey turned away before he could answer, and he moved soundlessly around the rock to crouch beside her. "You're a long way from home." He let strained silence fall between them; in spite of herself, she felt her skin shudder at his nearness, an awareness that cut through the apathy that wrapped her in a protective cocoon. She didn't want it. She didn't want to feel anything, least of all about him.

"Yes. I'm a very long way from home." She folded her arms against herself and stared out at the meadow without seeing it. "It seems to me that this wilderness is big enough that a person should be able to find some peace. Please—leave me alone."

She knew without any further comment from him that he had no intention of respecting her wishes. She pushed herself to her feet, muscles stiff from long sitting, and prepared to leave him there, as he had left her the night before. But he stopped her; his hand shot out and locked about her arm, holding her in place. From deep within the muffling folds of apathy anger flared, and she prepared to round on him; his voice arrested her as surely as his grip.

"You aren't alone any longer, Joey," he whispered. "Hold absolutely still and look to the north."

She looked. She obeyed his command without any thought of defiance and caught her breath. At the verge of the meadow stood two vast brown shapes, magnificent and ungainly. Two bull moose, crowned by impressive racks of antlers, faced each other across a span of trampled grass. One of them bellowed, stretching its neck and shaking its head in threat. Just beyond the adversaries a cow, demure and plain, stood by to witness the competition.

Luke spoke very softly close to her ear; his warm breath caressed the sensitive skin. "When you see moose in rut, you stay very still and very quiet. With any luck they won't notice us." His grip tightened on her arm, though whether in warning or reassurance she could not tell, and he maneuvered her until her body pressed against his. She would have cursed him soundly for his perfidy, but she had no time; with a crack of collision, the two bulls came together in battle.

Joey did not know what to expect. Would this be a fight to the death? She held her breath and forgot everything else as the animals disengaged, threatened each other with snorts and bellows, and charged again. Luke's arm had somehow found its way about her shoulders, and she leaned her cheek on his chest without thinking, all her attention on the drama before them.

It ended almost as soon as it had begun. Without warning one of the bulls danced away, tossing its head angrily, while the other charged after it. It soon became a rout, with the defeated party crashing off into the brush as the victor turned his attentions to the placidly grazing cow. Joey felt a blush rising at what she feared might follow, suddenly aware of the proximity of Luke's hard chest; but much to her relief the two animals merely wandered at a sedate pace to the far edge of the meadow, browsing as they went, and disappeared among the trees.

"It usually doesn't result in serious injury," Luke commented. His deep voice vibrated against her ear. He had not loosed his hold on her; if anything, it had tightened. Now her heart had begun to race in spite of her will; every last protective shred of indifference drowned in a flood of perception. Of him.

She clenched her fists and held herself rigid. He would not humiliate her again, he would not. . . .

"Animals have more sense than human beings," he said softly. Without quite letting go, he pushed her away to gaze at her, searching her eyes. He compelled her to look, and she did. He filled her sight and all her senses, no matter how hard she fought it. His hard face was almost relaxed, almost gentle; last night's ferocity was gone as if it had never existed. The fragile framework of her resolve collapsed entirely, and she could do nothing but feel him, though she wanted nothing more than to run and never see him again.

The grip of his fingers became a caress on her arm, trailing from shoulder to elbow. "Animals play games of dominance," he told her, "but they know when to quit."

His other hand released its hold and moved up to touch her face with feather softness. She closed her eyes and shuddered. She was melting in his heat, and she did not want it—and yet she wanted it so powerfully that everything she knew and believed in was disintegrating around her.

At last she gained enough control to open her eyes and face him again. "We're not animals," she whispered. "We're people. Life isn't so simple for us." She cursed herself for her vulnerability and for revealing so much, more than she wanted him to know. But she saw no triumph in his eyes.

His thumb brushed along her jaw. For a long moment he looked away, across the meadow and forest and beyond to the distant mountains. "Sometimes things *are* simple," he murmured. His hands moved back to her shoulders. "Joey, I've changed my mind. I'll help you find what you're looking for."

Joey's heart stopped. She stared at him, at an expression that revealed no hint of humor or calculation. She didn't know him, she reminded herself. She didn't know him; she had no reason to trust him. But she knew he was in earnest. She knew it with as much certainty as she had ever believed anything in her life.

There was no thought for what had made him change his mind, no time for lingering injured pride or doubts. Joey gave in to exultation and flung her arms about him. For an instant he was rigid against her, and then he was crushing her in a grip that almost drove the breath from her lungs. His face was pressed against her hair, his lean hardness molded to her body so that she could see and smell and feel only him.

When he let her go, setting her back on her feet, she was shaking. She had to hold on to him to keep from falling, and he supported her with his hands under her elbows, no more willing to let go than she. There were no bonds of logic to hold her back and bid her analyze the situation in coldly rational terms. There were no careful plans to consider. When his mouth came down on hers, she met it joyfully.

The heat now was like the heat in her dreams, all-consuming; the fire of his hunger for her met and mingled with her own desire. As in the dreams, nothing else mattered; the rest of the world faded to insignificance.

"Luke," she gasped against his mouth, and he pulled away to look at her with burning eyes, green licked with golden flame. For an eternity he did nothing but gaze at her with that strange and unfathomable stare, and she moaned as she wound her fingers in his dark hair, pulling him down again.

His arms lifted her easily, holding her so that every hard muscle of his body strained against her own. His mouth pressed her neck above the collar of her shirt and traced along the soft vulnerability of her throat and chin. Somehow the top buttons of her shirt came loose, and his lips were on the upper swell of her breasts while she hung suspended in his embrace.

Her hands clutched helplessly in his hair as his tongue moved over her, leaving a burning trail along her skin. Without conscious thought she wrapped her legs around his hips and felt the hardness of his arousal; she felt her body respond with aching need. He moved against her instinctively, as though no layers of clothes separated them, and his breath rasped in time to his stroking tongue.

When she felt she could take no more of his caresses, he let her slide down along his body and lowered his face to her hair while his hands cupped her buttocks and pressed her to him once more. The coarseness of his cheek rubbed hers as he caught her ear in his teeth, biting and sucking. The growing wildness within her demanded that she respond, that she return his caresses; but he held her so thoroughly captive that she could do nothing but accept what he wished to give.

Her breath had grown ragged, her heart pounding in time to the throbbing deep within that cried out for release. His lips traced over her jaw and found her mouth; long fingers pulled the tail of her shirt from the waist of her jeans and slipped underneath to burn against her ribs. They cupped under her breasts, sliding up to touch her aching nipples. His kiss deepened, almost overpowering, but it demanded and took from her something she was more than willing to give. She opened her mouth for him, accepted his searching tongue, met it with her own. He devoured her. He dominated her completely—and he burned. . . .

"Joelle . . ." His voice was a hoarse groan. She was too lost to hear anything but passion in it until his mouth left hers, his hands left her breasts and slipped free of her shirt. Her mouth was still wet with him, filled with the taste of him, and his withdrawal registered with painful slowness. "Damn it. No."

She focused on him at last, on the strange dull sound of his words. They made no sense. She reached out for him again, and he caught her arms and kept her away, the same easy strength with which he had held her close before.

"No." His breathing came as rough as her own, but it was no longer the breathlessness of rapture. The green-gold eyes were wild—no longer burning but narrowed in sudden and terrible awareness. They looked, not at her, but within at some vision that drew the denial from the depths of his being. His hands tightened on her arms until the reality of pain dispelled the last embers of passion, and her gasp brought him back.

She gazed at him, at the tangled gray-streaked hair, at the mouth that had so recently claimed hers, and at his eyes that widened with something almost like fear. That alone got through to her. It brought with it the first stirrings of rational thought. Suddenly she was aware of the cool evening air, the vast emptiness around them, and how thoroughly she had forgotten herself.

But she had no time to feel any of the emotions that struggled for attention. Luke was backing away; he had released her arms and stared at her now as if she were some terrible apparition and not the woman he had wanted only moments before. Every last hint of grace and confidence and power had deserted him. He half-stumbled over a hidden rock, righted himself without a glance, his eyes never leaving hers.

Belatedly Joey found her voice. "Luke, wait. . . ." She struggled to shape her confusion into words that made sense, that would make him explain—but before they came to her, he was gone. Between one moment and the next he had spun on his heel and bolted, and she was left with nothing but empty air to hear her questions.

For a long, endless span of time she stared after him.

"Why, Luke?" She let her knees give way and dropped onto the rock to bury her face in her hands.

Nothing made sense, nothing was clear anymore. "Why?"

Only the wild geese answered.

Luke ran. He ran until the sobbing of his breath forced him to a more reasonable pace, until the darkness challenged even his keen vision. He ignored the crashing tumult of his progress through the woods, unashamed of clumsiness he never would have tolerated in himself at any other time. At the moment he cared for nothing but the cleansing freedom of unfettered physical exertion.

The forest fell silent at his passage. He was not part of it now, not a natural element it accepted and welcomed. His run trampled ground unbroken by any human footfall, and he came as a despoiler, not a friend. Only the gradual return of sanity reminded him of his proper place.

The frenzy of his flight dropped to a new rhythm. His muscles relaxed into a lope that he could maintain for many kilometers, tireless and even. His mind found its balance again, a harmony with nature that gradually restored some portion of peace. Not entirely; that, it seemed, had been taken from him forever.

His feet unerringly chose the easiest path over broken ground, through thick stands of fir and pine and over open slopes where night-browsing deer stared after him. They knew his thoughts were not for them.

*She* still filled his senses. Though he ran now by instinct, she was with him. For those incredible moments when she had been in his arms, he had paid very dearly. It had been a most terrible revelation.

He had not guessed the half of it before, that first time he'd seen her. She was different—far, far more different than even his dreams had intimated.

He slowed as he approached a familiar arch of bare rocky ground, stopping at last just as he reached the place where it fell away into a deep valley. Here the land stretched out vast and wild; he dropped into a crouch and gazed at the mountains where they caught the light of a quarter-moon.

There was no man-made barrier here to sully the perfection of Nature. No sign of habitation, no ravages of clear-cutting and human carelessness. His own cabin was well hidden, where the lake glittered in the reflection of a perfect, star-laced arc of sky.

Luke allowed his breathing to steady and his thoughts to clear. It didn't seem as if they could ever be entirely clear again—but for now, for this moment, he had to remember who he was. What he was. Perhaps in so doing, he could forget everything he had come to realize about Joey Randall.

A lone, clear cry rose above the subtle noises of the night and the thud of his own heart. He raised his head to listen. They were near, speaking to him in their way. The single howl became a chorus. He wondered what she would think if she heard it. Perhaps she did hear it, even now, from the safety of her civilized world.

Crisp air carried the scent of autumn, the promise of another year's end spent in solitude. He tossed back his head and closed his eyes, longing to join the wolves in their song. But he did not give in to the yearning. Just as he could not give in to what he so desperately wanted. That moment of triumph when he had held Joey in his arms and felt her respond was the first and last time he would ever do so.

For her sake—and for his—he would never see her again.

Even the distant, uncounted, uncaring stars in the black pool of sky were a reminder of her. Like the glitter of gold in her dark eyes . . .

When the wolves howled again, Luke gave himself over to the wild abandon of their song, and to forgetfulness.

* * *

At the end of the first day, when Luke didn't show up in town, Joey wasn't particularly alarmed. Something very strange had happened, something she was still struggling to understand. The encounter had affected him as powerfully as it had her—his final expression as he'd abandoned her at the meadow's edge left no doubt of that.

But that explained nothing. From the very first time she'd seen Luke in the tavern, he had been a mystery. Giving in to his pursuit had only deepened the enigma. Relentless questions dominated her thoughts, awake and in dreams.

There was the question of why he had reacted as he did, when it had been so flagrantly clear he still wanted her. Why he had broken their kiss when, for the first time, everything had been right between them—and she had been so close to achieving her goals.

But the question that haunted Joey most was about herself. She had never believed it would be possible, even for an instant, to find herself at the mercy of something as simple as passion. Or as undeniable. It had seemed reasonable at first to tell herself it had been nothing more than gratitude and relief that her long months of search were at an end. But Joey had never been very good at self-deception. The clarity of her thinking, upon which she so prided herself, would not allow that comfort.

She knew it was not simple at all when it took no effort to remember the feel of his mouth on hers, to smell the wild masculine scent of him, to imagine herself as lost, again, as she had been then. When her dreams became impossibly vivid, and she no longer struggled to escape him at the end but turned willingly into his embrace and met his passion with one equally savage . . .

It was overwhelming. Joey had to admit she was out of her depth. Her reaction to Luke Gévaudan was like nothing she had ever experienced. And now, safe in the quiet rationality of her own room, surrounded by her maps and equipment, she could accept it as a puzzle that must eventually be solved—but not at the expense of her goals. The one thing that had kept her going, always, was the memory of what she had set out to do. Luke had agreed to help her. Whatever price she had to pay would not be more than she could handle.

If it happened that the price was one she could enjoy, so much the better. With a carefully constructed framework of logic, Joey boxed away the questions and consigned unnecessary emotion to the still place in the depths of her heart.

When Luke did not put in an appearance on the second day, Joey became concerned. She paced her room and the nearby woods and avoided everyone. On the third day she grew angry. And on the fourth she resolved that the waiting was going to end.

There were several people who could tell her what she needed to know; as it happened, she found two of them conveniently together on the afternoon she decided to take matters into her own hands.

Maggie and Allan Collier were talking in the middle of Main Street when Joey headed out for the bar. She blinked to see the redhead away from her usual station behind the counter, and in the company of the other person most likely to help. As Joey altered course and walked over to join them, they looked up. She had the distinct and uneasy impression that Maggie looked a little guilty; even Collier wore a peculiar expression. It didn't take much imagination to guess at the subject of their conversation.

"Hello, Joey." Collier examined her from head to toe as if he half expected to find her not quite all in one piece. "We've missed you over the past few days."

Maggie shot the doctor a quelling look, and her heightened color revealed a dusting of freckles over pale skin. "What Allan means is that—uh—you just hadn't come by the bar in a while, and I had sort of gotten used to your visits." She smiled rather lamely. Joey was even more convinced she had walked in on a conspiratorial conversation on the subject of herself—and, she had no doubt, Luke Gévaudan.

She forced a smile. "I'm sorry I've been scarce lately, Maggie. And stop giving me that look, Allan. I might have some reason to think you've been keeping an eye on me."

Maggie had the grace to blush, but Collier merely returned her smile. "It's always a pleasure to keep an eye on a very lovely lady," he said gallantly. Maggie rolled her eyes.

"I appreciate that," Joey murmured, "more than you know. Both of you." She hesitated, considering the best way to broach the topic of what she needed to learn. "You've both been good friends, and I've been neglectful. The fact is, I've finally made some progress in what I came to Lovell to accomplish."

Collier raised his brows, not quite concealing the smallest of frowns; Maggie did not bother to hide hers.

"Don't tell me . . ." the redhead began, but Joey broke in before she could complete her question.

"I found my guide, Maggie. I have a way now to do what I came here to do, and everything is just fine." She intercepted Collier's penetrating look. "I'm fine. Really. But I just need to take care of one more thing before my plans are settled."

Both her friends gazed at her, neither one looking particularly pleased. They both clearly knew who her guide was, even if they hadn't seen her since the day she had made her proposal to Luke. Maggie had made her doubts plain before, though they seemed to have evolved into something more serious. And Collier—

there had been that undercurrent during dinner the previous Thursday, another mystery among all the others. If she'd had time for it, Joey would have asked for explanations.

As it was, she wanted only one thing. She shrugged off further equivocation. "I hope that one of you can help me. I need to know how to get to Luke Gévaudan's cabin."

Her announcement had the expected effect. Maggie shook her head, and Collier's usually pleasant expression grew strained. She knew they were working up to lecturing her, and she had a fair idea of the subject of that lecture. Her nerves had been strained almost to the breaking point by weeks of disappointment and days of emotional turmoil. She had reached the end of her rope.

"I know what you're going to say, both of you. It's not something I need to hear." She deliberately fought to soften the hard note in her voice. "I really can take care of myself. I've been doing it for some time now." Old memories surfaced briefly and were pushed aside. "The only help I need right now is to find out how to track down my guide. He's already agreed to help me, and I just need to make sure he doesn't forget."

Collier closed his eyes. Maggie ran her hands through her mop of hair. Neither one looked reassured or convinced.

She waited for a long moment, gazing from one to the other. "If you can't help me," she said at last, "I'm sure I can get the information I need somewhere else."

There was another span of silence. Joey was preparing to turn on her heel and leave them when Collier cleared his throat.

"Very well, Joey. I can show you how to get to Luke's cabin. It's the better part of a day's travel by foot, going at a reasonable pace." His blue eyes traced over her. "I've no doubt you can handle it—if you're careful." His words carried many layers of meaning. "If you'll come with me back to my office, I'll show you." His glance shifted to Maggie, who hunched her shoulders and shook her head.

"I have to get back to the bar. It's in your hands." Without a single word for Joey, Maggie turned and left them, dodging a slow-moving truck with a swing of her hips.

Joey stared after her. With a soft sigh, Collier took her arm and steered her away from the street. "She's very worried about you, you know."

"I know," Joey muttered. Belated guilt rose in her, quickly suppressed. "And when this is all over, I'll explain everything to her. She's been a good friend."

They were silent as they walked the few short blocks to Collier's office. He greeted the assistant who served as both receptionist and nurse and pulled Joey into his study. Like him, it was comfortable and pleasantly mellow with age, lined with books and neat but just a little dusty. He sat her down in a worn leather armchair opposite his desk and studied a row of oversized folios stacked on a corner table, selecting one with a nod.

As he set the volume on the desk between them, he paused to look at Joey with a grave and measured concern. "Joey, you don't need to tell me it's none of my business. I know perfectly well it isn't. But, like Maggie, I don't want to see you get hurt."

Controlling the urge to grab the folio from his hands, Joey kept her tone level. "I could ask a lot of questions about why you seem to be so sure I'm in some kind of danger. And what was going on between you and Luke during dinner Thursday night." The flicker of surprise on his face told her she had scored a hit.

"But I don't have the time to indulge in questions, Allan. I'm too close." She leaned forward. "Only one thing matters to me right now. Will you help me?"

Collier dropped his eyes in answer and busied himself with the unwieldy pages of the book, flipping over detailed sections of map laid out in colors of earth, water, and forest. At last he paused, muttered to himself, and flattened the page before him.

"Here. This is Luke's land." His gesture encompassed a broad expanse that covered most of the page, dotted with the azure of streams, bordered on one side by a ridge of mountains, and on another, the side closest to town, by a large lake. "He's one of the biggest landowners in this area. Most of it is untouched wilderness."

Joey reached out to touch the page. So much land? Maggie had hinted about it before, but it was only one of many things she still did not know about Luke Gévaudan.

As if he had read her thoughts, Collier's hand settled over hers. "Joey—what do you really know about Luke?" The pressure of his fingers refused to let her dodge the question, and for once she had to acknowledge his very real concern.

She sighed. "I know what I need to know." She met his eyes and tilted her chin and did not look away, willing him to understand.

His hand lifted from hers. "Joey, Joey. There are things you should know, so much I should tell you. . . ." He stopped himself and shook his head wearily. "But I know when I'm licked. Now pay attention." At once he became brisk and businesslike, explaining the best route to Luke's land, pointing out landmarks that would guide her to where his cabin lay on the far side of the lake. He disappeared for a moment and came back with a photocopied duplicate of the map, which he proceeded to mark with a red pen accompanied by indecipherable notes.

When he had finished, Joey took the folded map and smiled at the doctor with gratitude she had no need to feign.

"Thank you, Allan. Thanks for your help—and your

concern. When this is over, I'll buy you a big dinner at the lodge." His expression was so glum that she weakened and reached out again to squeeze his hand. "Don't worry about me, Allan. I'll take care of myself. I always have." She turned away before emotion could weaken her resolve.

"Joey."

Her grip tightened on the doorknob, but she did not turn at his voice.

"Joey, take care. Take great care."

She closed her eyes and left the office without a backward glance, clutching the map in her fist.

# Chapter 5

The next morning was warmer than she expected. Loosening the collar of her jacket, Joey checked the contents of her light knapsack a second time and finished the last bite of muffin. She had forced herself to eat more than she wanted, but she knew she was going to need all the energy she could find during the day ahead.

Joey studied the map a final time, folded it neatly, and tucked it in her jacket pocket. She had a good seven miles to go over heavily wooded country just to reach the near side of the lake; that would be the easiest stretch, since she'd be able to follow a dirt road haphazardly maintained by the town. After that, she'd be passing onto private land—Luke's land. Three or four miles beyond the opposite shore of the lake lay Luke's cabin. As Collier had said, it was a good day's hike, but she felt nothing but anticipation and excitement at the challenge; it felt good, and right, to be finally doing something.

She did not dwell on the fact that a very insistent part of her longed to see Luke again. . . .

The sun had warmed the day even more since early morning; Joey shed her jacket and wrapped it around her waist, pulling the knapsack in place over her shoulders as she started for the road leading out of town. She'd gone a little way in that direction a few times during her explorations, particularly since it was roughly in the direction she had hoped to find the site of the plane crash. But she'd never gone as far as the lake.

Her steps were firm, and her heart beat fast with excitement; fresh mountain air cleared the cobwebs from her mind. The gravel and earth under her feet rolled and crunched as the road narrowed to a rutted path through the trees.

Joey had never felt quite so aware of the wilderness as she did now. The rich scent of the trees was delicious; birdsong seemed sweeter than any man-made music. The contentment she felt seemed to have no logical source, but for once she didn't ask for logical explanations.

By the time she'd been walking for several hours, Joey was beginning to feel less elated than tired. She'd determined to hold out until she reached the lake, just beyond the halfway point of her journey; according to the map, she should be close. Her stomach was rumbling with a reminder that strenuous physical activity required plenty of fuel, and for once she was more than happy to comply with its demands.

The first glimpse of water brought Joey to a halt where the path curved to begin its passage around the lake. Lac du Loup—Wolf Lake. Considering how many times the subject of wolves had come up over the past few weeks, Joey wasn't surprised.

In the past Joey had considered one wilderness lake very like another, but for some reason she found herself regarding this one with considerably more appreciation.

The noon sunshine sparkled like diamonds on the pristine blue surface; Joey had no doubt that the old cliché was completely appropriate. It was a large lake, and the far shore was no more than a greenish-brown haze of distant trees, flanked by the ubiquitous mountains.

Somewhere beyond the other side lay her goal: Luke's cabin. Joey squinted as if she would somehow be able to make it out, and then gave up in favor of searching for a good spot for a picnic lunch.

She wandered some distance along the lake shore before she found just the right place. The trees came nearly down to the water's edge, shielding the lake from the path. A number of large, flat rocks provided an excellent site for laying out her lunch and basking in the sun.

With a groan of satisfaction, Joey eased herself down onto one of the rocks and shrugged off her knapsack. A quick search of the contents revealed her sandwiches, only slightly squished and still edible. In fact, at the moment they looked like a banquet.

She was so lost in appreciation of her meal, and of the absolute peace of the lake, that the sudden intrusion of raucous noise came as a considerably unwelcome shock. Freezing in midbite, Joey held perfectly still and listened.

Voices—there could be no doubt of it—male voices. Quite a number of them, making no attempt at subtlety. She could not make out words, but the tone was enough to alert her.

Joey had no reason to believe the voices meant harm. But she found herself finishing the last of the sandwich and quickly packing away the remainder of her meal, tense with the awareness of how alone she was—and how isolated.

She had just stood up to pull on her knapsack when one of the owners of the voices put in an appearance. He was young—probably younger than she was, in his early twenties—and he was clutching a large bottle of beer in one hand as he plunged out of the trees. His hoarse, slurred voice called something unintelligible to his companions; Joey took an involuntary step back, her mind already on possible routes for escape. But she held her ground, refusing to give in to ridiculous and unfounded fears.

Those fears seemed a little more justified when the rest of the voices joined the first. There were five or six of them, young men in torn jeans and T-shirts, all carrying bottles that suggested an obvious reason for their loud conduct. She recognized a few almost immediately; a couple were regulars at Maggie's bar—so regular, in fact, that only now did she realize that in all probability they didn't have jobs. Employment wasn't easy to come by in Lovell. But that seemed small comfort as, one by one, the men focused on Joey where she stood, alone, at the edge of the lake. She stepped back again and felt water lapping at her heels.

There was a long moment of silence as the men regarded her. Some of them seemed far gone in inebriation, but one or two were still sober enough to fix on her in a way that she didn't like. She held quite still in the faint hope that, somehow, they would decide to be gentlemen and leave her alone.

Her hopes were short-lived. One of the more sober ones, a blond-haired man with watery blue eyes, made an unsubtle remark. Joey heard enough of it that she could not quite suppress a blush; one of the other men laughed. A third followed up with a comment that was unmistakably lewd. Joey set down the knapsack carefully.

"Well, what have we got here? If it ain't the pretty American girl," the first man said appraisingly. He looked her up and down and leered. "Ain't we lucky to have her visit us."

There was a chorus of agreement from the other

men, who moved forward in a ragged clump. Joey's eyes slid about in assessment. This was not going to be easy.

"Ah, she don't look very friendly, Billy," the lewd man slurred. "Kinda stuck-up, if you ask me."

"Yeah, she's not very nice, is she?" complained a third. There was general grumbling. Joey tried to convince herself there was no threat in the sound, and failed. "But you know these American-beauty types. Think they're God's gift and all."

One of the men made a suggestion about what kind of gift he'd like to have from Joey. The lewd man giggled. Joey decided she'd either have to make a run for it or try to take control of the situation. The latter had always been her preferred method, even with men— especially with men.

She kept her face serene and her voice level as she said, "I don't want to spoil your fun, guys. I'm just doing a bit of hiking, and they're expecting me back at the lodge in a few hours. So, if you don't mind, I'll just be on my way."

The men looked at each other. For a moment she thought the calm rationality of her voice might have gotten through to them; then one of the men guffawed.

"Ah, if they don't expect you back yet, you've got plenty of time."

"Yeah, we need a little 'feminine company.' You won't be spoiling our fun at all."

"That's right. You wouldn't mind partying a little with us, would you, 'Ms. Randall'? Just to be friendly?"

Joey listened to the chorus of comments and held back a shudder. "I'm sure you gentlemen understand, but I really have to be going. Maybe some other time . . ."

"Gentlemen! Well, I like the sound of that!" the blond man, Billy, commented with a broad gesture. "Too bad there aren't any here, huh?"

This elicited more laughter, and Joey knew no

amount of "reasoning" was going to get her a reprieve from whatever this bunch had in mind. Or would soon figure out . . .

As if on an unspoken cue, the men began moving toward her again, though one or two showed a little reluctance that might have been hopeful if there hadn't been just enough of them to encourage a mob mentality. Joey saw that they had fanned out in a pattern that would block an escape to the left or right, and that left one direction—back, into the lake. She was considering how best to jump for it when Billy plunged forward. She staggered back, but he caught her arm and held her poised with one foot in water and the other still on dry land.

Joey put all her strength into trying to free her arm, but the man seemed determined to keep it. He chuckled and leaned over to pull her out of the water, his breath hot and foul on her face.

"Not so fast, city girl. Not very friendly at all, are you?" His watery eyes raked over her at close range, lingering on the front of her shirt. "But you sure are pretty. Very nice. Huh, boys?"

There was a chorus of agreement, and Billy tugged her back. Joey dug in her heels and resisted. With his free hand he grabbed the front of her shirt and pulled. Buttons popped free, and Billy was sufficiently distracted by what was revealed that he lost his momentum. His hand moved down to grab at her chest.

That was all the motive and opening Joey needed. She brought every bit of self-defense she had ever learned into play and threw her weight against Billy, using him for support as she brought her knee up against his groin. His reaction was instantaneous and very satisfying. With a grunt of agony he doubled over and dropped his hold on Joey. She was ready. While he struggled to right himself, she plunged backward into the lake.

Joey was a strong swimmer, and she'd hoped to get a good lead on her tormentors. Floundering through the warm shallows, she made for deeper water, but even over her splashing she could hear pursuit. Her boots dragged her down, but she didn't dare to take the time to remove them. Water soaked through her jeans, slowing her further.

With a final burst of despairing energy, Joey dived forward as the lake bottom dropped out from under her feet. Too late. Something caught at her ankle; she tried to kick it free, but it clung stubbornly, and a moment later Billy's head emerged from the water. Joey didn't have to see his expression under the dripping blond hair.

She struggled fiercely as he clawed at her, winding his hands in her waterlogged clothing and catching her braid. She heard herself screaming in rage—a rage that totally eclipsed fear—and it took several violent moments before she realized the cries she heard were not hers alone.

Her captor realized it at the same moment. He froze, and Joey tensed for escape. But it soon became clear that Billy's attention was no longer on her. She followed his gaze back to the shore as his grip loosened and his mouth dropped open in shock.

There was motion at the lake's edge, frantic motion, signs of struggle and cries of anger and pain. The distance was too great for Joey to make out the words, but it was very clear that something had happened to distract her friends on shore—and Billy as well. She kicked free of him and swam a few yards away, but he did not pursue. He threw one threatening glance back at her, cursed viciously, and plunged back for shore.

Joey's heart was pounding with fatigue and reaction; she watched him go and stared beyond to the disturbance among the trees. Over the lapping of water she could hear the yelling, could see the movement of men running to and fro—and, suddenly, a pale, low shape among the darker forms. Joey blinked water from her eyes. She had seen that shape often enough to recognize it for what it was.

Catching her breath and gathering composure, Joey waited while, incredibly, the men on shore fled back into the woods the way they had come, pursued by a swift gray shadow. Their cries receded, and as silence settled back over the lake, Joey prepared to head back. Men or no men—wolf or no wolf—she couldn't expect to swim in place much longer.

By the time she had dragged herself up on the shore, only discarded bottles and scattered footprints marked the erstwhile presence of her unwelcome suitors. For a moment she sat, shivering, on one of the rocks and stared off into the woods. No human clamor came to her ears; the men were long gone. Joey closed her eyes and gave silent thanks to her unexpected savior.

She forced herself to her feet after a brief rest and began to search for her knapsack. It was not where she had left it; she found an apple core near the rocks and one of the bags in which her lunch and snacks had been wrapped; a little farther on, in a clump of bushes, she discovered her jacket and her empty pack.

With a frustrated sigh, Joey returned to the rock. At least it was early afternoon, not night; even so, it was going to be an uncomfortable walk back to town. Her boots were leaden weights, so she took them off and set them out, with her socks, to dry a little. The sun was still warm enough to keep the chill away from her wet body; the jacket, at least, was dry if a bit the worse for wear.

Her map was gone along with the few pieces of equipment she'd carried. Though she might have continued on by memory, she had no intention of showing up at Luke's cabin looking—and feeling—like a drowned rat. With an angry growl Joey pounded her fist against the rock so hard that it stung.

When the wolf appeared a few feet away, she almost didn't see it. It was a shadow among shadows, a little paler but unobtrusive, part of the landscape. *Her* wolf. The wolf that she had seen that day on the hillside. Perhaps the same one who had shown up at her window the night of her first dream of Luke. Her unexpected savior.

Joey wished she had something to give it, some way to thank it. As it gazed at her from the cover of the brush, she met its pale eyes and smiled in spite of herself.

"Well, wolf. We meet again."

It cocked its head and lolled its tongue in an expression ridiculously like a grin.

"Looks like I have you to thank for saving me from those roughnecks. I only wish I had some way to repay . . ."

She broke off when she realized she was talking to empty air. With a shrug, she slid down to the ground and made a makeshift nest against the rock with her jacket. Strange that she felt almost safe knowing the wolf might be near. Secure enough to relax for just a few moments . . .

Joey woke with a start. The sun had dipped to the west, and shadows stretched across the beach, hinting at the coming of evening. Her clothes and shoes were nearly dry, and she knew she'd have to get moving; she would be lucky to make it home before dark. The thought of being out here at night, alone, was motivation enough to pull her up with a groan and contemplate pulling damp boots over stiff socks.

While she tugged them on, she gazed out over the peaceful waters of the lake. How still it seemed, how unlike those men. . . . She froze in midthought. The water was not quite so still after all. There was something breaking the surface in long, regular strokes, cutting across the lake from the east. It didn't take long for Joey to determine that the form was human, a pale shape against azure. Her heart began to pound again; she searched for an object, any object, that might serve as a weapon.

She was considering a smallish rock as a last resort when the figure rose up in the shallows lapping against the beach. A dark head appeared, then broad shoulders, gleaming with rivulets of water. The lake fell away from a distinctly masculine torso, revealed a muscular belly and . . . Joey blinked. Long legs, quite as bare as the rest of him, strode onto shore.

Joey did not need much time to recognize him. *What a strange and unfortunate coincidence,* she thought as she wrapped her arms tightly about her chest.

It was Luke Gévaudan.

If Luke was the least bit concerned over his undressed state, he did not reveal it in the bold way he marched up the beach. To the contrary, Joey thought in some chagrin, he seemed totally unaware of the effect he was having on her. She could feel the slow flood tide of heat rising over neck and face as he stopped to look down at her from his imposing height.

Hugging herself even more tightly and shivering with far more than the late-afternoon chill, Joey tried to keep her eyes turned away. Her efforts were not successful. They kept straying, quite against her will, to the muscular legs at eye level: calves and shins with their masculine dusting of hair, sturdy knees and corded thighs, and higher still . . . Joey used every last shred of willpower to keep from staring at that very prominent part of him. It was rather difficult to ignore, as Luke's state suggested he was very much aware of her after all. His total lack of modesty made her own discomfort—and attendant resentment—all the more acute.

With a deliberate facade of nonchalance, Joey allowed her eyes to slide up, linger half-unwillingly on the bunched muscles of his rock-hard belly, and take in the powerful chest and shoulders. Naked, he didn't really look much different than she had expected; what she hadn't expected was that she'd be seeing him this way in the middle of the forest, or that he would make her feel both helpless and incredibly, amazingly ravenous. For him. And not just because she needed his help.

Drawing in a deep, shaky breath, Joey grabbed control of her raging hormones and allowed her eyes to meet his at last. He had been gazing at her the entire time, unmoving; whatever he thought of her examination of his well-displayed body was not revealed in his pale eyes. They were, in fact, as bleak and hard as she had ever seen them. There was no sign of any desire to seduce her, no will to continue the pursuit he had so suddenly broken off several days before. His expression, in fact, was coldly threatening, and Joey felt herself shiver for yet a third cause.

"You're trespassing on my land," he said, so softly it came out as a growl from the depths of his chest.

So shocked was Joey at this greeting that she momentarily lost the power of speech. Then the heat rose in her face again, this time a heat of outrage and emotions pushed to their limit.

"I'm terribly sorry, Mr. Gévaudan." She bunched hands into fists under her arms where they folded tight against her chest. "It just so happens I had wondered what had happened to you. When you didn't come back to town . . ." She cut off that line of explanation with an angry toss of her head. "The fact is, you had a lot more trespassers than just me. And right now I'm a little cold and tired, and I would like nothing better than to get off your land as quickly as possible." She debated making her point clear by getting up and starting back for town then and there, but something in his eyes held her in place.

"I heard noise on this side of the lake, and came to see what was going on," Luke offered softly. Some of the threatening harshness of his voice was gone, though his expression remained taut and cold. "Tell me exactly what happened."

Joey considered saying nothing just to annoy him; she didn't care for the casual way he commanded her. But she found herself telling him anyway—everything that had happened since she'd arrived at the lake. As she described her confrontation with the town rough-necks, he listened intently; when she told him the gist of what the men had said to her, how they had made their intentions clear, his already icy expression took on a remote savagery that made Joey falter. She could almost see his upper lip curl in a soundless snarl; his eyes narrowed to slits.

Wondering at the sudden alteration, Joey trailed off to silence. His eyes, which had taken on a distant expression not focused on her at all, sought hers again. "Go on," he ordered. Joey found herself grateful that the rage she sensed just under the surface of his toneless voice was not aimed at her.

"The wolf saved me," she concluded. "The same wolf, I think, that I met a couple of weeks ago." She paused to swallow and observe Luke's reaction, half-expecting disbelief or derision. But he merely stared un-blinkingly at her, as if she had commented on the weather. "I don't know what else to think about it. The wolf appeared and apparently chased all of the men away. After I swam back to shore, the wolf reappeared. It looked at me for a few minutes and then ran off. I haven't seen it since. And the men haven't been back."

Luke was silent. She could see no evidence of surprise or doubt on his face, even when his eyes searched beyond her to the forest. In fact—Joey shook her head mentally—she could almost swear that he was not surprised at all. That he had heard something he expected to hear . . .

Amazed at her own surmise, Joey found herself voicing it before she could stop herself. "That wolf—you *know* that wolf, don't you?" She was rewarded by his sudden full attention; his eyes grew suddenly paler as the pupils contracted in shock. That question, at least, he had not expected, and Joey felt a sudden flare of smug satisfaction. "Does that wolf belong to you?"

Her satisfaction and sense of having unbalanced him at last was short-lived. Suddenly he laughed—a deep chuckle that rocked Joey back in genuine astonishment. She had heard him make a similar sound before—brief, subdued, edged with cynicism—but this was a full-blown laugh. The laugh seemed as alien to him as this wilderness was to her. It briefly transformed his face from grim severity to something approaching warmth. And then it died almost as quickly as it had come, leaving Joey's ears ringing with it, and her heart pounding in confusion.

He looked down at her again, some of the humor still lingering in his eyes. "No one ever 'owns' a wolf," he said softly. "But you might say that particular wolf and I are on very good terms."

Joey took this in, with all its implications, while Luke's gaze slid back to the trees behind her. The last of the humor vanished. "I can see I'll have to do something about those men from town. They've come here once too often, and it's about time they learned to stay off private property." His eyes came to rest on her again with a significance she suspected she was missing.

"I think they may have learned their lesson, thanks to your 'friend,'" Joey said. She could not quite control the shivering that had come over her in earnest; some of its was still the aftereffects of her ordeal, but the air was not getting warmer, and neither was she. Luke's formidable shadow cut off much of the fading sunlight, and she knew she had little time left to get back. The thought of making the long hike to town, with the possibility of running into those men again, was becoming less appealing by the moment.

As if he had read her thoughts, Luke's gaze raked over her. She tried to stop her shivering but might as well have asked the wild geese to forgo their annual migration; she could see him take in her condition for the first time. She managed to draw some humor out of the fact that, like most men, he was so completely self-absorbed.

But he reacted. His eyes narrowed again with an entirely different emotion. "Perhaps. But I'll have to make certain of it in any case." She could feel him step forward even when she kept her gaze turned carefully away from his all-too-intrusive presence. "You've been out here too long," he muttered gruffly. "This is not the time of year to be sitting around in damp clothes."

Joey almost laughed in disbelief. "You're telling me that?" She couldn't help herself; she drank him in again from head to toe, and this time, for the briefest moment, the faintest color rose in his tanned face. But it was nothing to the blush that followed in her own when she realized how thoroughly she had once again acknowledged his unclad state. And that awareness of him had never entirely left her, not since he had appeared like a primitive wilderness deity on the beach.

She made haste to cover her discomfiture. "I would like very much to get back home and put on clean, completely dry clothes," she assured him in a deliberately emotionless voice. "But I have to admit that I'm wondering if those men might still be out there. If your wolf friend didn't chase them all the way back to town, of course."

She kept her chin high to keep from drowning in chagrin at having to admit—to him—that she was afraid. That she didn't want to go back to town alone.

It galled her incredibly to acknowledge such a weakness, to give him any power over her beyond what he already had. . . .

But he was staring beyond her again. His broad chest rose and fell with deep breaths that Joey might almost have called agitated, had his face not been so rigidly calm.

"I should go after them," he muttered, more to himself than to her, "and make sure they're hiding in their little holes."

With a deliberate effort he looked down at her, his expression softening in a way that made her bite her lip. "But not now. You can't stay out here." He put his hands on his hips and considered her. "And you can't go back to town. It's too far, and it's too late. And . . ." His gaze raked over her assessingly. "You look like a drowned wood rat."

Joey's mouth fell open in outrage before she could stop it. A thousand cutting remarks flew to the tip of her tongue and died there. She could beg him to take her back, of course; she could further put herself in his power and still have no way of securing his help. She could argue with him here, remind him he'd agreed to help her, and then try returning to town on her own in the dark. Or she could give up all hope of getting his cooperation and go home now, and forget all her hopes and plans.

None of these options seemed the least bit appealing. So she held her tongue until he said what she'd expected him to say. "You'll have to come back with me. My cabin is some distance away, but it's a lot closer than town."

Having come to this decision, it was clear to Joey he did not expect her to object. She bristled. She fumed. But she also realized that he made perfect sense; and his cabin had been her destination all along. That much hadn't changed. She still needed his help, and she still was bent on getting it, one way or another. That they weren't the circumstances she preferred had little to do with it.

"All right," she admitted at last. "I guess I don't have much choice." She pursed her lips and met his eyes with deliberate coolness. She *would* stay in control. "I should thank you for helping me out. And for your 'friend's' help, too." She thought back to the wolf and the way it had stared at her the way Luke was now.

"Later I'm going to ask you about that wolf." She made the statement a challenge, to let him know that she didn't give in easily—to anything. He might have her at a disadvantage, but she was still someone to be reckoned with.

She half-expected him to offer his arm in support, but he kept his distance. In fact, he seemed finally aware that she wore clothing while he had none at all.

"Wait here," he commanded, and before she could answer, he had bounded off into the trees.

She caught a flash of tanned skin among the deep green of the wood and then no more; pulling on her jacket, she squinted the way he had gone. She grew rapidly irritated by his absence as the sun sank lower in the sky and the wind grew ever more penetrating. But then, all at once, he was back. He was still bare from the waist up, but snug jeans now covered everything below.

With an uneasy start, Joey realized that the covering did not seem to make much difference. The awareness of him she had been fighting all along was not the least reduced by the addition of clothing. And he still showed not the slightest sign of being uncomfortable himself: Even his feet were bare on the damp gravel of the beach.

Joey thought she would have liked to be very disgruntled if she had been less cold and tired; she would have liked the option of turning and leaving now, even if she hadn't planned on doing so. But she shrugged it off philosophically. She was a practical woman, a realist. She'd always been and always would be, and even Luke Gévaudan didn't have the power to change that.

He started off, looking back at her inquiringly when she hesitated. With a last final glance around the place that had seemed so beautiful and peaceful, she zipped up her jacket and followed. She had a feeling it was going to be a long, uncomfortable walk. And the discomfort was not a matter of mere cold and weariness. She wished with quiet desperation that it were that simple.

Luke was painfully, irrevocably aware of her. Every one of his senses had been alive to Joey from the instant he had seen her on the beach and through everything that had followed. The very best of his intentions were being defeated one by one.

Even as he heard her grimly struggling to keep up without revealing any hint of weakness, his own heart was pounding with the strain of being so near to her. She seemed to dominate sight and sound and sense of smell, so that he hardly knew where he put his feet or consciously remembered to take the right path. Somehow his feet found their own way without any help from his mind. What there was of his rational mind was fully fixed on her.

Did she knew how she affected him? She must have seen at least some of it, though he had been careful not to let it show on his face, even when his body betrayed him. She had not shown any shock or horror at his nudity. For him it was nothing; for someone brought up as she had been, it surely must have been strange at the very least. But she had kept her composure—and made him lose his.

A breath of her scent came to him teasingly as they walked. Her clothes had clung to her skin; the shirt had been pulled open during her struggle with the brutes from town, and he was well aware that she wore no additional protective layers underneath. The cold sculpted points where her breasts met fabric; what the jacket covered he had no trouble imagining.

Pale, damp hair had been wrung out and twisted into her usual braid, and it was true that she had indeed looked rather like a drowned wood rat—but only because her peculiar vulnerability had forced him to find a defense of words. Even bedraggled and smudged with dirt, she was desirable. He had never expected her to look so lost, so in need of help. It had been easier to regard it all as an exercise when she had seemed so certain of her own invulnerability. Or when she was as determined to use him as he had been to seduce her.

But now she was simply alone and, he knew, frightened, however well she attempted to conceal it from him. Once he would have been gratified by that familiar reaction. Now he cursed it for making things worse than they had been.

Everything had changed with that kiss—that terrifying, exhilarating kiss so unlike any other he'd experienced. He'd followed his resolve not to go back into town, not to see her again; he hadn't counted on her coming after *him*.

She half stumbled on a fallen log, and he reached out automatically to steady her. The contact brought both of them to a sudden, startled halt. He dropped his hand instantly. He had felt the heat of her skin through the sleeve of her jacket; she stared at him now with brown eyes wide. Whatever had happened before—she still felt it, too. He knew why she had come after him, but he also knew her motives were not as clear-cut as she wanted to believe.

He wished he could have gained some satisfaction out of it.

Though he told himself he was taking her back to his cabin for her own good, his motives were no clearer than hers. Never had he been forced to face this kind of confusion with any of the other women.

They walked in silence. The shadows grew longer and the light receded under the canopy of trees as they passed in and out of the forest, skirting the lake along the deer track that the path from town had become. Occasionally he led her on a shortcut through unmarked land; he wondered if she had any conception of how few human feet had crossed there. Her face was set in stubborn determination; to prove, he thought, that she could keep up and didn't need him. That she wasn't afraid. She wrapped her arms about herself and refused his help, even when she might have used his steadying grip.

He had been concentrating on ignoring her to the best of his ability, forgetting the feel of her supple body in his arms, the uninhibited passion of her kiss and what it had done to him. But when she lost her footing at the edge of a creek and he was there to catch her, he knew it wasn't going to work.

She was too tired to fight him. Her body was limp in his arms for a long moment as her breath sobbed and her eyes screwed shut in unutterable weariness. He could feel it as if it were his own. The pale oval of her face was lovely even haggard with exhaustion; the lips parted with her breathing were just as enticing. The softness of her breasts lay against his arm while his own breath stirred her hair. When she opened her eyes at last, he was lost in them.

Taking a deliberate hold on himself, he eased her to her feet. She leaned against him just long enough to make certain of his downfall and then pushed away. She did not meet his eyes again. But the damage had been done.

He had determined to stay away from her, for his sake and for hers. She had, in a few short hours, managed to undo days of self-control. Nothing had changed;

he could not forget what had sparked between them, or what he had realized about her. But she had come to him, and his struggle was over.

He wanted her. He still wanted her more than he could remember ever wanting a woman, even in his time of strongest need. If she had been indifferent to him, perhaps he could have resisted—but he sensed her own desire, the desire she tried to hide even from herself. It no longer mattered that she wanted to use him for her own ends. She would give herself to him willingly, and he wanted what she had to give. So be it.

They stopped within sight of the cabin, up the slope from the lake amid abundant forest. The last rays of the sun struck sparks from the lake and caught the cabin in a welcome glow. Joey stopped and leaned over, hands on knees, staring at it with an expression Luke knew to be relief. He wished that he could feel that same relief now that he'd reached his decision.

But there was no comfort in it. He would ignore everything his senses, his mind, and his instinct told him so he could have her in his bed. So he could feel her body against his. Because he wanted her. And the consequences be damned.

Even as his body stirred in anticipation, he wondered if both of them would survive those consequences.

Joey didn't know what to expect as they walked into the cabin; from a distance it had seemed plain and practical, well-constructed of logs, small and unexceptional. As Luke held the door open for her, the first thing she noticed was the chill. She had expected a flood of comforting warmth after the cool of outside, but it was almost as cold within as without. She wrapped her arms tightly about herself and shivered.

Luke shut the door behind them, led her through the entryway and vanished through another doorway, leaving Joey to examine her surroundings. As exhausted as she felt, she was not about to relax until she had a very good grasp of where she was—and what she was getting into.

The room she stood in was probably the largest in the cabin, a central living area that seemed stark but somehow comfortable. Against one wall lay a fireplace, empty of wood or ashes. Lining the others were shelves alternating with impressive displays of antlers and pelts. A thick woven rug covered most of the wood-paneled floor, and there were a few pieces of furniture: a well-worn sofa, an elegantly carved rocking chair, a few small tables covered with various objects. At first glance it seemed very plain, but as her eyes traced around the room a second time, she began to absorb the details.

Before she had progressed very far in her study, Luke reappeared, a thick blanket slung over his arm. He had put on a shirt much like those he always wore, a brown-and-green plaid; his feet were still bare, noiseless on the carpet.

"Use this," he said, pushing the blanket unceremoniously into her arms. It was so heavy she almost dropped it. "I'll find some spare clothes for you." He hardly looked at her as he turned to go, his eyes focused inward and his posture reserved.

Joey shook out the blanket and draped it around her shoulders. "Do you always keep it so toasty warm in here?" she called after him. There was no reply. She tugged the thick wool closed so that it overlapped in generous folds and began a slow circuit of the room, trailing excess blanket behind like a train.

She had not known what to expect, and she found herself wondering again just how much—or how little—she truly knew of Luke Gévaudan. The cabin did not luxuriate in creature comforts, but there was a rich sensuality, a deep love of nature, in the few articles he had chosen to display. A roughly made, hand-painted table against the left wall exhibited a number of objects, chief among them several beautifully carved animals whittled from wood. There were two wolves, an adult and cub; each was so lifelike, even the fur had been rendered in finest detail. A moose stood off to the side, head raised under a rack of antlers that reminded Joey of the battle she and Luke had witnessed. Half-afraid to touch them, Joey ran one tentative finger over the strong back of the moose. The feel of carved wood was delicious even to her weary senses.

Beside the carvings was a collection of rocks of varied shapes and sizes and a small display case containing a multifaceted crystal. Joey gazed at it for a moment and moved on to one of the rows of shelves alongside the table. She had just begun to take in the sheer number of books they contained when Luke reappeared.

"Clean clothes," he announced as she paused to face him. Once again his arms were filled with fabric—a plain flannel shirt, jeans, woolen socks. He frowned at her as if seeing her for the first time since their arrival; his eyes swept over her critically. "Put these on. They should fit."

He paused again, and Joey wondered if he expected her to strip in front of him. She tightened her grip on the blanket. His gaze swept beyond her to the table with the carvings; dark brows drew together briefly. Then he looked back at her, offering the clothing with an impatient gesture. "Go ahead. I'm not going to bite you. Are you hungry?"

The abrupt change in topic startled Joey as she took the folded clothing from Luke while trying to maintain a precarious hold on the blanket. She failed, and it slipped from her shoulders to lie in a puddle about her feet. Luke crouched to pick it up; Joey found herself following his motion in blank fascination. Even now she was completely aware of the way he moved, the glitter of his strange eyes, even the corded strength of his bare feet.

He rose and stood with the blanket for a long moment of awkward silence. They looked at each other; Joey felt her pulse rising and wondered if he could hear the pounding of her heart. But he turned at last to lay the blanket on the sofa. "Are you hungry?" he repeated over his shoulder. All his attention seemed focused now on some fascinating flaw in the weave of the blanket; he did not turn again to receive her reply.

"Yes, as a matter of fact—I am," she said at last to his broad back. As if to underscore the words, her stomach rumbled loudly at just that moment; Luke cocked his head, and Joey had the absurd notion that if he'd had the right kind of ears, he would have swiveled them back at her.

"So I hear." There was the slightest trace of humor in his voice, though she could not see his expression. "I have venison stew; it's not fancy, but it's filling." Joey had the sudden impression from his body language—a language she was beginning to learn and which was far more subtle than she'd guessed—that he was almost on the defensive, as if he expected her derision at such simple fare. His shoulders were taut and almost hunched; his fingers had tightened ever so slightly on the blanket draped over the sofa back. The fact that he should care what she thought of his cooking disarmed her in an unexpected way.

"That sounds very good," she said softly. "Thank you." She saw his muscles loosen almost imperceptibly as she spoke, and his head lifted, so that the last rays of daylight from the near window silvered the strands of dark hair that brushed his collar. Before she could give in to the sudden, overwhelming impulse to run her fingers through that hair, he was striding away across the room and through the connecting door.

Wishing she had a space heater or even a fire to change in front of, Joey began to pull off her soiled clothing. She found herself unable to share Luke's obviously casual attitude about nudity, and half-crouched behind the dubious protection of the sofa to change. She struggled hastily out of her boots, socks, and jeans, debated briefly over her underwear, and decided after a moment to wad it up with the rest of her discarded clothing.

The new clothing was dry and clean if not much warmer than the rest of the cabin. The jeans she pulled on were quite obviously a woman's, though perhaps a size too large; Joey considered the probable nature of their previous owner as she zipped them up. One of Luke's many "conquests"?

The thought made her lips tighten with annoyance. She had to keep reminding herself she was here for a reason—for her *own* reasons. She wasn't any man's conquest unless she wanted to be. Least of all Luke Gévaudan's.

The shirt Luke had provided was deliciously soft against her bare skin as Joey shrugged into it. Like the jeans, it seemed more suited to a fuller figure, though Joey was not about to quibble on that score. It felt more than wonderful to be in clean clothes again, with dry woolen socks on her feet. She allowed herself to savor that feeling and temporarily abandoned all other concerns. The sofa was surprisingly comfortable as she settled into it, pulling the blanket up to her chin and staring into the empty fireplace. With a little imagination she could see it brought to life with leaping flame, turning the cabin into something romantic and mysterious. Suitable, she thought, for its occupant . . .

She'd hardly realized that she was sitting in near darkness when Luke's voice broke the silence. "I've started a fire in the stove, but it'll be a while before the stew is ready." He appeared beside the sofa, a dark form surrounded by deepening shadows. Joey could just make out a pair of lamps in his hands, and as she squinted to watch him, he cleared space on two of the small tables to either side of the room, lighting the lamps one by one.

At once a soft glow spread from the lamps to illumine the room; it wasn't enough light to read by comfortably but was more than enough to prevent accidents. Luke's face was strange and gaunt with hollows carved of shadow, his eyes hooded when they turned to her. In the darkness they seemed almost black.

"I'm going out for firewood," he said at last. The lamplight cast long, ominous shadow-shapes that preceded him as he moved to the entryway. "It would be best if you just stay here and rest. I won't be gone long." He fixed her with a final look, a long stare she could not quite interpret in the uncertain light, and vanished into the entryway.

For a while Joey sat and absorbed the peaceful stillness of the cabin, closing her eyes and allowing her aching muscles and battered sensibilities to bask in soothing quiet. But even bone-weary exhaustion was not enough to permit complete comfort in an unfamiliar place—particularly *this* place. When she felt quite warm, and the first edge of fatigue had worn off, she was ready to explore further.

Pulling the blanket up into a makeshift cloak, Joey resumed her study of the bookshelves. It was just possible to make out titles in the dim light.

She had been right in one of her first guesses about Luke; he was an educated man. The range of books he kept on his shelves was considerable: history, psychology, nature, and literature seemed among the most common topics but were far from the only ones. She found titles not only in English but a great many in French as well; her shaky grasp of the language enabled her to translate some of them. Like the others, the French books covered a wide variety of subjects, though there were many that seemed to focus on French-Canadian folklore and culture. They told her he was not only bilingual but fluently so. She wondered if he spoke French as flawlessly as he spoke English.

She took down one book, a fat volume about animals in mythology. Strange somehow to think of Luke sitting in this cabin, reading by lamplight. It was an aspect of him she hadn't given much consideration, something that made her feel oddly off balance. It suddenly seemed very likely that he had thoughts and feelings and interests other than alienating the townsfolk and pursuing women—that he might be someone she could genuinely like.

Joey replaced the book and rested her hand against the shelf as if her feet might give out from under her. She had never thought in terms of liking him. It had always been a matter of the physical; fending off his advances, then acknowledging the effect he had on her, if only in dreams—later coming to the realization that she could make use of their mutual attraction to gain her own ends. She had never really thought of him as a human being who could sit in a silent cabin and read by lamplight.

Even now she wasn't sure it was a matter of liking. She didn't think it would be easy to like Luke Gévaudan. Liking him, in fact, might be the worst mistake she could make. But perhaps she had more to learn about him than she had realized. And knowing that, she could armor herself against letting unexpected feelings get in the way.

She realized she was shivering again when she nearly tripped over the blanket that had fallen at her feet. She bent to retrieve it just as she heard the outer door open and slam shut; a moment later Luke edged through the inner doorway with a stack of firewood and kindling, only his eyes visible above the load. He kicked the door shut behind him and set the stack down before Joey could offer help. As he set to work placing the kindling in the fireplace, she dropped onto the edge of the sofa and watched.

The thoughts and feelings that coursed through her now were just as confusing and unsettling as everything else that had happened to her since she'd met Luke. The rampant physicality of him seemed a blatant contradiction to the intellect suggested by his collection of books; his cool purpose and pursuit of her had occasionally allowed glimpses of something gentler and more meaningful, even when she hadn't wanted to see it.

And then there had been his inexplicable flight after their first kiss . . . and the fact that he was, at this very moment, making her forget everything she'd set out to do was in itself a frightening discovery.

The sudden shimmer of newborn flame distracted her from brooding thoughts, and she realized all at once that Luke was studying her with the same quiet intensity that she had focused on him. She smoothed the frown from her face.

"Thanks for the clothes," she said, plucking at the sleeve of her shirt. "I didn't know what you wanted me to do with the old ones." She nodded in apology at the wad of discarded fabric in the corner. "If you have some sort of tub, I can wash them out. But I don't suppose you have a dryer. . . ."

Flashing him a hesitant smile, Joey let her eyes slide away from his and center on the growing flames as they licked at the wood. The fire sputtered and sparked as the first wave of warmth reached her. Like the clean clothes, it offered a purely sensual comfort that lulled Joey into a moment of pure happiness.

In that moment Luke vanished again, leaving her to contemplate the changing face of the fire. Closing her eyes to savor the warmth on her face, Joey allowed her senses to take control. She could smell the rich odor of Luke's stew as it drifted from the adjoining room; her stomach growled again, loud enough to make her grimace. The woolen blanket was slightly rough against her cheek, the flannel of her shirt soft where it touched her breasts. Shadows leaped and danced, fleeing before the light of lamps and fire. The sense of comfort and safety was so powerful that Joey gave up fighting it at last.

# Chapter Six

Warm breath brushed the top of her head. "Are you ready to eat?" Luke murmured from behind. Joey could feel him as strongly as she felt the heat of the flames, almost as if he had touched her. She anticipated his touch—almost welcomed it. But he kept his distance.

"There's a table in the other room," he added.

She turned to look up at him; for a dizzying instant their gazes locked, and then she found herself following him across the room and into the adjoining portion of the cabin she had not yet explored.

There were already two steaming bowls of stew on the rough-hewn table when Luke pulled out a chair and offered it to her with an almost gentlemanly gesture. She couldn't quite resist dipping a finger into the thick stew and pulled it out hastily; like the room itself, it was certainly not lacking in warmth. The old-fashioned wood-burning stove that was the room's primary feature seemed more than adequate to heat this portion of the

cabin, at least; Joey wondered idly why the cabin had
been so cold before.

As she waited for the stew to cool, she allowed her
gaze to drift around the room. Another impressive rack
of antlers hung above the small table, and she resolved
to ask Luke about them later; she'd seen no guns or
anything else to indicate that he was a frequent hunter,
though it made sense that a man living as he did would
have to track down his meals from time to time.

There was a basin set into a wooden counter on the
other side of the room, and a small pump seemed to
serve as the equivalent of a faucet. Before she could ask
Luke about it, he was demonstrating it for her, pumping
water into two earthenware mugs and setting them
down beside the bowls. The water was icy cold and
sweet when she sipped it.

Cupboards lined most of the remaining walls, and
a very few cooking implements hung in the vicinity of
the stove, but it was fairly obvious Luke didn't indulge
in a great deal of culinary experimentation. Reminded
abruptly of her considerable hunger, Joey picked up the
plain wooden spoon Luke had provided and dipped it
into the stew. The first bite assured her that while Luke
might not be a fancy cook, he could produce something
adequate to the purpose.

She smiled up at him as he sat down opposite her.
"It's good," she mumbled through a mouthful of venison
and vegetables. Her reward was the first real smile he'd
displayed since he'd appeared out of the lake that afternoon; it had a remarkable effect on the harsh lines of
his face and a surprisingly devastating one on her own
unbalanced emotions. The smile was the most genuine
and warm she'd ever seen from him, and it was directed
entirely at her.

Then he rose, his own stew untouched, and began
to move restlessly about the room. Joey concentrated on
filling her most immediate needs, finishing her portion

quickly. As she looked up to thank him, Luke ladled more stew into her bowl from a large cast-iron pot; she briefly considered not making a glutton of herself and then decided it was too good to pass up.

When the last spoonful had disappeared, Joey leaned back in her chair and was grateful for the extra room in her borrowed jeans. Luke was hovering in the vicinity, as he had done throughout her meal—never quite looking at her, never quite speaking, but always very much there. Only Joey's hunger had prevented him from completely unnerving her; now she didn't have that distraction. She noticed that he hadn't touched his own stew.

"That was delicious, Luke," she said with real sincerity. He stopped his pacing to meet her eyes. She dropped hers to study her empty bowl ruefully. "I can't quite believe how much I ate. Thank you."

"Do you need more?" he said, sweeping her bowl away before she could take it to the sink. "I don't have much here right now. I need to go into town for more supplies." His tone was gruff with what she guessed to be embarrassment; like his earlier smile, it touched her unexpectedly.

"It was fine—I couldn't eat one more bite," she assured him. Feeling at loose ends and very much aware of her own uncertainty, Joey got up to join Luke at the sink.

He rinsed her bowl and set it aside, responding to her inquiring look, "No hot running water here. It has to be heated." He gestured at the stove; a large open tank was attached at the side of it, warming water as the stove itself warmed the room. He retrieved his own untouched bowl, dumping the contents back into the pot. This he took with him through a door at the side of the kitchen, one that Joey presumed led outside; he was gone for several minutes, and he returned with an empty pot, which he rinsed and set with the bowls. Joey realized with a start that no electricity and no hot running water meant no refrigerator, either; the implications of Luke's lifestyle were beginning to make an impression.

It occurred to Joey that it said much for Luke's appeal to the opposite sex that he'd managed to lure a number of women up here for lengthy stays. The place wasn't exactly the lap of luxury; somehow or other Luke had provided those women with adequate compensation. As he turned to scoop hot water out of the tank alongside the stove, his arm brushed against her shoulder; Joey was reminded suddenly and powerfully of just how potently attractive he could be.

Luke finished his cleaning up in silence while Joey leaned against the table, letting herself admire him without the complications of questions and analysis. In the woods it had seemed natural that he should move so gracefully, but his spare gestures as he performed the simple domestic tasks hinted at the same smooth strength. When he put the last clean dish away and turned to look at her, he caught her eyes on him and froze in place; she knew he was aware of the train of her thoughts though the calm, remote expression of his face did not alter. Not at first—not until she began to drown in his amber-green eyes and felt rather than saw him move toward her with the slow deliberation of a natural predator.

When he touched her arm and steered her in a circle back into the main room, she found herself shaking her head in confusion. If he had made a single encouraging move, she would have fallen into his arms then and there—and she didn't want that. There was still the small matter of finding out why he had run away from her. Why he looked at her now with the old intensity but kept his distance when he had her where he had wanted her all along.

Even if she learned nothing else about him, she had to understand what he wanted from her, so that she could get what she needed from him—and not sacrifice more than she was prepared to give in the process.

Luke guided her back to the sofa and left her there while he checked the fire. It was blazing merrily now, but he stayed at the hearth, leaning against the uneven stone and gazing into the flames as Joey had done earlier. She perched on the edge of the sofa, unable to settle. Except for the crackling of the fire, it was incredibly silent; even the lodge had never been this quiet.

When the utter stillness became oppressive, Joey broke it.

"I want to thank you again, Luke, for helping me out today. I do appreciate it." Her voice sounded very small and strange even to herself, and as Luke turned his attention to her, she found herself babbling.

"In San Francisco you always know where not to go at night and what neighborhoods aren't safe to be in alone, but somehow it never occurred to me that I'd be running into punks up here. I've been learning about dangerous animals and how to avoid them, but I never thought I'd have to worry about the human variety." A nervous laugh escaped her. "It's a good thing I had basic self-defense classes. Next time those guys aren't going to get away with that kind of nasty behavior. I . . ."

"There won't be a next time." Luke's voice was soft and harsh. "They won't bother you again." The grim finality in his words stopped Joey's desire to chatter, and she met his eyes. They were glittering in the firelight; his face was set in an expression made ominous by flickering shadows.

"I hope you're right," she murmured, though she knew there was no reason to doubt it. Questions flooded her mind again, and she deliberately set them aside.

Under Luke's unwavering gaze she stood and began to move aimlessly about the room. It was warm enough now that she had no need of the blanket; she went to stand under the display of antlers and pelts that she'd noticed earlier. Rich fur in gray and black was both soft and rough under her stroking fingers. "This is beautiful," she said, burying her hand in the pelt. "I guess you must do quite a bit of hunting up here. This is all your land, isn't it?"

"It's my land," he said at her shoulder. Startled, she froze for an instant and then resumed her tactile exploration. She knew it shouldn't surprise her that he could move so silently. Not any longer.

"What kind of animal is this?" she asked at last, her tone deliberately light in spite of his disconcerting nearness. "I've never been that comfortable with the idea of hunting, but I imagine up here that it's one of the necessities of life."

"It is necessary, at some times and for some reasons," he said, answering so quickly that his words caught the end of hers. "That belonged to a good friend of mine. I took it from him when he no longer needed it."

Joey dropped her hand and turned to face him. "A friend?" The meaning of his words penetrated, and she might have laughed had his expression not been so serious. "Like our friend the wolf?"

"Yes. Very much like him." The utter sobriety in his eyes and voice made her falter. He reached up to run long fingers through the dark fur where hers had passed. "I keep it as a reminder." For a long moment he seemed lost in his own thoughts. Joey's eyes shifted up to the antlers above their heads.

"What about those? Were those friends, too?"

"Not friends, but respected adversaries. In nature, predators seldom hunt for any reason but necessity. There is never any certainty about the outcome." He spread his hand through the pelt and gripped it tightly.

"Sometimes the predator loses. It's only human beings who cheat on the rules of nature."

Looking at Luke, Joey knew there was far more behind his tightly deliberate words than she could guess. "But you never cheat on the rules?" she asked softly.

"Not if I can help it." His words were equally soft as his eyes met hers.

Joey could easily have found herself lost in them again, but she chose not to give herself the opportunity. Moving away with unhurried casualness, she stopped at one of the tables where one of the lamps cast its light, almost superfluous in the glow of the fire.

"These are beautiful, too." She touched one of the several wooden sculptures on the table: a bear rearing up on its hind legs, front paws displayed in aggressive threat. Even at this small size the power of the animal was evident in the lines of carved wood.

"Thank you." Luke had come up silently behind her, but this time she expected it. Even so, his words surprised her.

"You did this?" She picked up the sculpture carefully, turning it in her hands to examine the exquisite detail. Each tiny claw had been carved to a delicate point, and even the teeth looked sharp enough to bite.

"Yes." There was a long silence. Joey set down the bear and picked up a second carving that she guessed to be a cougar, graceful and sleek. "The winters are long here, and it's useful to have something to do." She heard him shift behind her, a restless whisper of bare feet on wood paneling.

"I've never seen carving like this." Joey picked up the third sculpture; like those on the table against the far wall, this was a wolf. Its head was flung back in a howl, ears laid flat and bushy tail straight. She could keenly remember the mournful cries she'd heard at the lodge. "They're wonderful. Did you ever consider selling them? You'd probably get an excellent price."

His chuckle was little more than a bark, but for once there was no grimness in it. "I don't need the money." He moved to stand beside her, his shoulder almost touching hers. "I do it because the winters are long and cold, and I have all the supplies I need. But if you like it . . ." He paused, and his hand brushed hers over the carving. "It's yours."

His touch was brief and fleeting, but it struck Joey with the force of a blow. Her fingers tightened on the carving until the sharp edges bit into her palm. "Thank you." She swallowed back a sudden painful constriction in her throat. "I'll treasure it."

He said nothing more, and she looked up to see him stalk away, circling in front of the fire. His muscles were taut, and the usual grace of his movements was lost as he paced, looking everywhere but at her.

Joey set the sculpture down among the others. It still wasn't time, too soon to demand explanations or press matters that needed to be resolved. She steadied her shaking hands, pressing them together as she moved to the next set of bookshelves. Like the others, it was filled with volumes of every description, and she sought among them for some harmless topic that would take them away from dangerous ground.

She found what she was looking for in a slim volume of European folk and fairy tales. The illustrations were quaint but lavish, and she paused at one depicting the story *Beauty and the Beast*. The Beast in this case was a creature with a head that resembled a cross between a bear and a boar, dressed in the finery of a past century.

"Your collection of books is impressive," she said into the silence. Luke paused in his pacing to glance up, though he stayed by the fire. "With the winters so long and cold and no electricity, I imagine books could go a long way toward keeping a person sane."

"When there are no other distractions," Luke responded. His voice was even, and his silhouette against the firelight seemed less rigid. Joey turned the pages carefully.

"I used to love these stories. My mother used to read them to me when I was young. . . ." She broke off before memories could trap her and continued, "You have quite an interest in mythology. I've always found that to be a fascinating subject."

Luke had moved halfway across the room, stopping at the sofa as if it were an unbreachable barrier. "It can be. Myth is powerful because it has roots in reality."

Joey cocked her head with a wry smile. "Yes. But it can also give us a nice, safe distance from reality." She closed the book and set it back in place, wondering why every subject of conversation seemed to carry an unexpected complication. "And reality has an unfortunate way of sneaking up on us anyway, no matter how we try to ignore it." She stared at rows of titles without really seeing them.

Luke's voice was so soft she almost didn't hear it. " 'There are more things in heaven and earth, Horatio. . . .' "

"Shakespeare, too?" She focused again and found a row of that author's works on one of the top shelves, out of her reach. "But *Hamlet* is a tragedy, isn't it? I never much cared for tragedy."

A sense of fragility came over Joey that sprang from equal parts unwanted memories, unrelieved tension, and a sudden and overwhelming sense of aloneness. She wanted desperately to recover her equilibrium, but it seemed lost and far beyond her reach. She turned her back so that Luke wouldn't see what she was sure her face revealed and circled the far end of the room, passing the darkened kitchen and stopping in the most distant corner.

It was something of a shrine—that was her first thought as she looked down at the tiny corner table. Beautifully carved shelves rose above it to form niches, each containing some small item. Two candles, unlit, completed the image of a place set off as a sanctuary. For memories? Joey wondered.

She stopped the thought by focusing on the objects. There was a hairbrush—the handle made, like the table itself, of intricately carved and painted wood. She picked it up carefully. There were still a few soft midnight-black hairs caught in the bristles. A woman's hair.

For an instant Joey wondered if it could have belonged to one of Luke's earlier lovers—one of those Maggie had warned her about. Surely not even the most arrogant of men would keep a shrine to his former conquests? The mere idea seemed ludicrous, but as her eyes traced over the items on display, there could be no doubt that they had belonged to a woman.

There was a mirror, a silver one finely made though simple, and a gold ring set with a single flawless ruby. Joey was almost afraid to touch them. The other shelves contained similar articles, but it was the table itself that displayed the most compelling object.

The music box that held the place of honor was exquisite. It had a classic design that suggested age but was in perfect condition: polished and, like the rest of the shrine, free of dust. Joey could not resist running her fingers over the silver and gold molding, the tiny picture carved on the lid that depicted canoes on a river surrounded by forest and mountains. Without thinking, she lifted the lid.

It was a lovely, sprightly melody the box played: an air with the sound of a folk song, unfamiliar but oddly captivating. Joey cocked her head and closed her eyes to listen. It was the kind of tune that called for joy, dancing, and happiness, and Joey felt the delicate strains begin to dispel her melancholy. The melody had begun its second repetition when it cut off with a sudden snap of the lid.

Luke's body pressed against her back, the lean hardness of him shocking her back to awareness. His hand clamped down on the music box as if to physically hold it in place there, and his breath came fast against the crown of her head.

Her first thought was to free herself and escape his almost suffocating presence, but he held her there as surely as he did the music box.

"I would prefer," he said very softly, "that you don't touch the things on this table."

There was a definite warning in his voice, but it was his closeness and not the subtle hint of anger that made her heart leap into her throat. She wavered between pushing him back so that she could turn to confront him or holding absolutely still in hopes that he would go away on his own; every inch of her was aware of him from the firm pressure of his thighs against her buttocks to the strong jaw alongside her own temple.

His voice vibrated above her ear, echoing through her body as he released the music box. "Don't touch this again." For a long, tense moment it seemed as though he would not release her, either, and then he stepped back. "Please."

The last word had the nature of an afterthought, but it served to take the heat from Joey's indignation. She turned quickly to face him, the edge of the table pressing into the small of her back as he had pressed a moment before.

"I'm sorry I touched something I shouldn't have, but I didn't mean any harm by it, and I certainly didn't do any damage." She lifted her chin and met his gaze squarely. "There's no need to fly off the handle."

Luke's face had been rigid with something approaching hostility, but now his features relaxed into the usual cool remoteness. Joey was almost grateful for the safe distance it put between them again. It might have worked if it hadn't been for the seesawing of her own emotions.

"Did I fly off the handle?" Luke's words were even and as distant as his expression, but Joey almost sensed amusement in their tone. She took a moment to slide away from him and the table to a more neutral location. She watched his face as he moved to stand where she had been; his fingers touched lightly a final time on the music box and caught at one of the long black tresses on the hairbrush.

The subtle shifts in his features were small, but Joey knew she did not imagine the change. Luke lifted the hair and wound it around his fingers, caressing it as his eyes grew unfocused. The harsh lines of his face softened; there was almost the faintest whisper of a smile on his narrow lips.

"Who did it belong to?" Joey found herself asking, needing to learn what could bring such an expression of—tenderness, yes, even that—to his face. She half-braced herself for a return of his cold anger, but it didn't come.

Instead, he seemed to find his way back from some faraway place to hear her words, and his response was slow and remote.

"It was my mother's." He offered no more, unwinding the dark hair from his fingers and pressing it almost reverently back into the bristles of the brush.

With an inward sigh that seemed to release a year's worth of accumulated tension, Joey felt her muscles relax. She leaned against the bookshelves behind her. Question upon question rose up, demanding release, but she pushed them back. The strange gentleness of Luke's demeanor now was worth patience; for once he might expose something no amount of questioning could ever force from him.

As if sensing the intensity of her concentration, Luke turned back to her. There was still a hint of the unguardedness he had briefly revealed, but it was now tempered by wariness.

"My mother died a long time ago. When I was still a boy. This"—he gestured with a short, restrained motion at the corner table—"is what she left." His absolute stillness except for the one brief movement forced Joey to shift in compensation. The smell of leather-bound books and woodsmoke mingled in her nostrils.

"I'm sorry." They were inadequate words, but Joey felt them keenly. She felt them with all the pain of her own loss, when she herself had been hardly more than a girl. In the brief time she'd known him, Luke had never mentioned family. He had never mentioned his parents, and the subject had never seemed important. Now it had a powerful significance. It made him, in this small way, like her. And she knew now that the momentary softening in his expression had been very real.

The painful lump that rose in her throat was as much sympathy for his loss as memory of her own. It frightened her because it made her vulnerable when she could least afford to be, and yet it gave her a small advantage. Even Luke was not without the ties of emotion, and his past.

With a motion as abrupt as it was noiseless, Luke pushed away from the table and strode back to the fireside. Joey continued her circuit of the room as she reined in her emotions, coming at last to the place where she had begun earlier that evening. Her eyes scanned the titles a second time without really seeing them.

"I lost my parents, too," she murmured, stroking the embossed cover of a volume of Donne's poetry. It was only a reminder to herself, to conquer feelings by trapping them with words. She had done that many times in the past when she felt close to being overwhelmed.

"Yes. We have that in common." Even in the quiet, Joey had not expected him to hear her whisper. She looked up where he stood by the fire, staring once again into the blazing light.

She found herself pulled by some irrational compulsion across the safe distance that separated them, stopping at the sofa, her fingers twisting into the blanket that lay tossed over the back. There was a shower of sparks in the hearth as Luke tossed a branch among the flames.

"Do you miss them?" she asked suddenly.

At first she thought Luke did not intend to answer, so long was the interval of silence. She clenched a fistful of blanket.

"I've been alone a long time," he said at last. "It was a long time ago." There was such an evenness to his tone that Joey knew it was not natural, any more than hers had been. But when she risked a glance at him, he was still staring, unmoved and unmoving, at the ever-shifting and indifferent face of the fire.

Joey found herself walking again, around the barrier of the sofa. She hesitated there, struggling with compulsions she did not understand. Her instinct was to comfort and be comforted—but her mind told her to be safe, to take no further risks. With a sigh she dropped onto the sofa and half-pulled the blanket around her, though it was almost too warm.

Her next words, when she broke the intervening silence, seemed to come from some other person. "My parents died in the crash when I was sixteen. Twelve years ago." The lump in her throat seemed intent on impeding any further conversation. With a deliberate act of will she forced it back. "I've been waiting—all this time—to find them. I never got to say good-bye."

She was horrified by the sudden break in her voice. The rush of words that wanted to emerge, that cried out to be said to someone who might understand, were stopped before they could betray her into tears. With rigid self-control, Joey composed her face into blankness and tried to pretend she had never spoken at all.

Like a flickering shadow, Luke was suddenly before her. He hovered there, blocking off the heat and light of the fire, balancing as if he had acted on an impulse he did not know how to carry through. Joey blinked and stared at his hands, wondering bleakly if he would try to touch her, and what she would feel if he did. Part of her wanted it desperately, to have even a man she hardly knew, a man as much opponent as friend or potential lover, make her feel less alone. But it would come out of weakness, not on her terms. She would lose the last threads of control.

Luke's hands clenched into fists at his side. For an instant he remained poised, and then he retreated as suddenly as he had come.

Joey was not certain how long he was gone. She concentrated on the moments free of him; to gather her balance and remind herself, as many times as necessary, why she was here. When he returned to thrust a hot mug of coffee into her hands, she was able to take it with perfect composure and smile up at him again.

"Thanks. Just what I needed." The coffee was at that perfect temperature somewhere between scalding and warm; she sipped at it and inhaled the steam. It cleared the last of the fuzziness from her mind.

She found Luke in the carved rocking chair, legs stretched out toward the hearth, his strong chin resting on folded hands. "You didn't have any?" she said, setting her own mug carefully on the floor beside the sofa.

Raising his head to regard her, Luke shifted his feet and almost smiled. "I only keep it for guests."

Whatever his intention, his words had the effect of making Joey content to keep silence between them. The quiet stretched for a long while; Joey could hear sounds outside the cabin she could not identify that made her glad to be indoors, even under these circumstances.

Once she was sure she heard the howling of wolves, and her eyes sought the pelts on the wall and the carvings on the two side tables.

Her eyes strayed again and again to Luke after that. For a while he sat as she did, almost unmoving, lost in thoughts she could not begin to guess at. Then he got up to pace—a restless series of turns about the room, seemingly without any purpose but to overcome some internal conflict. His expression tightened and relaxed, and had he been the sort to do so, Joey might have expected him to talk to himself. But he maintained the silence and returned at last to his chair with a half-carved piece of wood.

His deft, expert movements with the small knife fascinated Joey and relieved any threatening boredom. She watched him carve a long, narrow body, shaping short legs and a wisp of a tail, a foxlike head. She played a game of guessing what sort of animal he pulled out of the unremarkable block, and she realized how much time had passed only when Luke got up to throw more wood on the dying fire. In spite of herself, she yawned broadly.

Luke's keen gaze met hers for the first time in what seemed like an age. "Are you tired?" The sound of his voice after long silence was welcome. Joey shook her head. She could not yet afford to be tired, not while matters stood as they did.

"No, not quite yet. What time is it?" She realized belatedly that her watch had been lost sometime in the struggle with the men at the lake, and Luke did not seem to possess a clock in any visible location.

He cocked his head, looking off into space as if consulting some internal timepiece. "Close to midnight. Perhaps a little later." At once his eyes came back to hers, dark except for the glitter of firelight. "Is there anything you need?"

Joey considered the question and examined it for

double meanings. His look was so intent and focused, so like the ones he had turned on her when he'd first begun his pursuit, that she suspected more than one layer in the casual remark.

For a long moment she wondered if she should put things off a little longer, try to draw him out. But even she had limits, and this had not been an easy day. She drew in a deep breath and met his gaze.

"Yes. I need to know why—why you left the way you did last week."

The only reaction to her question was a sudden hooding of his eyes, a deepening of the lines between his dark brows. She knew with inward certainty that he had been waiting for that question; he raised his head and stared down at her almost fiercely. "I can't tell you that."

"Can't—or won't?" she challenged. There was a long moment when their wills clashed as gazes locked, a silent battle that was not the first of its kind between them. Joey knew it would not likely be the last, even when he was, again, the first to drop his eyes.

"I can't." It came out almost as a growl, angry and defensive. His broad shoulders were hunched, and tension radiated from his body as surely as if it had taken solid form. Then, all at once, the tense posture dissolved. He straightened slowly, looking up from under his brows. "It doesn't matter anymore." His tone had changed from growl to purr, and Joey found her own annoyance draining away.

"If it doesn't matter, does that mean you'll help me?" She was hardly satisfied with his answer, but on her list of priorities the most important thing was still clear. She pushed the memory of their kiss and its bizarre aftermath from her mind.

Luke left the fireside and covered the space between them in one long stride. Joey found herself pressing back into the sofa. He seemed huge standing there before her, all restrained power and unpredictability. Tilting her head back to face him, she repeated stubbornly, "Will you help me, Luke?"

The muscles of his face stiffened and relaxed, but his eyes remained fixed on hers. "I will."

Closing her eyes briefly, Joey heard the words and felt her muscles loosen. "Thank you."

The simple exchange seemed to release something in both of them, for Luke suddenly smiled—as close to a real smile as he usually came. Joey suspected genuine warmth in it, and she met it with one of her own. Before, she'd let her unrestrained joy at his offer of help push her to incautious behavior, and that wasn't going to happen again. But her relief and gratitude were very real nevertheless; she drew her knees up to her chest and rested her chin on them with a sigh of contentment.

Once again they let the deep silence lie. In spite of her pleasant drowsiness Joey found herself watching Luke with that same unwilling fascination as he paced restlessly before the hearth. There was nothing in his walk, or in any of the restrained motions of his body, that was not graceful. She reflected idly that it must come from living in the wild; he was a woodsman, well versed in the ways of Nature. Perhaps his growing up here, on the edge of civilization, accounted for the strangeness that both piqued and intrigued her in spite of herself.

It was easy to allow her thoughts to drift from idle speculation to admiration and then to recent memories. And to dreams. All at once Joey was remembering things she had tried to push away, distracting images that had no place in the scheme of her plans. She remembered the feel of Luke's body against her back when she had touched the music box, and days ago when— She tried to shut away the rush of sensation that came to her with the memories, but it suddenly gripped her with absolute and uncanny power.

Her face was suddenly far hotter than the fire warranted. She cast the blanket aside and shivered with something distinctly other than cold. Closing her eyes did not keep the images away: Luke with his powerful arms locking her in an embrace she had no wish to escape, his lips on hers, all of her careful control utterly abandoned. . . . That had been reality. For those moments in the meadow the entirety of the world had been a kiss unlike any she had ever known.

And then the dreams . . . they were worse. In the dreams she was lost utterly, completely vulnerable. The first dreams had brought fear, but since the kiss they had been so compellingly erotic that Joey had forcibly locked them away where they could not interfere, could not destroy her best-laid plans.

Until now. Now she was here alone in a cabin with Luke, aware of him in ways she had no ability to dismiss. Imagination took on greater power than she had believed it could—that she had not experienced since childhood, when she had learned how overwhelming reality could be and gave up dreaming.

Until now.

Now a new tension was building in her, wiping away the weariness and contentment as if it had never existed. She told herself it was irrational and worse to believe that Luke would be able to feel it, to sense the crumbling of her defenses. But when he met her eyes, again and again with increasing frequency as he paced about the room, she was almost sure he did. He had to know. He had been waiting for this moment. Whatever had prompted his inexplicable behavior after the kiss in the meadow, it no longer mattered.

Joey made one last bid to shore up her emotional walls and build them anew with purposeful rationality. She knew she had failed as soon as she began.

She watched him as he crouched before the fire, reflected light glinting off the chiseled planes of his face, the layered, rough texture of his hair. His worn jeans pulled taut across his thighs as he pushed a new log into the flames; she bit her lip and tried to ignore the tingling in the pit of her stomach. God, he was magnificent! The old plaid shirt he wore did very little to conceal the breadth of his shoulders, or the sleek, powerful muscle of his arms. She remembered that all too well, from her very thorough view of him on the lake shore.

She had wanted to stay away from men. She had expected to meet her goals without emotional complications. She had determined to keep control and keep Luke Gévaudan where she wanted him. She had lost herself once already. And none of that mattered.

Watching him in firelight—at this moment, suddenly—she wanted him more than she could have believed possible.

He turned abruptly from the fire and looked directly into her eyes. The green-gold of them was briefly eclipsed by a glow of red, like an animal's eyes in the flash of a camera. For a moment her heart was in her throat. That wildness about him—the way he crouched there, alert and wary. The smooth glide of his movements. The fierce intensity in his gaze. That gaze was locked on hers now, unwavering, challenging. . . .

She was being sucked into those eyes, pulled out of herself. And still he did not look away. It was impossible, impossible to concentrate or to have any hope of fighting it. His eyes glittered, but not the slightest shift in their gaze warned her of his intent. Before she could take another breath Luke was on his feet, moving toward her with a swiftness that held her rigid with startlement.

In another instant he was before her, his powerful hands locked on her upper arms, face inches from her own. His warm breath bathed her face. She could see the pupils of his eyes dilating, feel the quickening of her own pulse to the flutter of a trapped rabbit. Fear, shock, and desire struggled for dominance. Looking into eyes hot with emotions she suddenly understood, she knew too late she was completely out of her depth.

His grip tightened, drawing from her throat an involuntary gasp. The smell of him was wild and potent, and she felt the pressure of his fingers like burning brands on her arms. The dreams and the vivid memory of his kiss destroyed the last of her defenses.

Suddenly it was hot, far too hot; her clothes seemed like smothering bonds. She made a weak gesture to reach for the buttons of her shirt, to free herself. Free. The moan that escaped her seemed to come from some other throat. His face drew closer; her lips parted in delirious welcome. From somewhere far away she heard a deep rumbling, like the contented purr of some huge cat, but underlined with some subtle threat. His eyes were almost black now, all pupil; the powerful rush of his desire merged with her own. And then she could bear it no longer and shut her eyes in surrender, flinging her head back with a cry. Lips brushed against her throat, then the gentle pressure of teeth. It excited her beyond reason. She had left reason far behind.

His lips traveled over her throat, and his tongue, hot and slightly rough, stroked across her chin. Eyes tightly shut, she searched blindly for his mouth with her own. She was burning, burning with unrelenting heat, from within and without. His teeth caught her lower lip between them, tugging gently, and then his tongue followed to soothe where they had passed.

And then, at last, his lips were on hers, hard and yet incredibly mobile, dominating her as his eyes had done moments—ages—before. The rumble of a throaty growl vibrated against her as his tongue slipped into her mouth. Somehow his hands had left her arms and were around her, trapping her into immobility. His body was a lean, solid, supple cage from which she had no hope of escape. The pulse in her throat beat an irregular tattoo as his kiss deepened, claiming the innermost part of her, muffling her soft, urgent cries.

His hands were moving over her now, pulling at her shirt, tugging it from the loose waistband of her jeans. Her urge to help him was impeded by the pressure of his body against hers, but she cooperated fervently as the force of his lips eased, peppering his mouth and rough chin with tiny kisses. His fingers found the bare flesh of her back, stroked down, pushed the jeans around her hips. She managed to free one hand long enough to unsnap the front of them, hardly aware of what she was doing. She was all instinct now, and her instincts wanted only one thing.

In one smooth movement he eased her back onto the sofa, freeing her hands at last to tangle in his shirt, which had come half-undone. Trembling fingers worked at the buttons, brushed over the fine, mingled dark and pale hair of his chest. She pushed the shirt back from his shoulders, and he shrugged out of it as if it were an unwanted second skin. Her own shirt was trapped under her, open to expose her breasts to the heavy air; in spite of the heat, her nipples hardened almost painfully. His gaze—black, intense, unreadable in a way that should have frightened her—swept once over her body. It was as if his mouth and hands had touched every part of her.

For a long, agonizing moment he paused above her, his power like a storm on the verge of breaking. And then his lips came down on hers again, trapping the cry that rose to meet them.

There was no gentleness in him now as his mouth possessed hers. It was all raging passion released in a torrent, and it swept away the last fragments of Joey's rationality. With the freedom of primitive, unrestrained lust Joey accepted his ferocity and met it with her own.

Her tongue teased his and stroked over his lips, but he allowed her little chance to explore the limits of her own passion. Pinning her arms against her sides, his lips and tongue tasted her cheeks and chin, sliding down her neck with tiny nips and bites that made her writhe in pleasure.

When Luke's mouth found her breasts, Joey felt herself dissolve into a world of sensation unlike any she had ever known. One of his hands released her arm and covered one breast as his lips and tongue explored the other; his fingers were hot and callused as they kneaded and stroked her burning skin. His tongue trailed in circles over the soft swell until they reached the nipple; when he took it at last into his mouth, Joey arched her back with a cry that came out as a whisper. He teased her nipples, one after the other, until she was tossing her head in abandon, and only then did he grant her mercy and slide his lips down to taste the underside of her breasts, licking the hollows and moving to the taut sensitivity of her belly.

Joey's hands clenched and loosened in rhythm to his soft bites and kisses as he passed inexorably downward, circling each of her hipbones with teeth and tongue. His fingers found the center of her heat before his mouth did; they stroked over the acutely sensitive softness as she strained upward with breathless, soundless cries. From some distant place she could hear his breath coming harsh and fast, could feel his need like a living thing. He released her other arm and pressed his palms against her breasts as his mouth replaced his fingers; she reached down to tangle her own hands in his hair. He teased and caressed her, pulled her to the brink of fulfillment and then withdrew, again and again until she was sobbing with delicious agony.

For an instant his hard body pulled away from her, as his hands fumbled with the zipper of his jeans. The sudden break in unrelenting sensation brought Joey back to herself; her hands were shaking as she moved to help him. Their eyes locked for the first time since they had begun, and there seemed to be nothing rational or human at all in Luke's; they echoed what she herself had become.

When Luke was free of the restraints of his clothing, Joey's hands were there to take his hard length, stroking it with the same fierce desperation she had felt in his caresses. He stiffened, half-crouched above her, and for the first time he was as lost as she. He was fire and untamed masculine power in her hands, and she wanted that fire and power inside her to meet the burning of her own desire.

His breath came in audible rasps now, vibrating in time to the stroking of her hand. Without any agreement but one forged of instinct and need, she dropped her hand, and he positioned himself against her. The heavy shaft pressed her inner thigh, slid without hindrance along the slick softness of her skin, poised at yielding wetness. Joey lifted her hips to take him in, felt the delicious pressure as he prepared to enter.

And then it stopped. Joey opened eyes squeezed shut in unbearable anticipation and tried to focus on Luke where he lay, absolutely still, agonizingly motionless as his pale, wild eyes locked on hers again. Her body was taut with need for him, for his body on hers, for him inside of her—and he did nothing. She wanted to scream, to howl in frustration. There was no reasoning with her body now, or with his. With a moan she reached down for his hardness, wanting what only he could give, knowing he wanted it, too. . . .

He finally moved then, a jerk as if he'd been struck. The wordless cry he uttered was hoarse and harsh with denial, almost a snarl; his teeth bared in a grimace of rage and pain. Joey flinched and stared up at him, frozen in midmovement. His pupils had abruptly gone to pinpricks of shock. She stared in incomprehension as he flung back his head and made a sound of strangled, unmistakable agony.

And then, in defiance of human limitations and her own intense need, he was suddenly gone from above her. In the space of an instant she wa· left bereft, alone and abruptly, unbearably cold. Dazed, she turned her head weakly against the worn cushions, searching. He was there, in the darkest corner of the room, hunched and naked, only his eyes burning from the shadows in reflected firelight. Staring at her; staring, as he had before, but now with the bleak coldness of a stranger. Cold.

Joey shivered and plucked at the edges of her shirt, pulling it over her chest. Naked, suddenly vulnerable and frightened, she buttoned the shirt with fingers shaking now from reaction and returning sanity. Her jeans lay somewhere out of sight on the floor; to get them she'd have to sit up. Her eyes flickered again to the motionless shadow among the shadows. He was still staring, but his gaze seemed unfocused now. Closed off from her. She rolled upright and found her discarded jeans, moving as little as necessary to pull them back on. Again and again she glanced up to gaze blankly at the man she had desired beyond all reason, uneasy and frightened beyond comprehension. There was no desire left now—none but the last wisps of sensation fading from her sensitized body. She shuddered. It was so cold, colder than she would have thought possible. It felt as if she would never be warm again.

He shuddered. He shivered with emotion and need so far beyond control that there was no hope of relief. In the pitiful concealment of the shadows, Luke fought a compulsion so powerful that it took every ounce of strength he possessed not to become something that would destroy him. And her.

The small, weak part of his being that still possessed

the ability to think berated him in an endless litany of contempt. He had known the risk and had chosen to ignore it. He had known from the moment he had kissed her and felt her passion flare to meet his own. His pride had told him he would have her and be damned to the consequences. His mind had been determined to control his body, but his body had betrayed him.

He was still heavy with desire for her, and the only heat in his body seemed centered in the one place that could bring no ease. Every primitive instinct screamed for him to finish what he had started, but he could not do it. In the mass of contradictions that were his emotions, it was supreme irony that though his body had betrayed him, it was his mind that kept him now from completing the betrayal.

Turning inward, Luke gave himself to the interior battle and pushed the sight and smell and feel of her from his consciousness. She did not exist. She was not here. He was alone as he had always been. Only that nonsensical repetition allowed him to keep a grip on sanity and bring him back to some semblance of what he had been before.

When the chill in his soul had become no more than a tiny sharp point of pain and his body felt a cold that was of the purely physical realm, he found the world again. His eyes moved to the dying fire, little more than embers; around the familiar solid comfort of the cabin and, at last, to the form huddled on the sofa.

Joey lay where he had left her. She was dressed again and had managed to pull the edges of the blanket up around herself; he could see by the steady rise and fall of her chest and by the soft looseness of her body that she slept, a small mercy granted to them both.

It took all his will to compel his stiff body into motion, to toss more wood mechanically into the embers so that they would not die entirely by sunrise. It was morning already; he tilted his head with awareness of the coming day, though it was still several hours from dawn. Time enough, perhaps, for her to recover and for him to lock himself away beyond any hope of succumbing to her again.

He stopped above her, hovering there and regarding her with forced dispassion. The soft hills and valleys of her body, which he had begun to discover and explore, were forever barred to him. The gentleness of her features in repose, all the serious care and determined pride eased away by sleep, had become no more than another pretty face. The sweet mystery that Joelle Randall might have been to him would remain unsolved.

Luke bent down and gathered her into his arms, not smelling her or hearing her breathing or feeling her softness. He carried her across the bleak silence of the cabin and into the last room leading off the kitchen, where his bed lay. He undressed her carefully, wrapping her in a faded nightgown, folded and long unused, gleaned from one of the drawers. Her exhaustion was such that she did not waken; he could not have borne that when it took every ounce of strength he possessed to ignore her sweet, fragile nakedness under his hands.

The combined heat of fire and stove lent the room enough warmth to keep her comfortable throughout what remained of the night; she did not stir as he nudged her under the sheets and pulled the covers over her body. Once, as he threw the last blanket over the bed, she rolled her head against the pillow; her eyes fluttered, and the moan that came from her parted lips was filled with melancholy. Luke bowed his head and did not hear it. He turned away into the darkness and left her to her dreams, dreading his own.

She would wake and know the coming of dawn and find herself again; for him, there would only be night.

# Chapter Seven

The unsullied light that flooded through the sheer curtains of the window by the bed woke Joey slowly, warming her face with the gentlest of caresses. She stretched luxuriously, half-awake, savoring the light that traced across her cheek. She couldn't quite remember what today was, or what she had planned, but she could already smell the wonderful breakfast Mrs. O'Brien was making up in the lodge kitchen, and the sheer sensuality of the moment made her reluctant to think about much of anything.

With a sigh, Joey flung back her arms and arched her back. Her hair was spread loose over the pillow, and the feel of the flannel nightgown against her skin was another delicious sensation. After another long, lazy interval of peaceful contentment, Joey forced herself to open her eyes to face the day and the things that had to be done.

The first shock was the discovery that she was not in the bed in her room at the lodge. The second was that she was in a bed she had never seen before, in a totally unfamiliar room. The third was the realization that she was in Luke's cabin, in *his* bed—and the flood of memories that came with that knowledge.

She sat bolt upright, casting the heavy layers of blankets aside. The nightgown she wore, soft and infinitely comfortable, was not hers either. Her own clothes lay over the back of a chair beside a simple desk, along with the borrowed jeans and shirt and socks Luke had given her the night before.

The night before. The room was not particularly warm, but Joey felt an inner heat sufficient to drive away any encroaching cold. The memories came back in a rush: everything that had led up to a loss of control so complete that even now Joey felt desperately confused. What had happened? She knew the hard facts, the sequence of events, but in the light of day it all seemed like some bizarre fantasy.

She had let Luke make love to her. More—she had wanted him with a kind of savagery she hadn't known was in her. It had never happened to her before—certainly not with Richard. Never with him. Not that hungry need, that wild passion. With Richard she had never lost control.

Wrapping her arms about herself, Joey squeezed her eyes shut as if that simple action could shut off all remembrance. Make it all as if it had never happened . . .

But what *had* happened? There were enough questions to drive anyone crazy; for a moment Joey almost laughed at the image of herself indulging in a fit of hysterics. It was not just a matter of how she had gotten herself into that position—for the second time with him—but why he had ended it all and left her half-crazy with desire.

Again.

A clean rush of anger and indignation flooded Joey, firmly pushing chagrin and bewilderment out of the way. She clenched her teeth and felt them grinding as her jaw set. The bastard! First he'd agreed to help her, kissed her in a way she'd never been kissed before, and then abandoned her. Then, after not bothering to give her the slightest explanation, and after she'd had to go chase him down, he'd so graciously allowed her the hospitality of his cabin, only to repeat the same exercise—this time getting her to a point of such emotional vulnerability that the memory was almost beyond bearing. And then—he'd just stopped. He'd left her as if she had transformed into some kind of noxious snake—or worse.

His inexplicable behavior was bad enough, as was the constant uncertainty that seemed to be her normal state whenever she was near him. But this last blow to her pride was worst of all.

Clenching her fists in sheets still warm with the heat of her body, Joey swung her feet over the side of the bed. The floor was cold, but that was the least of her concerns. She stalked to the chair and touched her crumpled jeans and shirt. The last thing she intended to do was take any more of Luke's "charity" or wear anything belonging to one of his past conquests. She wasn't one of them.

She lost no time in stripping off the flannel nightgown—it also had belonged to some other woman—and began to tug on her own stiff clothing. As she balanced awkwardly with one leg half in the jeans, some sixth sense warned her. It wasn't noise or anything else so obvious that made her look up to find Luke in the doorway. The warning was too scant for her to do anything but cross her arms over her chest and glare at him with all the indignation she could muster.

There hadn't been time for her to have any expectations about what she would do when she saw him again, or what he would look like. If what had happened last night would show on his face. If he'd bother to explain himself. But now he stood in the doorway, filling it completely, fully dressed and ominously big and very silent.

Joey almost ordered him out, detesting her half-dressed vulnerability. The words wouldn't come. Instead, she stared at him, face hot with anger and embarrassment—and other emotions too appalling to bear thinking about. Even after what had happened, his mere presence did things to her that made her want to scream in unabashed rage.

Perhaps she would have given in to her impulse if Luke had said or done a single thing to provoke it. But he merely stood there, gazing at her with absolute blankness, not looking at her bare skin or reacting to her hostility. He dropped his amber eyes long before she could begin to engage him in yet another contest of wills.

"Breakfast is ready. I'll take you back to town after you've eaten." For a moment he paused, looking back up at her under his brows as if he debated more personal words. Then he turned on his heel and left her staring after him.

If Joey's anger had been hot before, it had become a veritable blaze now. She swore in a way that shocked even herself and pulled the rest of her clothing on with savage jerks. He wasn't going to get away with that—no, not a second time. She would make him tell her what was going on even if she had to risk life and limb to find out.

Luke was sitting at the small table over a bowl of oatmeal, across from a similar bowl before an empty chair. His posture, head dropped in one hand while the other stirred the oatmeal listlessly, was so alien to what she knew of him that Joey stopped to stare. It almost managed to defuse her anger. Until he looked up to see her, stiffened into rigidity, and sprang up from the chair, moving to the far side of the room as if she had a disease he didn't want to catch.

Joey spun to face him. "I've had enough of this, Gévaudan. I think it's about time you told me what the hell is going on here. Between us. If this is the way you acted with all your other girlfriends, I'm not surprised they didn't stick around. I came all the way out here to find you, and you . . ."

"Eat your breakfast." Luke's voice was no more than the softest of whispers. He was not looking at her. His back was pressed up to the far wall, hands spread against it like an animal backed into a corner.

Joey ignored the tone and the tension that twisted his imposing frame into a taut spring on the verge of release. "You aren't going to just ignore me this time, Luke. You owe me an explanation. You told me you'd help, and then you—used me and didn't even bother to finish what you'd started." Her face burned with chagrin at her bluntness, but anger had taken her too far to back down now. He had rejected her. . . .

"I can tell you nothing." Again his voice was deadly quiet, but this time he looked at her. His eyes were wide and piercing with some nameless emotion. "Eat, and I'll take you back to town. You won't see me again."

That was the last straw for Joey. The anger she felt was beyond anything she had ever experienced. She had always prided herself on her control and rationality, her cool ability to meet every challenge. All that went out the window as if it had never existed at all.

She found herself advancing on Luke, step by step, her fists clenched before her. "I won't see you again? Maybe I'd like that idea if you hadn't agreed twice to help me. Now you're going back on your word—again? What kind of man are you, Gévaudan? Maybe you're just the kind of coward who likes to pick on anyone you think is weaker than you are. Or maybe you're afraid of me. Is that it, Luke? You're afraid—of *me*!"

The absurdity of her own words shocked her into momentary sanity, but it was too late. Luke lunged at her with one incredibly swift movement and caught her arms so tightly that she cried out with the force of it. Her feet dangled as he lifted her, holding her as helpless as a newborn kitten while his eyes bored into hers.

His breath rasped, and his face was contorted into such an expression of bleak ferocity that Joey almost closed her eyes to block out the sight of it.

"I warn you, Joelle. Stop now. Eat your breakfast, go back to town, and forget you ever heard my name."

The shaking of his voice was that of barely repressed savagery, and Joey knew with the surety of instinct that he was one step away from a total loss of control.

It was not quite enough to defeat her.

"No."

She winced as his fingers tightened but met his eyes even though part of her screamed to run and keep running.

"I came here for the help you promised me. You *have* to help me. Damn you, you have to." She clung to that one goal that had never changed, discarded every personal consideration and every desperate question.

For a moment she thought he might get a grip on himself, calmly set her down, and agree to do as he had promised. He closed his eyes, and the break in his frightening stare was a relief. It lasted for only the briefest of instants.

"You don't know, Joelle. You don't know what game you're playing." The words were even, deliberate, cold. "If you push me far enough, you'll regret you ever left San Francisco. And you may never go back."

Before his chilling words could penetrate, he lifted her against the hard rigidity of his body and forced his mouth on hers. Struggling against him was like trying to stop a forest fire with a garden hose. There was not the smallest trace of gentleness in the kiss; it bruised her mouth as he forced his tongue between her lips with utter violence. She could do nothing against it, and when it ended, he dropped her so suddenly that she staggered.

As she clutched the chair back and straightened he stood over her, unmoving, unrepentant and unrelenting. The bitter tang of blood was in her mouth; her tongue searched and found the place where he had grazed her with his teeth. She backed up, ignoring the hard edge of the chair where it dug into her spine.

Luke was wild. His eyes blazed, and his teeth were bared; Joey kept very still while he struggled visibly to regain his composure. Joey battled for her own, and the first rush of alarm and fear at his attack subsided under the weight of returning anger.

Lip curled in defiance, Joey straightened to regard him with something approaching contempt. "Your threats and boorish behavior aren't going to work on me, Luke. Don't concern yourself any longer; I'm not about to impose on you for one more minute." She whirled on her heel and left Luke standing there, angry strides propelling her into the main room. She jerked at her hair and wound it into a loose knot at the nape of her neck, securing it with a bit of string from her pocket as she made for the door.

Luke was already blocking her exit when she reached it. Skidding to a halt, Joey narrowly avoided a collision; she hid reaction under a mask, of cool hostility. "You wanted me to leave; if you'll kindly step aside, I'll be going."

His eyes were still wild, his posture taut with threat. "Forget you ever met me, Joey. Go back where you came from—give up on this quest and return to your city. Don't come back."

"Oh, no." Joey matched the harshness of his tone with a ferocity equal to anything he could muster. "Not on your life. I came here for a reason, and I'm not going home until I've done what I set out to do."

Tensing in anticipation, she took a step forward until her chest almost touched his. "With or without your help I'm going to find my parents. If I can't find a guide, I'll guide myself. And neither you nor anyone else is going to stop me."

She had almost been ready for his reaction this time, but even so it was a shock when the steel grip of his hands fastened on her shoulders and forced her back, back against the near wall, pressing her there with the full power of his body. The harsh lines of his face were rigid, the amber-green glow of his eyes lambent with a kind of madness.

"No, you won't." His words grated, breath hot against her forehead. "You won't find a guide, and you won't go up into the mountains. You won't get yourself killed in *my* territory." He pushed her against the wall so that every inch of their bodies touched; Joey trembled with rage and fear and yearning.

"Why do you care, Luke?" She made the familiarity of his name into a taunt. "You could have had what you wanted, and you didn't take it. What does it matter to you what happens to me?"

A wordless growl rose from his throat, and he tossed his head back in a gesture of something like despair. His trembling vibrated in time to her own; Joey gritted her teeth as he dropped his feral gaze once again to hers.

"I won't allow it. *I will not a allow it.*" The words came like blows. "You will not go. Do you understand?" His fingers tightened hard enough to leave bruises. Joey felt her teeth bare in response; she struggled uselessly in his grip, nearly spitting with rage. No sane, logical response would come, nothing except irrational defiance.

"I can prevent you from going, Joey. Easily." Luke's tone had become almost even, almost reasonable, even as her own heart beat hard and fast in growing fury.

"You'd have to pass through my lands to get where you need to go, unless you want to spend a month doing it. And I won't let you. Do you understand me? I won't let you pass."

The last of Joey's tenuous control broke in a flood tide. The sounds that came out of her mouth were hardly words; they were cries of rage mingled with emotions that had heated to fever pitch. She beat at him with her fists, half-trapped as she was, and her feet struck blows on his shins and ankles. She tossed her head so that her hair came loose and whipped about her face in a frenzy; throughout it all he stood as unyielding and silent as one of his mountains.

As suddenly as it had come, Joey's eruption of madness subsided, and she felt the tears on her burning face. They lay glistening on Luke's, too, where she had flung them in her struggles; the sight shocked her more than his absolute stillness. Her arms and legs went limp, and had he not held her there she would have fallen. She lay against him, her head rolling on his shoulder in abject defeat. The tears came in earnest then, and she had no will to fight them.

Luke's shoulder made a hard pillow to muffle her sobs, but nothing so trivial—not even his victory— seemed to matter. Her tears soaked his shirt; her body shook and jerked like a puppet controlled by some indifferent hand. She hardly noticed when the pressure against her body eased, and arms caught her up and held her in the gentlest of embraces.

It was only after the final storm had subsided that Joey felt Luke's stroking hand as it caressed her hair, pressing her face into the sculpted planes of his chest. He supported her as easily as he might a child; his arms dwarfed and protected her as his cheek rubbed the top of her head. The utter emptiness of emotion, the bone-weariness Joey felt, did not hold that awareness at bay.

When the last shaking had stilled, Joey struggled to

summon the energy to wipe the tears away. Luke's big hand came up to cup her chin, raising her face to meet his. She tried not to look at him, not to let him see the aftermath of her ignominious loss of self-control. Her eyes felt swollen, face stiff with drying tears; before she could gauge his expression, he lowered his head to kiss the wetness from her cheeks. The feather-light touch of his lips was infinitely tender, infinitely different from all that had gone before. His tongue tasted her tears and stroked her eyelids. She closed them, and the soft gasps that came now were not of furious grief.

It seemed impossible, ludicrous, that anything could be left within her to stir at his touch. The rage was gone, but there was still something that could respond to the feel of him, to his gentle caresses. The utter contradictions that were Luke Gévaudan, and that comprised her own feelings about him, had no more significance than a single fallen pine needle on the forest floor. Her trembling returned, and with it a rush of sheer sensuality.

Perhaps it was the sudden sense of helplessness that broke the spell between them, that cut through the pure sensation to strike at the forgotten core of logic. Joey stiffened suddenly, released her hold, and pushed Luke away, using her body to repel him as she had accepted him only a moment before. He did not struggle to hold her. As he fell back with a single graceless step, his face was as stunned as if he had been struck. Joey looked away.

Luke said nothing. He stood motionless as Joey felt her way to the door, blinded by confusion and wanting only one thing, one solution to the almost unendurable chaos of her emotions. Her hand found the doorknob and twisted it; she stumbled through the tiny room that served as an entryway and opened the door to freedom. Sunlight dazzled her eyes. She reached up instinctively to shield them, staring with incomprehension at the arch of blue sky, the brown and green edge of forest. Her feet carried her from the cabin. It didn't matter that she didn't know the fastest and most certain way home; all that mattered was to get away, away from Luke Gévaudan and her own madness.

She had nearly reached the lake shore before Luke caught up with her. Knowing he was there without benefit of sight or sound, Joey froze; he came up beside her silently and handed her a small rucksack. She took it as if she had no will of her own, numbly assessing the contents through the canvas. Clothing—her jacket, perhaps—and smaller objects that might have been food items. Joey hardly cared; she did not meet his eyes, nor did he force contact. When she shrugged into the light pack, he backed away, face turned aside, and melted into the trees like a ghost.

Joey did not waste time on thinking or analysis or questions. Giving herself to the sane reality of physical action, she let her feet find the way to the path skirting the lake and followed it with steady strides.

Only one thought broke through the blankness of her self-imposed indifference. There was still one unassailable reality in her life that hadn't changed. She would find her parents, and no one—not even Luke Gévaudan—was going to stop her.

Drifting among the trees beside the path, Luke trailed Joey as she worked her way across his land. He sensed that she was lost to herself, much as he was; she did not notice when he used his subtle influence to turn her when she left the sometimes imperceptible trail. Always he watched to see that she came to no harm, though the mere sight of her was a pain almost too terrible to bear.

Before long the wolves came to join him, so silent in the forest that even he almost missed their coming. They flowed about him, weaving the patterns of their kind, keeping even greater quiet than was their wont because they sensed the presence of an outsider. They watched with him when Joey stopped to rest, dragged the food Luke had assembled for her out of the rucksack, and ate it with a listlessness that struck him to the heart. When she pulled herself to her feet and almost stumbled, only the wolves kept him from going to her.

It was late afternoon when Joey reached the outskirts of town. The wolves stopped before he did, wary of the haunts of man in daylight. Luke trailed farther on, until he saw Joey reach the manicured lawn of the lodge; even the people Joey passed did not see him. She seemed equally unaware of them as she took the steps up to the broad porch, leaning in utter weariness against the door before pushing it open and disappearing within.

He stood there behind the screen of trees for a long moment, pulled savagely in two directions, longing to go to her again and knowing he could not. He had made that mistake once before. At last he submitted to the silent call of his brothers and whirled back into the forest, rejoining them as they milled eagerly among the patterns of light and shadow that mottled the forest floor. Their call was compelling, and he did not fight it.

As before, he ran to clear the smell of her from his nostrils, to forget the feel of her in his arms, though now he did not run alone. The wolves leaped and bounded about him, and he shared the lead with the alpha female of the pack as they left the man-tainted lands and returned to the protected haunts of his domain.

They ran and then slowed again, to await the coming of sunset; the lead female caught the scent of prey, and they were off on the hunt. The deer that fled before them, incautious in its late-afternoon graze, was swift and valiant despite the flaw that had marked it as the wolves' chosen prey. They took the chance that nature gave them, to make themselves strong while keeping the deer tribe free of the individuals that would make it weak.

The hunt was successful this time, as it often was not. Luke sat off to the side as the wolves feasted; even the exhilaration and exhaustion of running long and hard had not freed him of her presence. The wolves knew it, for even they looked up at him and kept their distance, growling and groveling when he came near. He was always a little separate from them, but now he was truly alone. There was only one solution to his aloneness now, and for all time to come.

With a snarl Luke slammed his fist into the broken surface of the rock on which he sat. He had surely learned his lesson by now. He had paid—and made her pay—for his failure to heed the warnings his senses had given him. She thought he was crazy, or worse—and with good reason. That thought hurt more than he would have believed possible. Any other woman would never have forced him to endure this. He would have forgotten about her as he'd told Joey to forget about him.

But Joey wasn't any other woman, as he knew now to the marrow of his bones. And he knew her well enough to understand that, in spite of his warnings and threats, she would not give up on her crazy scheme, the one for which he'd promised his help. How easily he'd made that promise when he'd thought it was still possible to take her and let her go like any of the others.

Her words echoed in his mind. Coward. *Was* he a coward? Afraid to risk himself to help her after he'd given his word? But it wasn't that simple. He dropped his head into his folded arms and sighed. She had as much to lose as he did. And he had everything to lose.

For the first time in many hours Luke's mind settled into the rhythms of cold logic. He knew she would do what she'd planned, without his help, just as she'd threatened. So it came down to risks that seemed equally terrible: her very life—or her sanity, and his. He could stop her from crossing his lands easily enough, but she would find a way around them, pushing her quest into the dangerous time that came with the first snows. He could let her go alone, but he knew she would haunt him, and that would drive him to madness. He could not let her die because he had refused the help only he could give.

The solution, when it came, was as inevitable as the rising of the moon in the night sky. It brought with it no relief, no acceptance—but it was all he had.

The wolves were dispersing, bellies full with their meal. They came to him to pay him homage, ducking heads and flattening ears, from the alpha female to the lowest-ranked animal in the pack. Luke stood up to acknowledge it, asserting his dominance with looks and gestures the wolves understood with the ease of long familiarity. Then he dismissed them, and they trotted away to find their resting place as he watched them disappear into the deep shadows of the forest.

Luke tossed his head back to feel the cold bite of the evening breeze. With a sudden shiver of excitement Luke remembered the men at the lake, the roughnecks who had assaulted Joey. He had been too preoccupied to consider how best to deal with them, but now he had the time and the will to solve that little problem. The hair rose along the nape of his neck. Joey had thought they'd learned their lesson, but he doubted it. He doubted it very much. They needed to remember—to have it indelibly imprinted on their small, vicious brains—never, never to trespass on his land again. And never to touch Joey Randall.

The cry of triumph that lay trapped in his throat burst free. Baring his teeth in a grin, Luke turned in the direction of town. For the first time in a very long time things would be simple—and very satisfying.

* * *

"Joey . . . you're back!" The sound of genuine astonishment in Maggie's voice almost made Joey wince as she settled on a stool at the bar.

Joey managed a smile at the redhead. "You sound surprised, Maggie. The Big Bad Wolf didn't eat me after all." Maggie flushed to the roots of her curly hair and covered her discomfiture with a quick move to fill a glass with Joey's usual white wine.

Taking advantage of the brief lull before explanations would be due, Joey let her head drop into her folded arms on the scratched surface of the countertop. She was still drained and exhausted from the events of the day before, even though she had fallen into bed almost as soon as she'd reached the safety of the lodge. She'd hardly been aware of the curious faces of the guests as she'd stumbled up to her room, pulled off her dirty clothes, and dropped into bed and to sleep.

It was small mercy that the dreams did not come that night, as though all the reserves of her intellect and emotions had run dry. She had slept through most of the day, awakening to afternoon sunlight flooding the room—and to a powerful awareness of how much she needed a good shower. Nevertheless, she'd had to struggle to find the energy to wash the dirt and sweat from her body, forcing herself to eat a meager supper in her room.

It seemed more instinct than logic that she'd ended up here at Red's. The tang of the wine filled Joey's nostrils as Maggie set a glass down at her elbow. The redhead said nothing, but Joey didn't have to see her face to know she was bursting with questions and comments. Joey smiled again in resignation.

"Don't look so grim, Maggie. I'm fine. Everything's fine." She summoned up the brightest expression she could muster and straightened to regard her friend. "It's all working out just as I planned, thanks to your suggestion. I'll finally be able to make my expedition."

"Does that mean you went all the way out to Gévaudan's cabin and convinced him to help you after all?" Maggie asked. Her skepticism was all too evident.

"I did, and lived to tell about it," Joey said with a short laugh she hoped was convincing. "It's all working out just fine."

Maggie shook her head. "Sorry to sound like an interfering busybody, but I could have kicked myself after I suggested that crazy idea to you." She sighed, leaning her elbows on the bar, chin in hand. "We—Allan and I—didn't want to see you get into something—well, unpleasant. Damn it, do you know how worried we were about you?"

Unexpected emotion stirred in Joey's bruised heart at her friend's words. She had never been the touching kind, but now she found herself reaching out to touch Maggie's arm.

"I know. And it means a lot to me. Sometimes I'm not good at telling people things like that." She ducked her head. "But please don't worry anymore. Tell Allan—in case I don't see him for a while—not to worry, either. I'll take good care of myself." She did not draw away when Maggie grasped her hand tightly, her hazel eyes bright with concern. Joey returned the pressure and grinned.

"When are you leaving?" Maggie tossed her curls and smiled wryly at Joey's expression. "Even I know when to give up."

"Soon. I'm supposed to meet Gévaudan at the edge of his land the day after tomorrow." She hesitated, knowing it was best not to be too specific. Not when she didn't know how things would really turn out—when she'd make it back to town. Or *if*.

She concealed a shudder. "He figures it'll take us a number of days both directions, so I suppose I'll be gone a week or more. You were right about him, Maggie—he's just the man I needed for this. I'll be in good hands."

The redhead sighed and shrugged philosophically. "I know you won't listen to any more advice from me. As long as you know what you're doing. And don't take any chances with Gévaudan. I meant it when I said before he's got a . . . dubious reputation."

"Which is why you were surprised to see me back here so quickly," Joey teased. "But, as you can see, I'm all in one piece, and it all worked out perfectly. Gévaudan's no match for me!" With a cocky gesture she raised the wineglass, saluted her friend, and took a long drink.

Maggie's face was easily read, and Joey knew her act had not been entirely persuasive.

"He's really not as bad as they say," she added, setting down the glass. "And whatever happens, Maggie— it'll be my choice and my responsibility." Joey closed her eyes briefly, wishing she could risk fully confiding in Maggie, pouring out her doubts and fears and confusion, admitting that she was about to take a terrible gamble—that she'd be going into the mountains alone. But she could not be so cruel. She could only hope that Maggie and Allan would not hold Luke to blame if she never came back. Whatever her feelings about him, it was her choice alone to risk her life for the freedom from the past she so desperately needed.

When she opened her eyes, Maggie was returning from serving another customer. Joey sighed deeply and met the redhead's troubled gaze.

"Maggie, I've told you something of why I'm doing this, why I *need* to do it. But I've never really talked about it—in a way that might really explain." She searched for the right words. "All my life I've felt as if there was something undone, something that kept me from really living life—the way people like you live it."

The explanation seemed wrenched from a part of her that hadn't been touched in ages—a part of her that Luke Gévaudan had exposed and left raw to the very real possibility of pain.

Now she looked inward at that hidden place again, and her words were as much for herself as Maggie. "I suppose you could say I've been hiding all my life, so that no one could do what my parents did when they died and left me alone. Even my marriage was very safe. Richard was . . . predictable. Safe. I thought that was what I needed most—but one day it wasn't enough, and that was when I realized I had to do something to try and find some meaning. . . ."

She trailed off and swallowed; a watery laugh forced its way past the lump in her throat. "I had a decent life. I don't know why I couldn't have just accepted that. Everything was nice and orderly and safe. But when I realized I had to do this one thing, that was all that mattered. It became . . . a purpose. Something to fight for."

She risked a glance up at Maggie, whose face was drawn with a sympathy so open that Joey could not bear to watch it. She forced herself to continue. "I can't turn around and go home and forget about this just because it's easier and more practical to do so. There've been times when I've wished I could—but it's too late for that. I have to finish this, Maggie. It's my last chance to say good-bye to people I loved—but maybe it's also my last chance to find myself."

The words ran dry then, and she could not find any other way of saying what she herself was only beginning to understand. She'd never put it so bluntly even within the safety of her own heart. It left her trembling with the violence of a battle she'd hardly known was being fought. Within herself.

Maggie's hand covered hers where it clenched against the counter. "Don't say any more, Joey. I think I do understand. We all have things we have to do—no matter what the risks." The redhead broke off; Joey heard a catch in her voice that hinted of personal experience, and memory. "All I can say is that I want you to find what you're looking for. Just be careful. Be safe. Take care of yourself, okay?"

"I promise I'll do my best, Maggie." Joey managed a tremulous smile, and Maggie answered it with one of her own. Unclenching her hands, Joey took another long sip of wine and concentrated on the soothing liquid as it loosened the tightness in her chest. "And now I've got to go, Maggie. I'm going to get plenty of rest and gather up the rest of my supplies. I'll drop in and say good-bye tomorrow evening."

"That's a deal." Maggie swept away the glass and gave Joey a broad wink. "You rest up good, hear? And I'm going to want a full report the minute you get back."

Joey did not quite meet Maggie's eyes as she turned for the door. "I will. As soon as I get back."

Ignoring the flush of guilt at the trust in her friend's words, Joey could not quite shut out the small voice that taunted her: *If I get back.*

Joey turned in early that night, careful to avoid anyone who might subject her to questions she had no desire to answer. She spent the next morning collecting the remaining supplies she would need: additional clothing, easily portable foodstuffs, anything she had not already purchased that would stack the odds in her favor.

In the late afternoon she laid out her maps and spent several hours studying them, memorizing the shortest route to her destination. That meant crossing Luke's land. If he really did try to stop her—she slapped the palms of her hands against the map. She'd deal with that when the time came.

That evening Joey tried to rest before making her

last visit to see Maggie. Everything was as ready as it was likely to be, but the twisting thoughts that coiled in her mind would not be silenced. Though the dreams had not plagued her for the past two nights, she could no more drive memories away than she could forget Luke Gévaudan and everything that had passed between them. She had come no closer to understanding him, or herself; where he was concerned, there was only a black pit of confusion, pain, and longing.

Tossing on the bed, Joey fought for the determination that had always been her strength. Now that she was doing it at last—facing something she had worked so long and hard for—it was suddenly very frightening. And she would be facing it by herself, without even the practical help of someone who could guide her and get her there and back in one piece.

Joey was too much a realist—even now—to ignore the facts. What she was doing was foolhardy, insane, even suicidal. She would risk her life and betray the faith of her friends to chase a dream that might not even exist. She might die in those mountains, just as Luke had warned her.

It was small comfort to remind herself that, if she did, she wouldn't be entirely alone.

Joey spent more time at the tavern that night than she had intended, bolstering her courage and pushing back useless emotion in small talk with Maggie. After last night's encounter the redhead did not push for more details or further assurances, and Joey accepted that with mingled guilt and gratitude.

On her way to the bar Joey had run into some familiar faces that had momentarily jolted her out of her preoccupation. The pack of young men passed by in a blur at first, until she recognized the blond ringleader and then the others who had confronted her at the lake. For a long moment Joey had wondered if, in the middle

of the empty street, they intended to take up where
they'd left off; she'd braced herself and stood her
ground with more stubbornness than sense.

But they hadn't taken up her challenge. If anything,
their faces had reflected an unease so great that Joey had
wondered if she'd suddenly sprouted fur and fangs. The
ringleader had muttered something, but his companions
had dragged him away so quickly that Joey blinked in
astonishment.

Now, in the warm familiarity of the bar, she studied
Maggie's bright face and wondered if she'd see it again
after tonight. She'd thought long and hard about what
she would leave behind her if she never returned; the
redheaded barkeep and Allan Collier had come to mean
more to her in a few brief weeks than most of the ac-
quaintances she'd left in San Francisco.

Joey did not examine too closely how little she had
allowed her life to be touched by others after her parents had died. It was too overwhelming and far too dangerous a distraction. If she'd ever needed all her internal
strength, it was now.

Only the burning memory of Luke Gévaudan had the
power to chip away at her resolve. Somehow, he had gotten to the very core of what she held protected in her
heart, broken barriers she had not known existed until
he'd discovered them. Now she had to put him out of
mind as well, forget him as he'd commanded her to do.
Her thoughts of him held nothing of logic. And logic was
all she had to guide her and keep her alive.

Coming back to herself, Joey blinked as she looked
up at her friend. It was with a powerful feeling of déjà
vu that she caught the change in Maggie's expression as
the redhead paused with a half-full mug of beer in
hand, staring over Joey's shoulder at the door as cold air
swirled through the tavern.

The sense of him was so undeniable that Joey did
not have to turn around to know what had riveted the

barkeep's attention. She swiveled on the stool as Luke glided into the room and up to her as if they had parted only moments before.

The grim lines of his face did not soften as his eyes swept over her and up to Maggie. Caught in the fascination of Luke's nearness like a bird under the spell of a snake, Joey heard rather than saw the redhead's retreat, the resumption of normal conversation as the tavern patrons reacted to and shut out Luke's presence.

Luke's eyes dropped back to her with an intensity that banished anything or anyone but the two of them. Joey felt herself fast recovering from the shock of seeing him there; defensive anger rose to take its place, but she pushed that down and regarded him with forced calm.

"Well, Luke, this is a surprise. I didn't think I'd be seeing you before we began the expedition." She kept her voice light and level, exactly as if she and Luke had reached the businesslike understanding she had implied to Maggie. She had no intention of revealing to him when she planned to leave, but she knew by the tightening of his jaw that he understood the mocking challenge she threw at him.

The touch of anger in his face disappeared under a mask of cool indifference as blatantly false as her own. "I thought it would be a better idea to come in early, make sure everything is in order. No sense in taking any chances." His deep voice carried layers of meaning that Joey could not entirely read. Was it threat? Did he intend to make sure she didn't leave town, or was it something she could not even guess at?

Joey slid off the barstool. "In that case, maybe we'd better go discuss our plans." She turned her back on him with deliberation and searched for Maggie, who stood watching with her arms folded and her eyes wide and troubled.

"I've got to go, Maggie, take care of a few last-minute things." She smiled with all the warmth and sincerity she could muster. "Please don't worry. I'll be fine, and I'll tell you all about it when I get back."

Joey watched Luke's gaze track back to Maggie, almost a glare of warning; Maggie met it stubbornly. "I expect your guide to look after you. You'll do that, won't you, Mr. Gévaudan?" The redhead's voice carried its own warning. "You make real sure you take good care of Joey. We'll be looking forward to seeing her again. Soon."

With a last nod at Joey, Maggie turned her attention back to the bar, dismissing Luke as easily as he'd dismissed her.

Luke's tension vibrated in the air between them, making the hair rise along the back of Joey's neck. She turned away and strode from the tavern, knowing Luke was hard on her heels.

As the door closed behind them, Joey did not give Luke the satisfaction of a confrontation. She charged grimly across the street and headed back for the lodge as Luke kept pace in silence, a burning and implacable presence. It was only when they reached the vicinity of the lodge that Joey felt sufficiently in control of herself to face him.

"I thought the plan was to forget you ever existed," Joey mocked quietly as she spun to a halt. "You made yourself fairly clear. I thought I was doing a pretty good job."

The expected reaction didn't come. He merely looked at her without the remotest hint of desire or threat or anger. The amber-green eyes hardly seemed focused on her at all.

"I'm here to do what I said I'd do. Nothing more. I'll guide you into the mountains and get you back. Then you'll be free to leave."

The utter chill in his voice, as impersonal as if there had never been anything but business between them, penetrated even Joey's determined facade.

"I see. You've decided to help me after all. Is this decision subject to sudden reversals like the others?"

The taunt came out even when she tried to halt the flow of words; he stiffened almost imperceptibly. If his pride had been touched at all by her barb, he did not reveal it beyond that sudden tension and the merest flicker of his eyes.

"I give you my word that I'll get you where you need to go, and back again."

"In return for what? You've said before you don't need money. What do you want from me?" She searched the distance of his pale eyes for some flicker of passion, anything to hint that he still wanted her the way he had before their second disastrous attempt at lovemaking.

His voice was almost a whisper. "That's simple enough." He gazed up, beyond her, to the pale unreachable swathe of stars overhead. "When you have what you want, you leave. You never come back here again."

# Chapter Eight

Joey felt herself trembling at his words. She refused to acknowledge the deep pang of loss, the utter hopelessness that came with his offer. After everything else she had done to reach her goal, this was little enough to give up. And she'd be forever free of the unsettling enigma of Luke Gévaudan.

Looking up to catch his eyes, Joey nodded with slow deliberation. "All right. If that's what you want. But it seems unfair to you, after all, since I'll be getting all the advantage out of the arrangement."

Her final remark did not seem to affect him more than any of the others; he folded his arms in front of his chest and studied her calmly.

"I don't think so."

He held her gaze for a moment and then looked away again, toward the lodge. "If it's agreed, then there's no point in wasting time. There are things to be arranged and planned if we're to leave as soon as possible."

"I've done most of the planning already, as it happens," Joey countered. "I think you'll find everything in order."

"That's what I intend to find out." Without warning Luke began to walk toward the lodge, forcing Joey to jog a few steps to match his long stride. "Nothing can be left to chance. I want this to be as uncomplicated as possible."

"Excellent," Joey snapped. "Then we're in perfect agreement."

Luke did not answer as he bounded up the steps to the front door and flung it open. Trailing after, Joey was secretly relieved to see that the last late diners were gone, and she and Luke were able to make their way up to her room without suffering a single accusatory glare. None of that should matter anymore, just as her relationship—such as it was—with Luke was of no further significance.

Moving to lay out her maps on the bed, Joey paused as Luke scanned the room and its contents, dismissing all of it but the pile of equipment in the corner.

"I've got everything assembled," she offered, clamping down on an unwelcome surge of defensiveness. "What I didn't already have I bought yesterday in town; there shouldn't be anything to prevent us from leaving tomorrow."

Luke nodded absently, rubbing his jaw as he surveyed the items neatly grouped on the floor. "Let's hope not." He didn't seem to notice the shift in Joey's posture as she stiffened; before she could summon up an appropriate retort, he added, "I'll check through that later."

He swung around and, with that uncanny swiftness of movement, joined Joey by the bed to look down over her shoulder at the maps. He studied them silently for a long moment while Joey grimly ignored the radiant heat from the body inches away from her own. Instead, she focused on the maps and smoothed out the wrinkles with nervous strokes of her palm.

"This is the general map," she said at last, eager to break the silence. "These areas"—she indicated the red circles marked in several places throughout the map—"were the locations I determined most likely for the site of the crash." Her voice didn't quite catch on the words. "I knew the approximate area where they went down: Their last radio message broke up toward the end, but their description of the landscape narrowed it down. I know they were near a sizable mountain, and other landmarks they'd been passing over when they had to alter course; over the summer I've checked these other sites."

"And found nothing." Luke leaned on one of the posts of the bed canopy and traced over the map with a finger. "Didn't the authorities investigate this when it happened years ago?"

His voice, cool as it was, held no hint of challenge, and Joey felt herself relaxing as much as his nearness allowed. "Oh, yes, they tried. Unfortunately, it was during a late spring snowstorm, and it was some time before they were able to begin the search." A trace of bitterness crept into her words. "They told me their resources were stretched too thin to allow much time for one small downed plane. They made a few attempts, but once they decided it wasn't going to be easy, they more or less gave up."

"Twelve years ago. That was a bad year."

Joey looked up at him, his face a blank as he searched old memories. "There were many accidents that year." All at once he came back to himself, and his eyes deliberately avoided hers to rest on the maps again. "They found nothing at all?"

"Nothing. Even they didn't know exactly where the plane went down—the places they searched are the

same ones I've considered, though I was able to elimi-
nate some areas."

She swallowed and concentrated on facts as cold
and hard as glacier ice. "They believed that the place
might have been covered by an avalanche after the
crash, which would have made finding it almost impossible until the spring thaw. By then they had more important business."

There was a profound quiet broken only by Luke's
deep, measured breathing and her own, fast with suppressed emotion. She sensed something from Luke that
had nothing to do with cold facts and everything to do
with unreasonable emotion; for an instant she tensed in
expectation of his touch. Then the moment passed, and
Luke's words were as even and cool as before.

"If it went down under an avalanche, the plane
could be anywhere—the wreckage could be wedged
into a crevice or covered with a rockslide. You could
have missed it at one of these other sites—and it may
not be here, either." His finger marked the final location, the one she needed him to find.

"I know that." Hearing the steadiness of her own
voice, Joey knew she had passed the crisis point. "But
that doesn't change anything; I have to try."

For the first time Luke's eyes met hers. They were
unreadable, but there was a flicker of that old intensity.

"There are some . . . needs . . . that drive animals
beyond the limits that mere survival demands," he said
softly. "Human beings are no different."

His gaze dropped away, and Joey was left with the
obscurely comforting feeling that Luke had tried to tell
her that, in some way, he understood her compulsion.
The thought almost warmed her; she wrapped up the
feeling and hid it away with the others.

"In any case, this is the last place I have to check,"
Joey said at last. "There's no point in thinking beyond
finding it, is there?"

She had not expected an answer, but Luke echoed her words. "No. No point at all." He leaned over; Joey could smell the intensely masculine odor of his skin and the flannel shirt he wore. "And the other map?"

Joey pulled the smaller map over to the center of the bed. "This one covers the immediate vicinity of the site; you told me before much of the near area to the south is your land. That shouldn't pose any difficulty." She didn't look up at him, remembering all too clearly his threats to keep her from crossing his territory. And what had accompanied those threats. "The most direct routes don't seem to intersect the Provincial Park on the other side of the mountain—unless you think there's a better way than the one I've marked here."

Luke's finger followed the meandering red line she had used to sketch out the path she'd intended to travel. "Miller's Peak," he murmured. "The best route is close to the one you've indicated, and much of it does cross my land."

Frowning, Joey traced the area immediately south of the mountain, careful not to let her fingers brush his where they touched the map. "I wasn't sure about this part. I know it's private, but I haven't been able to locate the owners. Do you think that'll be a problem?"

The softest breath of a laugh made her look up at Luke in startlement. His grim-set mouth had relaxed into a wry half-smile. "No, I don't think that will be a problem. I know the owners of that land; they won't object if you're with me." He offered no further explanation, and Joey shrugged; explanations didn't matter if it meant one less obstacle to her goal.

"Good. In that case there's nothing to prevent us from getting this done as quickly as possible." Joey straightened, feeling a rush of genuine confidence for the first time in many days. Things were finally falling into place. . . .

Luke studied the map for another long moment,

seemingly lost in his own thoughts. Then he turned to fix her with a hard stare, the brief smile gone, his eyes pale and cold. "Don't misunderstand, Joey. It's not a great distance, not as we reckon distance up here. But it's wild country. The way to Miller's Peak covers ground from above timberline to heavily forested valleys, all wilderness. No civilization, and no conveniences. We aren't going to take any chances." Each word came with measured deliberation. "This will be done in slow, easy steps—and if there's any chance that you can't handle it, or if anything at all happens to make it too dangerous, we're turning around and coming back. Do you understand?"

The brief surge of confidence fled as Joey absorbed Luke's warning. She tilted her head and set her jaw. "I understand what I came here to do, what I *have* to do. One way or another, I'll do it."

Luke rose to his full height and took a menacing step forward. "Get this straight, Joey. You'll do exactly what I say at all times. You'll obey without question, and if I determine that it's too dangerous to continue, you'll come back here with me and stay here." His eyes locked on hers and did not look away; Joey refused to let him see the unsettling and unwelcome effect of his words.

"I told you before, Luke," she said softly. "I'll do this with or without you. If you won't go through with it, I will."

Joey had become so practiced at reading the language of Luke's body that she was able to note the faintest vibration in his muscles as he held himself absolutely still. His voice dropped to a whisper. "And I told *you*, Joey—I won't have you die in my territory, or come to harm in my care. If you don't do exactly as I tell you, I'll see to it that you never get within twenty kilometers of Miller's Peak."

Trembling with an inner rage she struggled to conceal, Joey held her ground. "I see. You're very good with threats, Luke—and if you're good at anything else, then you'll do what I hired you to do. Or is it all nothing but empty words?"

Luke spun away from her so suddenly that she flinched, backing away from the violence of his retreat. He began to pace the room like a caged panther, the slight hitch in his turns revealing what his face did not. The charged silence of the room grew heavy with tension; Luke came to an abrupt halt to fix her again with his icy gaze.

"Don't play games of dominance with me, Joelle. You can't win them." As if to prove his point, he shifted subtly into a posture rife with menace, one that made him look bigger than Joey had ever seen him; she felt herself mesmerized into immobility, all her limbs locked and beyond her control. She was drowning again in the cold yellow-green glow of his eyes, but there was no desire there to soften the experience. Her breath came hard and fast, from some distant place; for an endless moment she struggled against what he tried to impose on her and broke free with a gasp, trembling with exertion and indignation.

She waited until the shaking had stilled, until she could look at him again without fear of losing herself. With infinite, glacial chill, she said, "I'm not interested in playing games with you, Luke. Of any kind. I am interested in only one thing. Do your job, and I'll cooperate. Get me to where I need to go, and you'll never see me again. We'll both have what we want."

Turning her back on him, she knelt by the bed and began to fold up the maps with precise, deliberately controlled motions. Behind her, Luke said nothing; she wondered why she felt so little satisfaction that he had no answer.

* * *

There was a businesslike and perfectly efficient remoteness between them for the remainder of the evening. Luke set himself immediately to sorting through her gear, pronouncing approval or disapproval of the various items she had assembled over the summer and dividing them into two neat piles. True to her word, Joey did not attempt to interfere with his decisions, although she could not resist occasional comments on the necessity of paring down her already scant "luxuries." Luke reminded her that a lighter pack made travel that much easier, something she could not deny.

They came briefly to an impasse over her butane stove, however; Luke insisted that there would be more than enough dead wood on their route to supply fires of the handmade variety, and Joey's argument about the possibility of inclement weather didn't sway him. When he pointed out that they'd return home if the weather got that bad, Joey found it most prudent to clamp her mouth shut; Luke got his way and, with an expression of loathing at the gassy smell, consigned the stove to the farthest corner of the room.

"What about that?" Joey said as she adjusted the shoulder straps on her loaded pack, nodding at the larger pile of equipment that remained untouched where Luke had left it. "You aren't planning to carry it in your arms, I take it?"

Luke looked up with narrowed eyes that almost hinted at humor. "Not at all. My backpack is at the cabin; since it's on our way, we'll stop by and pick it up there. In the meantime . . ." He paused to gather up a large canvas sack Joey had used for laundry. "This will do until we reach the cabin." With total unconcern he dumped out the contents of the sack and began to refill it with items from the second, larger pile.

Joey undid the buckles of the hip belt and shrugged out of her pack, setting it down carefully before she replied. "If we need to stop by your cabin to pick up your gear, that's fine. But I won't spend another night in it."

Deliberately studying one of the zippers at the top of the pack, she sensed rather than saw the shift in his stance, the sudden stillness that followed her words. After a moment the efficient motion resumed. "You won't be," he growled. "The first night will be a good trial run to see if you're up to this. We'll camp a few kilometers beyond the cabin. Will that be satisfactory?"

Joey turned away from the chill of his words. "Quite satisfactory. I don't think you'll find that I'm any burden to you."

There was a moment of silence; she felt his eyes on her, burning into her back. "It's late, Joey. You'd better get some sleep."

Walking over to the window, Luke drew back the curtains and stared out into the night; Joey glanced uneasily at the bed. It was certainly big enough for two people—if they didn't mind close proximity. Luke showed no signs of leaving—or hinting that he expected to share it with her. After the night at the cabin and today's unsettling confrontations, Joey's feelings were so muddled that she could do nothing but stand frozen there, torn between an unremitting awareness of Luke and her own desperate uncertainty.

"Go to bed, Joelle." Luke's voice was soft, almost gentle. He leaned against the window frame, his breath condensing on the glass.

"What about you?" Hugging herself, Joey was appalled at the way her words emerged, small and vulnerable. The silence grew so complete that she could hear the faint whisper of his sigh.

"Go to sleep." He did not turn from the window, and at last Joey crept over to the bed, gathered up her night things from the bedstand, and closed the door softly behind her as she made a final trip to the washroom down the hall. The time away from Luke while she brushed her teeth, combed the tangles out of her hair, and donned her warm pajamas gave her a chance to put things back in perspective, and she was ready to face him again when she came back to her room.

Except for the single bedside lamp and the faint glow of moonlight sifting through the curtains, the room was dark. Joey paused to scan the room, searching for Luke's form in the dimness. She found him at last, stretched out on the floor under the window, head pillowed in his arms. His side rose and fell with the even breathing of sleep, and Joey padded quietly to the bed to pull back the covers.

She paused again with her hand at the lamp, watching Luke where he lay on the hard, cold floor. The overwhelming flood of sympathy and yearning that came to her then was something she wanted to reject utterly, something that could bring nothing but pain and more questions than she could answer. She struggled for a moment, but the struggle was brief. Tugging at the quilted bedcover, she bunched it up in her arms and let her bare feet carry her across the room. She stood over Luke, closing her eyes against the longing, and crouched down beside him to lay the bedcover over his shoulders, pulling it down so that its inadequate length covered everything but his feet.

He turned then, half-rolling onto his back with a sigh. Joey held herself still until the moment passed and he subsided; she knelt there and stared at his face where the faint haze of moonlight defined it, at the harsh planes softened in the gentlest of illumination. The grim line of his mouth had relaxed, stirring memories of the few times he had truly smiled at her with a warmth he hid from the world; a mouth capable of tenderness and possessive fury against her own. Lines of care between the dark slash of his brows had eased, and Luke's face in the utter repose of sleep was that of a man she didn't know and had barely glimpsed. A man she could want, even now . . .

It should have helped to remind herself that he had pursued her for his own ends, twice rejected her, treated her with careless negligence, and even come close to violence. It should have been possible to regard him with contempt, but she could not. The only resolution she could make was that he would never know her weakness.

She risked tucking the edges of the bedcover under the curve of his body and retreated before the feel of him against her hands could demolish the remaining fragments of her composure.

The bed seemed very cold and empty when she crawled into it at last. Sleep was long in coming; when it took her at last, the dreams had returned.

When Joey woke early the next morning, it was to a room as significantly empty as her bed.

She sat up in alarm, aware immediately that Luke was gone, along with half the equipment. Her heart began to pound with the certainty that he had left her once again, changed his mind and abandoned her without explanations as he had twice before.

By the time she came fully awake and could think more clearly, she realized how ridiculous that assumption was. He wouldn't have taken the canvas sack of her gear if he'd intended to leave her. A moment later her hand, fumbling for the small alarm clock on the bedtable, brushed against a loose sheet of paper.

*Meet me at the edge of the forest with your gear.* Those were the only words in the note he had left, scribbled impatiently in bold lines. Her hands almost shook as she crumpled the paper into a tight wad and tossed it into the wastepaper basket against the wall.

It was time. Joey tossed back the sheets and set her feet on the floor, mentally cataloging her final preparations. She pulled on underwear, a light shirt and a warmer wool one over it, sturdy wool pants, two pairs of socks, and boots. Two light wool sweaters, a medium-weight parka, hat, and windbreaker lay draped over her backpack; rain gear was already stowed away where it could be easily reached. A quick glance out the window revealed the biting blue sky of a cold autumn day.

She took her compact toilet kit to the washroom. The features reflected in the mirror seemed almost a stranger's. Dark hollows shadowed her eyes, and it took a conscious effort to smooth away the almost permanent frown that had settled between her arched brows. She schooled her face until it looked back at her with complete and remote indifference, and then she returned to the room for the last time to stow the remaining gear.

The edge of the forest loomed before her, a wall of trees that marked the final barrier between the world she knew and the one she had yet to discover.

Luke was waiting for her there as he'd promised, blending so completely with the wilderness that only Joey's ever-present sense of him kept her from walking past. He nodded to her once and turned for the woods in silence.

They followed the same route Joey had used to track Luke to his cabin; it was familiar to Joey, yet utterly different because this time she was not alone. Even as they walked in tandem, Luke slowing his long stride to accommodate hers, Joey could not for a single moment lose her awareness of him at her side. The lean grace of the simplest of his movements impressed itself on her, and she felt remarkably clumsy next to him; it did not add to her peace of mind.

But there was another, unexpected side effect to his presence. Before, when she'd hiked to the lake, she had felt almost at one with the wilderness that surrounded her, grasping in some tenuous way the fragile bonds that connected all life. With Luke that awareness was magnified beyond anything she had ever experienced. It was as if he possessed some mysterious power to make her see things she never would have seen otherwise, without any effort on his part, or on hers. The very forest around them seemed like a living entity, and Joey felt less like an intruder than a welcome guest in Luke's domain.

Even so, the time came when the silence, broken only by the cries of birds and the distant grunts of moose in rut, began to seem oppressive.

Slanting a glance at Luke as they walked, Joey broke the peaceful accord. "I've been wondering for some time, Luke—why don't the townsfolk like you?" She hesitated a moment, hearing the ill-mannered bluntness in the question. It was not something they'd ever discussed. "I mean—it seems to me that something strange goes on whenever you come to town. The reactions . . ." She trailed off into awkward silence.

Joey knew she'd struck a nerve by the tightening of Luke's jaw, the hardening of his profile as his strides lengthened. Joey skipped a few steps to keep up until he'd slowed again; he did not turn his head as he answered.

"That's old history, and none of your business," he snapped. All at once the tension rose between them again, an invisible force that repelled any risk of intimacy. A retort rose to Joey's lips, and then she flushed, knowing he had the right of it; she had deliberately provoked him. For a moment she tried to consider rationally why she had shattered their unspoken harmony, and found she could not face the conclusions that came in answer.

"I'm sorry," she murmured at last. Her flush deepened when he ignored her apology, and she ducked her head between her shoulders with a firm resolution to say nothing more for the remainder of the day.

She came up out of her thoughts to find him looking at her, his face still rigid but his eyes belying that hardness. They were almost yearning. . . .

"I'm sorry I pried," Joey repeated, dropping her gaze to the gravel path at her feet. "You're right—it wasn't any of my business." The words dried up in her throat, and silence fell between them again.

Joey never quite regained that sense of belonging she'd felt before her questions had disrupted the truce between them; they had almost reached the lakeshore when Luke called a halt. It was only then when Joey realized how the weight of a fully laden pack had made the distance seem far longer than it had before; her stomach made known its needs with embarrassing boldness.

Luke looked up, his face relaxed almost into amusement. He'd found a convenient rock to sit on, propping his feet on another with long legs stretched out between. Joey released the hip belt of her backpack, struggled out of it, and set it down with a sigh of relief. A few moments later she had a pair of slightly compressed sandwiches in hand.

"No point in eating jerky and nuts if you can have roast beef," Joey said lightly, holding the larger sandwich out to Luke. He looked at it a moment, nostrils flaring, and then shook his head.

"You eat both. You'll find you need them." At her dubious expression, he smiled. It was a real smile, albeit a small one. "Believe me, you'll need more food on this trip than you'd ordinarily eat in a month."

"What about you?" Joey frowned.

"I'll take care of myself. I had a very large meal yesterday." As if that provided adequate explanation, Luke leaned back in a bone-cracking stretch and turned his face into the late-morning sun. After a moment of vague annoyance Joey shrugged and bit into the first sand-wich. She supplemented it with juice from one of her plastic bottles and found room for most of the second sandwich, just as Luke had predicted.

As she finished, Luke got up and headed for the lake, gesturing for her to stay put; she watched until he disappeared. When he returned, his hair was wet, paint-ing his broad shoulders with watery brush strokes. "We'll rest here for a while, let you digest a bit. The first camp is a few kilometers beyond the cabin; we'll stop early tonight." He looked up and down critically, nod-ding to himself. "So far, so good."

Joey swept him a mocking bow from her seat on a rock opposite his, and he almost smiled again.

They took an easy pace after the meal. The lake danced in and out of view, a perfect echo of the achingly blue sky above. Gradually the sense of peaceful oneness with nature—and even with Luke—returned, and Joey resolved not to shatter it again.

They passed by the place where Joey had confronted the town roughnecks; she shuddered and felt Luke's presence as an unassailable protective force at her side. He never touched her and seldom spoke, but it didn't seem to matter, and for once Joey felt content enough to let the miles pass on in silence. The most delicate bird-call pierced the air with the intensity of a siren amid the profound quiet; even the fall of golden aspen leaves seemed to whisper secret messages. The forest embraced them, and the mountains rose up like distant guardians, and all was right with the world.

There was still a good hour until sunset when Luke led her to the place he had chosen for their first night's stop. Luke set about making camp at once, and Joey helped where she could; they put up the small tent and rain fly, and Luke set her to clearing an area for a fire while he collected tinder, kindling, and dead wood for fuel.

He nodded approval of her thorough elimination of all but bare ground and gravel where the fire was to be built, and together they gathered rocks to form a rough circle in which Luke set dry needles, bark, and twigs for tinder. Joey sat back on her heels to watch him as he built a construct of twigs and small branches; she almost jumped when he spoke.

"Matches?"

He almost grinned at her startlement. "You didn't think I'd do it the old-fashioned way, did you?"

Joey, who had been thinking just that, flushed and rummaged in her jacket pocket for the waterproof container. Luke got the fire started on the first try, something none of Joey's other guides had managed. She leaned closer to the fire instinctively as Luke nursed it into full flame.

He'd already rigged up a dingle stick—a long, sturdy branch balanced against a large rock so that one end hung high over the fire—and Joey pulled one of the pots out of her pack and filled it with some of the water Luke had collected from a nearby stream, suspending it from the end of the stick. As the water heated for coffee, Luke bagged the extra food and hung it from a high tree branch, where animals were less likely to reach it. By the time the water was boiling, the campsite had the look of a temporary home, more comforting than Joey would have believed possible.

Not greatly to her surprise, Luke declined the coffee she offered and crouched beside her as she sipped hers, his head tilted back as if to test the early evening air. Rays of dying sun painted the sky with vivid colors against the dark silhouette of the wood.

Joey savored the remarkable comfort of a hot drink and sitting absolutely still. A hush had fallen over the forest as day made transition into a darker and more mysterious country; the sounds that broke the silence were strange and haunting.

She hardly noticed when Luke vanished again and was content to do nothing but stare into the flames as she heated more water for soup. The cheese Joey had procured that morning disappeared quickly; she was amazed at how hungry she still was when Luke reappeared with a pair of sizable fish, gutted and cleaned.

Joey eyed the fish with considerable anticipation. "Those look terrific. I've got foil in the pack—learned how to cook them that way on my last trip." She couldn't resist a bit of pride for what she'd learned of wilderness cooking, but Luke shook his head.

"I'll show you how to do it the old-fashioned way." He set down the fish and produced a pair of flat rocks, which he set directly in the fire. Joey dropped her chin into her palm and turned to watch the sun slide behind the peaks of the nearest range, creating a pattern of deep blue silhouettes against the fading light. It was easy to get lost in the perfect beauty of it as the first stars winked into existence, heralding the brilliant display that overwhelmed these northern night skies. It came to Joey then that there was still something left in her to wonder at it; even she could not quite take it for granted. . . .

"Watch, Joey," Luke commanded. His voice reminded her of the growing chill and her unsatisfied hunger; she observed him as he pulled the hot rocks from the flames, salted and greased the fish, and set them on the rocks at the edge of the fire. Soon the rapturous smell of cooking filled the air, and when the fish was ready Joey had no qualms about eating it directly from the rock with her knife and fingers. She looked up to watch Luke eat his with momentary surprise, realizing it was the first time she'd ever seen him actually ingest anything but water; he seemed to enjoy the fish as much as she did, leaving nothing but bones to be consigned to the fire.

The quiet between them was companionable and

content. They cleaned up so efficiently that they might have been a team for years rather than a day; afterward Luke added more wood to the fire, and Joey watched the sparks fly up to mingle with the stars.

Luke's voice was very soft, hardly troubling the serene silence. "I have to go back to the cabin now, Joey. I have my gear to collect." Joey started and stared at him where he crouched, sketching formless shapes in the dust with a twig.

"You're going to leave me here alone?" Joey could not quite suppress the quiver in her voice; it summoned up irritation at herself that turned on him.

"By all means, go. I'll have a nice time here with the bears and wolves and anything else that might want a quick snack. . . ." The absurdity of her words changed her annoyance to humor, but before she could continue Luke had risen to tower above her, his face solemn in the flickering light.

"You'll be safe," he said gravely. "And you won't be alone." He turned on his heel, looking over his shoulder as he reached the edge of the trees. "Watch the fire—if you get sleepy, put it out as I instructed. And stay in camp." Without another word he bounded off, swift and silent as a stag in an alpine meadow.

Joey was left to consider his words: *You won't be alone.* Tugging on her second sweater against the growing chill of the night, she had the uneasy feeling that she knew exactly to what he was referring.

As if in mocking confirmation of her thoughts, a howl rose and echoed beyond the pitiful illumination of the fire. Joey turned her head, trying to locate the sound, but it eluded her; the darkness seemed suddenly alive, and very alien. It was then she realized how much Luke's presence had kept that terrible strangeness at bay. He was part of it, and it accepted him—and so it accepted her as well.

Now the only familiarity lay in the stars overhead,

and even they were more vast and fathomless than the domesticated variety that shone feebly in the skies at home. She stared up at them and tried to concentrate on naming the constellations as a second howl joined the first, and a whole chorus broke out around her. The uncanny serenade continued for an endless time as Joey huddled by the fire, and then just as suddenly fell silent. But they were not gone. Joey knew it as surely as she knew anything at all; they were still there. All around her. Waiting . . .

She was very far from sleep when Luke returned. Bolting upright in an excess of jangled nerves, Joey was fully prepared to give him a thorough tongue-lashing. But the desire to do so died almost immediately; beyond Luke, at the edge of the trees, she could see the eyes—eyes that reflected the firelight and glittered from a dark core of shapes that moved in utter silence. Eyes that focused on her and then turned away, winking out of existence one by one like fireflies. There was not so much as a rustle of brush to mark their passing.

Luke set down his pack and sighed as he joined her by the fire. Joey was still shaking with reaction, but her relief at having him back was so powerful that it overcame every other consideration. Without thinking, she went to him and touched his arm, feeling the welcome solidity of his hard muscles under her hand.

"I hate to say it, but I'm glad you're back," she said with a wry smile. "If those were your friends again out there, looking after me, I'd hate to see your enemies."

His arm was rigid, ungiving beneath her fingers, though he did not draw it away. "I'm sorry if you were frightened," he said softly, staring into the fire. "It wasn't my intention. You were never in any danger." Suddenly his tone grew remote and almost cold. "You didn't want to come back to the cabin, so there wasn't much choice."

Joey released his arm and backed away from the

heat and strength of his body. "You're right, of course," she said with equal chill. "Next time you should ask your friends in for dessert, or coffee at least. They've earned it."

In the small space that separated them Joey felt the gulf that lay between all she had known in her life and everything he was—everything she could not understand. Not only of him, but also of herself. She rose at last, unable to bear the dissonance between them, and retreated to the tent. She left its shelter just long enough to hang her day clothes out on the line for airing and hurried back to the warmth of her sleeping bag.

Sleep would not come. It wasn't the cold, though she had certainly been warmer; nor was it the utter silence of the night that lay beyond the fragile walls of the tent. Those simple things she had learned to accept. The thing that kept her from sleep was as complicated as only the human heart could make it. She could no more shut off thoughts of Luke, and her own confused feelings about him, than she could turn around and go home and give up on everything she had fought so long and hard to achieve.

It was almost a relief when the howling began again, more distant this time but very clear and almost sweet. Joey forced her muscles to relax, listening to the patterns as the cries rose and fell in their own ancient rhythms. She could hear no threat in the sound. It was natural, part of a world that was meant to be.

But it was no clinical desire to discuss the laws of Nature that brought Joey up out of her sleeping bag and made her don the parka she had set beside it. She tugged on the boots that lay just outside the tent and crept toward the fire.

He was still there, a dark, motionless shape against the dying embers. His head was tilted back, his posture so intent that Joey froze in place to gaze at him in wonder. As howls chorused the night, he cocked his head;

his eyes closed and nostrils flared as if savoring the most beautiful music. When he rose to his feet, it was with a single fluid movement so inhumanly graceful that Joey's breath caught; only then did he turn his head to look at her.

The green-gold eyes were swallowed up in blackness, pupils wide as they caught a splinter of firelight. Joey understood in that instant that he did not know her. His muscles bunched as if in preparation for attack, he quivered and gathered himself—and Joey gasped. "Luke!"

He froze in midmotion, perfectly, utterly still. Then recognition came, and the muscles that had tensed so ominously relaxed again. "Joey." His voice was momentarily dull and strange, as if it came from some great distance.

Tightening the parka about herself, Joey went toward him cautiously. "I didn't mean to startle you. I heard the howls—and since I couldn't sleep, I thought I'd ask you about those wolves."

Luke blinked. He seemed to come fully back to himself at last, and there was no sign of anger or antipathy. A slow smile altered the fire-carved planes of his face. "What do you want to know?"

The moon had risen and begun its slow arc across the sky when Joey found herself drifting on the seductive tide of Luke's voice, her eyes heavy as sleep coaxed her into surrender. She jerked and shook her head, stifling a yawn; Luke fell silent and regarded her from the short distance that separated them.

"You've had enough for one day, Joey," he said softly. "You need your sleep for tomorrow."

Her head spinning with images of wolves and Luke's nearness, Joey almost protested. A yawn overtook the words, defeating any hope of clinging to the contentment of the past hours; she half-smiled sleepily and lurched to her feet. She *was* bone-tired, with aches where she didn't know muscles existed.

"Good night, Luke," she murmured.

He met her eyes briefly and looked away, into the dying fire. "Good night."

Joey hesitated, longing for something she couldn't define. She wanted to recapture the ease that had been between them as he'd talked to her of wolves and the wilderness he loved; to see the lines of his face relax as he lost himself in another world she could only touch the fringes of. But he was closed off to her again, now, lost in a different way that excluded her completely.

With a sigh Joey turned back for the tent, shedding her boots outside and bundling up her parka in the corner of the tent. She took a sip from her canteen and zipped herself into her bag, certain that sleep would come quickly and grant her the rest her mind and body needed. But she founded herself waiting—feeling the empty space beside her like a void that stole sleep utterly and left her staring into the darkness.

She sat up at last, dragging the sleeping bag with her to the entrance of the tent. There was no light but the eerie glow of the waning moon; it was just enough for her to make out Luke's form as he moved about the fire, extinguishing the last stubborn embers. When he had finished, he settled back into a crouch, head dropped between his shoulders, as still as if he intended to spend the entire night in that lonely place.

"Aren't you cold?" Joey heard herself call out across the clearing. She shivered, pulling the edges of the sleeping bag up around her chest. "I am."

Luke started; he tilted his head without turning, and Joey knew he had heard.

He did not move for an endless moment; Joey strained for some tiny change, some indication of his intentions. At last she dropped back into the tent, closing her eyes with a defeated sigh. The sleeping bag was all that she needed, more than enough to get her through the night. . . .

It was some extra sense that warned her when he entered the tent, blocking the scant moonlight as he sealed the flap behind him. Only the faintest rustle of fabric attended his movements, as he unrolled his own sleeping bag and stretched out beside her, the soft sigh of his breathing mingling with her own. Her eyes saw only a shadow in darkness, but she didn't need sight. She closed her eyes again and smiled.

"Good night, Luke," she whispered.

# Chapter Nine

"Look there, Joey." Luke gestured across the gentle bowl of the valley that encompassed his lands. "Tonight we'll camp a little way up the slope of that ridge; tomorrow we'll be over it."

Joey squinted and reached for her binoculars, focusing them where Luke had indicated. Between tonight's campsite and the one they had just left, forest stretched out almost unbroken, rising here and there in gentle swells. The ridge of mountains they would cross dropped down into the saddle of a pass, a place more easily crossed than the high peaks to either side. Even those forbidding sentinels were dwarfs compared to some of the ranges beyond them.

"It'll take most of tomorrow to cross, and our stop after that will be on the other side." He said no more, shifting under the weight of his pack and briefly checking hers before setting the pace.

Comfortably warmed by the morning's breakfast and a good night's sleep, Joey felt more than ready to tackle the day's challenges. She listened with interest to Luke's occasional comments on the route they followed and the animals and plants they encountered. They startled a shy, late-wandering red fox into flight across their path, a blur of rust amid the green and brown of forest undergrowth. Black bears gorged on autumn berries, fattening for the winter; Luke and Joey respectfully detoured around them. The animals here had little fear of man; even the mule deer paused to stare as they crossed the meadows before bounding away with their stiff-legged gait.

And Luke belonged here, as much as any of the creatures they had encountered. This was his world, not that other domain of mankind. Joey tried to imagine Luke amid the towering skyscrapers of home and failed.

It was late afternoon when they began the gradual ascent up the side of the ridge that marked the pass through the mountains. Joey felt her muscles strain against the pull of gravity; she was glad now that Luke had insisted on carrying the greater portion of the load.

When Luke called a halt at the night's stop, she blew out a loud breath of relief and struggled free of her pack, flopping to the ground beside it. Luke looked as serene as if he'd taken a half-kilometer jaunt, his appearance not in the least worsened by two days on the trail.

Joey sighed and thought about her mirror. She was almost afraid what she might see in it—and more afraid of what Luke saw at that very moment. As if he'd read her thoughts, he turned to look down at her. There was no criticism in his eyes; they almost glittered, as if in amusement.

"I'll get a fire started and some hot water going. There's a stream that feeds into a small pool just beyond those trees; you're welcome to use it, though I'd ask you to skip the soap for the time being. Even that can pollute the water." Though his tone was serious, as it always was when he discussed such things, his eyes remained friendly; Joey grimaced at an itch that seemed to travel over the entire surface of her scalp instantaneously.

"I guess I look pretty awful, don't I?" she said wryly, tugging at her loosened braid.

He almost chuckled. "Awful? Not you. You hold up very well on the trail." His eyes were intent on her, sweeping along her body in a way that made her tense and shiver.

"As compared to whom?" she said lightly.

"Ah." He turned away, suddenly very interested in removing articles from his pack. "There could be no comparison."

The casual charm with which he said the words reminded her of when she had first met him, his attempts to pursue her as just another woman to share his bed. It jarred in a way she could not quite understand.

Something made her throw caution to the winds then. "You never talk about your background, Luke. Or your past."

He looked up again, and there was the first hint of a frown on his face. "There isn't much to talk about," he said with a shrug. "It's not important."

"I disagree." Joey stood up and brushed the dirt from the seat of her pants. "There's a lot about you I don't understand, Luke. And I'd like to." Ignoring the warning that sounded in her heart and the slow flood of heat that rose in her face, Joey plunged on deliberately.

"Maybe it's just that I don't like mysteries. But since we're stuck with each other for a while, I think it's reasonable to learn more about each other. Don't you?"

"Reasonable?" Luke's tone was almost mocking, though whether it mocked her or himself Joey couldn't guess. "Does reason have anything to do with this?" Suddenly he turned the full intensity of his hypnotic gaze on her, and she felt herself swaying under the impact. And then he released her, almost before she could realize what was happening.

Joey shook herself. "I don't know how you do that, Luke. But it only makes me want to know more. I like to know what I'm dealing with. Who I'm dealing with."

He stood up, a length of rope in his hands. "Have you forgotten, Joey, that this is a business relationship? I take you to the place you need to go, and when it's over, you'll be leaving town. That arrangement seemed to suit you when we left. I don't see that anything has changed." Turning away in dismissal, he strode across the rocky ground to rig the rope between two sturdy saplings; Joey felt the slow burn of anger compel her to follow.

"A business relationship. Is that truly all you think is between us?" Appalled by her own words, Joey stopped dead in her tracks, but it was too late. He swung around to face her, and the old menace was back in full force, cold and primitive.

"I thought you'd learned, Joey. There is nothing between us and can't be." He jerked from stillness with a snap as he forestalled the protest that rose, unbidden, in her throat. "No questions. I can't give you answers." His face almost contorted then, a brief flash of pain. "Until you leave my territory, there can be no peace for either of us. Don't you understand?"

In the silence that followed, Joey tried to assimilate a flood of thoughts and feelings and memories into some meaningful pattern. None of it made sense, and his words did not clarify anything. Anything at all.

"I *don't* understand," she said at last, softly. "I don't understand anything about this, or you. You've never bothered to explain. Why did you come after me in town, and then . . . act the way you did at the cabin? Why? Why am I so repulsive to you now that you want to see me gone? Don't you think you owe me the *businesslike* courtesy of an explanation?"

Luke shut his eyes, tightly, as if to block out the sight of her. "I can give you no answers." Each word was forced, drawn out from the depths of something like despair. Joey almost flinched, almost stepped back, remembering the bizarre juxtaposition of savagery and tenderness he had shown at the cabin. But he did not move, and she found within herself the courage to continue.

"I won't accept that. It isn't fair to expect me to. I need to understand, Luke—and somehow I will."

With the softest of curses, Luke spun suddenly on his heel and strode off into the brush. Joey stood there for a long moment and set about searching for stones suitable for the evening fire. The mindless task kept her occupied until Luke returned with firewood, and then she slipped off to the pool to bathe her face and rinse her hair.

When she had finished, she rocked back on her heels and twisted her hair into a fresh braid, shivering as drops of water spattered her cheek. Her reflection in the cold, pure water told her what she needed to know. If she had lost a large part of her certainty, the one thing she had not lost was her determination.

It was only a matter of showing Luke just how determined she could be.

Luke tasted the scents borne on the evening breeze as he made his way toward camp; Joey had already begun cooking a side dish and had heated her usual coffee—that much was clear half a kilometer away. He'd had unusual luck in his hunt that night, and the sizable hare he had caught was already gutted and skinned. The small predators of the forest who had watched him from a safe distance had quickly disposed of what he'd left.

The time away from camp, and from Joey, had given Luke time to think. No human being had ever had the distressing effect Joey Randall had on him; no woman had even come close. Her insistence on questioning him about his past had presented him with a problem he had no hope of solving. He could not tell her what she seemed so determined to learn; he could not begin to explain why she had driven him to behavior even he found inexplicable.

This had never happened to him before. He had no more control over it than he had over the indifferent stars that flickered in and out behind the lacy silhouettes of firs against the darkening sky. She had no conception of what her mere closeness did to him—and he could never take the risk that she might find out.

Shifting the hare in its skin sack over his shoulder, Luke bared his teeth. He had done everything possible to keep his distance, and for a time he'd hoped she would make it easier for him by keeping hers.

When he had left camp, after starting the fire and erecting the tent, he'd spoken to Joey not at all beyond warning her that he might be gone an hour or two; she'd merely stared at him with that familiar stubborn lift of her chin. He had felt her eyes tracking him, but seldom had he been able to bring himself to meet her gaze. That in itself was a deeply unnerving experience. It confirmed everything he had realized about her—and about himself.

He could still dominate her if he set his mind to it. But it was as if all his will to do so had fled, and in the long run it would gain nothing but further pain.

Pungent smoke drifted across his path as he crossed the border of trees and into camp. She was sitting by the fire, her expression turned inward, cradling a cup of coffee in her hands. She looked up as he approached, though he knew he'd made no sound that could warn her. One more proof that she could feel his presence with senses beyond those that humans usually possessed. One more proof, and one more burden.

He did not meet her eyes as he set the hare up for cooking, though never for an instant did he fail to sense her watching him, focusing her own undefined strength and pitting it against his without knowing what she did. Or what she was.

When his tasks were done and he could put it off no longer, Luke crouched across the fire from her, keeping that barrier between them. His defensive rage had leeched away, but it left him vulnerable; the direct reproach of her gaze told him she would not give up, just as she had promised. He knew that of her, as he knew it of himself.

He could maintain the silence, until she felt compelled to break it; he could continue to fight her off with all the carefully suppressed ferocity at his disposal. He knew neither method would work—not with her. There was one other way to keep her at that safe distance where she couldn't break his control. She wanted words. Words were not his favorite means of expression; they were man-made constructs that had no true place in his world. Usually, with the others, they hadn't been necessary, after the beginning. Joey wanted more than he could give—but he could give her something to make her believe she had what she wanted.

Letting his muscles relax into a pattern of indifference, Luke met her eyes. The gold-flecked depths of them, fringed by dark lashes, had the terrible ability to weaken his most powerful resolve; he braced himself against them and against the sight and smell of her and said, "You wanted to know something about my past, Joey."

She tensed in startlement; her eyes widened, the full curve of her lips parting on a breath. He remembered the feel of those lips under his own, the soft oval curves of her face, the silky texture of her hair. . . . He closed his eyes long enough to stop the litany and what it did to him. When he opened them again, her face was coolly expectant.

"I'd like to know more about you, yes," she said quietly.

He sighed, knowing he revealed himself by the flicker of her eyes. "What do you want to know?"

For a long moment Joey considered, her head cocked, as if she had expected him to launch into a detailed autobiography. He half expected her to demand that he tell her about the other women who had come before, but she surprised him.

"Tell me about your mother, Luke."

He stiffened instinctively, drawing up all his defenses, muscles trembling with the urge to fight or flee. One by one he brought the reactions under control again, before Joey could catch more than a glimpse of them—though he knew it had not entirely escaped her. Just as he knew he had little choice but to answer.

"My mother," he said heavily, feeling the weight of the word in his heart. He'd never spoken of her, not to anyone like Joey; but there had never been a woman like Joey before.

"You told me—that she'd died when you were a boy." Joey licked her lips, as if realizing at last the significance of her question. "I—I could tell she meant a lot to you."

"Yes." Luke dropped his gaze and stared into the fire, which seemed safer than Joey's sympathetic eyes. "If that's what you want to know, I'll tell you." He closed his eyes, casting back into memory, into a time when things had been simple, when he had been happy as only a child can be when his world is a known, safe place—and before, to a time he knew through stories and the soft, nostalgic words of others. And considered where to begin . . .

"There is a valley," he began slowly, "hidden in the mountains not far from here, where a small village exists much as it has for a hundred years. Few people know of it, and those who do seldom speak of it to strangers." He looked up to find Joey's attention riveted on him like a child hearing a fairy tale, and he almost smiled.

"In this village there are families, many related, all living in harmony with each other and with their world. They seldom need to go beyond its borders, but sometimes the villagers will send the restless young men out to the nearest towns to buy those few necessities the village can't provide for itself. Many years ago one of these young men grew to have a family of his own, and his only child was a beautiful girl that he named Marie-Rose."

"That's a pretty name," Joey murmured, her face warmed by firelight that turned her pale hair to molten gold.

"Yes." Luke gathered his thoughts again and continued, "Marie-Rose, like her father, was a restless girl. She wandered the forest from the time she was very small, and never listened to warnings that she should take care not to stray too far. She was as fearless as she was beautiful; when she grew to be a young woman, she was not content to settle down with one of the village boys. There came a time when she followed them on their expeditions into town, and so she found Lovell, and learned about the world outside the village.

"When her parents knew they could not prevent her from visiting Lovell, they did their best to prepare her for the things she might see. She made many trips there, often alone, to watch the peculiar life of the people who lived in a place so unlike her own. One day a stranger came to town."

He fell silent for a long moment, remembering. He remembered his mother, even from the time when he had been little more than a small child. And they'd told him what she had been like in those days; carefree, full of life and laughter, running barefoot through the forest as fleet as a deer and as fearless as a wolverine.

"The stranger," he said at last, "was from a country Marie-Rose had never seen, and barely knew of—a place far from the mountains. He had come as the leader and representative of men who wished to buy land, locate virgin timber to fill the needs of people in that other country. Marie-Rose didn't know of this at first, but she was drawn to the stranger and his smell of other places. She began to follow him, to make more and more frequent visits to the town, until one day he saw her. On that day he was captivated by her utterly, and she in turn gave her heart to him."

Again the memories overwhelmed words; Luke felt his muscles tighten, remembering the man who had changed his mother's life forever. He looked up at Joey, who sat absolutely still, her chest rising and falling with deep breaths of wonder. The newer ache of her presence pushed the old pain of the past aside, so that he was able to continue with detachment once again.

"The stranger courted Marie-Rose, and after a short time, unable to leave her, he decided to settle in Lovell and give up the things he had come to do there. Marie-Rose told her parents and the people of her village that she loved this stranger, and that she would stay with him. But they berated her, telling her this man had no place in her life and could only bring her pain and sorrow. Marie-Rose refused to listen to their warnings; at last they had told her that if she took this man as her mate, she would no longer be welcome in the village.

"With great sadness, Marie-Rose accepted the condition. She left the village forever and went to the man she had chosen, who built her a cabin in the forest and used his wealth to buy as much of the surrounding land as he could. Marie-Rose didn't know that he was rich with money had had earned by despoiling the wilderness she loved, but when he settled down with her, he put all that behind him.

"Their life together was happy for the first years; Marie-Rose continued to wander the forests, and her mate delighted in her love of life and freedom. He went away at times, to conduct business, but always came back with some gift for her, and all was well between them.

"On the day Marie-Rose discovered she was to have a child, the man could not do enough for her; he brought her special delicacies imported into town and watched over her devotedly. When their son was born, he had her dark hair and her eyes; he grew up to match the size of his father, and became a part of both worlds."

"You," Joey breathed. He felt her eyes move over him searchingly; he almost shuddered under the inspection, though it was not annoyance that he felt but something far more troubling.

"Yes," he admitted with a sigh. "For the first years the boy had everything he could possibly want or need; his mother taught him the ways of the forest, and his father took him to town and showed him the ways of civilization.

"The happiness was not to last." Luke closed his eyes again. "Marie-Rose had never lost her wildness, and once her babe was weaned, she would occasionally disappear into the woods, sometimes for entire days, leaving the boy in the care of her mate. At first this seemed no trouble, because the father's business allowed him to stay home to look after the boy, or to take him into town on those days his mother was gone.

"The boy was too young to understand when things changed. He didn't understand that the two disparate worlds of his parents were less compatible than even they had realized. He only learned later what had happened. . . ."

Luke heard his voice as it carried the story to its inevitable conclusion, recalling it with crystal clarity. He remembered waking that first time they had argued, hearing the sharp crack of angry voices in the kitchen, his mother's lapse into French—which she seldom did unless she was very angry or very happy—and his father's booming voice shouting back. He had crouched in bed, listening, fearful without knowing why, longing to rush in and stop them.

That had only been the first of many fights, conflicts that came one after another with greater and greater frequency. They were always careful to do it away from him, so he never heard much of what they said to each other; he only knew it hurt.

He began to catch his usually cheerful mother in tears, crying quietly where she thought no one could see; his attempts to comfort her made her smile but never took the sadness from her eyes. She began to disappear for longer and longer times into the forest, always returning with endearments and apologies, holding him tightly so that he could not be angry that she'd left him. But his father began to interrupt their quiet moments, to tell his mother she was not to go out, that she was to stay and look after their son and the house and forget her wild ways.

Luke had still not understood the anger between them, so potent that he felt it like a black cloud summoning a hard spring rain. But he saw his mother's sorrow, and it was her he turned to, her he grew closer to, protecting her instinctively from the threat he saw in his father.

A day came when his father grew so angry that he came at Luke's mother with a lifted hand prepared to strike; that was the day when Luke stood between them, holding his body as a barrier, defying his father with every ounce of a child's strength. The blow had fallen on him. And his mother had gone at his father with a rage

Luke had never seen before, so savagely that his father had fled the cabin.

That was the first of his father's absences. He, too, always returned, often with soft apologies for Luke, and even for his mate. But things were never right again. The arguments became cold silences, the disappearances by his mother or father longer and longer. One or the other always looked after him, but he learned what it was to rely on himself, to be prepared for new shocks in a life that had opened up an unknowable abyss under his feet.

One day his father left and did not come back. He waited, and his mother did, in weary silence. A year passed, and he did not return. He left no explanation, no warning.

Luke remembered when his mother accepted that her mate would never return. She never spoke to him of it, never explained—but he remembered her wild eyes that day, her tears as she held Luke and rocked him, even though he had grown too old—her black hair tangled and her voice ragged as she sang a lullaby in broken French. That day, it was as if the light died in her. The wildness faded. Luke never understood until much later why his mother had been so terribly broken.

Even after his father had abandoned them, life fell back into a rhythm almost normal, almost peaceful, a brief tranquillity after the storm. Marie-Rose continued to teach Luke the things he needed to know of her world; if anything, the urgency of her desire to make him truly a part of both worlds in which he lived grew even stronger. She saw to it that he attended the small school in Lovell, refusing to accept his youthfully fierce determination to stay by her side, protect her as his father had failed to do. Because she wished it, he had learned—focused all of his intensity on amassing the knowledge she insisted was vital to his future. It didn't matter that she herself knew little of the outside world.

Her son—he would know and understand the things that had so fatally eluded her.

So much of this he had come to grasp when it was too late.

He remembered the long days when he had struggled with his own alienation from the other children, doggedly working his way through years of schooling. He grew up with few friends and with no knowledge of the hidden village in which his mother had been raised.

Something—some subtle shift in Joey's posture, some night sound that broke the inward focus of his thoughts—made Luke suddenly aware of his own voice, reciting the memories as if they were no more than a tale of hypothetical characters in another existence, incapable of giving pain. He broke off, looking away from the hypnotic spell of the flames, away from Joey's rapt face.

"It was only because of my mother that I did well in school," he said at last. "Because she wanted it, I learned about my father's world." He heard his own voice catching on the word "father"; a word he had never voiced to anyone but her, and one other, in all the time since his mother's mate had left them. "He had left us money to live on, in his vast generosity—a tidy sum in the local bank, plus all the land he had bought for my mother. Sometimes new deposits would appear in the bank. She never touched it, except what she needed for me."

The mournful hooting of a great horned owl punctuated his words; he paused to listen, to a language far simpler and more honest than the one he'd found Outside. It seemed a melancholy and appropriate comment on his mother's fate.

"When I turned fourteen, my mother changed. She'd lived the past many years changed already, though I didn't know it then; I was old enough to see it on the day she began to talk to me about my future. I didn't care about any of that, but because it was important to her, I listened." Luke closed his eyes. "She told me there would be changes in me as well, things I wouldn't always understand. She explained that there would be things I would have to deal with, and she wouldn't always be there to help me. Even then I didn't realize what she meant."

Luke caught himself then, remembering the limits on what Joey could comprehend. There were things he had no intention of telling her—could not tell her, even now. Her lovely dark eyes never left his face; she could have no conception of what he left unsaid, the thoughts that went through his mind as he spoke so dispassionately.

He shook his head, dismissing what could never be. "My mother told me about the village she'd grown up in. She'd always kept me from exploring in that direction; only then did I learn that she had left the village and her family behind forever. But she told me that I could find my own people there, if I needed them." It was hard, now, to keep his voice level. "She apologized for all she had been unable to give me, made me promise to complete my education. None of it warned me of what was to come."

Silence fell, only the crackling and popping of the fire marring the perfect emptiness of it. "After she had talked long into the night of things I had just begun to grasp, she stood over my bed and waited until I'd fallen asleep. I remember her face in the darkness: all serene sadness, a face out of a medieval painting. There were tears, but I had seen those often enough in the past not to be alarmed."

Her cascade of rich dark hair had fallen over her face, veiling the depth of her emotion before he could know what lay behind it; he remembered squeezing her hand, trying to offer comfort even as he'd drifted off to sleep with the ease and innocence of the very young.

"When I woke the next morning, she was gone."

Luke lifted his head. He could feel his face settling into a perfect, indifferent mask of stone. Like stone, his eyes saw nothing. "She had left everything behind, but she never returned—not after that day, or the next or the next. I finally understood for the first time what she had done." Even the memory of the deep sense of betrayal, of adolescent rage at his mother, himself, the world— even that did not reach the calm surface of the face he turned to Joey.

"I went after her then. I tracked her with all the skill she had taught me. She had hidden her trail well, but I followed it. It led me to the village—the place she had spoken of.

"It was there I found her. There were many strangers, people I had never seen except for one or two I had glimpsed in town or in the forest. They looked at me without surprise. My mother was there, on the doorstep of one of the cabins; her face was more at peace than I had ever seen it. She seemed to be sleeping, but I knew." The image of her face, the echo of his wild howl of grief at her treachery in leaving him, reverberated to the roots of his soul, trapped there to die in memory. "The villagers tried to help me. They took me away while they put my mother to rest in accordance with their own ancient traditions. I never knew any of that until much later."

He wondered how he could explain to Joey those days of torment, when he had suffered in the grip of a raging fever born of terrible grief and the changes that were even then coming upon him. Her face now was tense with a reflection of the pain he could not show, as if she expressed it for him. No—even she could not know the source of that pain.

There was too much intensity, too much emotion. He had to end it now before it went too far to stop. Between them . . . and within himself.

"Later, when I recovered, they told me more about

my mother and how she had grown up there and come, at last, to leave them. They had taken her back, willingly, though too late—regretted having cut her off, grieved for her. Because of that, they accepted me and made me one of them. They never spoke of my father." The word grated, again. "When I went back to the cabin, I gathered up a few belongings and went to live among them for a time. I finished what education Lovell could give me, and when the time came I went Outside, as my mother had wished."

Those long years in the city, away from everything he loved, had been torment; the burden of constantly mimicking what he was not, what he had no desire to be—of fulfilling his mother's wish for him, in honor of what *she* had been—had brought him back wiser but with no love for his father's world. He could no more speak of those things, now, to Joey than he dared give in to his own dark yearnings.

Abruptly he ended it. "There's little more to tell." The sound of his voice came remote and detached to his own ears. "I came back, and never left again." He looked up to meet Joey's eyes across a fire that had grown small and cold; it was a relief to turn his attention to the simple task of building the fire up again.

He knew she was still watching him, waiting, even before she spoke.

"Thank you."

It was hardly more than a breath, though he heard it as clearly as a shout. "Thank you for telling me. I—" He knew when she looked away by the infinitesimal change in the soft lilt of her voice. "I was wrong to pry, and I'm sorry—sorry for everything."

The last words held a wealth of meaning. Luke met her eyes and was lost in the whirling gold sparks, like stars in a velvet-dark sky. He didn't want her sympathy, but he could not make himself turn away as if her concern did not matter, as if she were only a complication and not an obsession.

But he did break away at last, as the last branch he had fed into the flames caught and smoldered.

"I've answered your question, Joey," he said. It didn't come with quite the evenness he would have preferred. With deliberate care, he relaxed every tense muscle and stretched until the bones cracked. "Now it's your turn to answer some of mine."

She started. Her finely molded nostrils flared; the supple lines of her body hidden under bulky and practical clothing froze into stillness. Composure came back to her slowly, and with it the familiar, defiant tilt of her chin. "What do you want to know?"

He considered for a long moment. It came to him how little he really knew of her and had never needed to know, even now; where she had come from, what she had been before, seemed almost unimportant. If there had been some hope of a future—but there wasn't. In spite of that knowledge, the question that came to him now rose unbidden from the very compulsion he had tried so hard to deny.

"You said once," he began with deliberate casualness, "that you were married. Richard, I believe his name was. . . ." Watching as she reacted to his question, he felt his own anticipation like an unwanted hunger.

"Yes." Joey's voice was small. "I was married. I met him while I was still in college—he was a successful architect, a guest lecturer at the school. I was very young then." Her breath caught, and she bit her lip. He could almost see the inner debate as it tightened the lines in the soft oval of her face, wondering if he had revealed so much. "At the time he seemed to give me things I thought I wanted. The security—the stability—I needed.

"For a while it worked well enough. Life was comfortable with Richard. Predictable. Safe. Passionless.

Nothing dramatic happened to end it. One day I came to realize—" Her eyes opened again. "That it wasn't fair. Not to either one of us. It was a kind of trap. . . ." Her choice of words made Luke focus on her so intently that she dropped her gaze before he could read her meaning.

"It isn't important what happened. We agreed, eventually, that we had different needs. I'd come to realize then that there were things, things that I . . ." Breaking off, Joey stared into the fire; the glitter of unshed tears fractured the reflection of it into embers that burned at the tips of her dark lashes. "None of that matters anymore. We parted friends." She lapsed into silence.

Luke almost stopped then, in respect to her distress. But the prick of the compulsion drove him to demand more of her. "And before Richard?"

Joey met his eyes, her lips curved up into something approaching a smile. "There were no others. I didn't have time or space for them before Richard. Or after. I didn't even have space for him."

The rush of triumph that transfixed Luke then was not rational. "Jealousy" was only a word, too paltry to define what he had felt imagining Joey with other men. Ordinary men. But long practice kept the reaction away from his face where Joey could guess at its source.

He felt no need to ask more. There was relief in her, as well, when she realized she had satisfied him with with those few revelations. The tautness of her face relaxed; her lips resumed their usual calm curve. Luke looked away and listened to the night's language, to the cries of night-hunting owls and the rustling of small animals hidden in the brush. But he was drawn back to her again and again. With every heartbeat he lost ground he had little desire to regain.

For the first time in many years he wished for more than the ability to read the language of the body, the nuances of movement and expression that had always sufficed with the others, and with the townsfolk who shunned him. In the silence, he gazed at Joey and wanted to understand the thoughts that passed behind her composed, delicate features; the motivations behind her sudden bursts of temper; and why she responded to him in ways that tore at his resolve, why even now the primitive needs of her body called to his in ways that her cool rationality denied. He wanted to know, desperately, why she was the one. . . .

He only realized how long he had struggled within himself when Joey's head dropped wearily into her arms where they rested on drawn-up knees, her silver-gold braid catching moon and firelight as it slid over her shoulder. It had grown very late and very cold, and Joey shivered even as her body demanded its toll of rest.

Luke hesitated only a moment. He got up from his place across the fire and moved to her side with steps too silent to wake her. For one last instant he paused, inches away so that he could hear the sweet sound of her breathing and smell the rich femininity of her scent. Then he dropped down beside her; his arms closed about her so that she eased back into them without coming fully awake, her loose-limbed body a featherlight softness. She sighed, and her eyelids fluttered as she settled against him with complete and unconscious trust.

He held her there until the fire died, his face pressed into the silken spun-starlight of her hair. For those time-suspended moments he was able to believe there was no future to deny. "Joelle," he murmured against the gentle pulse at her temple.

Her name drifted out into the night, and the unasked question was answered by a solitary cry of a distant wolf.

# Chapter 10

The next morning dawned brilliant and very cold; Joey felt more rested than she had in many days. The luxury of waking to breakfast and coffee and hot water had added a great deal to the feeling that everything was working out far better than she could have hoped. Only the continual, nagging awareness of Luke and the memory of what they had revealed to one another prevented a lapse into a reckless state of sheer happiness.

Luke himself seemed unaware of the subtle change. He was reserved but friendly, casual but oddly intense in that way of his. As they started their day's hike, she caught him looking at her when he thought she wouldn't notice; always that intensity was there. She had almost grown used to it. Almost.

It was easy to fall deep into thought, lulled by the steady rhythm of the pace Luke set, relying on his watchfulness in place of her own. Sometimes she would stumble, and he'd catch her, chiding her for her inattention, but he seemed content to take the responsibility.

She was free to assimilate all he had told her of himself and his background, adding another piece to the puzzle that was Luke Gévaudan. It only made the other missing parts seem more vital.

Thoughts soon became more of a burden as their ascent up the slope of the ridge grew steeper; her feet struggled for purchase on the scree, and choosing each step took more and more of her concentration. Luke's hand was always there to steady her, his solidity a barrier against any fall. He almost insisted, once, that she transfer more of the contents of her pack to his; with a stubborn desire to prove herself, Joey declined and made the vow that she would keep up with him, one way or another.

It was harder work than she had thought, but she managed it. Her reward was Luke's appraising glance as they reached the summit of the pass, his slow smile of approval.

As they paused for a cold lunch, Joey caught her breath and basked in the feeling of accomplishment. And Luke's regard. Around them, the ridge was bare of trees, an open place where the wind was sharp and marmots whistled among the rocks. Joey shivered and pulled on the extra layers of sweater and parka she had discarded on the long hike up. A goshawk cried, sharp and sweet, as it rode the air currents in search of prey.

From here the valley that swept away below them was a canvas of rich green, unbroken save for a few meadows and the revelation of water where streams cut through the forest. The valley was small, well protected by mountains on every side. Joey packed away the uneaten food and savored the magnificent view.

"Is that still your land?" she asked, awed by the sheer scope of it.

Luke shook his head. "No—my land ends with this ridge. That"—he indicated the valley with a nod—"belongs to good friends of mine. And there"—his hand came up to indicate a series of low peaks at the other side where the land rose gradually from the valley floor—"that's our goal."

Joey stared at the place she had been struggling so long and hard to reach. It seemed very far yet, and there were still no guarantees that it would be the place she sought. But there was still a chance. She was almost there. . . .

"Are you ready?" Luke was hitching his pack up over his broad shoulders. Joey nodded slowly, her eyes still locked on Miller's Peak and the surrounding mountains, range upon range marching into the distance beyond them. She hardly noticed when Luke helped her into her own pack and started down the other side of the pass; she scrambled to catch up and concentrated on the uncertain footing of descent.

They soon found themselves once again among the trees, entering a land every bit as pristine—and primitive—as Luke's had been. Joey was considering how she could possibly have done this on her own when something very fast and very determined burst out of the brush ahead of them and flung itself headlong at Luke. She very nearly lost her balance under the weight of the pack as she jumped aside, but Luke held his ground, and when the small form was about to collide with his legs, he caught it up and swung it into his arms. Stunned, Joey only then recognized the very dirty and very wild face of a laughing child.

A moment later Joey was laughing herself. It was hard to believe such a little girl could move so fast. Shrugging out of her pack, she watched in growing amazement as the child chattered a rapid-fire patter in a language most distinctly not English. Luke was smiling. It was just about as close to a broad grin as she'd ever seen on his face, and that alone was enough to capture Joey's full attention.

She concentrated very hard on picking up individual words in the little girl's babble. A fragment or two she managed to catch convinced her it was French she was hearing; a moment later Luke's deep voice confirmed it, speaking in more measured tones. There was more genuine warmth in his voice and in his expression than she had ever seen. He shifted the girl in his arms as if she were as light as a feather, and she kept up her ceaseless chatter, tugging at his chin, giggling and squirming.

It didn't bother Joey in the least that she could understand only a little of what the girl was saying, and no more than a portion of Luke's brief replies. Watching them together was a revelation. Luke's full attention was on the child, his head cocked and eyes bright with amusement. He was utterly relaxed, the hard planes of his face shifting again and again in response to the girl's monologue. Joey thought he had entirely forgotten her existence, but even that did not annoy her. There was too much fascination in seeing a side of Luke she hadn't realized even existed.

Luke laughed once, a deep chuckle as the child asked him a question; he shifted her again in his arms and answered. *"Tu es devenue trop grande pour moi, Claire. Je vais devoir te remettre à terre."* A moment later he let the wriggling little girl slide out of his embrace to the ground, where she took firm possession of his hand and abruptly turned her full attention to Joey.

It certainly seemed odd that a child—no more than six or seven years old, with a dirt-streaked face, tangled black hair, and one finger planted firmly in her mouth—could focus that familiar, unnerving stare on Joey in much the same way Luke had. She felt as if she were being very carefully examined, judged, and sentenced by those wide green eyes. To counteract both the inspection and her uneasy reaction, Joey dropped into a crouch and smiled. "Hello, Claire. My name is Joey."

The little girl removed her finger from her mouth,

clutched Luke's hand more tightly, and thrust out her lower lip with uncertain belligerence. After another long moment of concentration she turned to look up at Luke with a loud and demanding question.

Joey didn't have to understand all the words to work out the meaning. She maintained her smile and waited while Luke set down his pack and tousled the little girl's curls with his free hand. He glanced for the first time at Joey; the smile was still there, but this time it seemed all for her—a reassurance, still tinged with warmth.

Luke answered the little girl slowly. Relying on guesswork and tone of voice to follow the conversation, Joey translated silently. *Joey est mon amie.* Joey is my friend. That much she understood very well. She basked for a moment in the warmth of Luke's gaze and then turned back to the girl.

The child looked dubiously from Luke to Joey. *"Est-ce qu'elle est gentille?"*

Luke's answer was firm but reassuring, telling Claire that Joey was indeed *"gentille"*—nice—and that Claire should be polite in return. *"D'accord?"* he asked softly.

The little girl sighed heavily. "Okay." The accent on the English word gave it a charming lilt; Claire tilted the corners of her mouth in a hesitant smile. Joey returned it and extended her hand. The little girl shuffled for a moment and then placed her own grubby fingers in Joey's with sudden gravity. *"Vous ne pouvez pas parler français, mademoiselle?"*

Joey looked helplessly up at Luke, who appeared very close to an outright laugh. He spoke to Claire in French and switched abruptly to English again, almost losing Joey in the process. "She only wanted to know if you spoke French." The gleam of his green-gold eyes was almost teasing.

Giving Claire's hand a gentle squeeze, Joey released it. "A little—but right now I wish I'd paid more attention in class," she muttered wryly. "I'll bet you're going to tell me that all your friends who own this land don't speak English, right?" She stood up slowly, working the kinks out of her legs while the little girl backed up against the solid strength of Luke's legs, the top of her head just reaching his belt. One of his hands dropped to rest on Claire's thin shoulder.

"Some of them speak English—of a sort—but there isn't much need for it here." At Joey's pained expression he shook his head. "Don't worry. We'll only be spending the night here—and as long as you're willing to be friendly, you'll be made welcome." For a moment there was an odd tone to Luke's voice, but Joey had no time to consider it. Abruptly he looked down at the top of Claire's head, tugging gently at one of the errant black curls. *"Maintenant, va dire aux autres que nous arrivons."* "Tell the others we're coming."

Claire grinned very broadly at his words, did an exuberant little whirl, cast a final uncertain glance at Joey, and dashed off before she could blink.

In spite of the feeling that she was on the verge of something unexpected, Joey couldn't help smiling after the girl as she vanished as quickly as she had come. She turned back to Luke, watching the slow metamorphosis of his face into the familiar, cool, unreadable expression she had grown accustomed to. Gradually her own smile faded; at that moment she would have given a great deal to have him look at her, again, the way he'd looked at the child—the way he'd looked at her in the child's presence. Now the mask was back in place, and it created an unexpected ache in Joey's heart.

As if aware of her melancholy, Luke glanced at her and just as quickly away. In the brief silence he lifted on his pack and adjusted it without meeting her eyes again.

"They'll be expecting us when we arrive—shouldn't take more than an hour." He waited until Joey had donned her pack and then started off without further explanation.

"Just so I'll know what's happening, would you mind telling me who 'they' are?" Joey breathed, catching up to him. "And who that little girl—Claire—was? You certainly seemed to know each other!"

Luke kept his eyes on the trail ahead of them as he answered. "We'll be spending the night in Val Caché—the village where Claire lives. You'll be able to sleep in a real bed for a change." There was almost a touch of dry humor in his voice. "Claire is my—our relationship is rather complex. We all find it easier to refer to each other as 'cousins'—even across generations."

Joey's mind skipped over his explanation and put several things together. "Val Caché. Cousins . . . This is the village you told me about last night—the place where your mother grew up!"

"Yes." For a long while he said nothing further, and Joey considered everything he had told her of his background and the hidden village where a wild young woman had been born and had come back, in the end, to die. "As I said before," he added at last, interrupting her thoughts, "few of the villagers speak much English, but that won't be a problem; I'll translate anything you need to know."

Casting him a dubious look, Joey reflected that not knowing what was being said around you couldn't be considered an ideal situation. But the prospect of a bed—and actually seeing the place where Luke had grown up—outweighed her doubts. Anticipation rose in her again; a fresh burst of energy carried her through the forest as they traveled the remaining distance to the village.

When they arrived at last, Joey stopped in her tracks and stared. She could not have imagined a more picturesque place if she'd tried. From the edge of the clearing where they stood, neat one- and two-story log and wood-frame houses clustered to either side of an unpaved area that served as a main road. Beyond the village proper was an open field, and distant moving shapes that might have been horses or cattle. The whole of it could have been transported intact from the previous century. There were no electric power cables, no cars, and no satellite dishes; even Lovell looked like the heart of civilization compared to Val Caché.

She was still absorbing this when Luke led her over the small footbridge that crossed a swift-running stream and into the village. It was only then that Joey realized there were people waiting for them—people who had materialized seemingly out of nowhere to wait, still and silent, in their path. Like the village itself, the people were dressed as if they'd come from another, simpler time—but the faces that turned to Luke and Joey were anything but simple.

It was almost a relief when little Claire burst out from among the solemn adults and danced up to them; she even spared a quick smile for Joey before grabbing Luke's hand and chattering away. Joey had almost gotten the hang of separating out the lilting words she spoke, even though most of the meaning eluded her. The girl made a dramatic announcement and pointed at Joey triumphantly.

Joey found herself edging closer to Luke almost unwillingly when the villagers turned as one to look directly at her.

Several sets of penetrating eyes stared at her unblinkingly. She returned their scrutiny with a tilt of her chin, straightening under the weight of the pack. Luke's presence at her back, though he did not touch her, was very welcome.

"Hello." Joey heard her voice crack and cleared her throat impatiently. "Hello, my name is Joey Randall."

If she had expected an effusive welcome or any reply at all, she was doomed to disappointment. The faces that gazed at her were impassive, though not overtly hostile; even now she could begin to see similarity in the features—to each other and to Luke. There was much black hair, some of it shot with gray that seemed to have little to do with age; planes and angles of jaw and cheekbone were reminiscent of Luke's. But it was the eyes that were most like his, in their intensity and strangeness—even though none matched the subtle power of his.

Joey shifted uneasily, wondering how to break the stalemate, when Luke intervened. "*Est-ce ainsi que vous souhaitez la bienvenue à une invitée?*" Joey heard the challenge and question in his tone: "Is this how you welcome guests?"

The villagers shuffled; one or two of them muttered, and an elderly woman, her face a webwork of deeply engraved lines, stepped forward. Luke turned immediately to her. His words were clipped and defiant.

Grasping one clear word among the others— "*Grand-maman*"—Joey watched with tense fascination as the elderly woman and Luke exchanged a long, steady look. She could just see the resemblance there, though the woman's hair had long ago whitened, and the sharp angles of her face were soft and careworn with age and long experience. Joey sensed a kind of contest of wills between them; neither one broke the stare for an endless moment.

Then, abruptly, the elderly woman glanced away. She peered at Joey, looking her up and down much as Claire had done. Joey endured this scrutiny as well; when the old woman's face cracked into a smile, it startled her.

"*Alors, petit-fils, c'est ça, ta dernière petite amie.*" The old woman put her hands on her hips and flashed a glance full of hidden meaning at Luke. Joey struggled to interpret it, startled when the dry voice switched suddenly to heavily accented English. "Didn't think you'd ever bring one here, boy. Something special, *hein*?"

Glancing at Luke in mute appeal, Joey suffered a

second shock. A dull red flush had appeared along the angle of Luke's cheekbone; his lips settled into a grim line. The old woman cackled, and Joey almost jumped.

"*J'ai raison, hein?*" Once again the woman's attention was riveted on Joey. "Well, do the introductions. Where are your manners, boy?"

Joey was aware of a sudden shift in the demeanor of the people who had watched the confrontation. It was as if all the tension had drained away, to be replaced by something approaching goodwill; all at once soft voices were exchanging comments and glances and nods as the small knot of villagers loosened.

The deep tone of Luke's familiar voice was a relief, even sharp with annoyance. "*Grand-maman*, this is my friend Joelle Randall." He turned to Joey for the first time, his expression easing just enough to reassure her. "Joey, this is my grandmother, Bertrande."

Searching Luke's face for some clue as to a proper greeting, Joey took a chance. "*Bonjour*—Bertrande. I'm very happy to meet you." When she extended her hand, the old woman took it in a surprisingly firm clasp. In fact, Bertrande's hand was so far from fragile that Joey blinked. The old woman grinned, revealing several gaps where teeth had been.

"*Joëlle.*" The way Bertrande said her name was like the way Luke had said it once or twice, with a rolling lilt at the end. "A good name. It may be you'll do." Abruptly she dropped Joey's hand and winked broadly at Luke. "I was right, *hein*? *Elle est différente. P't-être que c'est elle. . . .*"

Once again Joey was treated to the rare sight of Luke's blush. If circumstances had been only a little different, she would have demanded a full explanation then and there—but one careful look at Luke's face told her clearly it was not the time. Explanations would have to wait. She understood enough to grasp that Luke's grandmother was a person of importance in the village, and if she accepted Joey, the others would do so as well.

As if to confirm her guess, several of the villagers stepped up to greet Luke, many with hugs and slaps, which he returned with some reserve. In fact, Joey noted that there was always something a little odd in the way he met their greetings; with some, including the few children who circled about him like dervishes, he was openly affectionate, as he'd been with Claire. With the women he was gravely courteous regardless of their age; with the men there was more reserve, almost a kind of testing similar to what had passed between him and his grandmother. But none of it made much sense to Joey, and she allowed herself to be distracted from her thoughts when Luke brought a man of about his own age over for introduction.

"This is my cousin Philippe," he said above the chatter of conversation that flowed about them. "Claire is his daughter. I'll be staying with him tonight." Philippe met her extended hand with his own callused palm, nodding to her gravely; his hair was jet black like Claire's. He murmured a greeting to her in French, looked at her for a long, searching moment, and turned at last to Luke. With a few final words to his cousin Philippe moved away; one by one the other villagers followed his example, until only Claire and Luke's grandmother accompanied them.

It was then that Joey registered Luke's last sentence. "You said you'd be staying with Philippe. Does that mean I'll be staying somewhere else?" Her voice sounded challenging even to her own ears, but Luke hardly so much as glanced at her. His face was still grim and set.

"You'll stay with my grandmother, Joey. You'll be comfortable there." He deliberately avoided her eyes.

"But why? Why do we have to stay—in separate places?" Joey realized with a start what she was reveal-

ing with her words, but they came of their own volition.
Before Luke could answer, she felt her hand being
clasped once again in Bertrande's warm, crepey palm;
the old woman flashed her uneven grin.

"*Crains rien, petite.* I will take care of you." Joey bit
her lip and willed Luke to be helpful. He turned to
meet her anxious gaze at last and almost smiled.

"She likes you, Joey. If my grandmother likes you,
you have nothing to worry about."

Joey could have cursed his deliberate obtuseness.
She felt a tug on her hand and found herself being led
away while Luke trailed after. "That still doesn't explain," she called back softly between her teeth, "why
we're being split up."

In several long strides Luke came alongside her. "It's
the way things are done here," he said at last. There was
still something strange and remote in his bearing, and
he still looked everywhere but into her eyes. "The people here are very old-fashioned. Un—uh, unmarried
couples don't—live in the same house."

The awkwardness of his explanation was so uncharacteristic that Joey almost stopped; Bertrande tugged her
back into motion with the breath of a laugh.

"Oh." Joey tried to imagine this tough old woman
standing guard over her with a pitchfork or something,
guarding her virtue. The image was so hilarious that
Joey lost her bad temper all at once. She smiled at Luke
with honest amusement. "I see."

Abruptly the old woman let go her hand and came
to a stop so quickly that Joey collided with her. She was
surprisingly solid. She turned her penetrating, amused
stare to Luke and back, lightning quick, to Joey. "I was
right, wasn't I, boy? After all this time. *C'est bien
elle. . . .*"

Luke froze into utter rigidity where he stood, every
muscle taut and poised for violent action. The words he
spoke then were so rapid and harsh that Joey lost the

thread of them almost immediately; the mere tone of his voice and the ferocious light in his eyes would have shaken most people to the core, but Bertrande merely regarded her grandson with cool dispassion until the last of his angry tirade had run its course.

Then, as if nothing at all had happened, she grabbed Joey's hand again, grinned broadly, and nodded. While Joey looked helplessly back over her shoulder at Luke, who was shaking with barely controlled rage, his grandmother towed her firmly across the village clearing. Joey felt as if she were being swept away by some primal force of nature she had no hope of stopping. The expression on Luke's face as he stood staring after them told her that he was, in that moment, just as lost as she was.

Luke had been right about one thing; his grandmother made every effort to make Joey feel welcome. The small wood-frame house Bertrande brought her to was not unduly primitive, though it was heated by an old-fashioned cooking stove and lighted by candles. There were only two rooms, one of which contained both kitchen and living area; the attached sleeping room had two small beds, the frames beautifully carved and painted with forest animals.

It was only after Joey had had ample time to rest, to bathe with water heated on the stove and relax with a steaming mug of broth, that Luke came for her. Bertrande had already insisted, with gestures and a few words in French and accented English, that Joey should remove her soiled clothing; she was given a pair of overlarge but warm wool pants, long johns, and a bulky knitted sweater to replace them. The warm clothing wasn't fashionable, but it made Joey feel almost like one of the villagers, and that seemed important.

Luke arrived at the door, and it was only then that it came to Joey with a shock how strange it had been to be away from him. She hadn't noticed the lack until it was filled by his presence, as his big, lithe frame filled the doorway. Now for a long moment their eyes met and held; Joey felt her pulse rising to a crescendo that surely he would hear. . . .

Suddenly Bertrande pushed between them. *"Hé bien, allons manger!"* The old woman's voice was comically querulous. Luke rolled his eyes, smiled at Joey, and offered his arm to his grandmother. As Joey closed the door behind her, she found him waiting; his gaze on hers was as inviting as his extended elbow. The feel of his hard muscle under her hand sent a shock wave coursing through her, and for a moment she leaned on his arm because she would have fallen otherwise.

Luke seemed not to notice. He was casual, relaxed, as if the presence of family and friends had broken once again through his outer shell. "I hope you're hungry," he said, looking down at Joey. "You're going to get a chance to see how much the people of Val Caché like to eat."

A rather loud rumble of her stomach answered before she could. "Everyone eats together?"

"Usually." Luke steered the two women toward a building larger than most of the others, a long construction of wood from which light and noise poured in abundance. "This is a close-knit community. Meals are an important time for gathering, discussion, even doing business. And for the most part, it's more economical to prepare and eat meals in one place."

As Joey digested this, Luke stopped at the broad wooden door of the building and held it open, waving the women in ahead of him. The blast of heat, delicious smells, and raucous noise was almost overwhelming. Almost at once Bertrande detached herself and hurried across the room to gossip with a crony; Joey simply gazed about and tried to take it all in.

It seemed likely that every member of the village of Val Caché was here, laughing, talking and generally having a good time. There was a brief lull while the people acknowledged Luke's appearance, but almost at once the dull roar resumed.

Luke took her elbow and steered her over to a table near the front of the room, closest to the fire and the wonderful smells that emanated from the corner where the cooking was done. He leaned close to her and pressed a piece of bread into her hand; Joey nibbled it absently. A hundred questions came to mind one after another, too many to be asked; at last she gave up and simply accepted.

Only the serious business of eating seemed to quiet the rambunctious crowd. Matrons with gray-shot hair and a few younger women moved among the long tables, serving generous portions of stew, freshly baked bread, and corn to the people who had finally found their seats. Joey shut her eyes and breathed in the smell, so welcome after three days on the trail. Without realizing it, she leaned into Luke where he sat beside her. His warm solidity made everything perfect, completely right, and all at once she was no longer a stranger, but in some strange way belonged. . . .

Suddenly a small warm body pushed against her, and she found herself tipping sideways—somehow, in the process, ending up very comfortably steadied in Luke's arms. A laughing Claire materialized on the bench beside them; two other children accompanied her, a boy of five or six and another several years older. They were all talking at once, adding to the general din. The eldest paused to give Joey a long, appraising stare of the sort she was beginning to become accustomed to; then he fell silent and looked expectantly at Luke.

Easing Joey away from him gently, Luke smiled at the boy. "*Bonjour*, Jean-Paul. How are things at school?"

As if his words had been a kind of signal, the boy grinned while ducking his head and glancing up under long lashes. "*Très bien, cousin Luc. Mais les gens du De-*

*hors. . . .*" The boy broke off with an embarrassed glance at Joey. "I mean, sometimes things are strange Outside. . . ." Jean-Paul reddened and dropped his gaze.

Luke's eyes gleamed with amusement. "I know that well, Jean-Paul." He turned to Joey, still smiling. "Jean-Paul speaks fluent English—he's been attending school in East Fork. One of the few who's done so. That's something we have in common." He gave the boy a gentle, reassuring punch on the shoulder.

Jean-Paul shrugged with the awkwardness typical of boys his age, glancing shyly at Joey. "I am . . . very pleased to meet you, *mademoiselle*." The words were accented, pleasantly so; Luke had no accent when he spoke English, and Joey never would have guessed, knowing nothing of his background, that he had grown up with any language other than her own.

She grinned at Jean-Paul and said admiringly, "That's very good! I wish I could speak French as well as you speak English!"

The boy blushed deeply and, as if the praise were too much, backed away with a final half-apologetic glance at Luke. Luke waved him off, and the boy vanished, tumbling straightaway into a game with a small knot of children near the fireside.

Abruptly Claire, who had been listening to the conversation with impatient squirms, slid off the bench beside Joey and reappeared at Luke's side, worming her way into his lap. "*Raconte-moi une histoire des gens du Dehors, Luc!*" Her voice was demanding, but Luke shook his head.

"*Plus tard.*" And at the girl's pout, he added, "*Promis.*" Joey caught the gist of the words and envied the little girl that she could settle so comfortably into Luke's embrace and look forward to hearing him tell her bedtime stories—that their relationship was so warm and simple. So painless . . .

As if the brief exchange had satisfied her need for

attention, Claire wriggled free of Luke's arms and dashed off to join the others in their play, accompanied by the younger boy.

Joey sighed, her contentment tinged with melancholy. "Claire is a beautiful girl. She'll grow up to be a real stunner someday."

"Much like my mother," Luke murmured. "With the same wildness. She won't be content to stay here forever."

There was such sadness in his voice that Joey turned to face him. She longed to ask him then what brought that distant regret to his eyes, to link her arm through his and lean her head on his shoulder. But she contented herself with feeling his thigh and shoulder against hers, in knowing he did not pull away from the contact.

"The children here are beautiful, Luke. And it's pretty obvious they're loved." *And that they adore you,* she added silently to herself. "But there seem to be so few of them."

She knew she'd hit close to the mark when Luke focused on her suddenly, though without surprise. "Yes. Too few." He dropped his eyes to the half-empty bowl of stew on the table and lifted a spoon to stir it absently. "This is a very old village. It hasn't changed much in a hundred years. The people here are content to keep it that way." He looked up with the distant expression that meant he was gathering his thoughts. "They're used to hardship and to living the same way their forefathers did. They're survivors. But in spite of all that, the village is slowly dying."

Joey glanced around her at the clumps of chattering people clearing away dishes and making a game of cleaning up. Someone was tuning what sounded like a fiddle, and laughter rose frequently above the dull roar. It was hard to think of these people as dying. They seemed so full of life.

"It's because there are so few children," Luke said, so softly that she had to strain to hear him. "The people here are nearly all closely related. Very few women have more than one or two children. Often, sometimes every year, Val Caché will lose a young man or woman to the Outside. And Jean-Paul is not the first to be educated, to learn things that may tempt him to leave one day."

Drawing in a deep breath, Joey settled closer to Luke, resting her fingers on his arm. He hardly seemed to notice. "You came back, didn't you?"

"Yes." The word was heavy, laden with regret. Joey knew there was more to that one word than she could guess. She looked around again, at children clearly indulged and greatly valued, at adults who treated them with respect and open affection. But there were few of them—and fewer still of babies and toddlers.

Biting her lip, Joey hesitated on the verge of offering comfort she was not quite sure how to give. After a moment she decided she wanted to see him smile again, to regain that relaxed warmth the children had brought out in him. She squeezed his arm.

"The kids are very fond of you," she teased gently. "I didn't know you were the paternal type."

Her remark had the unexpected effect of making Luke duck his head in obvious embarrassment. "The children are important to all of us," he muttered.

Joey couldn't quite keep the amusement out of her voice. "And I've noticed that everyone pronounces your name differently here. 'Luc.' "

Clearly relieved by her shift to a more neutral subject, Luke looked up, the drawn lines of his face relaxing. "My mother named me Luc, but I found it more expedient to anglicize it when I grew older. Most Outsiders manage to mangle even so simple a name."

Joey drew herself up in mock offense. "Are you implying I couldn't pronounce your real name properly?"

At Luke's wry headshake, she added, "And do you think of me as one of these 'Outsiders'?"

The question carried more significance than she had meant it to. Luke's muscles tensed where her hand rested on his arm. For a long moment he looked into her eyes in that way of his, so intently that her breath caught, and she could not pull away. At last, with a deep sigh, he dropped his eyes again. "I don't know."

Almost of their own volition Joey's fingers slipped from his forearm. She felt stung by his answer, but also more deeply puzzled. As in the conversations she had witnessed between Luke and his grandmother, she knew there were subtexts to his words—vital ones— that she was missing. More missing pieces that must be found.

She deliberately turned away from searching for them. There was still time. "You should help me with my French, so I won't be such a stranger," she said lightly. The momentary tension between them relaxed. "Val Caché—that means Valley. . . ."

Luke shifted his elbow on the table to allow one of the village matrons to clear away his plate. "Hidden Valley." His smile was a little crooked, but it was a smile. "A simple name, but appropriate."

"Very appropriate," Joey concurred. "How many people even know about this place?"

Touching her shoulder lightly—a touch that sent a stab of sensation all the way down to her fingertips— Luke pushed away from the table and stood. "Not many," he admitted quietly. "And that's how the people here prefer it."

"Outsiders," Joey muttered. Luke seemed not to hear as he led her across the room, pausing once or twice to exchange *bonjours* with friends and family. At the door he paused, turning to sweep his gaze across the room as if to take it all in, lock it so deeply into memory that it could never be lost. As if he never expected to see it again. Joey shivered at the blast of cold air that invaded the room in the wake of departing villagers.

Luke's familiar, intense warmth kept the cold at bay as he walked her across the village common, his arm brushing hers, their footsteps falling into a safe and comforting rhythm. The quiet after constant noise was almost overwhelming, and Joey was content to savor it, as she savored Luke beside her. When he would have left her at the door to his grandmother's cabin, she caught at his arm, held him there with more will than physical strength, until he had no choice but to look down at her.

She felt herself beginning to lose her way in his strange, pale eyes, but now it brought no unease. A muscle jumped in his jaw, skin stretched taut across his high cheekbones—she knew instinctively that he was poised on the edge of flight. But he stood unmoving, and she waited until his hands came up slowly to brush her arms, to burn her skin through the sweater and pause there on the edge of embrace. She turned her face up, her breath coming faster, willing him to read in her eyes the things she could not say aloud. Her hands slid up of their own accord, resting on his narrow hips, moving up over the firm hardness of his torso, splaying on his chest. His heart pounded under her palms.

*"Y était temps que vous r'veniez!"* The cracking interruption of Bertrande's voice behind Joey made them jump apart in the same instant. Joey nearly stumbled; a firm grip caught and steadied her. The old woman's not-unpleasant breath puffed against her cheek. "Easy, my little owl. Time for bed." Bertrande turned to Luke, who hovered in the doorway looking considerably shaken and almost forlorn. "As for you—" Joey could not miss the gleam in the old woman's eye as she looked back and forth between them. "You will have time for *that* later. *Allez.* Go!"

Luke looked one last time at Joey—a long, oddly

vulnerable expression—and turned on his heel before she could open her mouth to speak. His grandmother leaned out the doorway and called after him, cackling. "I know what I see, boy! *Tu vas d'voir attendre un peu plus!*"

Too dazed to do anything but obey, Joey let herself be coaxed and gently bullied into preparing for bed. Her clothes had been washed, hung on a line to dry before the fire—not decorative, but certainly practical. The bed that she was given was surprisingly soft, stuffed, she guessed, with down—the quilts that covered it were works of art in themselves, and very warm. Bertrande chattered to her in incomprehensible French, casting her knowing, amused glances all the while, and it was only after Bertrande had blown out the candles and settled with a sigh into her own adjoining bed that Joey had the peace to think again.

The old woman's whistling snores filled the unfamiliar silence of the room. Joey lay wide awake, and all her thoughts were of one thing. It seemed almost frightening to realize how much she missed Luke, even now—even when he was only a few houses away. She wondered if he was thinking of her too. This strange game between them, this dancing back and forth, was driving her to the brink of . . . something. . . .

Tossing her head against the pillow, Joey muffled a groan of frustration with her fist. At one time it had helped to concentrate on the goal she was so close to reaching, forget about every other distraction. Somewhere along the line that simple solution had ceased to be effective. Somewhere along the line she had fallen over the edge.

When sleep finally came, it was a different kind of falling, and the dreams that followed consumed her and left nothing but ash.

# Chapter 11

Luke accepted one more embrace from his grandmother, who seemed unable to stop cackling and winking conspiratorially at him. "You be sure and come back soon, Luc—and you bring her with you, too, *hein*?" The gap-toothed, triumphant grin she turned on Joey made him long to lose his temper, but he'd done it once, and it hadn't done a damned bit of good. Not with her. As he should have known. Only one thing would make her realize how wrong she was, about him—and Joey. He'd have to come back once Joey was gone and show her. That her guesses were wrong, her expectations a kind of torture. . . . The mental image of her leering face falling in disappointment held little satisfaction.

What Joey thought of all this, what she must have thought of his grandmother's behavior, he could not guess. She seemed cheerfully friendly to the villagers who came to wish her well on her journey, unaware of deeper meanings. He was profoundly grateful, now, that she had not understood all the words that had been spoken of them, around them—words that might have made her grasp the significance of the knowing looks the villagers turned on her.

She was smiling as she came up beside him, her hair smelling of soap, eyes bright with excitement. He looked away before the whirling gold sparks could trap him. "This is the day, Luke, isn't it? The day we reach the mountain?"

Her voice was so filled with innocent enthusiasm that he could not quite hold back a smile. Or a rush of feeling he could ill afford. "Perhaps. Depends on how hard we push. But we aren't going to rush this, Joey. Remember, I want to get you there in one piece."

His admonition failed to quell her high spirits. "Fine. Whatever you say, Luc!" The way she gave his name the intonation of his mother tongue almost made him touch her, caress the soft pale curve of her cheek, draw his fingers down the arch of her jaw. But he stopped the action within his imagination.

"I'm glad you've learned how to cooperate," he said dryly.

She drew herself up, arched her brows, and folded her arms across her chest. "I beg your pardon, but I'm always cooperative. I know some people who aren't nearly as flexible." Abruptly she bit her lip, as if she'd said something she hadn't quite intended. Luke felt the slight burn of heat in his face as he searched her words for hidden meanings but was spared a retort by the sudden appearance of Claire, who flung herself with characteristic abandon at his legs and began to babble in French.

"Luc, are you going away already? Why can't you stay longer?" With a lightning-quick glance at Joey she added, "And are you going to bring that strange *mademoiselle* back with you next time? Is she going to be your . . . ?"

Luke quieted her with a hand on her shoulder. She

understood instantly, falling silent and gazing up at him with wide, suddenly solemn eyes. He dropped to his knees and held her tightly. "Claire, there are some things it isn't polite to ask about. You don't want to make Joëlle feel embarrassed, do you?"

Claire considered that with a cocked head. "But she doesn't even speak French!" she protested at last. Luke suppressed a chuckle, confining himself to brushing one of the tangled curls out of her face.

"You know that words aren't everything, Claire. There are some things you'll have to wait until you're older to understand, but I promise I'll explain to you one day. When I can."

With a somewhat belligerent outthrust of her lower lip, Claire nodded slowly. "Okay. But you better come back soon!"

Luke accepted her vigorous little girl's embrace, taking great care as he hugged her in return. "Be good, Claire."

"I'm always good!" the little girl declared. In a flash she dashed off, brushing by Joey without another word.

"I wish I had that much energy," Joey said fondly. The last of the villagers were departing now with final good-byes, last-minute offerings of advice and occasional smirks that Joey, fortunately, seemed not to notice.

For an instant Luke tried to imagine what Joey must have been like at that age. Even now she seemed almost carefree, with something approaching a child's innocence. He knew she was not an innocent, far—very far—from being a child. He had only to remember and the blood stirred in him, had only to allow his full awareness to acknowledge her and be lost to her seductive power. . . .

He set those thoughts carefully aside, knowing it would never become any easier, not until she had left his territory and his life. The ache of the thought was consigned to that same cold place.

His grandmother appeared suddenly to interrupt the disorder of his thoughts, breaking in, for once, at an opportune moment. She spoke in French, momentarily ignoring Joey. "I forgot to tell you, Luc—the doctor is coming later today. Sure you don't want to hang around and wait for him?"

Luke glanced quickly at Joey, noting with relief that she didn't seem to pick that one word—*docteur*—out of the others. "We have to be going, Grandmother—now, in fact." He bent down to pay the expected tribute of a peck on each cheek, which she accepted as her due before turning to Joey. The expression on Joey's face was almost comical when Bertrande gave her a loud, smacking kiss in similar but much more dramatic fashion; Joey peered up helplessly at Luke until the old woman released her.

Bertrande beamed impartially at both of them for a long moment, and then raised her head to sniff at the air. "The season is changing," she announced in English. "I smell something strange on the wind. . . ." Abruptly her mobile, weathered face grew serious. "Maybe you'd better stay here after all, Luc."

For an instant Luke registered her words and dismissed them before doubt could mar his resolve. Stay here another night—and listen to the suggestive comments, see the shrewd nods and insinuating smiles of the villagers, knowing what they expected and what could never be—stay here another night and find himself pushed to the edge, pushed so far that he would have no hope of recovering his balance—no. It was out of the question.

He gathered up his pack and hitched it over his shoulders. Joey donned her own pack before he could help; she grinned at him in total incomprehension of his inner struggle, and he forced his muscles to relax.

With a final nod to his grandmother—who pierced him with a final, narrow-eyed stare bereft of the usual humor—he touched Joey's arm and said, "Shall we go?"

"*Allons-y!*" Joey matched his steps so buoyantly that her enthusiasm, her sheer joy, reached the dark heart of his deepest fears and illuminated it for an instant, so that he was able to forget everything but her happiness. As they settled into a ground-eating, steady stride across the valley floor, the cold morning seemed brilliant with promise. It was her hope he felt, and for the moment it seemed enough.

Joey paused only once to glance back at Val Caché as the protective forest closed around it, veiled it from the world Outside. Her words were so soft, he knew he had not been meant to hear them. "Good-bye. I wish . . ." And then she turned again and filled the new day with idle chatter that rivaled the birds and eased the void in his soul.

They crossed the valley floor during the course of the morning and, after a noon break, began the ascent up the first of the slopes that marked the foot of the mountain range among which Miller's Peak stood. When they reached a meadow that provided a clear view of their goal, Luke pointed it out to Joey, watching her face change as she gazed at it, the stubborn determination that settled there. It served to remind him what she valued most, what truly mattered to her—what she had to do before they could both be at peace.

He told her, then, what the villagers had confirmed: that a plane had gone down there among those mountains years before, lost in a late-spring snowstorm. They had even sent men out to look, but they had found nothing, for the softened snows had buried whatever might have remained to be found. He saw the hope in Joey's eyes.

She was quiet after that, all her concentration focused on reaching the source of a year's worth of hopes and dreams. Luke did not welcome the silence. He could not fill it as she did with idle conversation, light comments to pass the time; it was not his way. But the silence became a terrible burden as it had never been before. It left him free to be fully aware of her—the rich female scent of her, the sound of her breath and the steady beat of her heart—the gleam of sunlight on her hair, the perfect curves of her body, made to fit his. . . .

It was all he could do to erect the barriers one by one, keeping the awareness so deeply buried that he felt bereft of his senses, blind and deaf, unable to feel at all. The kilometers passed by in a fog; only instinct kept him to the right course, and even so he stumbled and lost the rhythm of his stride again and again, clumsy with the need to stay tightly locked within himself.

Once, Joey touched him. It was no more than a brush of her hand, an inquiry or expression of concern—he never registered her expression. Within an instant he had rounded on her, snarling, nearly knocking her backward with the force of his turn. He did see her face then, frozen in astonishment, a flash of fear in her eyes before she disguised it with anger. She backed away from him, searching his eyes; what she read there set her expression into lines of utter coldness. After that she kept a careful distance.

So they continued with the wall firmly back in place between them. Luke felt it like the bars of a cage that he could never hope to escape.

Moving slowly and steadily up the slope, they began to pass into the realm of the hardier trees that ruled the higher elevations, leaving the protection of the valley behind. At the top of the ridge that lay between Val Caché and Miller's Peak, Luke stopped to survey the last portion of their journey.

Another valley stretched below them, the deep green of forest giving way to the brilliant blue of a lake that lay at the foot of Miller's Peak. The mountain itself rose steeply, a stony giant knee-deep in water and clad to the waist in a garment woven of fir and pine.

Joey came up beside him, and he heard the hiss of her indrawn breath.

"That's it, isn't it?" she whispered. She wriggled free of her pack and set it down on a bare patch of rock, raising a hand to shade her eyes.

"Yes." Luke kept his eyes from Joey's face and silently calculated the distance around the near side of the lake and to the foot of the mountain. "There," he said, pointing to the sheer cut of the mountain's face, ridged and striated and touched with the crystal fire of sun-struck glaciers. "You said the plane had been coming from the east. In a bad storm that portion of the mountain could be a deadly obstacle. A plane hitting anywhere on this side—"

He broke off, cursing the need for detachment that made his words so cold. But Joey only gazed at the mountain, breathing hard and fast.

"Yes. It fits." Her voice was strangely calm. "They'd said they were coming up on a large lake. They caught a glimpse of it through the storm just before they lost contact—" Luke heard her swallow. "This is it. I know it."

She bent down to retrieve her pack and was already moving past Luke as he pulled it on again. Her plunge down the slope toward the tree line was almost reckless; loose stones rolled under her feet and bounced down the rocky ridge with hollow rattles.

Luke pursued and overtook her, setting himself in her path. She skidded to a halt and looked at him, eyes brilliant and skin flushed with emotion.

"It's so close, Luke," she breathed. "So close . . ."

"Not that close." Luke held her gaze, refusing the response of his heart. "Distances are deceptive here. We'll go a little farther down, to the lakeshore, and around as far as we can before nightfall. Then we'll make camp and be fresh in the morning."

"But—"

"This isn't a suggestion, Joey. We may have days of searching to do once we reach the foot of the mountain. And even then—"

She lifted her chin. "Do you think I don't know?" Abruptly she looked beyond him, lips parted. "But until I'm certain . . ."

With every fragment of discipline he possessed, Luke stopped himself from touching her, holding her against the sadness that gathered in her eyes. "You need sleep to think clearly, Joey. If we start now, we can cover a good distance before dusk."

Her gaze lifted to his, and she nodded slowly. "All right," she said. "I can wait one more day."

Luke turned away and started down the slope again before he could betray his thoughts. He heard her following, moving with greater care as they reached the tree line and entered the forest. She was silent, pushing herself without mercy even when he set a slower pace. They rested briefly by the clear waters of the lake and continued along the shore as the afternoon waned.

By nightfall they had reached a point close to the foot of the mountain where the trees marched up the steep incline, obscuring the rocky mass above. They made camp without a word spoken between them; Joey was lost in her own world of memory, and Luke took the respite with bitter gratitude. He waited as she sat staring into the fire, seemingly bent on keeping vigil throughout the night. It was only when she surrendered to exhaustion, retreating at last to the tent, that Luke was free to escape.

He stalked into the night, following his senses and the instinct men called intuition. He loped through the forest to a place where scree had worn away from the mountain and cut a pathway through the trees to the water's edge, an unbroken sweep from the sheer face towering overhead.

He found what he sought as the moon began its downward path, just before the first eldritch light of false dawn. He wrapped the fragment of metal in his shirt and carried it back to camp cradled in his arms.

Joey woke with the dawn, and Luke was there when she emerged from the tent, her fair hair loose in her eyes.

"I found it," he told her softly.

Joey stood beside Luke in the early morning stillness, turning the rusted metal over and over in her hands.

"There may be more," he murmured. "I didn't make a thorough search."

She looked up, focusing on his face with difficulty. He was remote, as he had been since they'd left Val Caché, but there was a softening in his eyes. Almost as if he knew what she felt at this moment.

When he had led her here, she had expected—what? A sign to proclaim that she'd reached the end of her search at last? A whisper of lost voices to comfort her and send her, sorrows banished, on her way?

*If only I could be sure . . .*

She shivered in the shadow of the mountain and gripped the metal until it almost cut into her fingers. The small rocks that made up the talus slope, worn away from the mountain's face by time and wind and weather, rolled under her feet. Luke moved away, impossibly silent on the scree, and paused by a jumble of larger boulders wedged among the trunks of close-set pines.

"Here," he called. She trailed after him and crouched at the place he indicated. "The fragment was caught between these rocks." He looked up at the mountain. "The plane must have hit there, at the sheerest point of the slope. There wouldn't have been anything above the tree line to keep the wreckage from scattering and falling or sliding down into the lake. Except here."

Here. Joey set down the fragment carefully and began to search among the boulders, sifting through layers of pine needles and humus. She heard Luke working beside her, grateful for his presence, for the matter-of-fact detachment that reminded her of her purpose. There would be time for emotions later.

They found other pieces of metal, twisted and dull, as they worked their way down toward the shore of the lake. Joey gathered them into a neat pile, like a burial cairn, and returned to the search. Luke called a halt at noon, and they sat at the lake's edge, close but not touching, their reflections dwarfed by that of the mountain above.

"It's not enough," Joey said quietly.

Luke tossed a stone into the crystal water, and Joey watched the ripples arc outward until they disappeared. "You need to be certain," he said.

She looked at him across the narrow span of earth and rock that separated them. He understood. She could have reached out and touched him, asked him to hold her in this lonely place, and he would have understood. But she wrapped her arms around herself tightly and got to her feet, kicking more stones into the lake.

"This is your world, Luke," she said. "You've been right about a lot of things. But I never realized how hard it would be to make your world give up its secrets."

"Joey—"

She shook her head and began to walk along the shore, Luke like a shadow at her heels. The hollow ache in her chest grew more intense as the day waned. She felt the wilderness as a living thing, rejecting her, mocking her, refusing to yield what she must have. It had taken her parents, but it would give her nothing in return.

Something wild rose in Joey then. She flung her head back and stared into the setting sun. She opened her heart and her senses and set aside the rationality she had lived by all her life.

*Listen to me,* she told the forests and peaks and clear water. *Let me find them, let me be free, and I'll give you whatever you demand. . . .*

"Joey." Luke's low voice shook her from the spell she had woven about herself, and she jerked around to face him. His eyes were unreadable, his expression as stark as the mountain itself. "It's time to make camp. Tomorrow—"

"No, Luke. Not yet." Joey looked through him and beyond, her feet moving before she recognized the strange certainty that drove her. She retraced her steps one by one, letting her eyes search without focusing until they caught the glint of dying sunlight on metal.

The plaque was half-buried in pebbles and silt, traces of brightness still visible through the rust. Joey knelt and dug it out, rinsing it in lake water with gentle hands.

She traced the engraved words, still readable, with a trembling finger. *To Jameson Randall, beloved husband and father.*

" 'Free as Nature first made man . . .' "

Joey felt the warmth of Luke's breath as he knelt beside her. He read the quote like a eulogy, his fingertips brushing over hers.

"It was a gift," she whispered, her throat suddenly full and tight. "The plane was a gift from my mother, after Dad's old one gave out. She saved up for it for years. I remember when we gave it to him, and she had this plaque installed in the cockpit. . . ."

Words failed, and she bent over the plaque and held it tightly to her chest. *I found you,* she said silently. *I found you.* She looked out over the water and thought of her parents, sleeping beneath that still and lovely surface.

Warmth wrapped around her, real and certain. Luke pulled her back against his chest and enfolded her in his arms while the years melted away and she became a child again. She heard her parents' voices, their last words to her so long ago.

"I love you, Mom and Dad," she whispered. "I love you." And then the tears came, released from the place where she had hidden them. She turned into Luke's embrace and clung to him as he held her against the storm.

The sun had turned the lake to liquid fire when peace came at last. Luke released her without a word when she pulled away gently, touching his face with her hand, and got stiffly to her feet. He followed as she climbed up from the lake's edge to the cairn she had begun and helped her gather stones to cover the wreckage, until only the plaque remained.

In the hush of dusk Joey set the plaque at the top of the cairn and wedged it in place. Only then did Luke leave her side. She stood before the cairn, alone but no longer bereft. It seemed right that she should say her last good-byes as darkness fell, that she should feel the burden of sadness lifted with the coming of night.

She found Luke crouched at the water's edge.

"Thank you, Luke."

He looked up, a handful of earth sifting from his opened fist. In the dim light she could see nothing of his expression.

"Was it enough, Joey?"

She understood what he asked. "Yes," she murmured, kneeling beside him. "I feel—as if I know they're at peace now."

For a long moment she listened to the rhythm of his breathing, letting the new, unfamiliar contentment wash over her. "For the first time in years I feel free."

Luke looked away, his profile silhouetted against the afterglow that lingered on the water. "Then there's no reason we can't return tomorrow."

Joey froze in the act of reaching out to touch him. Less than an hour ago he had held her while she cried as she had never cried before, rocked her like a child and shared her grief as only another orphan could. Now his voice was distant, almost cold, and as he turned back to her he flinched from her extended hand.

She let her arm fall. "It's so beautiful here," she said. "If we could stay a few more days . . ."

"No." Abruptly he got to his feet, setting his back to her. "The weather could change any time. We've been lucky so far, but I want you out of the mountains and—" He broke off, but the word he would have spoken echoed between them.

*Gone.* He wanted her gone. Staring blindly at his back, Joey folded her arms across her chest.

She had what she had wanted of him. He had done what he'd promised. She had laid her parents to rest, and she could go on now—on with her life, looking ahead instead of behind.

But when she looked ahead, it wasn't her old job in San Francisco that she saw, or the constricted life she had left there. Luke filled her sight, a dark shape standing on the path that led into a limitless future. Waiting just beyond the void left in her heart when her parents had died.

*What do you want, Joey?* she asked herself. The questioned echoed in her heart and went unanswered.

Releasing her breath slowly, Joey rose and moved to stand behind Luke. His body tensed, muscles going rigid at her nearness, as if he had thrown an invisible wall up between them.

She might have backed away. It would have been a simple thing. But there was a strange new joy in her that would not be silenced, a sense of hope that nourished her natural stubbornness.

Luke had been a mystery from the first day she had met him, and that mystery had only deepened in their time together in Val Caché and on the trail. Luke wanted her gone, out of his life, for reasons she didn't understand.

Not yet.

*You won't find it quite so easy to get rid of me,* she told him silently. *I never give up until I find all the answers.*

As if he'd heard her thoughts, Luke jerked his head up sharply. His nostrils flared. "The wind is shifting," he murmured, almost too softly for her to hear. He pivoted and took several steps away, looking deliberately over Joey's head. "We'll make an early start in the morning."

He was walking away before she realized it. She stared after him, setting her jaw. "As early as you like, Luke," she breathed. "As early as you like."

Slowly she made her way back up the slope, pausing to brush her hand gently over the weathered surface of the plaque that was her parents' final monument. *Free as Nature first made man. . . .*

"You won't be disappointed," she told them softly. "You lived your life to the fullest, and so will I. I won't settle for anything less."

She smiled, remembering, and when she closed her eyes, she could see them smiling back.

# Chapter 12

Luke knew before dawn that the weather had changed.

The morning sun hid behind a sky drained of color. The outlines of distant trees were soft and blurred, and the wind had risen, carrying with it the promise of winter.

Luke broke camp quickly, losing himself in routine as he tried desperately to shut Joey away from his senses and his thoughts. He had left her alone in the tent that night, had lain awake by the smoldering fire, remembering her tears and the courage that had brought her so far.

Now she would leave him, as she must. He would give her no chance to linger, no excuse to prolong this constant torment. He recognized the subtle promise in her eyes; Joelle Randall had attained her goal, but she was not satisfied. She would reach for more, for all she could hold.

She shone more brightly than the invisible sun as

they began to retrace their path back to Val Caché. "I feel free," she had said, and she was. She was more deadly to him now than she had ever been. There was no sadness to dull her vitality, no other obsession to distract her. Or himself.

So he fought to shut her out as he had done before. She tried to engage him in conversation; he rebuffed her with gruff monosyllables and silence. Even that was not enough to dim her brilliance. He walked more swiftly to keep her out of view, and she caught up easily. He felt her watching him, always watching, waiting for a sign of weakness.

He could never afford to be weak again.

They had reached the top of the ridge above the lake when the first snow began to fall. Luke felt the gentle sting of a snowflake on his cheek and looked up.

He came slowly to a halt. Joey continued a few paces farther and stopped to look back; her face shone with such inner radiance that Luke could not meet her questioning eyes. One snowflake and then another settled on the wool of her cap, kissing her cheek with the lightest of caresses. He saw her raise her mittened hand to touch the places where they had fallen.

"Snow," she whispered. She grinned, whirling in a circle with her arms flung up like a child in her first snowfall. Perhaps, he thought numbly, it *was* her first.

He could not help but watch her. The muscles of his legs locked as she began to dance, as uninhibited as a wild thing in its element.

Trembling with unwelcome emotion, Luke dropped his pack to the ground and swayed in the grip of longing and desire. Joey's joy in the simple beauty of nature was very real; she was laughing now, almost silently, opening her mouth to catch the lacy flakes on her tongue. Luke followed the motions of her body with hungry eyes, felt self-control slipping away like melting snow through his fingers.

She whirled to look at him then, and his heart turned over. The warmth of her face might have melted the snow for a kilometer in every direction before it touched the ground.

"It's wonderful, Luke," she said. "Will it snow all day?"

Luke swallowed to force words past the obstruction in his throat. He broke free of her gaze and stared up at the sky. "Yes. The weather has turned. We have to keep moving."

If she heard the deliberate coldness in his voice, she gave no sign. Her grin was incandescent. "You can take all this for granted, Luke. I'm not about to." She spread her hand to catch a palmful of snowflakes and examined them.

An admonishment rose in Luke's mind and vanished again instantly. Joey pinned him with her gaze and moved toward him, reaching out. Her voice came to him like a distant cry lost on the wind.

"Give me time to feel this, Luke. I want to understand your world, become a part of it—"

He stopped her. He used all the force of his will to keep her back, and she drew up short, smile fading.

"That was never part of our bargain," he said harshly.

The look in Joey's eyes took on a dangerous cast. "We can always change our bargain, Luke," she said.

He could not answer. Looking away, he smelled the air and let the wilderness fill his senses. It would be dark within a few hours, darker still with the late-afternoon sun lost behind the clouds and mist. Ahead of them, a few hours' hike to the west, lay a number of rocky inclines, stable cliffs that would grant them a night's refuge. They would be moving gradually down into the valley and away from the high country, but he could take no chance of delaying their return if the weather worsened.

One more night before Val Caché, and a few more after that. He could bear that much. He had no choice.

Luke looked through Joey as if she weren't there and bent to retrieve his pack. "We'll push on," he said. "I want to make at least another ten kilometers before dusk."

He turned without waiting for her protest. But as he began to walk, his ears strained for the sound of her breathing and the creak of her pack as she moved to join him.

Moving alongside Luke as the snow danced, Joey felt the slow warmth of contentment melt the cold between and around them. Impossible to be angry when everything had become so beautiful; if Luke seemed to be doing his best to ignore her, she found it absurdly easy to forgive him. She hardly noticed when he began to pick up the pace, caught up in the wonder of something she had never before experienced.

The snow began to stick to the ground, first in small patches and then in an even, pristine blanket. Joey made a game of shuffling through it, kicking it up so that it clung to the toes of her boots. She wondered what it would be like when it was deep enough to wade through, how much fun it would be to build a snowman, or have a snowball fight—things Luke had probably taken for granted as a child. Common things, which to her were small miracles.

Luke was silent, doggedly leading her along the course of the stream that paralleled their way. Joey found herself drifting behind, hardly aware when Luke snapped a command for her to keep up. A snowshoe hare, still mottled brown in the molt that would alter its coat to winter white, bounded across their path. A browsing bull moose and his cow, moving down the slope to the more sheltered valley, briefly challenged them and then crashed off into the forest. Small birds quarreled over the berries that remained on currant and chokecherry shrubs.

It was all wonderful, and she only realized how tired she was when Luke stopped at last, in a level area flanked by stretches of bare rock and cliffs. The snowfall had been heavier here, already an inch deep under their feet. It lent the wilderness a profoundly peaceful beauty.

"We'll camp here for the night," Luke said, studying the terrain. He hardly glanced at her, dropping his pack to begin the first steps of making camp. Staring about the place he had picked, Joey thought it would be nice to rest here. She plopped down on a rock, dusting the snow from its surface. Easiest now just to let her mind go blank, listening to the familiar sounds Luke made as he began to set up camp. She should be helping him, really, but she was so tired. . . .

Some time passed; she was vaguely aware of it, felt it more keenly when she noticed the dampness of her clothing, the way it clung to her skin. Not comfortable at all. It would be nice to take it all off, she thought. Her body began to shake, and she could not seem to make it stop. Ridiculous.

With an irritable snap of her head she looked for Luke. What was taking him so damned long? She was hungry. She wanted a bath. She wanted . . . What did she want? She couldn't seem to remember. All she knew was that it was *his* fault—it had to be.

She giggled. Better go find him. She tried to stand, found that her feet wouldn't quite support her. So clumsy. Better not let Luke see that. The world spun sideways; she knew she hadn't been drinking, but it almost felt that way. Getting drunk without drinking . . .

It hadn't seemed so cold before. Maybe if she changed her clothes. Joey tugged at the zipper of her light parka, pulling it down. Her fingers didn't seem to want to work properly. She got the jacket open at last and tried to pull it off. Somehow she got tangled in it and gave a snarl of frustration as her arms twisted at painful angles.

"Joey." The word came from far away. "Joey, what are you doing?"

The sound of the voice was like the annoying buzz of a fly. With a furious wrench Joey got the parka off and flung it in the snow. Something touched her; she punched at it angrily. "Go away," she snapped. "Go away!" She tried to stand again, to escape, but she seemed to have lost her legs. And then she was falling, falling . . .

Luke caught her in his arms before she hit the snow. "Joey!"

She said something, the words slurred and strange. "I'm cold, Luke," Her mittened hands flailed out to bat at his face. "Go away. . . ."

Luke's heart nearly stopped in his chest. Hypothermia. He cursed himself savagely. For most of the day he had ignored Joey, convinced of her ability to keep pace with him no matter how hard he pushed. He had been lost in himself, intent on shutting her out.

He had succeeded all too well. In his cowardice, his fear of her closeness, he had failed to see the signs, failed to note the early warnings. Such a small thing— insidious, creeping up with deceptive gentleness on the unwary, experienced and innocent alike.

And hypothermia could be fatal.

Luke stared at Joey's pale face, blank and dazed, no comprehension in it at all. Closing his arms about her, he held her in a tight embrace, willing her his warmth, feeling the fragility of her body. He could smell the moisture on her, knew how it had happened—so easy for her to overlook the changes in the still air that seemed almost warm, forgetting her own limitations. He could only rage at himself for his own blindness and stupidity. For risking something as precious as her life.

No time now to finish putting up the tent, build a

fire to warm her. Instead, he draped his parka over her and zipped it up, keeping her close as he half-carried her across the little clearing to the rocky face of the cliffside. The shelter he sought was there: the half-obscured opening of a cave, a dark shape shadowed by a slight overhang. Boulders and smaller rocks were scattered about the opening, and he thrust them aside as he dropped to his knees by the entrance, pulling Joey down with him.

There was no time to hesitate or weigh the possible dangers. He smelled the telltale scents of animal occupation, not recent but strong enough that under other circumstances he might have searched elsewhere for shelter. Now that wasn't possible. Not with Joey half-comatose under his arm, in peril as great as any risk of confrontation with the former owner of the cave.

The cave was surprisingly warm, sheltered from the rising wind, the snow intruding only a scant few inches under the overhang that protected the entrance. Luke backed in, pulling Joey after him. She was almost limp; he set her down on the carpet of dried needles, old leaves, and gravel that made a bed on the cavern floor and held her against him. He closed his eyes and pressed his face to hers. "Joey! Joelle, do you hear me?"

His heart thudded heavily in his chest while he waited for her to respond. Her eyelids fluttered, and a faint smile moved across her face. "Luke?"

He gave silent thanks to the powers of life and caught her face between his hands. Her cheeks were like ice. "You must stay awake, Joelle. I'm going to get you warm again, but you have to help me."

Her body shuddered, her words broken by the chattering of her teeth. "I'm cold, Luke. Make me warm. . . ."

With a soft oath, Luke held her against his body. "I'll help you, Joey. But you must help me, too. Will you try very hard to stay awake for a few minutes?"

"Okay, Luke," she murmured, eyes unfocused. "I'll try to stay awake. But I'm so cold. . . ."

Luke cursed and laid her back down against the cave wall, struggling out of his sweater. He draped it over her, scant protection that it was, and backed out of the cave. He ran with every ounce of speed he could muster, hauling the two packs over his shoulders; the adrenaline rushing through his body made them feel as light as down. Thudding to his knees at the entrance once again, he dragged the packs in after him, putting his own up to block a large portion of the cave mouth to cut off any intrusion of snow and wind.

She was still awake, as he'd prayed she would be. Her eyes seemed to be trying to track him, not quite succeeding; with clumsy fingers he battled with the ties and zippers of both packs to free the sleeping bags and the extra blanket he had brought along in case of just such an emergency. He opened her smaller bag and draped it over his shoulders to warm it with his body heat while he stripped his sweater and parka away from her body, moving her unresisting form as if it were a doll's. He spoke to her all the while, a firm, insistent monologue that denied her the chance to give in.

The wool sweater she wore was almost dry, but the underlayers were damp with perspiration. He removed them one by one, shielding her from the cold air that blew in the cave mouth when the wind shifted. When he had stripped away the last of her damp clothing, down to the skin, he lifted her in his arms and placed her deep within the cocoon of his unrolled sleeping bag, wrapping it about her tightly and laying her open bag and the blanket over that until he had covered her with as many layers as he could find. Only then did he begin to drag off his own dry clothing, pushing his sweater, shirt, and pants back against the rear wall of the cave.

There was no time to think. No time to consider implications or should-have-beens. His mind was focused on one thing, and his anger at himself fled before necessity.

Her body was still icy cold when he joined her. There was room enough in his bag, just room enough for the two of them, pressed together spoon fashion. Her nakedness stretched along the length of his body meant nothing in those moments but a terrible vulnerability to be protected and healed at all costs; he wrapped his arms around her tightly, feeling the fading shudders that vibrated against his chest, willing them away with all his heart and mind. He pressed his face into the softness of her hair. His knees filled the hollows behind hers; the swell of her buttocks was soft against the muscle of his belly.

He knew he spoke nonsense. He kept up the ceaseless oneway conversation, demanding that she stay awake, needing to hear her murmured acknowledgments. When her body began to warm against him, he buried his face in her neck and felt her snuggle closer, pressing back with a sigh, shifting her feet to intertwine with his. Whether there was conscious design in her movement he could not guess; he struggled with his body's reaction and tried to recapture the simple determination to save her. It would not come. Every instinct told him that the danger had passed.

The stirring of his body was undeniable. He could not risk leaving her yet, though his mind screamed a warning; nor could he pull back from the curves of her body, from the feel of her skin, and the utterly feminine scent that intoxicated him. She would know it soon enough if she didn't already: the devastating effect she had on him, that he had been fighting long and hard without success.

As if to confirm his thoughts, she moved again; this time it seemed almost deliberate. The way the delicious curve of her buttocks, the small of her back, rubbed against his growing hardness was exquisite torture. He stifled a groan. Did she have the energy to tease him even now? His deepest instincts urged him to pull her against him, take her, enter her uniquely female warmth. To cup the breasts that lay almost under his hands, tease the nipples into hardness, make her ready to receive him. . . . He bit down on his lip savagely and denied the instincts one by one. It nearly took more willpower then he possessed.

For long, tortured moments he held himself rigid against her, refusing to let the weakness take hold. He knew she was awake by the soft sound of her breathing; there was a slight shudder to it that had nothing to do with the dangers that had passed. He kept his arms still where they embraced her, his lips unmoving against the nape of her neck. It was only when he felt her struggle to turn that he released her with a shaky breath.

"Luke?" Her voice was soft, uncertain. She twisted until she was almost on her back, able to look over her shoulder at him; loose pale hair drifted about her face. Her cheeks were flooded with healthy color now, perhaps more than mere warmth could account for. The full curve of her lips were parted, her dark eyes focusing slowly on his. "What—what happened?"

The sensible nature of the question relieved the last of Luke's worries. She was lucid again, and her skin was warm and dry. With greater speed than he had dared to expect, her body had accepted his warmth and begun its recovery. The new worries that rose in him now had nothing to do with her physical safety.

He struggled to form words. "You've been very ill, Joey. Hypothermia . . ." He broke off as she registered what he told her, the sweet oval of her face abruptly paling under the flush. "You had to be made warm as quickly as possible." The flustered feeling that rose in him at the expression on her face made his voice harsh with chagrin. "Unfortunately the treatment in a case like this involves body-to-body contact for maximum warmth. Now that you've recovered somewhat, we can get you in dry clothes, and I'll build up a fire."

The practical list of tasks relieved the unaccustomed anxiety he felt as she watched him. He began to ease his way out of the sleeping bag, doing his best to ignore the soft slide of her body along his, when she stopped him with the lightest of touches. He froze halfway out of the bag.

"I don't understand, Luke. How did this happen? How did I get hypothermia? I don't remember any of it. . . ." There was such genuine distress in her voice that Luke longed to take her into his arms again. Instead, he let his eyes focus on the cave entrance, where a growing darkness revealed the lateness of the hour.

"I'll explain all that later, Joey," he said gruffly. "Right now there are things that need to be done so that we'll be comfortable here until morning." He pulled himself from the sleeping bag and paused to tuck the edges of it about Joey, filling in the space he had left behind. She stared up at him.

"I remember a little snow. . . ." Shaking her head, she seemed at last to consciously register his state of undress. Her eyes slid over him, widening at the appropriate place. Luke suppressed an entirely foreign desire to cover himself. But there was no castigation in her expression—quite the contrary. Luke had to look away again very quickly.

Turning his back, he pulled on the pants and shirt he had discarded earlier, aware of her gaze burning into him from behind. "I still don't understand how I managed to get . . . why didn't I see it coming? There should have been symptoms, some warning—"

Abruptly Luke whirled to face her. "You can blame that on me, Joey," he almost snarled. He caught hold of himself and smoothed his features with deliberation. "I haven't done a very good job as your guide. But I'll make sure I don't slip up again."

Before she could react he strode past her, pausing at the cave entrance only to admonish her, "Stay in the bag and keep warm. Later you'll have to move around a little, but for now stay put. If you need clothes, there's an extra shirt of mine and a sweater behind you; the rest will have to be dried." He swung around.

Joey called after him. "Where are you going?" Her voice was very small. He stopped with his hand on the cold rock wall of the cave entrance.

"Out for firewood. I'll try to build a small fire at the cave entrance; you'll need hot liquids and something to eat as soon as possible."

He didn't pause again when Joey's final words trailed after him, shredded on the wind that buffeted snow against his face.

"I knew we should have brought my stove!"

Joey huddled back into the warmth of the sleeping bag as Luke disappeared, wondering if he'd heard her rather weak attempt at humor. It was hard to be funny when she was just beginning to realize that something very serious had happened. Not only the hypothermia, but something even more frightening.

She remembered coming out of a daze, one she'd hardly been aware of, to feel Luke's hard body pressed into hers from behind. The shock of it had penetrated slowly, and by then some of the soft words he had spoken had connected. Stay awake, stay awake, he'd told her gently, over and over. She had obeyed without realizing it. When she'd come back to herself, to full realization, the first thing she knew was that Luke was most definitely aroused.

It had been utterly impossible not to notice the firm male length of him trapped between their bodies. The confusion had passed quickly, and even before she could ask him what had happened, her own body had reacted to the feel of him. A rush of desire had momentarily blocked the logical need for answers. For a nearly unbearable instant she had been certain he would know how very ready she was for him, how much she wanted to feel him inside her. When she'd finally been able to turn and face him, his eyes had been so bleak that she had pushed back the primitive emotions and settled for practical questions instead.

Even then he'd been obtuse about the whole thing. Joey felt herself flush with mingled discomfiture and a very definite desire to feel his body against hers again. It was hard to say which feeling was stronger. Just another of many moments of confusion she had experienced since the first day she'd met Luke Gévaudan.

Joey rolled over in the bag, very much aware of the appealing male smell that permeated the half of it where he'd lain beside her. She pressed her nose to the lining and breathed it in. She still didn't have a full grasp of what had happened, but she knew Luke hadn't stripped her, and himself, for their mutual pleasure. He'd spoken of something even she knew was dangerous.

Luke had been angry, though whether with her or with himself hadn't been clear. It had been something of an overreaction, like so many of his moods—like the brittle way he'd kept his distance ever since they'd found the wreckage. The message she had begun to glean from all that she'd learned of him began to make sense. He was afraid, that was clear: but of what? Of being hurt, of being abandoned—of opening himself? Joey drew the edges of the bag more tightly about herself and grimaced. That was something she understood all too well.

A slow resolve came to Joey then. It wasn't safe or logical, but it was most definitely real. It had been growing with every day they'd spent on the trail together, had begun to coalesce at the foot of the mountain where she'd laid her parents to rest. This last experience had confirmed the undeniable truth of it.

She had asked herself what she wanted, and now she was certain.

She wanted Luke. That much was fact. As for the rest—it was still too new, too overwhelming. There were some things she was not yet ready to face.

Reflecting on the unsettling changes that had come over her, Joey slipped out of the sleeping bag long enough to don the shirt and sweater Luke had indicated in the rear of the cave. There were no underclothes and nothing to cover her legs; Joey felt as if she were swimming in the shirt and sweater, which reached well down her thighs. But it was definitely better than nothing. She snuggled quickly back into the bag.

Lost in her thoughts, Joey didn't hear Luke at first when he returned, brushing snow from his clothing. He tossed his hair out of his eyes and gazed down at her with a frown. Joey felt his anxiety like a physical thing in the brief moment that their gazes locked. What he saw in her face seemed to satisfy him, for he turned away again and busied himself with setting up a small fire just outside the mouth of the cave.

Joey knew in that moment her feelings had been right. They might be crazy, but they were most definitely right. She smiled to herself as she watched Luke coax a fire into life, cursing softly under his breath when he was forced to use several matches before he got it to catch. Even the slight heat of the newborn flames was a real comfort; as Luke moved away from the entrance, Joey could see where he'd made a kind of wall out of the tent just beyond the fire, blocking the wind and leaving space for smoke to escape.

Luke worked quietly and steadily, pulling gear from the packs and dumping fresh water he'd found into the largest of the pots, setting it to heat over the fire. He strung a cord between outcroppings on the cave wall and hung her damp clothes to dry. After he had done all the small things necessary to make an overnight stay as comfortable as possible, he brought an assortment of food over to Joey and crouched beside her to offer it.

Even the most dry and tasteless trail food was immensely tempting. By the time she had finished, the water was boiling, and Luke made her mugs of steaming tea and bouillon, insisting that she drink several until she protested she could not hold another drop.

Luke returned to check the fire, and Joey sank back into the sleeping bag, warmed inside and out. Whatever the effects of hypothermia, she seemed to have gotten off lightly; she felt incredibly good. Good enough so that her eyes found their way without hesitation to Luke's back where he crouched by the mouth of the cave, gazing out into the darkness and swirling snow.

She thought again of the lean hardness of his legs touching hers, the arch of his hipbones, the flat planes of his belly, and the strength of his arms about her. He was wearing only a shirt and pants now, not even so much as a sweater, and she wondered at his ability to endure the cold, as she had wondered about so many other things. Having cared for her so well, he sat stubbornly across the length of the cave and seemed very far away. Too far.

"Luke," she called softly.

He stiffened.

"Oh, don't be so blasted antisocial for a change! I liked it better when you were friendly." She knew it was the wrong tack when he stayed quite rigidly where he was, stirring at the fire with a half-burned twig. An errant snowflake escaped the heat of the fire and crossed the daunting distance to settle on his hair.

"Please," she coaxed at last. "Won't you come over here? You may think it impresses me to show how immune you are to cold and hunger and the things that affect us mere mortals, but it only makes me feel inferior. You don't want to do that, do you?"

There was a slow relaxation of the taut muscles of

his back, visible through the thin wool of the shirt. At first he was silent; then, with a slow shrug, he turned his face half toward her, so that his profile was illuminated by the fire against the backdrop of the tent beyond. "No. I wouldn't want to do that."

With the natural grace that always made her stare, he rose to his feet, keeping his head bent to avoid the low roof of the cave, and came toward her.

Joey's heart began to pound with the force of her resolve and his undeniably powerful effect on her. She was entirely aware of the extra room beside her in the bag but knew it was too soon to push her luck; instead, she wriggled forward so that she could lean against the cave wall, shrugging the blanket over her exposed upper body. She patted the soft bed of needles and leaves beside her.

Luke took the invitation. He dropped, at first, into a restless crouch, as if he would spring up at the slightest provocation; Joey gave him a long, reproachful look, and he slid down at last to stretch his long legs and rest his head against the cave wall.

For a moment Joey was content to study him. His face was careworn—because of her, she realized. Concern—fear—for her. She didn't question her certainty. It only increased her determination. She found herself looking at him now with a stirring in her heart and deeper, in her soul, touching something that had been long concealed. There was one last protest from her crumbling barriers, and she ignored it.

She remembered the first time she'd seen him. He'd been impressive even then, but now he was familiar, though just as charismatic. Now she understood a little more of him—not enough to solve his mysteries but enough to fill her with a powerful new longing. His profile was strong, shaped by discipline and years of aloneness, hardship, and simply being part of the wilderness he loved. Even in the scant light of the little fire, it was compelling beyond any face she had ever known.

His hair was damp with melted snow, but he seemed not to notice. When the time was right, she'd brush back that errant lock where it fell into his eyes. She'd touch that hard arch of cheekbone, run her fingers over the slight dark stubble that had begun to appear on his chin and along his jaw; trace the grimness away from the narrow curve of his lips, smooth the lines between his straight dark brows. She would see those eyes turned on her with that burning, all-consuming need, for her. . . .

Luke turned to meet her gaze. For an instant she thought there would be no need for caution, that he would at last give in; but he looked away again, to stare at the floor between his knees.

"You were very lucky," he said softly, "to come through that as well as you did."

"Thanks to you," Joey replied. She felt the heat radiating from his body, as intense as that of the fire. More so. "You saved my life, didn't you, Luke? I might have died."

"Yes." His voice was suddenly sharp, and his eyes glittered in a brief, intense glance. "I thought you understood the basics, but it was my fault you got to the point you did—my responsibility."

Joey dropped her gaze, feeling the rising flush. "No, it was my fault. It was all so beautiful, and I—I should have known better. I told you I did, and you trusted me." There was a beat of silence. "It won't happen again."

"You're damned right it won't," Luke said between gritted teeth. There was a very real warning in his voice; now he was most definitely staring at her. "I won't let you do anything to kill yourself. Ever. You'd better understand that right now."

In an earlier time Joey might have risen to the bait,

met his proprietary rebuke with defensive anger. Instead, she reached out, very slowly, to rest her hand on his leg. The muscles grew taut and slowly relaxed again under it.

"I think I do understand," she murmured. Luke looked away, and in the dim light it was hard to tell if the color in his face was merely a reflection of the flames. "I want to thank you again, Luke. For taking care of me, and for saving my life."

Luke was very quiet. He looked at the cave walls, at the ground, at the flames—everywhere but into her eyes. Joey bit her lip. "If you were really serious when you said you would keep me safe. . . ." Luke jerked his head sharply to frown at her. "Actually, I feel a cold spell coming on again. I don't think these sleeping bags and blankets are quite enough."

Opening his mouth and shutting it again with a snap, Luke stared at her. She could see impending signs of one of his internal struggles, perhaps trying to determine how serious she was. Or what hid under the surface of her words . . . Suddenly the fight seemed to go out of him in one long rush. He sighed; slowly, with visible reluctance, he moved closer to her, so that their legs touched from hip to calf, and looped his arm over her shoulder.

Joey closed her eyes with a matching sigh of utter contentment. For a moment she simply savored the feel of his hard shoulder under her cheek. The pleasure of that, and the soft puff of his breath stirring the loose hair at her forehead, was enough to last her for a good span of time. When it was no longer quite enough, and the silence had taken on the peace of deep accord between them, she allowed her head to roll onto his chest and brought her hand up to rest beside it.

Predictably, he stiffened again—but this time the relaxation came more quickly and more easily. As if she were gentling some wild, skittish forest creature, Joey moved her fingers very cautiously over the hard swell of his chest. The beat of his heart increased, ever so slightly, under her ear as her stroking hand traced the muscles and found the small masculine nipple under his shirt.

His indrawn breath told her all she needed to know. He did not push her away. She caressed his chest with the lightest of touches and risked a glance up at him; his eyes were shut, his head leaning against the cave wall. The expression on his face was one she had never seen before, lost and on the verge of surrender.

To speak now would break the spell. Carefully, ever so carefully, Joey slid her fingers between the buttons of his shirt. His skin was burning hot under the wiry curls. His heart lurched and settled again into a rapid, urgent rhythm beneath her palm as she undid the buttons from the base of his throat to the place where they disappeared into the waistband of his pants.

Now her hands were free to caress his skin, with no barrier between. The feel of him was beyond anything she had ever experienced, could even imagine experiencing. Only in her dreams—those incredible dreams—had she come close. His body was perfect and solid and masculine, filling her with need.

His breathing came more deeply as her palm slid up to push the shirt half away from the marvelous breadth of his shoulders. Those arms, which could carry a heavy load as if it were nothing, which were so strong and sure about her; she let her fingers trace the arch of muscle between shoulder and neck, tickling the hollow between his collarbones, moving up to caress the hard edge of his jaw.

She could feel the pulse in his throat. There was resistance in his posture, as if he would lower his head to look down at her, but she kept him still, turning more fully to him so that she could bring her other hand into play. His arm about her was rigid, but she hardly noticed the sudden powerful grip of his fingers. With both hands she drew patterns from the high cheekbones and down into the hollows beneath, sweeping over the firm planes of his face, drawing out the tension and care. He shuddered but did not twist away. Teasing the lobes of his ears, she found the lightest dusting of hair at the upper rims and followed her original plan to brush the errant black locks away from his forehead.

There was a new tension building in him now, visible and undeniable. She knew the instant that he would have broken free, to flee or take her into his arms, but again she stopped him; she brought her mouth slowly down to the places her fingers had traveled, lips caressing the fevered, silky firmness of his skin.

The hair on his chest was surprisingly soft against her cheek as she kissed him there, tickling and teasing. Almost timidly she licked at his nipple; he jerked with a gasp. She smiled against the hard muscles and teased him further until she felt ready to give the same attention to the remainder of his upper torso. Only then did she move up, to kiss his shoulders, sample the masculine taste of the hollow of his throat, move her tongue over the stubble of his jaw so that the roughness made her tingle.

She was just preparing to give his right earlobe the same treatment when, with a sudden groan and a movement so swift and powerful she had no hope of resistance, he turned on her. Suddenly she was crushed against him, her face lifted to his; for an instant the full, seething intensity of his eyes was locked on hers, and then he lowered his mouth to claim her lips.

The yielding softness of Joey's lips sent a jolt of uncontrollable desire through Luke, and he knew the edge of sanity had been reached. Some faraway part of him screamed to stop, to end it before it was too late, as he'd ended it twice before. But it was already too late. He could no more have broken off what Joey had started than he could stop the fall of snow beyond the cave's primitive shelter. She had finally succeeded in doing what he had never believed any woman—any human woman—could manage. The siren call of her body and the undeniable bond forming between them was more powerful than his resolve—or than either one of them.

Too late. Her mouth blossomed under his, the lips like petals parting to be tasted. Without ending the contact, he pulled her onto his lap, dragging her free of the sleeping bag until she straddled him, her bare thighs to either side of his. She was trembling, but not with cold. His heart rushed in his ears. Her eyes were closed, her fragile neck arched back, her hands pressed against his chest and trapped between them.

The taste of her was exquisite as he explored the hidden warmth of her mouth with his tongue. Her own rose to meet it, danced along it as their breath mingled; he pressed harder and more deeply as if that alone could seal what had grown between them. Her soft groan came from the very heart of her, vibrating where his lips moved on hers. There was an urgency there that matched his own, but he maintained that much control; the last shreds of rationality held him back. Now there would be time.

His teeth grazed her lower lip, tugged at swollen fullness. Her hands struggled to free themselves, sliding over his bare chest and up to his shoulders; he allowed her fingers to clutch at him and then pressed into her again, exploring her delectable mouth until he knew every part of it. Then the sensitivity of his tongue moved on to taste elsewhere—sliding over her delicate chin, along the fine jawline, pausing to tease the lobe of her ear as she had done with him. She gasped, her head flung back in complete surrender. He tangled his fingers in the pale gossamer of her hair, loosening the last remnants of braid, and brought his mouth to the vulnerability of that soft neck so gloriously exposed.

When his teeth closed lightly on it, she stiffened; for the barest moment her nails dug into his shoulders with surprise. But he was gentle, mindful to leave no marks, establishing his dominance with utmost care. And she accepted. Perhaps she didn't understand the language he spoke with his body, but she accepted.

His excitement grew to an unbearable pitch, but still he held back. This time it would be right. His teeth and tongue traveled down her throat to the gentle hollow, where her borrowed sweater hid the beauty beneath; he untangled his fingers from her hair just long enough to help her pull it over her head.

The open neck of the shirt he had given her shadowed the swell of her breasts, rising and falling with the rapid rhythm of her breathing. He pressed his face into the soft skin where neck and shoulder joined, smelling the woman scent of her where it mingled with his own in the worn cloth. The smell of her alone could drive him to madness. He breathed it in and closed his eyes until the lurching of his heart settled again.

Her arms had come up around him, gripping the loose fabric of his own shirt where it bunched against the cave wall at his back. He let her pull it off, twisting his body until he was entirely free of it. The touch of her fingers on his back, on his shoulders, were like pinpoints of fire. Her eyes came up to his, insensible, wanting, needing, the gold flecks like embers; her parted lips were swollen with his kisses. He forestalled her silent demands, lowering his face once again to the arch of her collarbone, while his fingers came up to loosen the buttons one by one.

She arched back with a gasp as he pushed the open shirt away from her body, pulled it from her shoulders. Her breasts were small and firm and incredibly beautiful, the nipples already hard in anticipation of his touch.

For a moment he could do nothing but gaze at her, until with a cry she caught his hair in her fists and pulled him down to her.

It was sheer wonder to explore what she offered. He kissed her first, gentle kisses that traced the rich curves in ever-smaller circles around the thrusting, ready center. When at last he took her nipple into his mouth, she cried aloud, arching high as he began to tease it with lips and tongue. He was thorough, savoring the tautness of it with gentle nibbles, sucking, licking it in time to her gasps of pleasure. In the brief moment that he paused to transfer his attentions to the other breast, she twisted her fingers in his hair so tightly that at another time he might have winced. Now the slight discomfort was part of the pleasure, like the heavy weight of his arousal.

He took his time with her, until her breathless moans were more than he could bear. Only then did he press his lips into the valley between her breasts, licking up the delicate moisture gathered there, stroking the underside of each one before starting the inevitable path downward.

Joey's body was no longer within her control. It had become a wild, unruly thing of pure sensation, of burning hungers. The indescribable feel of Luke's mouth on her breasts, his tongue on her nipples, had brought her to the brink of ecstatic madness. And now his burning mouth was moving down, caressing the hill of her ribs, trailing like fire across her belly. She quivered under him.

It was her body that cooperated so fervently when Luke moved lower still, pausing to bury his face in the skin just above the center of her need. She lay back on his taut thighs and arched against him as she had before, shamelessly, wanting him to taste her, to caress her, wondering if she could survive his touch. Once he raised his head; his eyes were nearly black with desire, reflecting her own instinctive responses, forging something between them beyond her understanding. She wanted to speak then, to say something, anything to prove she was more than merely a creature of wild and uncontrollable urges. But then his mouth moved lower, and she was lost.

The tip of his tongue was like solid flame as it touched her where she was most sensitive, most vulnerable; with expert caresses he teased her until the hot moisture of her readiness overflowed. He tasted that as well, stroking over fullness as the gasps were torn from her one after another. And when at last his tongue found the aching place made so ready for him, she cried aloud.

Luke heard her cry like music as he savored the sweetness of her, relished the taste of her readiness. His tongue pushed gently and then with greater, more rhythmic force into the giving entrance to her body; she closed about him, opening herself for him with unstinting abandon. His senses were nearly raw with absolute awareness of every part of her.

It took every ounce of willpower for Luke to hold himself in check, to keep from tumbling her back onto the cavern floor, free himself, and sink deeply within her hot and willing body. He would have continued to stroke her with lips and tongue until she begged him for what he himself wanted so desperately, but suddenly her hands were sliding up once again to his shoulders, and she was using them to lift herself, to meet him, her nipples caressing his chest. It was her mouth now that claimed his, her hands that moved between them to the hardness that strained against the unwelcome bonds of his clothing. She traced over his trapped length with her fingers until he groaned, and she laughed softly, with a woman's triumph, against his mouth. The wildness rose in him, and he bruised her lips with his, but she had suddenly become equally savage and met him with matching ferocity.

There was no gentleness in her when she tore impatiently at his trousers, pulling loose the buttons one by one until he was free. She did not wait to take him into her hands, and the jolt of her fingers there was beyond any previous sensation. Distantly he knew there had been others, some skilled in their lovemaking—but none, none had made him so utterly helpless. Now it was she who dominated, who demanded, who teased to a sweet, agonizing fever of hunger. She needed no skill to bring him again and again to the brink, always stopping before he could lose control. And he dared not lose control—not yet. Not before he had made her his.

Somehow, in her fragile strength, she had tugged him down, straddling him, her glorious nakedness a vision filling his sight. After the final barrier of his trousers was discarded and forgotten, she paused to gaze at him, the delicate oval of her face flushed with passion, her eyes wide and wild and bold as they raked over his body. And then she followed her gaze with her mouth and caressed him, her gossamer hair brushing his belly to the point of madness, taking him in so deeply that his fingers gripping her arms sank with bruising strength into the soft flesh.

Joey felt his grip, a pain indistinguishable from pleasure. The delightful response of his body, the firm, unyielding length of him, was a temptation she sampled again and again. She paused once to watch his face, so completely abandoned that the taut grim lines of it had relaxed and reformed into tension of a very different kind. She felt her power over him, gloried in it and in the raw, wild savagery she controlled, knowing in this instant it was she who held dominion.

At the moment that she was most confident of her mastery, that she had him tamed to her will, she lost the fragile victory. He pushed her back with undeniable strength, as if she were no more than a creature of fire-light and heated air, back across his thighs until her body lay once again open to him. He held her there so tightly that she could not move, and his eyes caught at hers with such feral madness that for an instant she was almost afraid. The moment passed quickly, for there was no room for fear in what followed.

Somehow, in a movement too swift to perceive, he had eased her back onto the abandoned sleeping bag, kneeling between her thighs. His hands were burning brands against the most sensitive skin as he pushed and lifted them; had she wanted to deny what would follow, she would have been utterly helpless to do so. There was no humanity in his eyes. She tried to reach up to him, to gentle the ferocity, but he pinned her arms to her sides and lowered himself atop her. He hovered there, and for a brief instant the blackness that had swallowed up the pale green-gold of his eyes receded, so that she recognized what she saw there; he recognized her, he remembered who she was. Remembered the time before . . .

There was a single suspended moment when she believed he would abandon her again, jerk away, deny her and himself. He shut his eyes and flung back his head; a soundless cry seemed caught in his throat, his jaw working in silence. And then he met her eyes again, and there was nothing but passion and uncomplicated desire. And acceptance.

She did not understand, but there was no more time for understanding. Only sensation as he descended, caught the soft skin of her shoulder between his teeth, pulling her against him as his surging hardness unerringly found its mark. She cried in pleasure and relief as he entered her, sank so deeply within her that it was only then she realized that the void had been filled at last. When he began to move, she felt her fingers clutching the fabric beneath them in time to each thrust, heard her gasping breaths caught up in the rhythm until there was only that one primal beat in all the world.

Luke could hear the tattoo of her heartbeat under his, her breasts under him firm as they rose and fell with each ragged breath. She was more deliciously hot and tight than he could have imagined, made so perfectly to fit him that he knew then it had been destined. The thing he had been fighting had been as inevitable as the flow of seasons and the coming of snow.

She arched and moaned under him; when he freed her arms they came up to rake his back, searing trails of fire. The two of them together had become incandescent, merging together into a flame that heated the cave beyond the ability of any mortal fire. Her legs were strong where they came up to close around his hips, urging him on. He needed no urging. He let the rhythm take him, holding himself from the brink, sucking the place at the hollow of her shoulder where he had bitten, soothing it with his tongue. Even the taste of her brought him too close to the peak, so he withdrew for a moment to look into her eyes. They were wet with tears, and he kissed them away; he knew they were not tears of pain. There could be no pain. Only pleasure, as he brought his hand between their bodies to caress her delicate folds and seek out the erotic core of her sensation, stroking while she shuddered and tightened about him again and again.

The time came at last when he knew he could restrain his body's demands no longer. Her movements against his caressing fingers grew more urgent, and he held himself until she convulsed in a molten flood that carried him with it, crying his name as he plunged within the embrace of her body's fiery core and found his own release.

Only the sound of their breathing accompanied the aftershock of passion. Luke held himself within her, careful not to let the full weight of his body trap hers, savoring the feel of her, unwilling to let her go. Her fingers splayed over his back; she began to stroke his skin where her nails had raked him as if to soothe the tiny hurt. Her eyes were heavy-lidded as they gazed up at him. Bending to kiss the arch of her brows, he rolled onto his side and carried her with him, still sheathed comfortably in her warmth, so that one hand was free to stroke away the damp strands of hair that clung to her cheek.

Her head pillowed on his arm, Joey pressed her face into his chest, and he caressed her hair until the last of her shuddering subsided. When she looked at him, her eyes bright with quiet joy that he felt to the marrow of his bones, he knew every one of his fears had been useless. Even his grandmother had recognized it: This woman in his arms had been the only one from the moment he'd seen her. He wanted to keep her a part of him forever, bringing his leg up to hold her there as if she would escape. But her arm came up to drape over his shoulder, and she moved her own legs so that they were intertwined, one perfect whole.

They gazed at each other in the same wordless communication that had come with their lovemaking; her eyes were so beautiful that the emptiness in his soul was filled to overflowing. She alone had filled it. He wanted to kiss her again, explore every last curve and hollow of her face, her body; but the sweet languor and deep peace between them was too wonderful, too fragile, to risk.

It was done; she was his, and he was hers. The bond was sealed between them. For a moment he looked away from her, shutting his eyes against the sudden fear that surged within, unbidden and unwanted, in spite of this new completion. She didn't know. She couldn't know what had happened, how thoroughly they now belonged to one another.

If she did . . . He shut the thought out behind clenched teeth. He could not bear that thought, that she might learn and reject it and abandon him.

Too late for doubts. He would have to hold her, make her stay with him. He would give her whatever she wanted, so that she would stay. But if there was any chance she might escape him, he would use whatever means necessary to prevent that terrible, unthinkable, and fatal possibility.

"Can we move a little?" Joey's voice cut through his grim thoughts like a soothing balm. "My arm is falling asleep."

Luke felt his lips curve up into a smile in spite of every unanswerable question. He lifted her and carried her with him so that she sprawled across his chest. "Better?"

She sighed deeply and rested her cheek on his shoulder. "Much better." After a moment she propped her chin in one hand and grinned at him. "No complaints at all."

He couldn't quite reach her lips, so he satisfied himself with the gentlest of kisses on her forehead. "I'm glad to hear it."

"You see? It wasn't so bad after all." She reached up to tug at the hair that had fallen into his eyes. "Unless I'm very much mistaken, it wasn't entirely horrible for you either—was it?"

Luke almost chuckled at the hint of insecurity in her tone. "No. Far from horrible. Incomparable."

She dropped her eyes and peered up at him coyly from under her lashes. "I'll bet you say that to all the girls."

The smile eased from his face. He felt his fingers tighten where they rested on her upper arms. "There are no others. Never again." He willed her to understand what he dared not say. "Only you, Joelle. Always."

She searched his face, her own grin fading. "You

have a way of getting so blasted grim sometimes. You're going to keep playing mystery man, even now that you've had your way with me?"

Sighing deeply, Luke closed his eyes. Even now, he could not tell her. "There are some things—things that I can't explain, Joelle." He opened his eyes and traced her cheekbone with one finger, as delicately as he would caress a snowflake. "Just be with me. Stay with me."

Her brows drew together in a puzzled frown, but she could not maintain the expression long; she dropped her chin to his chest and stretched her arms to either side of his head, tangling her fingers in his hair.

"Someday I'm going to figure you out, Luke Gévaudan. I've never met a puzzle I couldn't solve."

"Take all the time you need, Joelle," he murmured, pulling her up so that her cheek brushed his. So incredibly soft. "Take a lifetime."

For an instant her body grew rigid in his arms and then just as quickly relaxed. Her breathing took on the slow, deep cadence that comes just before sleep; he stroked her back from the base of her spine to the nape of her neck, gentling her beyond the need for questions.

"Luke?" Her voice was lazy music. "Say my name again. I like the way you say it."

He trembled with the intensity of his need for her. "Joelle." He breathed her name as he breathed in the unique fragrance of her hair. "Joelle." Her muscles grew loose against him, her body languid with sleep. "Never leave me, Joelle. Never leave me."

His words echoed in darkness and silence.

# Chapter 13

Joey's fingers brushed across the raw-silk texture of his skin as she woke. For a moment, her eyes still heavy-lidded with sleep, she took in the feel of it, inhaling the warm masculine scent under her cheek. Her senses were so finely tuned, even now, that a thousand subtle messages came to her at once: the deep, gentle pulse of his heartbeat, the bite of cold air kept at bay by the heat of their intertwined bodies, the scents that were uniquely hers and Luke's mingled with those of the dry needles and leaves that lay scattered under them. Luke's breath tickled her hairline, his big hand resting with infinite tenderness on her shoulder. She could feel each place where his body touched hers with such delightful intensity that it made the various aches and scrapes and bruises fade to insignificance.

Luke stirred. The very pleasant pillow of his chest hardened as he arched and stretched; she shifted to accommodate his movements and matched them with a long, luxurious stretch of her own. When he was still again, she snuggled against him and sighed deeply, her breath teasing the wiry hair under her cheek as she drew her fingers down over his ribs and the hard-ridged planes of his belly.

This time Luke's motion was far from casual. His hand came down to stop the exploration just shy of its mark, flattening to trap hers. He dwarfed her everywhere, and that was no exception; she let her hand rest where he held it under his and arched her fingers just enough to register a protest.

Luke made a half-choked sound. Looking up under her lashes, Joey decided it had been more laughter than an indication of ticklishness. Nevertheless, she felt suddenly very curious to find out if he was as sensitive in that way as he seemed to be in others.

Relaxing her hand in surrender, she waited just until the tension went out of his and then began her sortie, darting up to flick her fingers back over his ribs. He stiffened and gasped in genuine surprise. "Joey!"

"You *are* ticklish!" she cried in delight, and momentarily forgot her intent to demand his total surrender. The lapse gave him all the time he needed. Before she could do more than squeal in surprise, he had lifted her until she straddled him, her legs along his, her breasts against the arch of his ribs. She knew instantly that her teasing had had a most satisfactory effect on him, even if he'd managed to counteract her assault. The feel of that significant and very admirable part of him trapped between them made her shiver with pleasure.

"Now you know my terrible secret," Luke growled ominously. His lips curved upward in a smile that made her heart squeeze into a fist and loosen again, forcing the blood through her veins in a rush like the flow of heady wine.

"And you can bet I won't forget, either," she warned with an answering grin. "You'd better stay on your guard from now on."

"I will. I most definitely will."

As he gazed at her, amber-green eyes intent as if she were all the world, the rare smile faded. Joey reluctantly abandoned her plan to suggest a sequel to last night's activities. There could be no doubt he was more than ready; the hot length of him against her belly was adequate proof of that. And the mere feel of his body under hers from ankle to chest was enough to make her wish they had nothing to do but make love and let the rest of the world shatter into nonexistence.

But it was the look in his eyes and the gradual return of his features to the familiar set pattern that made her bow to reality. Her own as well as his. Closing her eyes, she let her head drop to his shoulder, her lips at the hollow of his throat.

"I wish we could stay like this forever," she murmured against him.

She felt the tightening of his muscles, shifting in his arms and growing rigid where his chest rose and fell in measure to her own. "Do you, Joey?" He drew a deep breath and let it out again. Suddenly he tumbled her over on her back, pinning her beneath him. The intensity in his gaze held no hint of playfulness.

Joey stared up at him, alarm singing through her. Her body reacted, tensing and resisting instinctively, like an animal caught in a trap. But Luke held her as surely with his will as with his strength, and only when she closed her eyes did he break the invisible bonds that imprisoned her.

She felt his palm settle against her cheek. "Joey," he breathed. "I would keep you here forever if I could." And then he released her, moving up and away before she could open her eyes again, his back turned as he crouched over the pile of their discarded clothing.

Joey pushed herself up and struggled to clear her mind. The moment of alarm had vanished, and all she could think of were absurdities and the absence of Luke's warm body touching hers.

"And only yesterday," she joked a little breathlessly, "you couldn't wait to get rid of me."

Luke lifted his head, his shirt draped over one bare shoulder.

"Everything has changed," he murmured, as though he spoke only to himself. The simple statement made Joey shiver. Everything *had* changed—and she was a long way from understanding what those changes meant. To her life, to her future, and to her heart . . .

"You don't make things easy on a man, Joey."

She looked up. Luke stood over her, his fists on his hips, and he smiled—all the grim intensity gone, a rueful curve of his mouth that raised the temperature in the cave by several degrees. It was as if a summer sun had found its way from the far side of the world, piercing her heart with warmth and an unfathomable joy.

"I never intended to," she answered, grinning back.

There was a beat of silence, full of hidden meanings, before Luke turned away. She couldn't quite help following him with her eyes, his graceful lithe walk and the sheer masculine beauty of his body. Before her mind could move on to the next logical thought, she shook herself and searched the dim cave for something practical to occupy her mind and set it in order again.

She was constantly aware of Luke moving about the entrance of the cave, gathering up discarded gear and stowing it in the packs he had used to block a portion of the opening. A quick glance told her that the morning was quiet beyond the cave; the cold air that penetrated was ample evidence of the temperature. She found her dry clothes where they hung along the rock wall and pulled them on as quickly as possible.

Luke vanished outside and returned soon after with wood to light a fire. The smell of hot coffee made Joey feel strangely content, as if she were in the one place in the world she most wanted to be.

"If we leave soon and make decent time, we'll get to Val Caché by nightfall."

Luke dropped into a crouch beside her, gazing as she did through the smoke into the morning visible beyond. "It's clear—no sign of more snow. Not deep enough to slow us too much." He turned to look at her thoughtfully, dark brows pulling down. "If you get tired—or overheated, or cold—you tell me instantly. Understood?"

Joey could not hold back a wry smile of acknowledgment. "Quite understood."

Luke's palm brushed her shoulder as he rose to step over the fire. The casual intimacy of it made her shiver; she wiped out her cup and packed it away with trembling fingers. After a moment Luke returned, and his face was open as he extended his hand for hers.

She stepped out into a world of perfect beauty. The snow was brilliant in the morning sun, even and smooth except where it tripped over rock and boulders and seedlings, brushed like icing on the branches of pine and spruce. Her feet made whispering sounds as they sank down several inches to find a purchase on the ground beneath; her breath frosted the air in a graceful plume. Luke tightened his grip on her hand and watched her as she took it in.

Joey gave herself up to the sheer joy of it, flung her head back so that the puffs of her breath obscured the crystalline blue of the sky. She realized after a moment that she was laughing. Without thinking, she dropped down to gather some of the snow in her gloved hand, feeling it shift and condense between her fingers.

When she turned to glance at Luke, his expression was so absurdly pleased that she had the feeling he was taking personal pride in her reaction, as if he were solely responsible for what nature had provided. Her fingers tightened on the ball of snow her hand had formed; her wicked grin was not quite enough to warn Luke of her intention. The snowball caught him full force in the middle of his chin.

The comical look of surprise on his face lasted only long enough for Joey to catch her breath, and then he was stalking her, head low, teeth bared in a snarl of mock ferocity. She backed away, half-afraid in spite of the game, while he crouched low enough to grab a handful of snow in his fist. As he straightened, he grinned slowly and with great satisfaction, hefting the snowball suggestively; Joey looked around for somewhere to hide and fell into a ridiculous fit of giggles that effectively demolished her ability to escape. She planted her feet and braced herself for the coming impact.

The blow that came staggered her with unbelievable pain, and she felt herself falling—knocked off her feet with such force that her teeth rattled and she hit the ground hard enough to stun. She lay there with cold snow under her cheek, her chest squeezed in searing bands of agony, her vision blurring as she struggled to focus on the impossible.

A huge dark form loomed above her, nearly black against the snow. Vast ragged plumes of hot breath condensed in the air as the huge grizzly spread its paws wide in a killer's embrace.

Joey had no time to consider her final moments of life; before the grizzly could reach her, an explosion of gray fury scattered the snow between them and hurled itself at the huge animal like a sparrow harrying an eagle. In the agonizing seconds that followed, Joey grasped only bits and pieces of the drama that played out before her: the low grunts and angry roars of the bear as it maneuvered to face its attacker; the snarls of the wolf that whirled like a demon about the bigger animal, and once a single yelp of pain as the massive claws struck home; the unmistakable smell of animal heat and blood; the cold caress of the snow that spattered her face. And always, over and under all of it, the pain that urged her not to breathe, to let go . . .

She tried to call out his name, to use that one word as a focus that might keep strong the desire to live. The sound caught in her throat, though her lips moved in the snow; she tasted blood. The hot flow of it traced paths over her temple and burned like acid into the chill white that cradled her head.

Perhaps it was the shock of seeing her own blood in the snow that enabled her to come back to herself. She clung to awareness and stared at the place where the deadly struggle had played out; the bear was gone. The snow was marked with the struggle, torn away from the ground to expose the raw flesh of earth beneath. There were dark splotches that Joey knew the deadly meaning of. She used the last of her will to focus, to search for the one thing she wanted so desperately to see.

The wolf was there, suddenly, filling her vision. Even now she could spare enough thought to admire it: the heavy coat in disarray, erect along its spine; the sheer magnificent size of the beast; the eyes that burned into hers with the familiarity of an old friend. Familiarity. Joey squeezed her eyes shut and slowly opened them again. The wolf was staring. But her eyes were playing tricks on her, because it was also changing. Changing so gradually and so subtly that it took several long moments before she realized the impossibility of what she was seeing.

She knew then she was truly dying. Only a bizarre end-of-life vision could account for this. Still she stared, unable to look away, while the wolf blurred and shivered and became something else. Something she could not believe and yet had no choice but to accept.

The wolf was Luke.

He was the last thing she saw as she let herself descend back into the peaceful sanity of oblivion.

Once again he had failed her.

He cradled her in his arms while her blood dripped into the snow, and for an eternity that single numb thought overwhelmed all the world. The howl that rose in his throat choked him, but it brought back sanity: the sanity of the need for survival. The sanity his wolf's nature demanded. The need to take his mate back from the embrace of his dark and ungiving rival.

He snarled as he lifted her and carried her back into the cave, defying death to take her from him. Enough of the nature of his man's form remained to enable him to find the first-aid kit, to clear away the clotted blood that matted her hair and streaked her body, halt the deadly escape of her life's blood before it could carry her away with it. He located the deep gash at her temple and bound it up, and then patched the lesser wounds, tearing up his spare shirt when the bandages ran out. Her breath came slight and soft, but it came; he paused to bend his head over her and call upon the spirit of life to keep that one steady rhythm unbroken. The cold certainty of her condition did not leave him, but when he had done all he could, he was able to gather up the vestiges of human logic and weave them into resolution.

There would be no time to run for help. He could not hope to carry her back to Val Caché quickly enough, and she needed more attention than he could give.

And he could not bear to leave her. He knew the risk of concussion was great; Joey might slip away from him and never waken unless he used every ounce of his will to keep her.

Luke closed his eyes and brushed his lips over Joey's, pressing his cheek against her forehead. "Joelle. Listen to me, Joelle. You must wake up."

He waited an agonized, endless moment for her to

stir, to respond to the insistence in his voice. Then he shifted so that her head fell back onto his thigh and gathered her face in his hands. "Joey. Wake up." Every instinct screamed denial as he shook her, lightly at first, and then with growing urgency. "Joey!"

She was silent. He knew she was slipping away, torn from him by that deadly rival who lured her with promises of peace and rest. His breath caught, and a sound escaped him that penetrated his fear. A sound that had never passed beyond the place deep in his heart, buried and savagely guarded, since childhood. When he felt the moisture gathering in his eyes spill over and the first drop fell, to tremble like a living crystal on Joey's cheek, something within him broke.

"Joey." He forced the words out past the raw pain that made them crack and waver. "Joelle, don't leave me." He tasted the strangeness of his own tears on her face as he kissed and caressed her. Her skin was cold and lifeless, the pulse in her throat so distant that he could feel her retreating with every beat.

With sudden fury the desperate helplessness that paralyzed Luke shattered and reformed within his heart; his muscles tensed with the need to change, but he did not submit to it. Instead, he drew on the spirit of the wolf within, drew on the determination to survive. The weakness left him, and the cold rage that was neither entirely wolf nor man locked it out.

His voice was a deep growl as he gripped her face between his palms.

"Wake up, Joey. Now. I won't let you go."

He thought he heard the slightest change in the shallow cadence of her breathing, and it fed the savage determination.

"I won't let you leave me, Joey. You're mine." The words grated in his throat like ground glass.

"Understand this, Joelle; as long as we live, we are

bound. And I'll do anything to keep you. Anything. Even if it means following you."

She trembled. It was almost imperceptible, almost something he could have dismissed as imagination. But the bond between them was too strong, his need too great. He slapped her, no more than a love tap; it shocked him to use even that much force against her, but he did it again. And then again, as he spoke.

"Do you want that, Joelle? Because I'll come after you wherever you are. If you don't fight now and come back to me, we'll lose everything. Both of us. It's your choice, Joey. Your choice." His last words were little more than a hoarse whisper—but they were enough.

This time the movement was unmistakable; her lips parted, her blue-veined lids fluttered so that dark lashes danced against the deep hollows beneath her eyes. She gasped in pain that he felt as if it were his own, so closely were they bound at that moment; he lifted her up and held her gently to his chest and rested his mouth on hers as if to breathe all the power of his double life into her.

Her body convulsed, and her eyes opened to fix unerringly on him. "Luke?" The sound was faint but gloriously lucid; Luke held primitive exultation in check as he warmed her with the heat of his body. "I did something stupid again, didn't I? I'm sorry."

Luke almost laughed, so great was his relief, but he nuzzled her ear and cheek to hide the emotions that warred inside him. "Joey. Joey."

No other words would come. He felt her lift her hand, stroke his hair lightly; her breath caught again in unmistakable distress.

"It hurts, Luke. I can't breathe—it hurts so bad." The childlike confusion in her voice pierced him so deeply that the rage returned and swept away the gratitude and joy, replacing it again with a feral and primitive purpose.

But he managed, somehow, to keep his voice gentle. "I know, Joey. But you must do two things—until we can take away the pain. You must breathe, and you must try very hard to stay awake." He gazed into her eyes and willed her to obey. "Do you understand, Joey? If you can keep breathing and stay awake, you'll be all right. I promise."

Joey shook her head, her eyes blurring and drifting away from his. "I feel so strange, Luke. I had dreams—" Her voice faded, and he gripped her chin again so that she could look only at him. She smiled, though her gaze was distant and soft, lost in some inner vision. "You would think it was funny, Luke. I saw a wolf change into you." Her breathy laugh ended in a crack of pain. "My dreams just keep getting stranger and stranger. . . ."

There was no time for this. No time to explain to Joey the nature of her "dream"—or of what he was. "Joelle, you must listen to me. You have been injured, and we'll have to get help for you as soon as we can." He shifted her in his arms, and the movement seemed to grab her attention.

"You won't leave me? Luke, don't leave me!" Suddenly there was such focused anxiety in her voice that he knew she had grasped at least some of his words. Taking great care not to put pressure on her damaged ribs, he held her as close as he dared, feeling the grip of her fingers sliding on his skin as she sought to hold him. Even in her weakness, determination vibrated through her. Joy swelled in his heart; he put it away in a place of safety like the rare and fragile thing it was.

"I won't leave you, Joey. Never." He murmured to her until she quieted and lay once again passive in his arms. The ragged gasps of her breathing slowed again. "I need to do one thing, to bring help for you. I need you to be strong for me, not to give in and to keep fighting. Can you do that?"

Joey searched his eyes, her own dark in the dim filtered light of the cave, almost black with pain and fear. "I'll try, Luke. I don't want to—to go."

Fighting back the vulnerability that had no place in what he must do, Luke kissed her brows. "I'll hold you to that, Joey. Keep fighting. Don't give in. If you do"—he drew a deep breath and stared into her eyes— "I'll go with you."

For a moment her face drew into a frown, as if she were trying to make sense of his final words; then she almost smiled, in spite of the pain he knew tormented her with every breath. "I never was one to go down without a fight." She closed her eyes and Luke let her rest, knowing he had done all that he could. Only one thing remained.

He lowered her slowly, with infinite care, down to the thick bed of dried leaves and needles he had made for her, wrapping her in his parka and the spare blanket so that no cold could penetrate. She opened her eyes once, but they were no longer fearful; there was utter trust in them, complete faith in his protection. In him.

That thought galvanized him with more determination than he had ever felt in his life—except for one time long ago; and that old resolve blended with the new until they were inseparable. Luke kissed her one last time, urged her softly to be strong, and left the cave.

He padded through the snow, ankle-deep in it, unheeding of the frigid bite on his bare feet. When he stepped into the center of the little clearing, the prints he left behind obscured the marks of battle, brushed over the scrambling footfalls of his other self; he noticed them no more than the wind that assaulted his furless, naked body on every side.

Closing his eyes, he willed the change. It hurt so terribly that he clenched his teeth, but he endured the agony of shifting through his muscles screamed in protest and every instinct told him that his body was not ready. The wounds he had taken from the grizzly tore and bled anew; resources exhausted by battle and need struggled to give up their last remaining shreds of energy.

It was just enough. He opened his mouth in a soundless cry that became a low growl of effort. His paws did not feel the cold under them; the heavy fur turned the wind away as he shook himself. The world was altered through his wolf's eyes, but his senses grew painfully sharp in that instant after the change. He could smell Joey—on himself, on the ground where she had lain, within the cave where she waited, trusting, for him to save her.

The thin veneer of humanity remained unbroken even while his instincts raged at him to run, to find the others and bring them back, to do anything rather than wait in helpless impotency. But he settled back onto his haunches and pricked his ears to catch the messages borne on the autumn air. He closed his eyes, lifted his head, and howled.

He howled until it seemed that his soul had been torn out with the desperation of it. He keened his demand and his need at the hard sky until he heard an echo: the achingly distant answer of his brethren.

He answered them and heard their acknowledgment. His feet gave out from under him, and he collapsed to lie in the cold; his pants of exhaustion coalesced into white plumes that danced and shredded apart on the wind. In spite of himself, his tail thumped in the snow.

Joey's scent came to him on a curl of the breeze. With a grunt he heaved himself up. He willed the change once again; he fought with it and pleaded with it.

It would not come. Snarling in frustration, he turned about on himself and smelled his own blood, the slashes that had weakened him beyond returning. He needed time to heal, time to renew his energy and the hot force of life that was the source of his double self. There was no other choice.

He turned back for the cave, recrossing the tracks left by human feet. There was fear; fear of the woman who lay within the cave, whose labored breathing and smell of pain struck him like a blow as he paused in the entrance. He sighed and forced his feet to carry him to her side.

She was awake. Her eyes were half-closed in exhaustion, but she saw him at once as he stood over her.

If she had screamed, or gasped in fear, or flung out her hands to ward him off, something deep in his heart would have died, though he would not leave her when she needed him. But her eyes locked on his and, for an instant, were clear as she murmured his name. "Luke."

Then the rich depths of her eyes clouded and glazed over, her hand reaching out even as her head rolled back among the leaves. "Stay with me, Luke." Her fingers clenched in his fur. "Stay with me. . . ."

As her hand slid back he went with it, easing down beside her until the length of his body stretched out along the blankets. With infinite care he rested his head on her shoulder; her hand stroked over him once more as she sighed and turned into his warmth. He shivered from nose to tail at her touch.

There was nothing but waiting after that. Joey rested fitfully, falling into brief periods of sleep from which he woke her when they seemed deep enough to be dangerous. He took great care not to do more than nudge her gently, but she never seemed afraid, even in those few times when her eyes focused on his. It was as if she saw only his eyes and knew him with the instinctive understanding that linked them on a level beyond mere human senses.

The sound of human voices woke him from a light doze. He lifted his head from Joey's shoulder and called out, a bark in place of words. They heard and answered. With a shuddering sigh, he gathered his strength for the long run home.

# Chapter 14

Joey felt the passing time like a string of beads, little hard fragments of painful consciousness linked by long spans of oblivion. Her body wanted the oblivion, but something in her mind refused it; she had vague memories of a familiar voice pleading and raging, commanding her to stay. Obedience came in spite of the lure of the void.

Even so, there was a price. Each breath was a torment, with bands of fire forcing her lungs to contract away from the pain. If it hadn't been for the voice, and the eyes, she might have given up breathing entirely.

And there were the strange visions. . . . Visions that swirled in and out of dreams and awareness without regard to the dictates of reason. The one thing that linked all of them was Luke. Luke, and the wolf. There were times when she could separate the things that had really happened—the attack of the bear, her rescue by the wolf—and the things that made no sense. And there were other times when the two flowed together indistinguishably, so that they seemed equally real. If not for the more demanding reality of pain, Joey might have questioned her own sanity.

As it was, it took all of her concentration to lock the agony away when the men came for her, lifted her onto the stretcher between them, and bore her away from the safe place. When she was aware, she could see the perfect black serenity of the night sky overhead, and sometimes the face she knew to the core of her soul would block out the glitter of stars, the green-gold eyes would capture hers, and she would hear the voice soothing and demanding and saying her name. Over and over, so she could not forget it.

She heard things that made less sense: the howling of wolves, the musical lilt of a language familiar but incomprehensible, the soft words that spoke of a bond more powerful than death itself.

A time came when the jarring torment ended, and she felt herself cradled against hard warmth, felt a soothing whisper of touch along her cheek as her body came to rest on luxuriant softness. There were more voices then, buzzing like flies; out of all of them, only one mattered. *His* voice was a constant, and even when the protective contact of his hand dropped away, she knew he was still there. She hugged that one certainty to herself through all the hurt that followed.

Turning on his heel for the hundredth time, Luke swung about and charged back across the small room. The others had left long before—even his grandmother, whom he had chased off with a warning she had the good sense not to challenge. He had not needed to explain himself to any of them. They understood already and knew well enough not to test him now.

His lip curled in a snarl. He knew he was behaving like a wild beast, without the dignity his wolf-spirit demanded. It made no difference. He had threatened

Collier—his old friend—with bodily harm, with violence if the doctor did not see to it that Joey came through alive and well. It said much for the man that he had stood up to Luke and had nearly managed to shame him with his calm assurances.

But Luke knew he was very close to the end of his rope. If Collier didn't come out of that room very soon and tell him that Joey was going to be fine . . .

The door swung open before he could finish the thought. He leaped across the room and slid to a stop as Collier closed the door behind him.

"Tell me."

The doctor did not flinch at the grating harshness of the words, or at the proximity of Luke's rigid body and glaring eyes. But he had the very good sense not to take the risk of keeping Luke in suspense. "She'll be fine, Luke. With a little vigilance and care she'll be good as new."

Only force of habit kept Luke on his feet. He drew a deep breath to steady himself. Collier made use of the slight withdrawal and continued, "It was very fortunate that I was here on my monthly visit; you did well in caring for her, but she needed more treatment than you or the village could provide." He paused to frown at Luke, his expression deeply thoughtful. "She's a strong girl. She hung on, and a lot of the credit goes to her. What I don't understand is how this happened, how you let her . . ."

Luke surged forward, twisting in midmotion to avoid slamming the doctor out of the way as he reached for the door. Collier stopped him, catching his arm before he could open it; Luke turned on the older man, holding himself in check, fighting back the almost nauseating waves of violent anger. His muscles vibrated with it, and Collier's eyes flickered uncertainly to the rigid muscles of Luke's forearm under his hand. But he held firm, and Luke willed the blinding fury away, the part of him neither wolf nor man that longed to hurl his old friend aside like so much chaff. Instead, he waited until he could make coherent sounds again before he spoke.

"I have to go to her," he said, hearing his voice almost even, almost reasonable. "Let me go, Allan."

He felt Collier register the warning, but the doctor met his eyes and stood his ground. At another time Luke would have admired, as he often had in the past, the older man's fearlessness. Now he was an obstacle that Luke was not in the mood to deal with. He prepared to wrench his arm away and shove Collier aside, but again the doctor forestalled him.

"She needs rest, Luke." The calm concern that had made his friend's reputation for an effective bedside manner caught Luke's unwilling attention. "She's been through a great deal—as you well know—and I've only just now allowed her to sleep. As it is, she'll have to be awakened every hour or two, because of the concussion; she needs all the rest she can get in between." Luke read the firm compassion in Collier's mild blue eyes and looked away, setting his jaw against a desire to ignore the doctor's gentle rebuke and common sense. After a long, tense moment he let his fingers slip from the door handle, pulling out of Collier's grip and retreating several paces across the room. His body demanded immediate, violent action, but he held himself still until the doctor relaxed and moved away from the door. They stared at each other; at last Collier sighed and settled himself on one of the carved stools by the stove, rubbing his forehead wearily.

"You did well, Luke, in taking care of her until we found you. She could have lost a dangerous amount of blood from the scalp laceration; as it was, the real danger came with the concussion. Thank God you handled that correctly and kept her breathing." Collier looked up, and Luke watched him steadily, focusing on the words that declared Joey safe. "The cracked ribs are exceedingly painful, but I was able to give her a direct injection of anesthetic. That'll help her to breathe until the danger of concussion is past, and we can move her to oral painkillers. In the meantime she'll need some careful watching, but she'll be all right."

Turning away, Luke stared out the cabin's single window, careful that the doctor couldn't see the effect of his words. The soft blanket of snow had created a fairy-tale village that might have been populated by heroic woodcutters or wicked witches. As it was . . .

"What I don't understand, Luke—how could this happen?" Collier's voice cut into his thoughts like a knife and twisted the blade. "I'd never have believed you'd have allowed her to be exposed to that kind of danger. Even if there was nothing else between you—I can't believe you'd be capable of such carelessness."

The absolute control with which Luke restrained himself sent a shiver through his clenched muscles, and the hair rose along the nape of his neck. He trapped the visceral ferocity of immediate response in his throat for those few instants of silence, hearing Collier's breathing accelerate, aware that the doctor recognized what he was seeing.

When he was certain of his ability to make the words form in sequence, Luke turned back to his friend. Reminded himself that Collier was his friend, and not an enemy.

"It was my fault," he whispered. In spite of his efforts he could not keep the subtle threat out of his voice. "I should never have taken her. But it's done now. Too late for your lectures now, Allan. Much too late."

He met Collier's eyes and stared him down; the doctor looked away, but it gave Luke little satisfaction. The energy that had gathered in his body like an impending storm demanded release, and so he began to pace, letting the force of it drain away. Fighting to keep it from turning on Collier in its irrational violence.

"Well." The doctor's voice was very soft. "It doesn't matter now. The point is that you did what had to be done, got word to us soon enough that there was no lasting damage. Had her injuries been worse, or if they hadn't been treated promptly, I would have had to try to get her to a hospital. . . ."

In a few strides Luke reached Collier, and his hands shot out of their own volition, dragging the doctor up from his seat. He held the older man suspended in mid-air, the sound of his own pounding heart loud in his ears.

"No hospital." He snarled the words inches from Collier's face. "Hear me, Collier. She's not going anywhere." The color had drained from the doctor's ruddy complexion, and his blue eyes were wide with shock; that rare sight alone almost disarmed Luke, but he felt himself shaking the doctor as he would a defiant rival. "She's not leaving me."

All at once Collier became a dead weight clutched in his fists. Turning his face aside, the doctor looked down, his breath very shallow, docile and yielding; Luke responded to the silent language instinctively. With trembling arms he lowered the older man until his feet touched ground again.

The primitive fury that had come over Luke was gone, turned aside by Collier's wordless appeal to the wolf nature within him. His fingers twisted free of the doctor's shirt as he backed away, forcing himself to settle into a crouch at a safe distance where he could steady his breathing and his racing heart. Collier sat absolutely still on the stool; his eyes were turned carefully away, but the tightness of his jaw and the palpable tension in the tall, wiry body revealed his anger.

Luke ran a hand through his hair and dropped his head between his shoulders. "I'm sorry." It was all he could do to say the words. "I'm sorry, Allan."

Collier looked up slowly. The color had come back

to his face, heightened by indignation, but with Luke's muttered apology the sharp edges of taut bone and muscle began to relax.

"I don't suppose," he said mildly, "you'd care to explain what that was all about."

Feeling a perverse desire to run away with his tail tucked, Luke compelled himself to meet his friend's eyes. It was a rare experience for him to find difficulty in matching stare for stare. "I can't—it wouldn't make sense to you, Allan."

"Oh no?" Collier leaned forward to rest his elbows on his knees and winced. "Next time you decide to go wild on me, son, do me a favor and give me a little warning." Luke flinched, but Collier was not finished. "So, you don't think I'd understand—after all these years, and given what I know?" He shook his head, tutting under his breath. "You're a lot smarter than that, Luke. And I know there's something very unusual going on here. With her." He nodded toward the door behind which Joey slept in blissful ignorance.

Resisting the impulse to fling himself to his feet, Luke sighed reluctant acknowledgment. "It's not something I can talk about, Allan. Even to you."

His carefully restrained answer should have been enough to discourage Collier from prying, but this time too much was at stake. He knew it when Collier would not look away.

"Try me." There was a sudden sadness in the older man's voice. "You used to come to me when you wouldn't trust anyone else. Have we both changed so much?"

Luke closed his eyes. "*You* haven't changed, Allan." He opened them again, and this time he fixed his friend with a deliberately challenging stare. "But now everything is different. You know more about us—about me—than any other Outsider. But there are some things you cannot understand."

"Because I'm only human?" Collier's lips curved up in a bleak smile. "There was a time I would have given anything to be what you are."

The memories that came with his soft words almost made Luke look away. "There were times when I wished *she'd* chosen you," he said evenly, concealing emotion. "But it's not always a matter of choice with us. Sometimes it becomes"—he drew in a deep breath and let it out again—"a compulsion. And once the compulsion has been fulfilled, there is no turning back from it."

He watched Collier's expression change with the first dawning of comprehension. There was a part of him that wanted Collier to know, all of it—to know and accept as he'd done long ago, surrogate father to a proud and angry boy. But there was no rationality where Joey was concerned. Even Collier was a threat, with his mild, reasonable words and desire to help. There was no reason in this and nothing of mild humanity. Even Collier could not be trusted.

There was no hope of keeping it from the doctor completely; he was far from a fool and knew the ways of the *loup-garou* as no Outsider ever had. But Luke had no intention of making it easy for him. Before the doctor could probe further, Luke was on his feet and headed for the outside door; by the time Collier had opened his mouth, he had turned in the doorway. "Let it alone, Allan. For your sake, and ours. Do your job and heal her—then let it alone." Even as Collier stood to protest, Luke forestalled him. "I owe you, Allan. For her life. I'll never forget that debt. But don't forget what I am. Don't make me forget what I owe you."

Collier's reply was caught behind the door as Luke closed it. He stood for a moment, letting the solid wood take his weight, until he could think clearly again. Then he looked out across the expanse of snow that glittered in the morning sun. He needed to run, to free himself of human emotion. There would be time before he could see Joey again.

He paused only long enough to discard the hindrance of clothing and was already running as the change began.

The sight of Luke made Joey's heart lurch awkwardly as he paused in the doorway. He was looking at her as if he had never seen her before—or as if he had never expected to see her again. The flood of memories, dreams, and visions that overwhelmed her in that moment demanded more attention than she could give them, with Luke there filling her sight—but the emotions focused into sudden clarity. Gazing into the shifting strangeness of his eyes, Joey lost the lines of division between them. There was receding fear, relief—was it hers, at her own lucidity after being so near death, or his? Was it her powerfully physical awareness of him that made her pulse race, or the echo of desire she saw in his eyes? And the other feelings, the ones she was half-afraid to name . . .

There was no more time for analysis, for in a move too swift for her to follow Luke was at her side, and she was in his arms. He said nothing, holding her so gently that she hardly felt her body being shifted so that he had neatly taken the place of her pillow. She sighed and closed her eyes. He was considerably harder than a pillow, but much nicer.

Luke's warm breath bathed her face an instant before he kissed her, the pressure of his lips on her forehead and cheek as light as the touch of a butterfly's wing. She felt the tension in his body, as if he were holding some immense power in check in an effort not to crush her; she almost laughed. With the anesthetic Dr. Collier had given her, it would be a while before she would know if someone punched her in the ribs. And for that she was profoundly grateful.

The serene comfort of feeling well and safe came on in a rush; she felt tears gathering in her eyes. A soft caress brushed a single escaping drop from her cheek.

"Joey."

His voice was achingly familiar but strange, catching oddly on her name. "You're safe now, Joey. You won't ever be hurt again."

She looked up slowly, into his eyes. "Luke . . ." She tried to find words, but the choking fullness of her heart made it impossible. The green-gold of those intense eyes was suspiciously bright, though they never looked away from hers. "I'm all right." She said it for him, but also for herself; he dropped his head to press his cheek against her hair above the bandages. He hadn't shaved, and the stubble of his gray-shot beard caught in the loose strands. It felt wonderful.

"Joelle." He breathed her name, and then again, as if to acknowledge a miracle. The big hands tightened where they clasped hers.

"I'm here," she murmured, sensing some profound need within him. "And I'm glad you're here, too."

There was a long silence; Joey basked in a feeling of such complete contentment that it was hard to believe it wasn't one of her fever-dreams or bizarre, fantastic visions. There were things she knew had not been dreams or visions: the one she remembered now made her powerfully aware of the feel of Luke's heat burning against her, and no amount of exhaustion or abuse could short-circuit that instinctive response.

It soon became apparent that the reaction was not one-way. She shifted and lay back, tilting her head to gaze up at the bunched muscles of his jaw. Freeing one hand from his, she raised it to trace over the hard edge of his chin with her fingers. The tension seemed to flow out as she touched him, though the definitive indication of his desire for her showed no signs of departing. Joey grinned in spite of the pull of stitches.

"It's all so strange," she began at last, settling back more comfortably in his arms. "The last thing I remember—before I started having the strange dreams—was throwing a snowball at you. Remember? I scored a direct hit." She couldn't quite keep the smug satisfaction out of her voice, but the memory of what followed was sobering. "And then—something hit me, very hard, and knocked me into the snow. I remember that it was a bear, but the rest gets pretty fuzzy. Except that it hurt."

Squeezing her eyes shut, Joey concentrated on the fact that most of the pain was blessedly gone. "After that, I guess I went in and out of consciousness; I remember seeing you a few times, but nothing really got through." Her frown made the stitches pull, and she smoothed it out quickly. "I had the strangest dreams, so real. . . ."

She broke off, as puzzled now as when she had first awakened to find an anxious Dr. Collier bending over her. "All I know is that you saved my life, Luke. Again. Thank you."

She could feel the growing tension in Luke's body as she spoke, warning her even when she could not see his face. "I *risked* your life. I almost lost it." His voice grated in self-condemnation, all tenderness gone.

Joey would have twisted in his arms, but he held her too tightly. "Do you think I blame you, Luke? Because we were attacked by a grizzly?"

His posture was still rigid with distress. "I should have seen it coming, just as I should have recognized the hypothermia. There was no excuse for my mistakes."

"Luke . . ." Joey bit her lip, wondering how to ease his strange sense of guilt. "Those things were beyond your control. You tried to warn me of the dangers, and I wouldn't listen. In any case"—she turned her hand in his to grip his fingers—"you're only human."

His reaction caught her entirely off-guard. There was an instant when she thought he would have leaped right out of the bed like an erupting geyser if it hadn't been for her inhibiting presence. As it was, the strangled sound he made might have passed for a bitter laugh.

"Only human. I wish I had that excuse."

As Joey puzzled over his meaning and began to formulate the obvious response, Luke brought his hand up to brush her lips, the touch of his fingers halting her desire to speak. For a moment she relaxed into the caress, forgetting everything less important. She had almost dozed off when he spoke again.

"Tell me about your dreams, Joey."

The question was so unexpected that the first image that came to Joey's mind brought swift heat to her face. Even though the reality had far outstripped her early, unwilling fantasies of making love with Luke, she was not quite prepared to share them. Not yet. It was a great relief when she realized it was the other, more recent, and far more bizarre illusions to which he referred.

"You're probably going to find this rather funny, Luke. But I guess it's not so strange when you admitted you have wolves for friends."

Luke was silent. Joey knew that the silence had meaning, as all his moments of stillness did. "It started," she continued slowly, "after the bear attacked. It was a wolf that saved me." She narrowed her eyes as if that would make the internal vision clearer. "That part was real, I think. Something drove the bear away. But for some reason I couldn't find *you*." The thought arrested her, and she twisted again to look up at Luke. "You were there. I *know* you were—I felt you." She shook her head in confusion. "What happened, Luke?"

His body shifted under hers. "Tell me what you saw, what you dreamed, Joey. Then I'll tell you." There was more behind his words than Joey could grasp, but she had grown used to his obscure comments. Even when they drove her to distraction.

"Well—this is the part that will make you laugh." Ducking her head in embarrassment, Joey watched his face from under her lashes. "I thought I saw the wolf . . . change. Turn into you, in fact."

The words came out in jest, but Luke did not seem to find the humor in them. His eyes had that lost, far-off expression, and his jaw was still tight with tension. Joey faltered. "Luke?"

"Go on," he said in a husky whisper.

Joey let out her breath in a long, shuddering release. "After that, it becomes very strange. You—after you had changed from the wolf—picked me up. Mostly I remember the pain, that I couldn't breathe, but I know you were there. I heard you talking to me—that's one thing that came through when nothing else did. Your voice." Warmth radiated through her, and she closed her eyes. "Your voice kept me going. I don't remember the words, but I knew you wouldn't let me go."

His arms tightened gently. "Never."

"Mainly I remember the pain, but there was one point where I heard howling—wolves howling—and after that when I looked for you . . ." Frowning in concentration, Joey wriggled her fingers so that they interlaced with Luke's, as if his hand held special significance. "I knew it was you, but you'd become a wolf again. I wasn't afraid—for some reason the fact that you were a wolf didn't matter. I think I slept after that, and eventually I heard other voices and knew help had come."

There was a pause in which the only sound was Luke's deep breathing and her own, almost in tandem. She tightened her grip on Luke's hand and rubbed it against her cheek. "You were there the whole time, Luke. I think if it weren't for you . . ." The words that wanted to come then frightened her. Before she might have taken refuge in anger, or behind walls that she had constructed out of fear and pain and loss. Those walls had crumbled in the cave with Luke, reduced to rubble so fine there could be no hope of rebuilding.

"So what do you think?" she said at last. "Do you suppose I've tapped into some primal symbolism here?" She disentangled her hand from his and separated his fingers to examine them one by one. "I don't suppose it's very flattering to be thought of as a wolf, considering the double meaning, even in a dream, but . . ."

"It was no dream."

It was not the words but the absolute conviction in them that struck her dumb. Then she laughed, even though she knew it was the wrong response—wrong because Luke was in deadly earnest. She felt it in every line of his body that contracted all at once into hard knots beneath her.

Somehow, without her awareness or cooperation, she found herself lying on sheets warmed to fever heat and Luke half a room away. She blinked and shook her head, disoriented and vaguely angry. Her hands plucked at the blankets as if to find in them the comfort that Luke had so suddenly withdrawn.

He was pacing the room in short bursts, all the smooth grace gone, a clumsy marionette with broken strings. When he stopped to fix her with his hard, familiar stare, she stammered out the first inadequate thought that came into her mind. "What did you say?"

His gaze never wavered. *"It was no dream."* He drew the statement out so there could be no misunderstanding, word by deliberate word. "What you saw, Joey, was real."

The breath caught in her throat, between laughter and protest. If there had ever been a time wrong for laughing, it was now, and she was not prepared to chance it again. But what he said made no sense. Surely it made no sense at all.

"Are you saying," she said at last, with a deliberation equal to his, "that you turned into a wolf?"

For the first time he looked away, jerking to a halt. If it were possible for a man to look more dangerous, Joey did not want to know about it.

"That's exactly what I'm saying," he growled.

Joey closed her eyes, trying to reconcile his utter sincerity and what she knew of him with the insanity of his words. There had been wolves—several times, with him, there had been the strange proximity of the animals, and she had come to accept that with remarkable ease. That he had somehow been accepted by them, as part of the wild land he loved. A mutual respect she had not found the need to question. And he had freely admitted the relationship.

But this . . .

"I know about the wolves, Luke," she said carefully, opening her eyes but not quite meeting his. "It never seemed as strange to me as it should have, your relationship with them—the times we saw and heard them."

Luke was suddenly there before her. "Yes," he murmured, his pale eyes glittering. "Some of those were *real* wolves."

She heard the words without comprehension. "And the rest are . . . *werewolves*?" She flung it at him without thought, finally giving a name to the thing he implied. And he answered with the same grim sobriety.

"We call ourselves *loups-garous*. It means essentially the same thing."

Joey realized then that her muscles were as clenched as Luke's, but she could not make them relax. "You are saying," she said very calmly, "that you are a werewolf."

"Precisely," He bit off the word. "And the bed you're lying in belongs to another."

A sudden and inexplicable rage gripped Joey, strong enough to make her gasp with it. "What kind of game are you playing with me?" She snorted, almost bitter. "I see. All of this was some kind of elaborate amusement for you, wasn't it? All that back-and-forth, agreeing to guide me, the cave—I'll grant that you couldn't have been responsible for the bear, although if you can talk to wolves, I suppose . . ."

"Joey." The growl of his voice wasn't even human. It paralyzed her in the midst of the tirade. "Be quiet."

The words might as well have been bonds of steel. It was as if her mouth were muffled, her eyes clouded, her senses suspended, so that she could do nothing but stare at him in impotent helplessness. His eyes seemed so cold that there was nothing so recognizable as mere anger in them. All at once she understood the source of his power, the same power that made the people of Lovell avoid him, that made him so capable of fascinating and repelling at the same time. The power of a predator over its vanquished prey.

"If you won't believe, I'll have to make you understand, Joey," he said from a great distance. "Everything you see and hear will be real. I didn't want to do it this way."

In a few quick motions he had discarded his clothing and stood naked before her; before her eyes he began to change. She had no choice but to watch in powerless fascination as the familiar planes and subtle curves of his body began to shift, blurring, making her blink when suddenly there was nothing there to focus on but a haze like the shimmering illusion of water on hot pavement. And then Luke's eyes were staring up at her, unchanged except in shape, from the face of a magnificent gray wolf.

She knew the wolf, knew it from countless shifting dreams and visions. Knew it from the first time when she had met it on the hillside; recognized in it the ghostly shape that had howled under a bright moon on the neatly manicured lawn of the lodge; saw in it the animal that had so conveniently come to her rescue by the lake. Just before Luke had appeared, with equal convenience, to take her back to his cabin.

Her eyes told her what her mind could not grasp. There was one absolute certainty, one simple fact that beat its way into her stubbornly incredulous brain. Luke's eyes. They were Luke's eyes. His heart was in them. And in the moment that indisputable reality struck home, the wolf flung back its head and howled.

The mournful cry wound itself around her, worked its way deep into her soul and pierced her heart. She knew that voice as she knew Luke's; it had penetrated her dreams, and in the dreams she had understood the wordless message.

She had only the barest instant of comprehension before the door to the room burst open and a little dark-haired girl plunged through it, hurling herself immediately at the wolf. At—even now, her mind could not quite form the thought. Even when she knew it was true.

*"Qu'est-ce qui n'va pas, Luc?"* Claire's voice was strident, and she flung her small arms around the great shaggy neck, burying her face in the lush fur. The wolf shifted to nuzzle her cheek, and then two sets of alien eyes turned to regard Joey unblinkingly.

Claire frowned at Joey. It was in that moment that the invisible bonds that held her snapped free, and Joey gasped. The full force of what she had witnessed nearly stopped her heart. It lurched and resumed its normal rhythm as everything settled into an inevitable pattern.

"Luke." There was no fear, only dawning wonder. "Luke?"

With a gentle push the wolf disentangled itself from Claire and padded to the side of the bed. At this proximity it—he—was so huge and menacing that any sensible person would have frozen instinctively into paralyzed shock. As it was, Joey saw her hand moving independently of her will, descending, hesitating just above the black-tipped fur of a massive shoulder.

The wolf pressed into her caress, and the green-gold eyes slitted with unmistakable pleasure. Her hand sank deep into the rich pelt, marveling in the texture. Her fingers remembered the feel of it, and suddenly she recalled a comforting presence when she had lain, dazed and hurting, in the cave. Eyes that had looked at her as these did now, from a distinctly inhuman face. She had known him then. Her heart had known when her mind had been too far away to interfere.

A small, warm hand stopped hers in its motion. Claire made a short announcement, demonstrating her words by crooking her fingers and scratching Luke just behind his large, triangular ears. With a distinctly human sigh of contentment, Luke closed his eyes completely and rested his impressive jaw on the edge of the bed as Joey followed Claire's example.

Lost in the marvel of it, Joey never questioned when the wolf became Luke in her mind; she hardly noticed when a tall, dark figure entered the room and stood silently in the doorway.

*"Papa!"* Claire's voice made her look up, and even in her bemusement she recognized Luke's cousin, Philippe. He regarded her gravely from across the room as Claire ran to him and demanded with words and gestures to be lifted into his arms.

"Are you all right?" Joey was more startled by Philippe's accented English than by the bizarre conclusions she had finally reached. The man's green-gray eyes flickered uncertainly from her to Luke and back again; there was tension in him, as if he were concerned but had no desire to interfere.

Interfere—with what? Joey hardly understood her own assumption, but when Luke moved out from under her hand and turned to face his cousin, the tension in the room grew palpable. She stared in fascination as, in absolute silence, wolf-Luke gazed up at man-Philippe; the hair rose along his spine, and a growl rumbled from deep within the impressive lupine body.

Whatever wordless communication had passed between them, it was enough to make Philippe back away, Claire squirming in his arms; he paused only long enough to glance at Joey before vanishing as silently as he had come.

There was almost no time to reflect on the little scene, for suddenly the wolf shape began to blur and shift again, and then Luke was standing in the center of the room, shaking himself like a wet dog. Wet wolf, Joey corrected herself, and the beginnings of an almost hysterical giggle threatened to break her nonsensical calm.

The sound bubbled up as a choking cough that had Luke by the bedside in an instant, his hands almost as hot as live coals on her face. "Joey!" he said sharply. She stared into his eyes—the exact same eyes—and wondered why she had so completely failed to see it before.

She reached up to take one of his hands, turning it over and over as if it alone could yield up the secret of what he was. Knowing she must look and sound incredibly foolish, Joey grinned at him and let the sudden tears spill over. "You could have warned me, you know."

His exasperated cry was muffled as his lips pressed into the hollow of her throat. She tangled her fingers in his hair and saw in it the variegated strands of black and gray and white that she had never recognized for what they were.

They rested there, each adjusting to the monumental changes between them, Luke with his head on her thigh while she gentled him with her hands as she had caressed the wolf he had been. For once in her life Joey didn't question. For once in her life she felt no need.

The suspended time of magical acceptance could not

last; Joey sighed as Luke straightened, his callused thumb hot on her skin as he brushed the loose hair from her eyes. "I'm sorry, Joey. I didn't know any other way to make you understand." There was genuine contrition in his tone, but also very real worry; he searched her eyes for something he feared to see—condemnation? Loathing? Something caught in her throat as a new realization came to her, the first of a series of realizations that tumbled one upon another like dominoes.

"Oh, Luke. I was stupid not to have seen it before. It's just that they don't teach us much about werewolves where I come from."

His rough chuckle almost managed to surprise her. "It's not an easy thing to learn, or accept—even for us." Abruptly his eyes grew serious again. "We don't choose this. It's in our blood, Joey. But we don't reject it either."

Again he was studying her with such intensity that she knew he needed her answer. "I will admit," she said softly, "that it will take some getting used to. But"—she grabbed his hand and raised it to her lips—"what I'm most worried about is how I'm going to repay you for saving my life—or my virtue—several times."

Luke's sudden grin was truly wolfish. "I'm sure we can think of a way." The warm caress of his words made her suddenly, achingly aware of the sleek curves and angles and planes of his bare chest so close to her cheek, and of what lay just out of sight beyond the side of the bed. The heat that flooded through her with the very graphic image had nothing to do with the natural warmth radiated by Luke's arms and hands against her skin.

As if she had spoken her thoughts aloud, Luke released her and dipped briefly out of sight to collect his discarded clothing. She suppressed the flare of disappointment; hot on the heels of desire came a far more prosaic sensation, and suddenly she had to lean back into the pillows to resist a sudden wave of nausea.

Luke reappeared, his shirt half-unbuttoned in a way that did much to turn her mind away from less pleasant considerations. He leaned over her, frowning. "Are you all right, Joey?"

She managed a smile in response to his concern. "I think I need to rest now, Luke." Her eyes began to close in spite of every effort to keep them focused on him. "I'm sorry . . ."

Luke muttered something savage in French under his breath. "I shouldn't have forced you to—"

Joey stopped him with her outstretched hand, fingers on his lips. He engulfed her hand in his own and held it against his mouth, the warm breath caressing her skin until it tingled. "I'm glad you did, Luke. And there's still a lot more I want to know. For instance, why . . ." Her words were lost in a yawn. This time it was his fingers that stroked her lips to silence her.

"I'll tell you everything, Joey. There will never be any more secrets between us."

"I'm glad," Joey murmured. Luke's hands caressed her, but in a way that subtly relaxed rather than aroused. She surrendered to it gratefully.

"Luke." She heard the familiar, urgent voice from a great distance, but it jarred the peaceful lassitude just enough that her eyes edged open, the room blurred between her lashes. "For God's sake, Luke, what's been going on here? I've been hearing . . ."

"She's sleeping." Luke's voice was a nearby rumble; she felt rather than saw him move away. "Whatever you have to say can be said outside, Allan."

"What are you trying to do to her, Luke?" Collier's voice was a harsh whisper. "Instead of letting her recover, you show her things she can't be ready to deal with. Have you already told her the rest, Luke—about the position you've put her in? What you plan to demand from her, because you couldn't control—"

The words cut off suddenly. "Out." The barely suppressed ferocity in the single syllable cracked like lightning. Then there were no more voices, no more words, and Joey was left with the fading sense of something not quite right. Something that had yet to be resolved.

That was the last troubling thought that carried Joey into healing sleep.

Bounding over broken ice left by the night's freezing rain, the wolves hunted. It had been a long time since Luke had run at the head of the village pack, and there was an exhilaration beyond human comprehension in being once again among his own kind.

The communication that passed between them needed no inadequate human words. It pulsed on a far deeper level. Among real wolves, the language was simple and straightforward; among the *loups-garous* there were layers of meaning that surpassed the tongue of animals, or of ordinary men.

Luke knew the hidden thoughts of his brethren, understood the subtle change of his position among them. Because of Joey. He had always held himself apart because he could not fulfill his rightful place as alpha, with a mate at his side, fathering children to keep the traditions and blood of his people strong. That task had gone to the others—but their blood was not as potent and pure as his. The weight of that responsibility, and the torment of their unfulfilled expectations, had kept him from the most essential part of what he was.

Now, as he gloried in the primitive joy of sheer movement, of muscles bunching and stretching, of air so cold that it trailed in ragged plumes behind them, he exulted, too, in the knowledge of the woman who had changed everything. Joey could not know—not yet—what she meant to him, or to the village. To the people, the *loups-garous*, of Val Caché, she was hope for the future. A chance to keep the bloodlines whole. To him—Luke spun on one of his hind paws abruptly, and the others followed without once breaking stride—to him she was far more than even they could understand.

It was easy to let himself imagine that she was there with the pack, running beside him; her pale fur would catch the sun like new-fallen snow, the delicately sculpted muzzle raised to taste the icy air. Her eyes—her eyes would be dark gold, overwhelming in the change all deeper hues. She would be incredibly graceful, laughing in the way of his people, nipping at him and bounding ahead with her elegant white plume of tail trailing behind. . . .

Luke almost stumbled, and Philippe, a black shadow against the snow, brushed his shoulder. For a moment they ran in tandem; the tension of the previous day's confrontation was long gone, for it was not in their nature to hold grudges among themselves. It was not the way of the wolf-spirit, and there were far too few of them.

Philippe had not forgotten his place in the pack as second to Luke, however, and after a while he dropped back as they slowed to a trot. The prey had escaped, as it so often did, and the pack would rest before seeking other game.

They paused on a rocky slope, overlooking the untouched sweep of forest that hid Val Caché from Outside. Home. It had been a long time since Luke had thought of it as home, because he had been afraid to settle there with his heart lost to hope of finding a mate, or of finding peace. The others milled about him, nuzzling each other or panting as they rested, but Luke did not notice. His senses were tuned to one thing, one woman who meant more to him than life it-self.

He lifted his head in a deep, carrying howl of joy. The others joined it, one by one, and the chorus reached up to the sky until the entire valley rang with his triumph.

# Chapter 15

Hobbling around the small room on Allan Collier's arm, Joey lifted her head at the familiar sound. She smiled, and Collier paused to glance at her; he steered her to the nearest chair and helped her into it.

For a moment Joey was content to sit quietly, out of breath and aching from the effort. She would have preferred to remain in bed, but the doctor had made it quite clear that only regular movement would keep her healthy and healing, warding off the danger of pneumonia brought on by her cracked ribs. There was still considerable discomfort in spite of the painkillers, but only time would mend that; the side effects of her concussion were almost gone.

"You're coming along very nicely, Joey," Collier said, echoing her thoughts. The howling had stopped, and Joey turned her full attention to him, her smile still in place. "I must admit you're an extremely quick healer, and I've seen some very fast ones in my time."

"I'm glad to hear it," Joey said with a grimace as a

deep breath caught her unawares. "Just don't expect me to make a good case study for you, Allan, because I have no intention of ever, ever, letting this happen again."

The doctor shifted, and Joey caught a glimpse of something in his face, something deeply uneasy beneath the mild amiability of his demeanor. "I doubt *he* would let it happen again," Collier murmured, almost too softly for her to hear.

Joey remembered then what she had put out of her mind: the hushed conversation between Luke and the doctor that had given her the sense of something not quite right—between them, perhaps with her as well. She hardly knew what questions to ask, or if Collier could answer them; would he be willing to speak to her of subjects Luke seemed all too eager to avoid? There were still too many mysteries. Until now she had been content to set them aside. Until Collier's expression reminded her.

She had just opened her mouth to speak when Collier said, "What has Luke told you, Joey?" His posture was relaxed, but she knew, without understanding her certainty, that it was all bluff.

She sat up straighter in the carved wooden chair. "He told me what he is." She watched Collier close his eyes and nod slowly, without surprise.

"That I know. It was all over the village the instant he howled." The pliant lips curved in a slight smile. "Rather melodramatic. I hadn't been sure—before—how much you understood. You didn't show any reaction that would tell me how much you knew, or remembered—and Luke's behavior was not quite reliable enough for me to guess how much he'd revealed."

Reflecting on the lightning-quick changes in Luke's temper since they had come back to the village, Joey could only nod. "I do remember some of what happened. I saw him change before—but I thought it was all a fever dream, and later I put it down to my concussion. Until he did it again while I was wide awake and didn't have any excuses—except, perhaps, losing my sanity."

"And that," Collier said softly, "is not in any doubt. It's all very real, I'm afraid. And I can only marvel that you can accept it so well."

Joey sighed, resisting the urge to scratch at the neat row of stitches on her upper arm. "I don't really have much choice." A laugh bubbled up. "I've always considered myself a realist, a skeptic. But it's hard to deny something that happens right in front of you." She looked deeply into the doctor's eyes. "And by the time I learned . . . what Luke is . . . I think it was too late to matter."

She dropped her eyes from the concern in Collier's and twisted her hands together in her lap. The sound of his sigh filled the moment of quiet.

"I see. I had hoped—I had wondered what was happening. Between the two of you . . ." There was a constricted quality to Collier's voice that betrayed his discomfort. "I'll be honest, Joey. I didn't think it would be any different with you than with any of the others."

Struck by his words, Joey looked up quickly. "I remember your . . . warnings."

He smiled. "I tried, even though I'm very fond of Luke. I've known him a very long time, as I'm sure by now you've guessed. But Luke—" His laugh was short. "Luke is, as you now know, very different. He never let any of his previous 'interests' touch his heart. Oh, he never hurt them, not in ways that would have done lasting damage to any of *them*. But, and I hope you won't mind my being very frank, my dear—when I met you, I knew he might be capable of injuring you in ways he could not understand."

Biting her lip, Joey tried to take it all in, all the things at which Collier had hinted. Some of them she had suspected before; that Luke's involvements with other women had been casual, and that she had been intended as just another diversion. But later, somewhere in the midst of their sparring, and then at last when they had made love, that had changed. Irrevocably changed—and not only for her. Her life had been turned upside down by Luke Gévaudan, but he had not emerged unscathed.

"When he called us to come for you, I knew it wasn't that simple. Not like the others." Collier's voice had become grave. "Joey, you have changed him. You have touched him in a way that no other woman has done. And I don't know whether to be grateful or frightened by it."

The ominous tone of the last sentence caught Joey's attention. "What do you mean, frightened? Allan, I'm very thankful for your concern. I still don't know what I did to earn it." Smiling, she reached for his hand and rested her fingers on it in a light caress. "It means more to me than I—sometimes I'm not good at saying these things." Collier turned his hand to grip hers reassuringly. "I've been obsessed with one thing for a very long time. That was all that mattered to me. Now—other things have come to matter too. And it's because of you and Maggie"—she swallowed—"and Luke." Shaking her head, she sighed out the words. "I wish I were better at explaining, but when it comes to matters of the heart, I . . ."

"I understand, Joey. You needn't try to explain." She looked up into his smile. "I'm more glad than I can say that you've found some—something that brings you happiness." He broke off, and his face changed as if he were about to say more; Joey felt the echo of unspoken words between them. But then he merely sighed and leaned back, stretching out his lean legs.

Retracing his earlier words, Joey examined the significance of everything he had told her.

"Allan—you said you've known Luke a long time. And this village—Luke said few 'Outsiders' knew of it. But you said when I first woke up that this was part of your regular monthly rounds." She cocked her head at Collier expectantly, and he pursed his lips with a nod.

"I am," he said slowly, "one of the fortunate few who are permitted knowledge of Val Caché. My relationship with the village goes back many years—as does my acquaintance with Luke."

"And you've known all along about Luke—what he is?" Joey leaned forward eagerly.

"I've known since before he did," the doctor admitted. "I knew his mother."

Everything stopped in the moment that Joey put the facts together. "Marie-Rose? You knew her?"

Collier lifted his head. "Luke has told you about his mother." There was wonder in his voice. "He never speaks of her. For him to tell you . . ." The mild blue eyes were bright with something that might have been hope.

"I know," Joey murmured, "that what happened with her hurt him deeply." The image of Luke speaking, soft and distant, in the flickering firelight softened her voice to a whisper. "But he never mentioned you."

"I'm not surprised. It's far more characteristic of him not to speak of it at all. As you said," he said sadly, "it hurt him deeply. But he never shows it. Except to you."

Joey savored the sudden warmth that rose to bathe her heart in gentle flame. It was still too new and too strange to take on the solidity of words. "If you knew Luke's mother—then you knew Luke as a boy."

"Yes." His eyes turned to stare blankly out the window. "I saw little of him for the first years of his life, when his father was with them. Later—" His voice caught. "Later, when he was alone, I was able to give him my friendship, and receive his in return."

"So he wasn't entirely alone," Joey murmured. All

the things Luke had told her settled into new patterns. "He had you."

"At times that wasn't enough." Collier turned back to her, his face drawn. "Of course, by then the village had accepted him, and he spent some of his time here. But as he grew older and saw more of the outside, his experiences changed him, and he no longer seemed to fit in either world."

Joey understood the sudden image that sprang to her mind. "A lone wolf."

"Yes." Half-smiling, Collier gazed at her without quite focusing. "And for him, that word has more significance than you can imagine."

Sifting through the things she needed to ask, Joey frowned thoughtfully. "Luke is . . . a '*loup-garou*,' " she said at last, molding the words with care, "but he said there were others. His mother—"

"Was what he is," Collier affirmed gently. "A lovely girl and a graceful she-wolf with fur as black as midnight." Concealing her start of surprise, Joey watched the doctor's face transform into that of a much younger man. A man speaking of a woman he loved. She could not find the words to reply, but he continued, "None of us knew what would happen when she chose Luke's father. We could not protect her after it was done."

All the questions dammed up in Joey's throat. The silence was filled with poignant memory, and it was some time before the doctor's eyes came back to hers, still brushed with the sheen of old grief. "I tried to be a kind of father to Luke, but he was a very high-spirited boy. He would only accept so much from me, or from anyone else. Until you."

Joey understood the deliberate change of topic, but she could not shake the impact of what Collier had revealed. She leaned back in her chair, ignoring the ache where her ribs pressed into the carved wooden rungs.

"Marie-Rose was a werewolf," she breathed wonderingly, "and this village—" She sat up again quickly. "Are all of them werewolves, too?" Claire, with her lightning-quick delicacy; Philippe, tall and brooding; bashful and studious Jean-Paul—and Luke's good-natured and rough-spoken grandmother? The image of Bertrande changing into a feisty old she-wolf was enough to dispel the sober tone of her thoughts.

Collier shook his head before the laugh could escape. "Not all of them—some bloodlines are stronger than others, and some have been lost forever. Sometimes the change skips generations entirely. Luke's mother carried the true blood, as did *her* father. There are enough adults now to make a sizable pack." There was a sadness in his tone, and Joey recalled the same sadness when Luke had spoken of his people.

"And the children?"

Dropping his head, Collier closed his eyes. "Until they reach puberty, we never know. The change is hard on them. Some simply don't change at all." At last he looked up, and his eyes were earnest with melancholy. "Each generation there are fewer children. Val Caché is growing smaller. Someday . . ." He broke off. "I fear the time of Luke's people is passing."

Swallowing the unexpected lump in her throat, Joey blinked. "I'm sorry." She thought of the people she had met, and of the children and Luke's obvious devotion to them, even when he would never have admitted it. It seemed strange that it should matter to her, that she could even accept the incredible story she had heard. But it *did* matter, and she did accept it. There was a thing deep in her soul that responded with such undeniable certainty that she had no choice. None at all.

"I'm afraid I haven't done a very good job of explaining things, Joey," Collier said into the quiet. "I'd hoped—this would be possible for you to understand. I am immensely grateful. . . ."

"That I can accept it?" Joey shook her head with a

wry smile. "Allan, I'm the one who should be grateful, to have a friend like you." She reached out again to grasp his hand; he returned the pressure gently. "Things have changed so quickly, sometimes I think nothing could surprise me anymore."

Gripping her hand more firmly, Collier searched her eyes. "If something does—if something surprises you, or frightens you—if you ever need any help at all, Joey, I want you to know I'm here."

Joey blinked away sudden tears. "I know. Thank you, Allan."

The chair creaked under him as the doctor shifted, loosing her hand as he rolled a kink out of his neck. "And now, I think it's time you do a little more moving around before going to bed. Don't be too overconfident—your body still needs plenty of time to heal. You're in good shape now, and since the freezing rain has ended I'll be able to call my transportation in to pick me up. I'm behind schedule as it is."

He rose, and Joey pushed herself up with a groan to grasp his arm. She walked with him about the room several times, and at last he said, "Have you given any thought to where you'd like to do the rest of your recovering?" His voice was cautious, and Joey looked up from the ground ahead of her feet to his face.

"You shouldn't push yourself too hard, since you do need time to heal completely—but in a week or so you can be moved out of the village. I would recommend waiting a few more weeks before making any lengthy journeys, however." The last words were almost a question, one that Joey did not quite understand.

Moving slowly to the side of the bed, Joey sank into the downy softness of the mattress while Collier examined her stitches. "I haven't thought about it at all," she admitted with a frown. "I—" The emotions that rode hard on the tail of the doctor's question made her falter. Luke—that was the first thought. Luke. She could not seem to clarify the sudden turmoil of her thoughts. She hadn't thought of "after"—not in all the time she'd been here in Val Caché.

She tried to think of going back to the lodge, going home—but even the word "home" made no sense. Not anymore. It sat like a leaden weight in her stomach and rose to constrict her throat so that no sound could pass.

"Hold still, Joey," Collier said gently. She realized then she had been shaking her head in denial of something she could not begin to grasp, let alone accept. She could accept the existence of werewolves, but this mystery within her own heart was beyond comprehension.

"Good evening, Doctor." In spite of Collier's warning she jerked at the sound of Luke's voice; when she looked up her eyes found his instantly, as if some invisible thread of emotion connected them beyond reason. The amber-green of his gaze was bright on hers. "Joelle."

She relaxed under the warm caress of her name. For an instant she was oblivious to Collier as he moved aside, his legs pressed against the bed. Then she looked away from Luke's compelling eyes and saw the tension that held the doctor rigid, facing Luke with focused wariness as the younger man approached the bed.

After the revelations of their talk, Joey could no more ignore her friend's demeanor than she could the mesmerizing heat of Luke's presence. She knew instinctively that there was much she still had no understanding of; the way Collier's eyes had grown grave as they followed Luke across the room was a testament to how very little she did understand. But she did not know what to say or do or how to ease the situation, and Luke's touch, the lightest brushing of her shoulder with his fingers, drove everything else from her mind. It was her body that was responding. . . .

"Don't forget, Joey." Collier's voice was gruff with strain. "If you need me—for anything—or if you have questions, I'll be here, or in Lovell." Joey felt Luke's hand pause in its caresses; she watched as he turned slowly to confront the doctor. For a taut, almost painful moment they regarded each other, and Joey knew there was threat in Luke's very posture—saw the older man try to conceal an unwilling flinch. It was Collier who looked away, to Joey, the sadness back in his eyes.

"Remember, Joey." He moved slowly away from the bed, pausing at last in the doorway. "Let her sleep, Luke." There was no surrender in his voice. This time it was Luke who dropped his eyes.

Collier was gone before Joey could answer. The bed groaned as Luke sat on the edge, the heat of his body radiating in almost palpable waves. She made room for him, sliding sideways so that the narrow bed could accommodate them both; he hesitated only a moment, and as he stretched out beside her she pressed against him, settling her head on his shoulder. His arm came up around her, careful of her ribs, and Joey forgot every concern that her conversation with Collier had raised in the blissful contentment that followed.

She knew she had dozed, lulled by Luke's fingers stroking her hair and by the steady beat of his heart under her cheek, when his hand stilled to cup the back of her neck. The oddly intimate touch made her shiver to sudden wakefulness.

"What did he tell you, Joey?" Luke's voice was very soft, but there was no mistaking the intensity in his question. Joey opened her eyes and splayed her fingers across his chest, feeling the undeniable quickening of his heartbeat.

"That's exactly what he asked me," Joey murmured.

Luke stiffened under her and relaxed almost in the same moment. His fingers slid into the hair along the nape of her neck. He held her in place with that slight pressure when she would have pulled away to look at his face.

"He explained more to me—about what you are.

About Val Caché . . ." She hesitated, biting her lip. "And about your mother. That she was like you." She felt his heart lurch and settle again into a rapid, even rhythm. "And about the children—" Reaching across his chest, Joey felt for his hand, remembering all that Collier had told her. "I'm sorry, Luke." She closed her fingers around his, as far as she could stretch them, as if somehow she could protect him from the pain he had suffered as a boy.

His hand turned to capture hers. "Then you understand, Joey." It was a statement of belief. "You understand how it is with us." For the first time he withdrew his hand at her neck so that she could shift to look at his face. "How it is with me." His eyes were bright and alien as they met hers. Not inhuman, Joey thought dazedly. Something *more* than human.

Her ribs were aching as she sat up and braced herself against him, but she ignored that minor discomfort when she saw the tension in his expression, the—fear, she thought with a start—of something beyond his control.

"I think I do understand—as much as any 'Outsider' could," she said, resting her palm along the side of his face, fitting it in the hollow under his cheekbone. He shuddered and leaned into her caress; his eyes flickered shut and opened again. "A lot of things that never made sense to me before have become clear. But there are still so many things I *don't* know, Luke—things I want to know. About what you are, and why you exist . . ." She grinned wryly. "I never was able to just accept things. I guess you know that by now."

"I know." The two words were heavy with meaning, but there was a faint smile relaxing the grim line of his mouth. He slid his arm around her and pulled her against him gently, and she settled her face into the hard curve of his neck where it met the arch of shoulder muscle. There was silence for a span of time; Luke's heartbeat had slowed again, but she sensed—she knew in the way she had learned to know Luke's body—that he was far from relaxed. There was something that remained undone between them.

She was ready when he spoke again. "Did Allan tell you—did he explain—" With uncharacteristic hesitation Luke drew in a deep breath and let it out very slowly. Again he held her in place so that she could not see his face. "Did he tell you how we—"

He got no further in his stammered question; without warning Bertrande appeared in the doorway, a wooden tray of food in her hands. She set it down without ceremony on a nearby stool, put her hands on her hips and regarded them both with gleeful satisfaction.

*"Hé bien, Luc, je vois qu'ça s'est arrangé ent'vous deux!"* The old woman's voice held the same tone of gloating satisfaction; she leered at Joey unabashedly. "About time. No excuse not to do your duty, boy—as soon as she is up to it, *bien sûr!*" Bertrande chuckled and rolled her eyes. "I have a feeling it will not take long with you two." She spoke to Luke in French, too rapidly for Joey to follow.

Luke growled something incomprehensible; he had gone rigid under her, and she was able to push free of his restraining arm to watch the exchange. Bertrande's words were a puzzle, and there was something under their surface, something that brought that strange tension into Luke's body.

*"Bon, bien*, I will leave you now." Bertrande's eyes had not lost their twinkle in spite of Luke's obvious discomfort. For a moment she focused on Luke intently, spoke to him in soft French that Joey only half understood. *Don't worry*, the old woman told him. And something else, about leaving . . .

Bertrande turned suddenly to Joey, and there was an incongruous touch of gravity in her voice. "Take care of him, Joëlle. Let him take care of you. You cannot refuse what you are." Then, with a final flashing grin, she left the room with a cheerful *"Bonjour."*

Luke was up and headed for the tray before Joey could demand an explanation. He busied himself with it far longer than necessary, and at last Joey sat up against the stacked pillows and cleared her throat. "I'm rather hungry, Luke—do you suppose you could bring that over here?"

His back stiffened, and he turned at once with the tray in hand; the lines of his face were tense and angry, smoothing before her eyes into the familiar, distant neutrality that meant he was hard at work pushing emotion far below the surface. Joey understood that process all too well. She contented herself with the fresh bread and cheese, sipping the broth and cold water until her hunger had been appeased. The hunger that remained could not be satisfied so easily. Luke hardly touched the food; he gulped down the water in one long pull and ignored the rest.

"I guess you prefer meat?" Joey offered cautiously after she finished her last bite of cheese.

She'd meant it as a joke, but Luke turned to her and answered gravely, "Sometimes we do—but we're as much human as wolf." There was a strange sharp tenor to the words, as if Luke were trying to remind her—or himself—of his double nature. That he was still very much a man.

Joey set the tray down carefully. "What was she saying to you, Luke—what did she say that made you so angry? And what did she mean about . . . not refusing what I am?" She watched his face as it flexed in a series of emotions too rapid to follow. His eyes were hard as chips of amber-green stone as they met her gaze.

"Do you want to know, Joey?" The words flew like splinters of that same cold stone. "Do you really want to understand what I am—what we both are?" Before she could answer, he shifted and grasped her upper arms in his hands, tight enough to hold without hurting. The tray clattered to the floor. "I'll tell you. My grandmother was congratulating me. Congratulating us." Joey opened her mouth, and his grip tightened fractionally. "Not for any simple or obvious reason. Not for any human circumstance."

Joey sat on her knees, held more surely frozen in place by the savage look in his eyes than by his hands. "She said," Luke continued with harsh deliberation, "what all the village knows. What even Collier understands. You and I—we are joined, Joey. From that moment in the cave. By the blood of my people, we have become mates."

She felt her mouth working, but no sound would come out. "Collier didn't tell you that, did he, Joey—that among my kind, there can be only one true mate. Once we have found that mate, the bond is for life. It *is* life, to us." His words came in a barrage, cracking like gunshots. "Something we share with the true wolves, but different, because we are human as well. But not entirely." His eyes glowed with an alien heat. "What we are means that we cannot mate and mate again as Outsiders do. Not once we've found the true bond. As I have with you."

Shivering in sudden, uncontrollable jerks, Joey struggled for comprehension. She heard the words, but it was his eyes, boring into hers with inhuman ferocity, that made her shudder with a primal fear beyond controlling. "Luke, I don't . . ."

He cut off her gasped attempt at speech with his mouth, stopping her lips with his own, the burning heat of them moving on hers in a kiss that held nothing of tenderness. Her body responded while her mind was still grasping helplessly at what she could not understand. He withdrew before anything other than primitive lust could penetrate her confusion; there was almost a smile on his face, a ferocious triumph that chilled her more thoroughly than anything that had gone before and doused the heat of her body with frigid lucidity.

"You see, Joey. You feel it, too. You are mine, and your body knows it. Your heart knows it and your soul, even when your mind resists." His voice had become so rasping that there was little of the man left in it. "She said we cannot fight what we are. I tried to fight it when I met you, once I knew—but it was already too late. For both of us." The restrained power in his hands gripping her arms could have snapped them like twigs. "We can't fight it. You can't fight what *you* are, Joey."

She felt the blood drain from her face. The last words penetrated like acid into the roiling confusion of her thoughts and emotions. Full understanding came all at once, and she jerked free of him so suddenly that his hands hovered in midair where her arms had been. She turned on him then, feeling such wildness within herself that there was almost no surprise when he dropped his eyes from hers, fleeing the savagery of her reaction. There was a power rising within her such as she had never known, so thoroughly overwhelming logic and rationality and all those careful human boundaries in which she had prided herself that there was no hope in fighting it. She let it take her. It was that terrible power that propelled her forward to thrust her face into his, no softness that would yield to him or to any weakness within herself.

"*I am not an animal*," her voice hissed from the mouth of that alien self. "I am a human being. I control my own destiny. And I don't belong to you." The savagery that welled up to choke her belied her words, but she hardly noticed the contradictions. She knew only one need: to refuse submission, refuse surrender, refuse to lose the last vestige of control she had fought so hard all of her adult life to gain, over emotions and vulnerabilities that could lead only to unbearable pain. Refuse his demands and his insane assertions, refuse the identity he tried to give her. An identity that would make her lose what little certainty remained in her life . . .

Luke was trembling so hard that his body vibrated in sympathy to her own, an unwilling connection between them even in the extremity of their conflict. His eyes were on hers again, his face so rigid that it might have been carved like one of his wooden beasts. They did not touch; the battle was one of locked gazes and will, unbridled power that Joey used without comprehension.

Some small, faint aspect of what she had been scratched feebly at Joey's frozen rage. It asked her why she could not simply turn and walk away, why she could not speak rationally and deny what could surely not be true, soothing Luke with words that brushed the surface and held him at bay until the time came to go back, resume the life she had known before.

But there *was* no before. Even as that distant rational Joey tried to reason, the new power pushed it back. The tiny voice became a breeze shredded by a blizzard: Why? Why are you so frightened? Why is this so unlike Richard, so unlike everything you've ever known? Why does this man who is not a man make it impossible to use all the safe, sane explanations that protect you from hurt? Why is there so much pain—the pain that only comes with something called love. . . ?

"No," she gasped. The realization shattered both feral rage and distant voice in one terrible blow. Joey jerked back and away, a marionette suddenly cut loose from all familiar support—even the final surety of a carefully warded heart. She fell back, floundering, drowning in loss, and it was Luke's hands that caught at her and kept her from falling. There was no strength left to fight. She panted against him as he drew her into his arms, so drained of all sensation that even her treacherous body did not react to his nearness.

When her gasping had eased, she felt herself moved, set back from the support of his body, her chin tilted up so that her eyes had no choice but to follow. Even through the utter blankness of her mind she could see the pain in his eyes, as blatant as the raw, bleeding place within her heart where the living walls had been torn away.

"No," she said hoarsely. "This is too much. I can't. I can't . . ." She tried to pull away, but he refused to release her. "Let me go, Luke. Let me go."

"Oh, Joelle." The words were dredged up as if each one carried its own burden of despair. "I can't let you go. I wish I could make you understand. I wanted you to stay with me for your own reasons. I hoped . . ." He cut off with a snap, and a glaze of coldness filmed his eyes when he opened them again. Suddenly there was no more sadness. Nothing but the tearing pain that echoed hers.

"I don't understand what's happening," Joey whispered, turning inward, escaping his burning intensity. "I need time to think. I need to . . ."

"You won't leave me, Joey," he insisted in a raw, tormented whisper. And he caught her face in his hands, turned his gaze full on her then, that stare she had first seen in the tavern uncounted ages ago in another life. She knew the stare as she had recognized the stirring of that new and terrible power within herself; she knew it even as she felt the first effects of it, and something within her struggled to resist. But there was no more strength. No more will to fight the compulsion of those eyes and the things they promised and demanded. Joey felt her gaze unfocus, was pulled surely and inevitably out of herself to a place that offered peace and safety and protection from the turmoil her life had become.

When he released her, she lay against him as weak and helpless as a newborn kitten. There was no desire to do anything but be held in his arms. All the fear was gone, but Joey could no longer remember what it was she'd been afraid of; it all seemed nonsensical and unimportant. She was where she wanted to be. She felt Luke's warm breath stirring her hair, his hands caressing her back until her eyes began to drift closed of their own accord. So tired . . . and she was safe. Luke was there to take care of her.

"I'm sorry, Joelle." Luke was very far away. "I'm sorry." And she felt him bury his face in her hair as the meaningless words carried her to a place of peace.

Luke sat on the floor against the wall, willing his heart to slow and the instinctive reactions of his body back under sentient control. The shame he felt for what he had done choked him again and again, but there was no question of going back. No point in asking himself how he could have done it differently, better—so that she would have stayed of her own will.

He tried to tell himself that she would not suffer for it. Her clear intellect, her range of emotions, those would remain untouched. She would not lose any part of herself that was true, or forget anything that had meaning. Not permanently. He had helped her—to live as the wolf lives, as most of his people did—one day at a time, without dwelling on a past that could not be changed, without the fear of an unforeseeable future that so often poisoned the lives of Outsiders.

It had poisoned his life as well. He feared that unknown future so deeply that he stole part of his mate's very will and locked it away where she could not find it. Hid it from her so that she could not make the choice to leave him. A choice he could not accept and dared not risk. The choice his father had made, that had killed his mother.

He slapped his fist against the dusty floorboards so hard that his bones ground together with shooting pain. Having lost himself so completely, he had bungled the one thing in his life that should have brought joy and wholeness to both of them. For he knew that Joey felt it too—but not with that cool rationality with which she had always kept the world at bay. With the deeper needs she did not dare to acknowledge within herself, the same needs he had, an empty void of heart and soul that only he could fill.

As only she could fill his. . . .

He heard Collier's quiet step and smelled him before the doctor opened the door. Luke didn't feel the cold that flooded the room, overwhelmed as it was by a far more biting inner chill. He looked up bleakly as Collier closed the door behind him and leaned against it to regard his younger friend from the illusory safety of a few meters' distance.

"Don't worry, Allan," he said with an astringent smile. "I won't bite you." His tone belied his words, but it seemed reassurance enough for Collier; the doctor moved closer and settled on the stool nearest the hearth. Luke took in the tense posture and smell of apprehension. Collier, he reminded himself again, was not the threat.

"I've called in my transportation, Luke," Collier said with careful neutrality. "He'll be out to pick me up this afternoon." There was an expectant silence; Luke only stared, and at last Collier cleared his throat and continued, "I shouldn't have stayed this long, but the freezing rain and fog kept Walters grounded; Joey's out of any danger now, and I'm urgently needed back in Lovell." He stopped again and shifted on the stool, the slight movements and twitches of his normally placid frame revealing his unease.

"Then go, Allan. I'll take care of Joey." Luke's voice was harsh, but he could not soften it; the edge of his guilt and need and anger had honed it to such sharpness that it cut the inside of his throat. With deliberate effort he remembered his debts. "I told you before—I'm grateful, and I won't forget. You saved her." Honesty and the memory of a former closeness compelled him to admit what Collier surely understood. "You saved both of us."

"Does she know?" Collier spoke so quickly that Luke knew that one question had been his sole purpose, why he regarded his almost-son as he might an unpredictable, half-tamed beast. Which, Luke thought grimly, he was. Without intending it, Luke bared his teeth in an entirely humorless expression that was far from human.

"She knows." The half-lie came with remarkable ease. It was a matter of survival, and it was the wolf-spirit that pushed aside the useless guilt. Even the human part of him knew there was some truth in it. She had known—for a moment she had truly *known*.

Collier almost relaxed, but his eyes were still wary and searching. "Does she really understand, Luke? What it will mean to her, how it will change her life?" Biting back a snarl, Luke turned away, but Collier's voice was relentless.

"She must have a choice in this. You must allow her to choose her own destiny, Luke. She didn't grow up all her life preparing, hoping for the possibility of what has happened." Luke shut his eyes as if that small act could keep out the words.

"Do you think I can't comprehend your feelings, Luke?" The older man's voice was suddenly warm with compassion. "I do know. I wish I didn't. I wanted so much . . ." He broke off as his voice caught, drew in a deep breath, and continued.

"Even your mother had to make her own choice—"

"And it killed her," Luke snarled. Suddenly the bombardment of self-loathing became so great that the only defense was to turn it outward against the only available target. "You think *you* understand?" He fixed the full power of his stare on Collier, showing his teeth in contempt. "You know nothing about it. You wanted a woman you couldn't have—because you don't carry the blood. *She* had no choice at all. As I have none."

The doctor flinched, jerking away in an instinctive need for flight. Luke watched him settle deliberately back, the pale blue eyes narrowed with slow-wakening anger. "You're afraid, Luke—and so you hide behind this compulsion as if you're not human enough to control it. But I know better." The last four words were blows. "You're not an animal, Luke. You're not merely a creature of instinct. And she is worth far more than what your instincts would make of her—a female to carry on your bloodline and bear your cubs." He used the term intentionally, and it had the desired effect.

Luke sprang to his feet before he could will himself to stop and halted a bare instant before he could hurl his old friend across the room in his rage. His fingers were curled into claws, but he kept them at his sides until he could trust himself to answer.

"Damn you, Collier. That isn't what she is to me." He swallowed the bile that had dammed in his throat and cut off the stream of imprecations that rose to take its place. "She is . . ."

The words wouldn't come. He jerked his eyes away from the expression on his old friend's face, unable to bear the pity he thought he saw there.

"You can't force love, Luke. It comes in its own time and in its own way. If you try to force it—if you hide behind lesser things and hope they will be enough—it will die before it has a chance to grow."

Luke felt Collier's hand on his arm and had no will to shake it off.

"You don't have to tell me what she means to you. But don't make the terrible mistake of destroying what you may have found. Don't let your fear and your need replace the only thing that matters."

With deliberate calm Luke stepped back. Collier's

hand slid away. He stood there, absolutely still, until the hairs along his neck lay flat and the desire to attack and rend was reduced to no more than a twitch in his fingers. When he looked into Collier's eyes, he was almost composed.

"She wants to stay, Allan." He heard the evenness of his tone with bitter satisfaction. "Of her own will, she wants to stay with me."

This time the lie was complete, and it sealed the terrible guilt behind unassailable walls. The needs of the wolf-spirit, he told himself, demanded it. But it was the fully human part of him that could so twist reality to suit his own desires. As he had bent her will to his.

Sighing heavily, Collier dropped his eyes. Luke braced himself for accusations, but none came. "I have no right," he said softly, "to interfere with your life. But I will speak to her before I go, Luke—to make sure everything is all right." When he looked up again, his eyes were bright. "I care about her, too. As I care about you."

He was up and turned away before his words could penetrate Luke's icy calm. Luke could see only his long physician's hands, clasping and unclasping behind his back; with deliberate care Luke moved to place himself by the outer door, leaving the way to Joey's room unimpeded. "Go. Talk to her," he offered tonelessly. "Ask her yourself. And then leave us in peace."

Collier turned slowly to regard him, and then his gaze slid away as he walked to the connecting door. There was only the slightest hesitation—his hand tightened on the doorframe, as if he would turn and speak—and then at last the older man stepped through.

Unmoving where he stood, Luke listened. He could have perceived every word spoken had he chosen to do so, but it was enough to hear the tone of them: Joey's light alto, Collier's baritone stripped of its usual ease. It was a short conversation; when Collier reappeared, his face was drawn and strange, and he looked at Luke long and searchingly.

"It seems you were right, Luke," he said, his eyes never wavering. "Or so she says."

Luke felt his skin shiver where absent hair tried to stand on end. "Then you've done your duty, Allan," he said very softly. "You can leave her in my hands."

"Can I?" Collier whispered. He stood in the doorway as if to guard the woman within. "How well have you taken care of her, Luke? Have you really left her with any choice at all?"

The words struck at Luke so savagely that he almost changed then and there, the stress attempting to shift his muscles into a form made for instinctive response. Instead, he molded the power into one single unerring focus, turned it on Collier, and loosed it as he had done before.

"Listen carefully, Allan. Joey wants to stay with me. She is happy and has no desire to leave." He laid down the compulsion carefully, refusing to think, rejecting the human shame that would have stopped him. "When you return to Lovell, you will know that she is safe and well. Nothing is wrong; if you are needed, you will come, and you will see everything as it should be."

The blue eyes trapped by his were glazed; Luke tried not to see Joey there, and what he had done to her. "You will tell no one that she is with me, Allan. If anyone asks, you'll say she was taken to the hospital in East Fork and flew home from there. Do you understand?"

Nodding slowly, Collier leaned heavily against the wall as he began to shake. Luke recognized the signs; Collier was fighting the compulsion, unable to break it but aware in some distant part of himself what was happening. It would make no difference. Luke lifted his lip in self-contempt. How easy it was to control them when he wished to, and how ironic that the two people he loved most in the world were the first to be so privileged.

He turned away before he could strike out in blind rage, and as the contact broke, he saw Collier stagger and drop into the nearest chair.

It took some time before he could smooth his expression and pretend as if nothing at all had happened. He forced himself to sit on the stool Collier had vacated earlier and regarded the doctor across the room. "Didn't you say you had a ride to catch this afternoon?" he said with a lightness that tasted like acid bile on his tongue. "You'd better be going; I think I hear the plane."

Still half-dazed, the doctor blinked. He tilted his head and nodded slowly. "Yes. It's strange . . . I don't know what came over me just now." His eyes cleared; a hesitant smile replaced the slack expression on his handsome, weathered face.

"You worked hard to help Joey, Allan," Luke said, sincere in spite of his bitter self-contempt. "I hope you'll find time to get some rest. You've earned it. There's nothing more to worry about here—I'll take good care of Joey."

"Yes." Collier blinked, and for an instant his brows drew together in a frown. Luke tensed expectantly, but his friend relaxed again almost at once. "Well, I definitely hear my transportation, and I have a kilometer to walk yet." He stood up, leaned sideways, and caught his balance with a chuckle. "I must be getting old."

"Not you, Allan." Luke rose and moved to steady Collier; the doctor gripped his arm with obvious affection, and it was all Luke could do not to curse himself aloud. "I'll go with you, at least to the edge of the clearing."

With a grin the older man let himself be led to the door. "If this were an ordinary French-Canadian village, I'd swear my cider had been spiked with some particularly potent strain of moonshine." He leaned against

Luke heavily. "But I've never known any of you to drink anything stronger than water."

As he turned the conversation to Joey's care and recovery, Luke closed his eyes briefly in silent thanks. For the moment he was safe. Collier was well and truly persuaded that all was as it should be. By the time he broke the influence—as he inevitably must, being the man he was—it would be too late to make any difference at all.

Chapter 16

They said their good-byes where the villagers had first greeted them, at the outskirts of the village where children ran in energetic circles about them in the slushy snow. Joey leaned on Luke's arm, returning the smiles of Luke's people and feeling almost sorry to be going. She'd almost gotten used to having most of the conversations go over her head, used to the lyrical sound of a foreign tongue filling the air like the chattering of exotic birds. She resolved to ask Luke to speak French more often, just because she liked the sound of it.

The young men flanked them, on either side of the makeshift litter they'd assembled for her. Allan had made clear that, while she was fit enough to be moved, a hike up and over the ridge and back to Luke's cabin would tax her healing body too greatly; Luke had found plenty of volunteers willing to help him carry her when the going got rough. Joey felt faintly embarrassed at her own helplessness, but the grins and winks of the young men, and their cheerfully incomprehensible comments, made it impossible to feel ill at ease.

The farewells were effusive and noisy, accompanied by hugs and slaps and punches, though the ones directed at Joey were restrained in respect for her injured ribs. But there could be no doubt, now, how thoroughly she had been accepted by them, and the knowledge warmed her beyond all reason. Gone were the cold, staring, suspicious eyes; the pack had taken her in.

It made it doubly hard to leave, except for Luke. There was one thing she wanted more than to stay, and that was to get Luke alone.

Claire darted out from a tumbling mass of children and hurled herself at them both, scooting aside at the last moment to avoid jarring Joey and colliding full force with Luke's legs. *"Es-tu obligé de t'en aller, Luc? Pourquoi Joëlle et toi vous restez pas?"* Joey heard her name, said with such familiarity that she felt a stab of unexpected emotion. Even Claire accepted her. As Luke murmured a reply and ruffled the girl's midnight hair, wide eyes turned to regard Joey. The little girl chattered its rapid-fire French.

Joey felt heat in her face as she picked out a few pertinent words. *Bébé*—she'd definitely heard the word "baby." Involuntarily she glanced at Luke, whose expression seemed to smile; but there was no real warmth in it, and it never reached his eyes. Did that grim coldness mean he didn't want children? Did *she*? They were questions she didn't want to consider, not now. Too difficult to dwell on the future, on events that had no meaning in the present. *Now* was all that mattered.

The certainty and rightness of that conclusion made her long to pick the little girl up and swing her about, but Claire had already vanished again, her breathy goodbye lost in the general clamor. Joey contented herself by slipping her arm around Luke's waist and breathing in the smell of him. She could not remember any time in her life when she'd been quite this happy—but it took too much effort to think of the past. The past was gone, and memories were of little use to her now.

One by one the others made their farewells: Philippe, whose grave face cracked into a smile for her; Jean-Paul, who flushed deep red as he stood on his toes to offer her a kiss on each cheek; others she had met and had only begun to know, until the last of them came forward— Bertrande of the ever-present smirk and knowing eyes.

She spoke to Luke, who nodded gravely and replied in monosyllables to her raspy monologue. Joey could feel the tightness of his muscles; she consigned it to that same tension he always seemed to display around his grandmother—something, undoubtedly, to do with the village pack pecking order. That was something else she had only begun to understand, but there would be a time for that another day. She ran her hand up and down Luke's back to soothe him, but the tautness remained as Bertrande turned her sharp blue gaze on Joey.

"You are one of us now. Never forget. *J'vous souhaite beaucoup d'bonheur et beaucoup d'enfants.*" The old woman's eyes were suspiciously bright, though she turned away before Joey could see tears. Bertrande muttered one final string of words at Luke, and turned away without another glance at either of them.

Joey looked up at Luke's face in time to see the muscles of his jaw bunch and relax again as he watched his grandmother's retreating back; it was a long moment before he was aware of her scrutiny. He smiled, and this time there was real warmth in it, though there was an echo of something else she could not quite understand. "Are you ready to go, Joelle?"

Joey looked around one last time, at the people who raised hands in farewell as they turned back to their daily tasks. The fragrance of woodsmoke and breakfast mingled with the sharp scent of conifers and a brisk autumn morning; it was the smells she thought she'd carry with her until they returned. She smiled up at Luke. "I'm ready if you are."

With his arm around her to steady her, Luke nodded at the three young men, and the five of them set out among the trees. They were going home.

Home . . . Joey tasted the word as half-melted snow slid and whispered under her boots. It would be good to be home, and to have Luke entirely to herself.

The journey to Luke's cabin, fourteen miles over rugged terrain and up and down a mountainside, was made in a day. Luke and the other young men were virtually tireless. They moved so rapidly and smoothly that she felt no jarring but observed the land moving by in a blur; it was almost a shock when they were suddenly there, the setting sun bathing Luke's cabin in orange light.

They set her down before the cabin door. Luke helped her up, and she cautiously stretched cramped muscles, wary of stitches and healing ribs, while Luke made his farewells. She was rubbing her eyes and yawning when the three young men, calling out cheerful and undoubtedly suggestive good wishes, stripped without inhibition and began to change. The process was still too new and wonderful to be taken for granted; Joey froze and watched in fascination as blurred human forms took on the shape of wolves, one black and two gray, who milled about them for a moment with yips and barks before turning as one to dash across the clearing for the trees.

Luke's arm slid around her shoulder. "Does it frighten you?" he asked softly. Joey heard the unspoken plea in his voice; she reached up to grab his chin, rubbing her fingers over the rough texture of it.

"No, Luke," she whispered. "It's part of what you are." Before he could reply, she had pulled his head down to hers.

It was the first real kiss since the cave. Luke's response was immediate and definite. If she had initiated it, he was more than ready to take over. His arms pulled her against him, so tightly that every available inch of their bodies touched; his lips came down hard and softened when she responded with an enthusiasm that matched his own. He caressed her with his tongue, and she returned the favor by catching his lower lip between her teeth, tugging gently until he pulled free and took her mouth again so thoroughly that her breath stopped. It was only when his arms tightened in an effort to bring her impossibly closer that she was aware of anything else.

"Luke!" she gasped as painful reality intruded. "My ribs!"

He released her immediately with an oath, burying his face in her shoulder. "Joelle—I'm sorry," he mumbled into her skin.

There was such stricken remorse in his voice that Joey felt an overwhelming surge of protectiveness. She held his face against her and stroked his hair, ignoring the awkwardness of the position. His hands smoothed and caressed her sides as if to ease the discomfort, but the stroking touch had quite a different effect.

After a moment, when the ache of her ribs had eased and the other had built to an almost unbearable pitch, Joey laced her fingers in his hair and pulled his head up. She kissed his chin.

"I have an idea," she said with an imp's grin, "that should make us both feel a whole lot better."

Luke's slow smile revealed his understanding; his pale eyes were hot with desire that she could read as surely as the more obvious indications. "I will do anything in my power to make you feel better, Joey." His hands slid up to her shoulders, thumbs drawing lazy circles on her collarbones where the edges of her shirt parted.

"Oh, this is most certainly within your power," she assured him, shivering. "But don't think it's going to be a one-way experience, mister—the idea I have in mind will definitely take two participants." Suiting action to words, she reached down to touch the most blatant expression of his arousal; he let his breath out in a long sigh as her fingers traced the outline of it through the heavy fabric.

"I want you, Joey," he breathed. His hands tightened on her arms, his breath coming hard as he looked into her eyes.

She ended her teasing to slide her palms over his hips and up the broad expanse of his back, feeling the vibration of his rapid heartbeat. "And I want *you*, Luke—as soon as possible."

He almost crushed her against him then, but his face abruptly lost its intensity as he set her back down.

"But, Joey, your ribs . . ."

"I'm a fast healer—remember?" She stared challengingly into the glow of his eyes. "That's what the doctor said. And it so happens that I'm quite sure I won't feel entirely well again until I've had a great deal more exercise. The kind I have in mind requires a certain amount of cooperation from you. I'd rather not waste the time— but if necessary, I'm perfectly willing to convince you that I'm as up to it as you are."

She dropped her eyes significantly, and whatever resistance Luke had felt obliged to put up fell rapidly by the wayside. With a wordless growl that might almost have been her name, he swept her up in his arms and made for the cabin door, leaving the packs and litter on the ground behind them.

The door was unlocked as he kicked it open, but the cabin was bitterly cold. The temperature had a slightly dampening effect on Joey's ardor, but it soon became apparent that Luke had matters well in hand. He deposited her on the bed, threw several blankets over her, and disappeared into the adjoining kitchen, where the sounds indicated a very rapid session of fire-building in the cooking stove. Anticipation kept Joey patient as she huddled under the blankets; weariness claimed her in spite of it before Luke came back to waken her with his warm breath and the touch of his mouth on hers.

"Is it warm enough, Joey?" he breathed against her lips. The heat of his body made it impossible to judge; she flung off the blankets and pushed into the solid wall of his chest, savoring the masculine scent of him as her lips found the hollow of his throat.

"Oh yes. It's definitely warm enough." She felt him shudder as her tongue stroked along the concavity between the tendons of his neck. "In fact, it's getting so hot that I don't think we need all these clothes."

Her fingers suited actions to words, carefully undoing the top button of his shirt. The rough hair of his chest tickled her nose as she kissed the skin revealed. She unbuttoned her way down, trailing kisses until she could tug the tails of his shirt free of his trousers, her palm lightly brushing lower where his body's reaction was shamelessly evident.

"Joelle," he gasped, but when he would have returned the attention, she slipped out of his grasp and maneuvered him awkwardly but firmly back down onto the bed. His resistance was token at best; Joey grinned triumphantly and straddled him.

"You see?" She straightened her arms and spread her palms on his chest, sliding them over his burning skin to push the shirt to either side. "The idea is that I can get my exercise without having my ribs crushed. Don't you think it's a good one?"

Luke's expression was answer enough, but he managed a somewhat dazed smile. "An excellent idea. But . . ."

She silenced him with her fingers, stroking over his

lips until they relaxed and his tongue darted out to touch them. "Right now," she said in a husky whisper, "I'm afraid you'll just have to restrain yourself from anything that might aggravate my condition."

As she spoke, she began to move her hands over the hard, ridged planes of his belly and chest, light sweeping caresses interspersed with deeper pressure to work the tension out of his body.

At last he sighed and closed his eyes, giving himself up to her ministrations. "I can tell," she continued gravely, "that you're not used to being at someone's mercy." Her fingers found the whorls of hair that surrounded his small male nipples, already rigid when her thumbs slid over them. The soft catch of his breath made her focus attention there for a long, lazy stretch of time.

"No," he said raggedly, "I'm not." He opened his mouth to continue, and the words were lost in a soft hiss of breath as she bent down to close her lips over the sensitive nipple, so unlike and yet so like hers.

Her tongue flicked and teased it, and suddenly the muscles in his belly clenched and rolled as he tried to surge up against her. "Joelle," he rasped, an ineffectual threat; she was sure in her own power now and pushed him down easily.

"Well," she drawled, "you're just going to have to learn to take it. It just so happens I'm not like those other women." She grinned, almost sharply, showing her teeth. "I can't be so easily dominated. And I'm going to prove it to you, so you don't make the mistake of forgetting."

Luke's eyes snapped open to meet hers; for an instant they locked wills, and then Luke gave up with a groan.

"You see?" Joey whispered. She stretched out along his length and began to explore the powerful swell of his chest, the arch and hollows of shoulder and throat.

The tension in him now, as her lips and tongue and teeth did their insidious work, was not of resistance. She gloried in the subtle reactions, the shifts in his expression, the unevenness of his breathing. It was *her* power, and his body acknowledged it; acknowledged that she was his match. Joey did not stop to consider why that seemed so important. For now, it didn't matter.

She sucked at the skin where neck met shoulder, not too gently, hard enough to leave marks, while he arched against her. When her tongue slid up the corded column of his neck, his hands rose up to grip her upper arms; she could feel his attempts not to drag her more tightly to him, crush the bones in his response. "Easy," she murmured. "Relax."

He made a sound of considerable skepticism, choked off when she caught his earlobe between her teeth. For the second time she noticed the fine hairs that grew neatly along the rim of his ear; she stroked it with her tongue. "Your ears," she breathed into his skin, "are a dead giveaway—didn't any of those other women ever notice?"

When Luke pushed against her this time, it was with sufficient force to set her back where he could see her face. "None of them knew, Joey," he growled, "None of them meant anything."

Joey gazed into his eyes, dark with passion, and felt her heart turn over. "That's good. That's very good."

She used her will to carry him back down to the bed. There were no more coherent words from him for some time after, as she turned her attention to the carved, mobile planes of his face, moistening his lips with her own, tracing the edge of his jaw, his trembling eyelids with her tongue. The heat spreading through her, emanating from the place where his arousal pushed against her through the inadequate barriers of clothing, made it more difficult to keep up the light patter of conversation she needed to hold him down and at bay. The words began to catch on breaths that had become shallow and rapid with an almost unbearable awareness of him.

"I'm still not sure why I didn't recognize you the very first time," she managed at last, pressing a series of feather-light kisses along the straight dark line of his brow. "Your eyes should have told me. And then your behavior . . ."

She stopped an indignant response with her mouth, pushing hard, as hard as he had done those times when he had been so set on claiming her. He answered fiercely, lacing his fingers through her hair to trap her against his lips. For a blazing instant he almost took control away, and their kiss became a battle; his tongue thrust deeply into her mouth with such harsh possessiveness that she wrapped her own around it to still it, pushing it back and following its retreat. She traced the sharp white keenness of his teeth.

"Even your teeth," she breathed into his mouth, "should have given you away after that first kiss. You remember that, don't you? Only this time, you aren't going to find it quite so easy to run away."

The physical attributes in question closed over her lower lip, ever so gently. "It's too late to run, Joelle," he murmured roughly when he released it. "For either one of us."

If the demands building within her had been less overwhelming, Joey might have pursued the conversation. But there was a far more urgent communication making itself known rather forcefully in a very receptive location, and Joey answered without words, trailing kisses and bites back down the path she had followed, pausing to stroke each nipple and tease the sensitive skin at the base of his belly.

Luke's muscles bunched so tightly as she worked at the buttons of his jeans that they shuddered with the strain. His hands moved almost helplessly over her arms, the fingers settling at last on the buttons of her shirt, undoing one and then another. By the time she had the final obstruction cleared, he had pushed the shirt halfway off her shoulders, and for a moment his hot, callused hands closed over her breasts. Joey stiffened, closing her eyes at his touch, faltering with her hands inches from their goal; warm air licked over her skin like his fingers, and then she drew back out of his reach with firm discipline.

Her objective was firmer still. It was heavy and impressive against her palms as she stroked it, lightly at first, savoring the contrast of textures and the incontrovertible proof of her effect on him. She tried to remember if she had ever enjoyed the feel of a man's arousal so much, but memory remained a blur that refused to sharpen into focus; much easier to accept that the mere touching of him roused the need within her to an unbearable ache. She wanted more than to hold him in her hands. She wanted to feel him far more thoroughly than that. . . .

Somehow she found the strength to tug his trousers down and away, so that none of him was hidden; she cupped the part of him that seemed made to fit the curve of her palm and slid down, down, until her breasts brushed his thighs and her mouth slid over his yearning length.

He surged against her so powerfully that she got more of him much more rapidly than she had intended, but she adjusted quickly and grinned around the hardness as her tongue tested the subtle ridges and varied patterns. She closed her eyes to savor the familiar strangeness of it, and his harsh breathing that was an accompaniment to each movement of her seeking mouth.

"Did I ever tell you," she began, pausing for breath, "how magnificent you are?" His answer was a groan as she plunged down again. "I mean, when you change, of course."

Luke muttered a curse in French. "There is one change," he managed at last, catching her hair in his fists, "that I have no control over. With you. Joelle . . ." He arched up as she gave him her full and undivided attention, until he was vibrating and pulsing with every stroke.

Joey would have been content to go on for some time, reveling in her power; but Luke had other ideas. As if he'd read her triumphant satisfaction, his hands closed like vises on her shoulders, pulling her up and away, all the pale light of his eyes shadowed with dark passion. "Don't forget," she gasped, hardly noticing the savagery of his grip, "my ribs!" It was a token protest; she was too lost in the wild need in his eyes to care.

"One way or another," he rumbled ominously, "your clothes are going to come off. I don't care if they stay in one piece." His hands were already gripping the fabric of her shirt; she hastened to help him, twisting out of the sleeves just carefully enough to avoid unnecessary violence to her healing torso. He moved with feverish impatience to the waistband of her pants, but she beat him to it; her fingers were clumsy with excitement as she struggled with them, undoing the front and rolling sideways to kick them off as Luke supported her.

There was little time to think and even less to anticipate before she straddled him again and plunged down onto slick hardness. The gasp torn from her echoed his; he filled her so completely that for a moment she could do nothing but feel him, as she had not truly been able to do that first time in the cave; unmoving, only the innermost part of her flexed to caress him as he swelled to fit the molten cradle of her body.

He shuddered under her, long waves that pushed him impossibly deeper. "If you intend," he whispered, "to stay in control, I suggest you don't wait too long."

His ragged sigh shook both of them, and his heart drummed under her hands as she braced herself on his chest. His eyes opened suddenly, fixing on her with total awareness. "No one but you could do this to me, Joey. Enjoy your dominion while you can." His slow smile promised a sweet retaliation that made Joey shiver, the inner fire convulsing about him again and again. He shut his eyes and arched upward.

There was no more talk of control. Joey was helpless to stop either one of them as they began to move together, passing beyond the first awkwardness to find a rhythm uniquely theirs, unlike any other in all the world. Luke's hands caught her hips, pulling her down again and again, with greater and greater urgency; she could feel him penetrating into her very soul, deeper and deeper to a place beyond the physical realm. When his fingers moved to touch the aching part of her that guarded their joining, the cry that came was wrenched from that same ethereal place. But the sensations he aroused with his caresses, moving unerringly over her slick softness, were very much of the flesh.

She quivered and burned and pulsed until she felt the coming peak, knew she could not keep it at bay any more than she could stop Luke's fierce and demanding possession of her body and soul. As she arched back, he caught her and kept her from falling at the same moment that his body convulsed within her, driving him hard and fast as the throes of her climax, and his, overwhelmed her.

It took a very long time to come down. She bent forward, leaning over him, her loosened hair brushing his chest and chin as she caught her breath. Luke's hand spread to sift it back from her face, his other cupping her breast as the aching pleasure subsided. After a moment he pulled her down to his chest, and Joey made a small sound of protest as the motion separated them.

"Don't be concerned, Joelle," he breathed, heat caressing her temple as he stroked her hair. "It's only a temporary retreat."

Joey forced heavy-lidded eyes open to gaze at him. His profile was relaxed with satiation, and something more; his touch was infinitely gentle on her hair and shoulder and bare arm. She propped herself up, half on the bed, cupping her cheek in her palm and pulling gently at the varicolored hairs of his chest with her fingers. "You mean you still don't know when you've been beaten?" She watched his eyes, pale again but more gold than green, the color warm with amusement.

His fingers tangled back in her hair and pulled her down for a kiss, lazy but firm. "Joelle," he said as he released her, his voice thick with unspoken feeling, "I warned you once not to play games of dominance with me. . . ."

"But you didn't take into account how stubborn I can be," she finished. "You also told me once that with wolves it's often the female who takes charge—sometimes even over the alpha male. I wanted to see how much that applies to werewolves."

He grew suddenly very still beneath her. "It applies," he whispered, almost too softly for her to hear, "more than I would have believed possible."

Joey's smile faded as she tucked her head under his chin. There was no bantering humor in his voice now. "Are you admitting I have power over you, Luke?" The attempt to recapture the lightness was forced. "It's about time somebody did. After all . . ."

The utter silence, the way his breath caught and did not release for an alarming span of time, stopped her short. When she sat up again to study his face, it was flat and free of emotion, as harsh and cold as in the days when they had fought so hard to be free of each other.

"Too much power. Too much for either of us."

The way he said the words, his eyes staring into

space at some deeply troubling vision, told her that it was not her statement he was answering. Her fingers tightened involuntarily into claws, scoring his chest. It seemed to get through; abruptly his eyes flickered to hers. "Joelle," he said hoarsely, and in an instant he was pulling her face to his again, and his tongue was tasting her even as she could feel the stirring of his body between her thighs.

She knew she wanted him again even before the rush of wetness where his arousal touched her confirmed the thought. She moved her legs against him; he slid his hands down her back to press her more deeply into his demanding length. This time he would take and give; she read it in the tautness of his muscles along her body, in the way his lips and tongue possessed her own mouth so fully, tasting her everywhere. Almost before the kiss ended he was pulling her up higher, creating an exquisite friction as their bodies slid skin on skin, his tongue forging a fiery path down her chin and throat. He settled her and held her in place straddling his belly, drew her down to envelop her breasts with the heat of his breath and then his lips.

She was above him, but it was he who now commanded her responses. Her breasts were heavy against his mouth as he teased the nipples one by one, thoroughly, leaving no inch of yielding surface untouched. Joey arched her back and thrust against him with ragged cries. He released her once, looking up between her breasts, compelling her to meet his eyes. "Dominance is deceptive, Joelle," he purred. "Who controls now?" Before she could answer or beg him to continue, he found her aching nipples again and caressed them until she was wild with wanting.

Her body was limp and hot and moist in his arms when he shifted under her, holding her easily above him as he sat up against the headboard, laying her back onto the damp sheets and stroking the slickness of her inner thighs until they parted for him of their own accord. Her eyes snapped open when he bent over to burn her with the tip of his tongue, sipping from the cup of her body as she gasped his name. His touch brought her again and again to the brink; she had forgotten anything so insignificant as half-healed ribs as she caught at his hair, his shoulders, tried to pull[1] him up and into her before she caught fire.

But Luke held back. When she could bear no more and told him so in broken words and gasped phrases, he turned her again—gently, ever so gently, sliding her around to lie alongside him, easing himself down on his side, drawing her back into his chest so that his body cupped hers. It was only then that he ended her torment, gliding in from behind in one long stroke.

It was a more complete possession than anything that had come before, and Joey lost all thought of control—control over Luke or of her own body's response. She gave herself up to his cadence as one hard-muscled arm cradled her head and the other arched over her side, his hand kneading her breast in time to the motion. She was being rocked against him, carried away on a ride unlike any she had ever known as his touch slid down to where they joined, easing in a slow caress forward and back where the hot core of her body begged most urgently for release.

The release came even more powerfully than before, jolting them both as Luke buried his face into the sodden tendrils of hair at the nape of her neck, licking the salty wetness away, his hand stroking her hip and buttocks while she tightened and released in concentric waves of pleasure. She was still gasping when his hand settled on her cheek, thumb brushing the tears that had escaped without her knowing.

"Joelle," he said, caressing her name as he did her skin. "The power is yours." She could feel him shudder, the vibrations breaking in tiny shock waves against her back. "Use it wisely." The words were a plea phrased as warning, and though Joey did not grasp the message, she understood the underlying vulnerability. She tried to turn, but he held her gently in place, still part of her. His breath came slow and heavy and deep as it stirred her hair. "Joelle, there is something I must tell you."

Hearing the soothing richness of his voice more than the words, Joey pushed herself back as if she could melt into the solid muscled heat of his chest and belly and thighs. "Hmm?" Her movements seemed to affect Luke in unexpected ways; he closed his teeth very lightly on the back of her neck where it blended into her shoulder.

Abruptly he released her. "Joey, this is important. I . . ." There was a note of half-concealed desperation that almost brought her out of the dreamlike lassitude that had stolen the will from her sated body. She half-opened her eyes and smiled at the feel of his renewed stirring within her.

"And I thought I talked too much," she murmured. "Just hold me, Luke. I have something to tell you, too, but I think"—she yawned luxuriously—"that it's going to have to wait."

His hand flexed on her hip, but whatever answer he made was too soft for her to hear.

# Chapter 17

Luke tested the weight of the fully laden pack as he sealed the last parcel in the upper compartment. The storekeeper, shifting audibly and nervously behind him, cleared his throat.

"Will that be all, Mr. Gévaudan?" Luke almost smiled, however grimly, at the unmistakable desire to see him gone revealed in the man's voice. He half-turned his head without meeting Jackson's eyes; he had made it a point with the storekeeper, as with the others, to avoid confrontations. Joey had had that effect on him. For the first time in memory Luke found the half-fearful, half-resentful attitude of most of the townsfolk more a source of disquiet than grim satisfaction.

"That's all, thanks." He hoisted the pack onto his shoulders. "I'll be back for the things I ordered next week." He was almost to the door before Jackson spoke again.

"What—uh, what if they haven't arrived yet?" The

ordinarily voluble and cheerful Jackson was gazing after him anxiously, wringing his hands.

Luke managed a smile—a real smile, if restrained, his teeth carefully hidden. "Then I'll have to come back later." Jackson's face went slack, and Luke used the opportunity to slip out the door. It was entirely too unsettling to think that he might actually go out of his way to charm the townsfolk instead of, at best, tolerating them; he wasn't sure he was up to it yet.

The late-autumn morning was cold, but Luke shed the cold as easily as he did his clothing when the change came. Patches of half-melted snow lay clumped under shadows and in inconvenient icy patches on the sidewalks of the main street; he avoided them neatly and glanced up at the sky. There would be more snow soon; next time he came to town, he'd likely need snowshoes. Far more convenient to run as wolf, but a wolf didn't have hands to carry supplies.

The one disadvantage of being *loup-garou* was that you forgot your limitations.

Luke crossed the street to avoid the clump of young men wasting the day in drinking and idle conversation in front of the town bar. He shook his head, amazed at his own desire to steer clear of obvious conflict. Even though Joey was not truly one of them, she had friends here in town, people she cared about; that was enough to make him drift in and out of town as lightly as the first gentle snows of the season.

He was too preoccupied at first to hear the light footfalls until they were very close. The smell and soft patter told him who it as before she caught up to him.

"Mr. Gévaudan . . ." Joey's friend Maggie stopped short as she reached out a small hand to catch his attention, falling silent in confusion as he pivoted to face her. Her hazel eyes searched his; whatever she saw there must have reassured her. The perpetual animated cheerfulness Luke had noticed on several occasions sparked in those eyes, but her expression remained almost grave. "Mr. Gévaudan—"

"Luke," he interrupted with his most reassuring smile.

"Luke." She almost frowned, then caught herself. "I won't waste your time in small talk, Luke, since you seem to be in a bit of a hurry." Her sharp, observant gaze fastened for a moment on the bulging backpack. "I just wanted to know," she continued, "if you'd heard from Joey."

Luke held himself very still, studying her face. Did she know, or suspect? Had Collier broken the influence, or shown his confusion sufficiently to arouse Maggie's suspicions? Maggie was the type of woman whose loyalty was fierce, as stubborn as a wolf bitch guarding her den. Luke thought it through quickly and shook his head almost as soon as she'd finished speaking.

"Collier didn't tell you? She was injured and had to be flown directly to the hospital." He had no real trouble keeping his voice smooth and even with false sincerity. He'd had a lot of practice.

There was a subtle shift in Maggie's features. Her short jaw set and a hand came up to brush red curls from her forehead.

"Yes, he told me," she admitted with narrowed eyes. "But—and you'll forgive me for being frank, Luke—I can't help but feel there is a lot more to it than that."

"Maybe there was," Luke said softly. "But it's over now. I haven't heard from her." There was a sudden and unexpected twinge over the lie that made Luke's muscles tighten in defensive anger. "If you'll excuse me . . ."

"Then why hasn't she been in touch? It's been over four weeks. She promised to give me a full report."

Her hand darted out to catch his arm, and the audacity of the gesture brought Luke to a halt. He pushed back the desire to shake her off.

"I can't answer your questions. She hasn't written me, either," he said with utter truthfulness.

Maggie dropped her hand away, and her full mouth twisted. "Doesn't injure your pride at all that she didn't tumble into bed with you like the others, eh? Or maybe you've had enough time to recover."

She had stepped back neatly, and Luke caught himself to consider with cold rationality why she'd wish to provoke him. She wanted him to break down in anger, admit something that would confirm what she seemed to have guessed. Suddenly Luke found himself smiling at her nerve and the kind of loyalty she must feel to risk goading him.

Apparently she hadn't expected quite that reaction. Her hands settled on her hips. "If you know anything— anything at all—about Joey, I want to hear it. I'm her friend. She wouldn't just disappear and never even let me know she was alive and well."

Resisting the impulse to disarm her, Luke maintained his smile. "She's alive and well. That's all I can tell you." He turned away once more, starting for the edge of town.

"Is it really, Gévaudan?" she called after him. "Why is it that I don't quite believe you?"

The last words were so faint that Luke knew he had not been meant to hear them. Maggie didn't know about his hearing. And she didn't know how far he was prepared to go to keep Joey by his side. Luke's lip curled. He found himself liking Maggie; best for her if she never found out.

Joey was reading by the fire when he returned to the cabin at twilight. She was up and in his arms before he had quite gotten through the door, a greeting that startled and warmed him with its intensity, something he had hardly begun to get used to and doubted he ever would. It was a proper kind of greeting among his people, who like true wolves were as effusive in their affections as they were swift in conflict and resolution. Luke had known for many years that he was one of the few who seemed capable of holding a lifelong grudge; perhaps that was why every welcoming embrace, each kiss, came as a shock of joyful belonging, the kind he had never felt within his own pack. Each time they made love, it strengthened their bond and his need for her.

She was happy. He knew she was happy, knew it in the way he knew so much else about her, felt so much of what she was feeling, bound to her by more than mere physical desire or primitive instinct. It was enough, most of the time, to keep the guilt pressed far enough back so that she couldn't see it, so that it did not destroy the very real joy between them. Almost enough to make him forget his fears.

He had tried to tell her, once. Tried to clear away that one shadow on their happiness. She had stopped him, and he had never again found the courage. Now, as he pressed his face into her hair to inhale the compelling and unique fragrance, he let himself forget in the sheer rightness of having her in his arms.

Her eyes were bright with anticipation, the gold flecks dancing, as she stepped back to watch him open the pack. "What did you bring me?" she said with a grin. "I've been having this incredible urge for chocolate. . . ."

He put the box of fine imported truffles into her hands before she could finish. She sighed dramatically as she read the label. "I'm impressed! I never indulged myself this much." She stretched up to kiss his cheek. Even so light a touch affected him profoundly, as it always did. He busied himself unloading the rest of the pack, laying out all the things he had brought for her. For the first time he wished he had a vehicle capable of transporting larger items; he wanted to give her so much more than these few small luxuries. Perhaps after the snowfalls were regular enough, he could borrow Val

Caché's single antique snowmobile, or rig up a *travois*. . . .

"Music," Joey breathed as she found the cassettes. "And more batteries." She laughed softly. "I'll have to restrain myself, or we'll be swimming in batteries."

Luke dropped down behind her, wrapping himself around her like a cloak, nuzzling the soft skin behind her jaw. "Never restrain yourself, Joelle," he murmured against her. She turned in his arms and kissed him. Hard.

"I won't. I absolutely promise that I have no intention whatsoever of restraining myself in anything."

They were delightfully preoccupied for the next several moments; Luke groaned softly into her mouth at the inevitable result of her touch. "Unless you're deliberately trying to torture me, I suggest you stop," he growled, nibbling her chin. "Or there won't be any supper until very, very late."

"I think we have a glass of wine and a loaf of bread somewhere." She grinned. "And considering my current appetite, that should be plenty." Her words caught on a half-stifled laugh as he swept her up, the sweet weight of her body against his heart as light as new-fallen leaves and as profound as the one word neither one of them had yet learned to say.

When she lay cradled against him, the taste of her still on his tongue and her skin cooling under his stroking hands, her voice cracked the lazy, sated silence.

"There was something I wanted to tell you, Luke. Somehow I kept getting distracted."

He could not see her face, tucked under his chin; her body shifted, and one small hand reached down to lace through his. "I love you, Luke."

After a while his heart resumed its cadence, and he knew he would live. But it was a very long time before he slept.

\* \* \*

Happiness was not an entirely new thing to Joey. She knew that there had been a time when she had felt almost this happy, almost this loved and protected. But she also knew it had been in another place and time long ago, almost beyond memory. And memories had become fragile, uncertain things; like the past and future, they flickered in and out of reality, formless as ghosts.

Days or weeks or months might have passed without her knowing it; she felt the changing of the season, understood Nature's perpetual cycle, but the counting of time by the calendar had become meaningless. Luke owned no clocks and needed none. Joey gave herself to a rhythm of life older than mankind.

And Luke indulged her. He brought her small luxuries and sometimes bigger ones. One day, impossibly, there were flowers brought in from some distant place, reminders of far-off springs and summers in a world of endless cold. On another, he arrived with a number of cookbooks and a set of culinary equipment that he promptly, if somewhat apprehensively, put to use in learning more creative ways of preparing the "exotic" foods he brought in from town. Joey was impressed by his successes and sympathetic to his failures; his chagrin always made her determined to make him feel better, and that was far from a bad thing. Eventually she took pity, and they formed a partnership in the small, primitive kitchen that actually resulted not only in edible meals, but also in very pleasant—and enthusiastic— desserts.

As the days grew shorter and the autumn nights lengthened into winter, Joey's life with Luke settled into a comfortable routine. The lovemaking was the one thing that always held a hint of surprise, never the same, never dull; as the nights stole away the daylight hours Luke became, if anything, more energetic than before.

"It's our way, the way of my people," he'd told her once, after a long night of passion. "In the winter and early spring we become—" He had almost blushed then, and Joey had finished for him.

"Insatiable?"

He had laughed, and there'd been no more time for explanations. And when he drew back to ask if it was too much, Joey had been the one to laugh. She'd found within herself such a fierce passion for him that sometimes it took no more than a glance of his smoldering eyes or the faintest touch of his fingers to make her ready. As often as he demanded her body, she matched his lust with equal enthusiasm. They could not get enough of each other.

That, Joey often thought on the long days when Luke had gone hunting or to town, was adequate compensation for being snowbound and treated to so few of the comforts of civilization. She seldom thought of that hazy outside world, but when she did, it was hard to miss things she used to take for granted. Oh, yes—there were more than adequate compensations.

Her thoughts were running rather heatedly along those lines one misty afternoon when she heard a thump on the door. Joey jumped to her feet with a little thrill of expectant desire. When Luke returned from his runs, he always appeared at the door in human form. Generally stark naked.

Anticipation made her grin as she opened the door. A pair of shadows flowed past her, and a warm puff of breath brushed over her hand as she shut it again. She blinked, adjusting to the unexpected sight of Luke and Philippe in wolf form as the smaller, darker wolf dashed off into the back room. Luke sat on his haunches by the fire and yawned, showing rows of very sharp white teeth, and grinned at her. Wolves couldn't grin, of course—but Luke could, and there was no other word for his distinctly unlupine expression.

"You didn't warn me we were going to be having guests, Luke," she said with hands on hips.

Luke cocked his ears and waved his tail in a way that told her he was in a very good mood. It had been a long time, too, since he'd seen his family. The signs of the change began to manifest themselves; Joey's eyes had trouble focusing, and the impressive lines of the graceful predator's body blurred and shifted.

"Wait!" She held out a hand to forestall him; the blurring stopped. While his bright feral eyes watched her, she retrieved her sketchpad and sat down cross-legged in front of him, tapping her pencil against her lip thoughtfully. "Stay just like that for a while, Luke."

His expression became suddenly alert and intent as she began to sketch; Joey got the distinct impression that he was deliberately presenting his most noble wolf-ish aspect, though he made such a magnificent wolf that it was impossible to be other than impressed with him at any time. Or in either form, for that matter.

Joey brought her attention back to her work, roughing out the proportions, the triangular ears, the heavy ruff of fur flowing back from the sides of his head and about his neck, the green-gold eyes focused on her. She was momentarily distracted by those eyes, so distinctly his no matter what form he took. They were arresting in any situation, but when they were trained on her in that particular way . . .

"*Bonjour*," a familiar baritone called out. Joey turned to see Philippe emerging from the kitchen, buttoning up one of Luke's spare shirts, the borrowed clothing loose on his lanky frame. His gray-green eyes were smiling as he moved around behind her to look down at the sketchpad in her lap. "*Très bien*, Joelle. It looks very much like him."

Flushing a little at the compliment and at having her rough sketch on display, Joey smiled up at Luke's cousin. "I just do it for fun. But I'll bet there are any number of wildlife artists who would kill for a chance like this."

Philippe was silent, absorbing and undoubtedly translating her words, as Joey resumed her work. Luke suddenly shook his head, bristled the fur along the nape of his neck and gave a low, melodious growl; Philippe laughed softly.

Joey's pencil skidded on the paper. "Did I miss something? Hold still, Luke!" She frowned back and forth at the cousins. "Why do I always get the feeling that most of the conversation is going right over my head?"

With a stretch and a sigh, Philippe sat down on the edge of the sofa. "It—loses something in the translation," he said, hesitating slightly over the English words.

Luke made a sound that could only be described as a "whuff," and Philippe sat up a little straighter. "Luc reminds me that you could learn to understand it, if you wish to do so."

The line Joey was drawing wobbled off in the wrong direction. It was not only the words but the tone that caught her attention; Philippe was clearly uneasy, though the emotion did not reach his face. His eyes tracked from Luke to Joey and back again, as if he were trying to read some significant and unspoken message.

"I could learn—what? Luke's been teaching me some French, but that's not what you mean, is it?" She turned to stare at Luke, who had stretched out sphinx-fashion, his big forepaws extended before him. "You can understand each other when you're wolves, or even when only one of you is, right?"

Philippe nodded, almost reluctantly. His eyes were now warily fixed on Luke, as hers were.

"Luke never discussed it with me before." Frowning, she put the sketchpad aside. "How do I learn this mysterious language of yours?"

This time there was no mistaking Philippe's discomfort. "We are born to the understanding of it. It would be possible for you to learn, but it would take a certain ..." He trailed off; Luke abruptly sat up and fixed his ominous challenge-stare on his cousin. Philippe cleared his throat. "It would be necessary for you to become as we are. If you were to go through the change, understanding would come to you." He stopped abruptly, his eyes, as they met Joey's, both relieved and anxious.

It took several moments for Joey to absorb his meaning. "You mean ... change into a wolf?"

Her voice came out as a squeak. Rubbing her palms on her thighs, she licked suddenly dry lips. The thought was at once so ridiculous and yet so strangely compelling that she could hardly find the words to respond. "But I'm not—I'm not—" She swallowed hard. "Why do you think I could do ... what you do?"

Philippe's unease was as manifest as her own as he shifted on the sofa, looking everywhere but at her, or Luke. His voice was very soft. "You carry our blood, *cousine* Joelle. You have the gift within you."

Joey stared at Luke, eyes widening. "You're not saying that there is some truth to those old legends—you bite me, and I turn into a werewolf, too?" The words carried a faint edge of hysteria barely shaped into humor; she struggled to keep her breathing steady and her mind clear. Luke growled deeply. He shook his head in a gesture clearly intended to mimic the human one.

"No, it is not like that," Philippe put in hurriedly. "The gift cannot be given. It is born into the blood. You have this within you ever since you came to us." His expression was earnest, asking her understanding; Joelle wondered dazedly why he spoke with such urgency. Why Luke merely watched her with those cold lupine eyes ...

She stared at Philippe uncomprehendingly. "I don't understand. You can't be serious."

His eyes held no hint of a lie, or of humor. They were the eyes of a man; more than a man, steady and bright with the natural honesty of the wolf he could become. He was something impossible. He spoke of something equally impossible. Surely she would have known. Surely Luke would have told her. . . .

It made no sense. Her past—what she remembered when she thought of it—revealed nothing to justify Philippe's impossible claim. Why then, did she find herself accepting it—without proof, without fact, as if someone had whispered it in her ear long ago in some vivid yet half-forgotten dream? Why did her very blood beat with the truth of it? It was as if every critical faculty of her mind had been stripped away to reveal a primitive certainty that made her muscles clench in sympathy, preparing to shift and change. . . .

She shook her head, mouth forming words that gave no sound. Denials rose and fell, stopped by that same cold certainty. Somehow she gathered her shattered composure, looked again at Philippe, managing somehow a faint reassuring smile; the look she turned on Luke was not quite so tranquil.

She had no time to confront him. Luke seemed to have reached the conclusion that she needed a moment of privacy to assimilate what she had been told; in one graceful move he was on his feet and trotting toward the back rooms of the cabin, leaving her alone with Philippe in an awkward silence.

It was, surprisingly, Philippe who broke it. "I am sorry, Joelle," he said softly. "I did not know before that Luc had not told you."

Drawing in a deep breath, Joey forced her rebellious body to assume the fragile calm of the expression she turned to him. "It's . . . all right, Philippe. Like everything else, it's going to take some getting used to." She almost laughed at his obvious relief; the absurd humor of their situation saved her. "I wonder if Luke drove everyone in Val Caché as crazy as he drives me."

Philippe's grin, a rare expression on his ordinarily serious face, was answer enough. "You know him well, *cousine*." As suddenly as it had come, the grin faded. He leaned forward, long-fingered hands dangling over his knees. "Are you happy here, Joelle?"

The change in topic caught her up short. There was very real concern in his voice—concern that reminded her unexpectedly of friends she had not seen in many weeks. She considered his question even after the immediate, obvious answer rose to her lips; all at once there were layers of complexity she had forgotten, little pricks of uncertainty that teased at her mind but could not be seen or confronted.

"Yes," she said at last. "I am happy."

The words were true, in spite of the unfamiliar ambiguity that Philippe's question—and his revelations—had unleashed. "I *am* happy." She looked up into Philippe's green-gray eyes and smiled with sincere warmth. Her fingers cupped over his hands in silent thanks. "Don't worry about me, Philippe."

He sighed, taking her hand and lifting it to his lips in an antique but charming gesture. "I am glad to hear it, *cousine*. We all wish you to be happy. Ever since you came to us, we have seen the changes. . . ." He stopped for a moment, considering his words. "We have seen what you have done for Luc. For that, we are grateful. But Luc can be *intimidant*," He shook his head. "Overpowering. We also wish that it is . . . right . . . for you."

Joey followed his careful words, deeply touched. She squeezed his hand and let it go, getting to her feet with a soft groan at the painful unclenching of her muscles. "I'm more grateful than I can tell you—for everything you and the others did to help me. I wish I knew how to thank you."

"There are no debts among kin," Philippe said gravely.

She shivered at his words. Kin.

"And you have repaid us a thousand times by what you have done for Luc."

Almost frightened by his words, Joey looked at her feet. What she had done for Luke. The words meant more than she could grasp, but the deeper meanings slipped away even as she reached for them. She looked up slowly. "I hope we can be friends, Philippe."

With the gentlest of touches he clasped her hands and planted a light, whiskery kiss on each cheek. "We are all your friends, Joelle. We are your family."

She blinked away tears and managed a smile. "Thank you." It seemed inadequate, but it was all she could find to say. Family. The word was almost painful in its intensity. It conjured images of laughing faces, arms that kept her safe and made her feel wanted. Things she had lost, had almost forgotten. . . .

Strong arms pulled her back from the edge of the void. She gasped into Luke's shoulder, rigid as stone under her cheek. When the swirling darkness subsided and her vision cleared, she looked up, still tightly locked in Luke's embrace. Philippe stood motionless against the sofa, his eyes turned aside.

The tension was palpable; it pulled Joey out of herself instantly. She shifted in Luke's hold, which tightened even further, a clear nonverbal message she was not quite prepared to contest.

"Um—gentlemen, I don't know about you, but I'm getting rather hungry." Joey could hear the shaking in her voice and spent several seconds getting it back under control. "And Philippe is going to think we are lacking in the hospitality department. So, if you'll just let me go, Luke . . ."

"There won't be any time for that now, Joey." Luke's

voice held an edge that stopped her from pulling away. "Philippe and I are on our way into town."

Joey twisted against him with a frown. After a moment just long enough to make his control abundantly clear, Luke loosened his hold. She stepped back to a place at an equal distance from both men and raked them with her glance, taking in the two parkas draped over the sofa behind Philippe and the snowshoes propped against it.

"Isn't it a little late to be going out again?" she asked. "If you've run all the way from Val Caché, I'm sure you could both use a rest." The words she wanted to say— begging them to stay with her, not to leave her alone— were painfully locked in her throat.

Luke's expression was unmoved and almost stern as he met her eyes. "We'll spend the night in Lovell; I have business there, and I don't want to keep Philippe away from his family." For a moment his gaze moved to his cousin, who seemed quite content to look in the opposite direction.

"You'll be all right, Joey," Luke said at last, turning back to her. His eyes still held a challenging sharpness, but gradually his expression softened, as if he read her hidden distress; his muscles tensed as if to cover the short distance between them, but he turned instead to retrieve the parkas and snowshoes, brushing by Philippe without a word.

His back was to her as he pulled on his parka. "Be sure to lock up, and bank the fire as I showed you; we'll be back tomorrow as soon as we can."

As if that alone were sufficient good-bye, Luke tossed one of the parkas to Philippe, who donned it silently; in another moment both men were heading for the door, Philippe casting a half-apologetic glance back over his shoulder.

"Wait a minute." Joey shook herself and trotted after them, pulling Luke around with a firm hand on his arm. "You're just going to leave me alone here after what you told me, about"—she swallowed heavily—"what I am?" The words came out with some difficulty, but they came; she was amazed at her own calm. "Don't you think it's just a little unfair to leave me with only half an explanation?"

The sudden flood of moisture in her eyes startled her more than anything that had come before. Without warning, Luke pulled her into his arms and pressed his lips against her forehead. After a moment he took her chin in one callused hand and pulled it up; the thumb of his other hand stroked away an escaping tear.

"I will explain, Joelle—when I can. There's nothing to be afraid of. You are still what you always were." He dropped a kiss on each of her cheeks, then on her mouth with gentle tenderness. "I'll be back soon." Even as he spoke, he looked deeply into her eyes, in that way that always made her lose herself; she was smiling and forgetting whatever it was that had been bothering her by the time he dropped his gaze. He kissed her again, with sensual promise, and then released her. "Sleep well, Joey."

She watched him as he and Philippe left the cabin, peering out the small front window as the two men strapped on the snowshoes, produced a large wooden sled from somewhere just out of sight, and set off at a steady pace over the lush white powder of new-fallen snow. Luke turned once to wave; she raised her hand, and as they disappeared, she frowned at a sudden twinge that made her lean heavily against the paneling of the wall for support. It passed quickly, but she was left with a disconcerting sense of wrongness that kept her awake and wondering far into the lonely night.

Few words passed between them as they made their way across the snowbound wilderness of Luke's land; Luke was acutely aware of Philippe's unease, and he concentrated on keeping his instinctive response in check. He had no desire to quarrel with his cousin, in spite of the fact that he suspected Philippe had guessed far more than he would dare to admit.

If he caught Philippe interfering . . .

Luke stifled a curse as they kept up a steady pace over the untroubled snow. His cousin was far more tenderhearted than he let on, and like the rest of the villagers he seemed to have adopted Joey without reservation.

They were not slow-witted, and neither was Joey. Luke cursed himself for the thousandth time, nearly stumbling over a half-buried snag. There were moments when he was sure she would break free, begin to think again of the world outside the one he had created for her. He could not risk it. It was too late to go back. Joey was so deeply in his blood that he knew it would kill them both if he were to let her go.

He shook off useless speculation as he shook the snow from his boots when they arrived at the outskirts of Lovell. His business was conducted early the next morning without complications, and he and Philippe started back for home with their newly acquired burden.

At the door of the cabin Philippe said his farewells with a rough hug and grave smile; Luke was as sincere as he could be in asking his cousin to stay the night, but Philippe only laughed and shook his head before discarding his borrowed clothing and dashing off, a wolf black as midnight against the pale landscape. Luke watched him only a moment before turning to the door, pulling it open as he pushed his bulky burden through.

The sight of Joey's astonishment was worth the weariness of his long run and almost worth the night of separation. "Luke! What in the world . . ." Her face, bright with joy—at seeing him, he thought with that same perpetual wonder—shifted into a different expression as she found her path to him blocked by the thing he carried.

"A bathtub?"

She edged in alongside him, her hip and shoulder against him as she tried to take some of the weight from his arms. The feel of her body almost made him drop it, and she nearly lost her balance before he caught himself. He eased it away from her long enough to wrestle it down to the kitchen floor and then turned in one swift motion to take her in his arms. Her mouth was soft and giving under his, a more certain home than any he had ever known.

"Luke," she gasped at last when he let her up for air. "A bathtub?"

"You prefer the barrel?" he teased gently, winding his fingers in the fine silver gold of her hair. "If you don't like it, I can take it back."

Her eyes widened as she pulled free of his arms and stepped back to examine his acquisition. "That's why you needed Philippe. But I'm still not sure how you two managed to get it here. It's huge!" She looked it over thoughtfully. "There's a drain in the bottom; I presume you're going to rig something up. . . ."

Luke interrupted her with a feathery kiss on the nape of her neck, gathering her hair out of the way. The taste of her was intoxicating. "Eventually. Later." She sighed and leaned back into his caress as he nibbled at her neck and shoulder, pulling her shirt aside to breathe in the compelling scent of her skin.

"You know," she said after a moment, her words gratifyingly breathless, "I think I could probably use a bath right now. What about you?"

Grinning into her shoulder, Luke ignored the demands of his body's immediate response. "A very good idea," he agreed in a husky whisper. With considerable reluctance he let her go. A soft sigh of protest escaped her, heightening his arousal even further. "I'll get the water."

"I'll help you." Joey's eyes were bright with desire, and as the two of them set about filling the tub with water warmed in the stoveside tank, it was all Luke could do not to forgo patience entirely. Each time they touched, brushing against each other not quite accidentally, it was like fire licking along the nerves, igniting his body to fever heat; her skin was as hot as his own, flushed with the same urgency.

With deliberate control he disciplined himself to complete the task at hand. Only when the tub was filled with water, and steam clouded the air, did he turn to look at her and allow the full force of his desire free rein.

She looked back at him with naked emotion in her eyes. It almost frightened him, that emotion, those words she had once spoken after their loving. It sobered him enough now that he was able to check his lust and channel it into something gentler, something that could allow him to give back some small part of what he read in her eyes.

She flowed into his arms and met his mouth with her own, giving herself freely as she always did. She was not merely beautiful or desirable. She was life itself, and the promise of life that he had never before come close enough to touch. Trembling with his need for her, Luke worked the buttons of her shirt loose and found the weight of her breasts with his palms, taking a moment to stroke the impossibly delicate skin. The centers of them were already hard, and he bent down to kiss one, savoring it with his tongue, delighting in the taste of her. Her gasp drew so powerful a response from him that he stopped to rest his head in the cradle between her breasts as her small hands, entangled in his hair, relaxed.

Then, before he could recover, it was her fingers undoing his buttons, her hands that stroked and caressed his chest. Her hands. He stopped one in its motion and brought it to his mouth, kissing each finger, trailing over the soft palm with his tongue. She broke away and grabbed the edges of his shirt as if for support, almost shaking him.

"I want my bath, Luke. And if we don't stop, we aren't going to make it to the tub." Her voice was as unsteady as he felt, but she was smiling, and the dark mystery of her eyes glowed with sparks of gold, embers of a fire that might consume them both.

Luke said nothing as he pushed the shirt away from her shoulders, his hands lingering on the curve of them before letting her slip free. Words were artificial constructs, shallow and meaningless within the deeper communication of their bond and their need for each other. He was silent as she helped him shrug out of his shirt, only the gradual quickening of his breath speaking for him when her touch traced down from chest to belly and lingered there, teasingly, before working free the buttons of his jeans.

She captured him with her hand in the instant when he would have returned the favor, holding him still and rigid with the lightest of touches until he thought his control would break. The sound that escaped him was hardly a word at all, but she seemed to understand; she grinned, a slow, sensual smile of triumph, and released him, moving to free herself of her own jeans before he could assist—or, more likely, tear them from her body.

When she rose, the gentle glow of fire- and lantern-light caressed her skin and painted the curves and valleys of her exquisite form in a mystery of shadow. Luke caught her up in one motion and held her against him, breathing in her quiet gasp as he kissed her. He lifted her easily, marveling in the gentle weight, the perfect way her body fit his, savored the texture of her breasts against him, the warm caress of her belly where it cradled his arousal. He kissed her eyelids when they fluttered closed, the tip of her nose, her chin; he would have lifted her higher still to taste the sweet column of her neck and the gentle hollow where it met her shoulder, but he knew if he did so, it would break the final shreds of control, and he would pull her down onto himself and end it too soon. Already her thighs were clenched around his, the compelling scent of her own excitement and her moisture on his skin driving him inexorably to the brink.

There was only one solution. Carrying her to the tub, he tested the water with one finger and unceremoniously dumped her in.

"Luke!" she sputtered, shaking the wet strands of her hair and spattering him with silvery drops. The word held more of laughter than outrage; he took advantage of the moment to calm his racing heart and overloaded senses.

"Do you mind if I join you?" he said softly. The way she looked up at him, trying to mold her exquisite features into stern disapproval and failing with a giggle, made it suddenly easy to forget the demands of his body. His throat seemed strangely blocked as she held out her hand to take his.

Suddenly she tugged, and half the water in the tub sloshed onto the surrounding floor as he fell in. There was just room for two, as he had planned; even so, knee-to-knee was not the position he most favored.

"Come over here," he demanded roughly. She only smiled, brushing water from her face, before scooting around and settling herself against him. Her sigh was blissful with contentment as she let her head fall back on his chest, her damp hair under his chin; the water rose up to lap at her breasts. Luke shut his eyes for a long moment, feeling her, feeling the pleasant ache where her back trapped his arousal between them.

"It's a little lumpy," she complained lazily, shifting in

a way that made him open his eyes with a soft oath. "But I don't suppose there's much we can do about that."

Luke groaned into her hair and bit the top of her ear. "Not unless you'll settle for a very short bath." She moved again, a gentle torture that made him grab her hips to hold her in place; her breath caught.

"Maybe you're right, Luke," she murmured huskily. "I really would like a chance to enjoy this." He could feel her deliberately easing the tightness from her muscles, loosening against him, though his own tension remained and showed no signs of departing. He would have had to be dead or kilometers away not to react to her, and even distance was no sure remedy.

But he leaned back into the sloping surface of the tub and breathed deeply until he could find simple pleasure in their touch without the driving urge to alleviate his hunger for her. Her breathing steadied, and her hands settled onto his thighs where they cradled her on either side; the touch was simple and without erotic intent. Brushing the damp tendrils of hair away from her face, Luke listened to the sound of their heartbeats and let himself be soothed by the rhythm and the heat of the water and by the wholeness that had replaced the broken void in his soul.

It was Joey who spoke first; she moved very carefully and woke Luke from his doze. "I need to talk to you, Luke—about what Philippe said yesterday. About—" She broke off for an instant, drawing in a deep breath. "About my being like you."

Luke came to full wakefulness. He sat up, pulling her with him, wanting to see her face but unwilling to let her go long enough to make it possible. His heart began to beat again with a rush of adrenaline. "What do you want to know, Joey?" he said very softly.

"Philippe said—he said I could learn your language, the one you use as wolves—if I learned how to do what you do." Her voice trembled; her hands tightened on his thighs, the short nails lightly biting his skin. "He said I had the ability to change. That I carry your blood."

Closing his eyes against sudden fear, Luke considered his answer. He had started this, urging Philippe to reveal what he had deliberately made her forget. A test, he had told himself. A test to see if she could deal with any part of the truth beyond what little she already understood. A test of how much she remembered . . .

"Yes, Joey. It's true." He felt her stiffen in his arms and relax again, too quickly for the fear or denial he had braced himself to deal with. Luke expelled the air trapped in his lungs. So she *did* know, in some way, the truth of it. But was her seeming acceptance due to the hidden memory of what he had told her that day in Val Caché, or a more certain inner perception? "You have the ability," he continued gently. "You carry the blood. But it's not *my* blood—it is, and has always been, your own."

He waited for her response, feeling the helplessness of knowing she was, now and in this, beyond his influence. "You mean," she said in a very small voice, "that I've been this all along. What you are. A werewolf." The flatness of the words almost chilled him. "And that can't be. Nothing ever happened—nothing—my parents were normal, and I was normal. . . ." She trailed off, dropping her head. He cradled her face in his hands and pulled her back against him, stroking her high cheekbones with his thumbs.

"You couldn't know, Joelle," he murmured. "It must have been hidden in you, in your family." He stopped himself quickly, fearing to summon up the demands of her past. "The blood and the gift are rare. Occasionally we hear of others, *loups-garous* outside of Val Caché. My father . . ." With an effort he continued. "My father didn't know what he was when my mother chose him."

He stopped again, shutting off memory of the man who had sired him. Who had refused the call of his blood, had been unable to accept what Joey was learning now. "It's a rare thing, Joelle, but not unknown, even in your country. And it is nothing to fear."

Her breathing was quick, but for the first time he sensed something other than trepidation.

"I *should* be afraid," she said hoarsely. "I should be screaming, if I had any sense. And I can't quite figure out why I'm not." She chuckled, a lost little sound. Wrapping his arms around her, Luke pulled her into himself as if that alone could give her the peace and courage to accept what she was. "I know it's true. I don't know why I know, but I do." She burrowed against him, hard. Her body trembled in his hold. "I suppose the only way I'm ever going to understand this is to prove to myself—to see it with my own eyes. Feel it . . ."

"You can do it if you wish to, Joelle," he said, willing her strength. "You have the power within you." Her silver-blond hair was soft where his lips brushed it. "You would be as beautiful a wolf as you are a woman."

A long tremor shook her, as if the picture he had conjured up in his mind had communicated itself directly into hers. It was not beyond the realm of what was possible between them. He kept her tightly against him as he closed his eyes and thought of what it would be like to have her running beside him, a pale and graceful she-wolf almost the color of snow.

"In the winter nights," he mused, his cheek to her hair, "you don't feel the cold. Your fur is made to turn it away, and the snow shatters out from under your feet as you run. Your sense of smell is so intense that it's as if the whole world has crossed your path, the scents like thousands of colors without names splashed over the landscape like paint on canvas." He heard her breathing catch again and knew she felt the things he described.

"Your ears pick up every sound, and it's as if every

melody ever composed by man is some poor imitation, some distant memory of what you hear around you. Your packmates speak to you without words, without any need of them. The moon is so bright that even a night-blind human could find his way; when the hunt begins, it is you the pack follows, because you are strongest, but there is no resentment or jealousy or pride. There is a pattern—a weave to existence of which you are only a part—that sets the course of things as they should be, and even the beasts you hunt give up their lives to that pattern when their time comes."

He fell silent, listening to the rapid beat of her heart. "Often," he said at last, "the pattern lets the prey escape, and you have run for many kilometers with only an empty belly at the end of it. Your breath clouds the still air as you rest, accepting the defeat because it is not the first and won't be the last, and because the wolf-spirit gives you understanding. There is no rage or bitterness to shadow the sweetness of the night. The pack draws in around you, enfolding you, one with you, and when you cry out it is for joy and for the binding of the pack. In that moment, when the pack raises its voice, there is such perfection that your heart aches with the beauty of it, and with sadness because, like human contentment, it cannot last."

Staring into emptiness, he ignored the warning of his own words. "When the chorus is ended, you return to the rendezvous site hungry and wait for another day."

Cooling water lapped around them as Joey slid her palms over his thighs, raising goose bumps. "I can feel it," she said softly, "as if I had done those things."

Luke nuzzled the nape of her neck. "Because of what we are," he whispered, "we are blessed with two worlds. The true wolves live in innocence, even when they kill. But they are helpless to control their world or fight it when it breaks the pattern and turns on them. We have the ability to choose our destiny, to run as wolves but not be bound to the harshness of their existence. It is the gift we have been given. Not to use that gift . . ." He broke off when her fingers came up to grip his forearms with desperate intensity.

"I'm not ready." Her breath shuddered. "I'm not ready to be what you are, Luke. Not yet."

He soothed her with his voice and hands while her trembling subsided. "Don't be afraid, Joelle. There will be all the time you need to accept the gift and make it a part of you."

"And if I can't accept it?"

Her question made him close his eyes. This thing, this one thing, must be *her* choice. He had taken too much from her already.

"No one will force you, Joelle. You must want the change to make it happen. Only you can control it."

That much was absolute truth, and he savagely rejected the powerful desire to release her from her fears and make her want it, as he had freed her of the demands of past and future. To know and feel what she was, and never to have her run beside him—that would be a loss and a tragic waste, but not beyond bearing. Not as long as she stayed with him.

He knew his words had penetrated, for her body loosened again, sliding along his until the water almost touched her chin. "Thank you, Luke," she murmured. "For explaining and for understanding."

The stab of guilt he felt then pierced his heart. She believed she had something to thank him for. In her innocence she trusted him. She had given everything, and he had taken what she offered and gone beyond to steal what she did not yet know how to give.

Suddenly the savage pain of his thoughts twisted within him, and he felt his hands moving down to her hips, sliding up to her waist with an urgency impossible to deny. He knew it when she came to full awareness, her nipples already hard as his hands closed over her breasts, pulling her against his rigid flesh. He growled her name into her neck, biting her there not quite gently, hearing her gasp and knowing it was excitement and not fear by the heat of her body when he touched the place he longed to possess.

She gasped again, hard and ragged, when he pulled her up with him, the water streaming in rivulets over her tantalizing skin. He pressed into her softness as he licked the wetness from her shoulders, her neck, the delicate and sensitive flesh that trembled under his tongue. When he turned her in his arms and sucked the drops that clung to her nipples, she arched against him and cried out, burying her fingers deeply in his hair with a frenzy that matched his own. She wanted this, without gentleness, as he wanted to take without asking. Her breasts rose and fell sharply as he stroked them, drawing the water away until none remained, following the curve of her body to her belly as he lifted her. Her thighs clenched around his hips, silken bonds that claimed him as he cupped the sweet curve of her buttocks in his hands.

Her body was like fire when he thrust into her, one hard stroke into her molten core. She flung back her head and clutched his shoulders, moaning as he carried her across the room and through the door, so deeply inside her that he could not conceive of withdrawing. But his body was demanding release, and so he moved; he watched her face, eyelids fluttering, lips parted in passion, her breath coming hard and fast in time to his driving rhythm.

He stopped once, to ease her back onto the bed, pulling free of her long enough to feel the ache that could only be relieved by losing himself deep within her. It was her hands that urged him down, her eyes swallowed in black and gold fire that begged for her own sweet release.

"Do you want this, Joey?" he growled, hovering at

the entrance of her body, stroking the quivering, moist flesh with his own hardness. "Do you want me and everything I am?"

Her eyes opened, and for a single blazing instant they looked deeply into his soul. "Yes."

There was a certainty and acceptance in that one gasped word that came from a place he could not touch, beyond the reach of his influence, beyond even the rule of her own intellect. "Yes, I want you, Luke. All of you."

With a groan of overwhelming need Luke plunged down and sank deep within her. Her body arched to accept him, and in that moment she made a gift of what he would have taken, so that his guilt and fury were shattered in the sublime and terrible moment of release.

# Chapter 18

Winter arrived to grip Luke's world with its perpetual cold and endless snowfalls, providing ample opportunities for use of the new bathtub, and sometimes even for long, hot soaks that Joey appreciated as the blissful luxuries they were.

Luke spent the days with her, except when he went for his runs, alone or with either of the two packs that accepted him: that of the village, and that of the true wolves whose territory overlapped the boundaries of his land. In the evenings Joey worked her way through Luke's extensive collection of books as he carved his graceful wooden beasts, and they often talked by firelight long into the night before making love.

It was during these quiet intervals that Joey drew Luke most completely out of himself. She learned that he was as intensely interested in discussion and debate as she was and as fully capable of it; they fell frequently into long silences that never seemed awkward, but for the first time Luke seemed as ready to fill the quiet as keep it. Their lovemaking made him gentle and fiercely vulnerable and sometimes exposed more of him than he might have wished, but their long evening talks revealed his intense curiosity, his hunger for knowledge, and his driving need to understand what he was.

One night while Joey was curled up on the sofa, frowning over a passage in a particularly large and imposing volume, she looked up to find him watching her from his chair across the room, such an unguarded expression of tenderness on his face that the text fled her mind in a rush. His eyes transfixed her, and she stuttered out the first thing that came into her head. "Silver bullets!"

Luke raised his eyebrows in question, almost smiling. "I mean," she amended quickly, "the legends all say that silver bullets . . ." She trailed off as heat rushed into her face.

"Kill werewolves?" Luke supplied amiably.

Joey felt her flush deepening. "Well, it doesn't seem very logical to me, but—"

"Neither does anything else," he finished for her. Setting his most recent carving aside, he stretched his long legs toward the fire. "That's a legend with very little truth to it. There are no particularly deadly qualities to silver bullets, not for us." Abruptly his face grew serious, and he glanced aside at the two wolf pelts hung on the wall. "A sufficient number of the regular kind will do the job." There was enough bitter memory in his words that Joey felt no desire to pursue the topic.

She flipped a few pages of the book in her lap and changed the subject. "What about full moons?" She said it playfully, trying to win back his smile; he turned his attention to her and visibly relaxed. "I haven't seen any evidence so far that one is required," she added with a grin.

Luke surprised her by laughing, a brief, dark chuckle. "The change isn't subject to the phases of the moon or of any other supernatural force." His eyes sparked on hers. "It comes with the end of childhood and, barring certain circumstances, is under our control entirely after that."

Shifting to ease a cramp in her legs, Joey gnawed her lower lip. "Then where do you suppose all these legends started—silver bullets and full moons and the like?"

"We don't know all the answers." Luke nodded toward the shelves of books that lined three of the walls. "Ever since I learned what I was, I began to collect books, magazines, anything that could tell me the things I needed to know. All I found were scraps, most so distorted that they had no bearing on our reality."

"Such as," Joey consulted the text in her lap, "a lust for human blood?"

Luke grimaced. "Humans fear what they don't understand. That never changes. Though it's possible," he added reluctantly, "that some of our kind, our ancestors in Europe, went rogue and took the easiest prey." His expression was grim. "Which makes us no worse than humankind."

Joey swallowed, knowing that his "us" included herself. Not quite human—or *more* than human.

"As for full moons," he continued, "it may be that we were simply more visible then. European peasants didn't have the benefit of electricity. You've seen what the light of a full moon can do out here."

Leaning an elbow on the armrest of the sofa, Joey dropped her chin in her hand. "It's breathtaking, the way the moon and stars light up the night sky. Back home . . ." She blinked, suddenly confused. For a moment she struggled to regain her train of thought. Whatever she had been about to say drifted away like windblown snow. "I can see you've given this a lot of thought," she said at last, smiling into his eyes. "Which is exactly what I would have done if I—if I had known."

Luke rose to his feet, moving to the hearth to stare into the fire. "When I first learned what I was—just after my mother died—I was too isolated to understand all the changes." He gave a harsh laugh. "Too many things happened too fast. I'd lost my mother, found Val Caché—and changed, all in the same brief span of time. I knew I had to keep what I was hidden from the other kids in school, even though there were several occasions when I was sorely tempted to change right in the middle of class and chase a few bullies around the room."

Joey laughed, imagining just such a scene, and Luke's smile was less strained as he looked at her. "About six months after my mother died, there was a series of old movies shown in the theater in East Fork. One of them was *The Wolf Man.*"

"The one with Lon Chaney, Jr.?" Joey asked.

"Yes. And of course I had to see it, thinking I might learn something. I badgered Allan for days to take me into East Fork."

"Don't tell me," Joey said with a grin. "He kept saying no, and you never left him alone until you got your way."

Luke arched a dark eyebrow. "I usually do."

There was a sudden sinister quality to his voice that made Joey shake her head.

"Allan finally found the time to take me in for a matinee. I remember feeling stunned by what I saw on the screen. I didn't know whether to laugh or take offense. Even then I knew enough to realize how much they'd twisted what we were."

"You didn't see it as a curse," she said softly, as much statement as question.

"Being what I am?" Luke shook his head. "No. Even though it had killed my mother." He turned away quickly so that she could not see his eyes. "Even when I didn't understand it, it was a marvel to me. But after I saw the movie, I had a hunger to know more. To see the truth behind what I was. That evening when we returned to town, I tried to make myself become what I had seen."

Joey started. "A *real* werewolf? The kind that . . . ?"

"Is neither man nor wolf, but something in between? Yes." Shuddering visibly, he looked back at her again. "It was not pleasant."

"Then you can't take that form—the one that all the legends seem fixated on?"

"It might be possible," he admitted, lifting his upper lip, "but I would never want to try it again. It was exceedingly painful. Unnatural. That was my first real lesson."

*Unnatural.* Joey tested the word. "Being what you are," she said at last, "is natural. Part of the pattern."

His eyes brightened at her understanding. "We live within the pattern, as much as we can." All at once the green-gold of his gaze darkened to dull verdigris. "It gets harder every year. When I was old enough to use the money my father had set aside for me, I bought up as much land as possible, as many acres as money could buy. To protect the wilderness, my people, and the true wolves who held this land before we did."

Joey closed her eyes, too many thoughts and emotions crowding together behind them. There was silence for a long moment, and then Luke's weight settled on the sofa beside her, and his arms drew her in. His presence and his warmth stilled her brain's mad whirling, and she opened her eyes to the silver beam of the moon trailing a bright path from the near window, drawing them close in gossamer bonds of light.

The bond between them grew stronger as winter threw up almost impenetrable walls that locked the cabin in a world out of time; the snowbound woods became the bars of a sweet cage Joey had no desire to escape.

She heard the eerie whine of the wind's lament at night when she lay beside Luke after their lovemaking, unafraid because it could not reach her, kept at bay by the sturdy cabin walls and the steady cadence of his heartbeat under her cheek. She thought at times she almost understood the gale's language; it hovered just beyond her grasp, like the vague memories and faded images that haunted the edges of sleep. It was only when the wind cried and snow slapped against the windows, deep into the night, that she reached within herself to find the stillness and wonder why it seemed to hide uneasy secrets.

But the days always came too brightly to permit the presence of shadows.

There were still countless new things to be learned from Luke, and about him—and for him to learn of her. And there were surprises; the bathtub had been only the first of many gifts he brought her through the long season of cold.

The second surprise came at a time of the year that Joey had almost forgotten, so little had she noticed the passing of the days and nights. One morning she woke to the sharp, resiny scent of the forest, and when she got out of bed to trace it—and Luke—she found him flat on his back in a corner of the main room, muttering softly to himself as he worked at the base of a small and very fat fir.

"No peeking," he commanded, spitting out needles. "Go back to bed and stay there until I come get you."

The implication of the tree, and the overwhelming emotions it evoked, gave Joey little inclination to argue. She sat up in the bed and pulled the blankets up over her knees, listening to the tattoo of a hammer, Luke's almost inaudible footfalls, and her own rapid heartbeat. She had nearly forgotten. There were teasing, haunting images again: of Christmases long ago with her parents, trees that towered above her head, dazzling with light and promise. The past . . .

It was a blur, almost lost, almost without meaning. But the tree had shaken her unquestioning content- ment, revealed things that had been hidden, and she felt her eyes filling in response to emotions that hung sus- pended within her, bereft of the anchor of concrete memory.

When Luke came for her, the tears were gone, and the images had faded again. She was left with little time to brood. He stood back to watch her as she took it in: the chubby little tree hung with strings of berries and with his animals—dozens of them, small delicate wooden figurines strung over the branches—simple but profound beyond words. She flung herself at him so hard that they almost went down together amid the fallen needles, and it was some time before she had any desire to speak. She hadn't meant to cry again, but the tears came back in spite of her sternest efforts. Luke held her tightly until the last of them had dried.

"Do you like it?" Luke asked gruffly. She looked at his face; it was carefully blank, as if he were preparing himself for a painful rejection of his gift.

Her heart melted. "Luke, whenever I start to think you're the most unusual man I've ever known, you ask a question like that. Of course I like it." She flung her arms around his waist and dropped a kiss at the base of his neck; he pulled her up and returned it enthusiasti- cally.

"How did you know?" she said softly after she had caught her breath again. They had settled down on the floor before the tree; the smell of fir was pungent and wonderful. "I'd almost forgotten . . ." She blinked sev- eral times. Whenever she thought of passing time, or the past, or the future, it was as if the corners of her mind were lost in shadow. "I've always loved Christmas trees."

Luke arched his jaw along the top of her head, his voice vibrating into her bones. "I knew. I guessed. Does it matter?"

Shaking her head, Joey leaned back to gaze at the tree, not missing electric lights or glittering tinsel. At last she found the gifts, wrapped in plain brown paper, half-hidden under the lowest branches. "Are those for me?" she whispered idiotically. She turned into his chest and hid her face there, too moved and too vulnerable to do more than shiver.

He pried her away and cupped her face in his hands. "I wish I could give you more, Joelle. Everything. All the things you deserve." His kiss was gentle, tender rather than sensual. Her heart skipped a beat, and she spread her hands against his chest for support.

"And . . . is it Christmas yet?" she murmured, knowing how absurd she must look and sound, knowing that Luke didn't care.

The smile he gave her was a gift in itself. "Tomorrow. Today is Christmas Eve."

"Then I guess I'll have to wait," she sighed, leaning back into the cradle of his arms.

Luke chuckled into her hair. "Somewhere in the world," he reminded her softly, "it's the right time." He eased her away from him and retrieved two of the gifts— each a flat box, neatly but plainly wrapped, a cluster of autumn's bright leaves at the center in place of ribbons— and presented them to her gravely.

Her fingers were trembling as she opened the first. The long chemise was of sheerest silk, flowing like water in her hands, pale silver-gold in the filtered light. There was nothing deliberately risqué in the cut of it, or in the delicate matching robe she found in the second box. Nothing but the sensual sheerness of it that stroked her skin like Luke's kisses. "The color of your hair," Luke explained, his lips caressing her cheek.

"It's beautiful," she whispered. Luke had never cared

that all she wore each day were the same jeans and oversized shirts, but suddenly Joey felt genuinely worthy of the gift. Genuinely as beautiful as he claimed. She closed her eyes and rubbed the wisps of silk against her skin. The feel of it kindled a warmth deep within her; she opened her eyes to see the same heat reflected in Luke's.

She leaned against him, letting the silk flow into her lap. "I don't have anything for you," she admitted sadly.

"Oh, yes, Joelle. You do." His touch turned the warmth into a blaze. There were many gifts yet to be given.

That night they walked hand in hand over the frozen lake under a moon so luminous that the brittle winter stars were overwhelmed by its brilliance. The ice was uncertain under Joey's feet, but Luke was always there to hold her, whispering the secrets of his world into the stillness. The winter was a world in waiting, dormant until the coming of spring; only the wolves and the animals upon which they fed braved winter's harsh and austere beauty.

It was the first of many such walks. Luke took her out into the woods, by day and by night, teaching her to see and hear and smell, testing the limits of her senses. Confirmation of that newborn inner truth—of what she was—came to her slowly. It settled into her bones, into her heart and into her soul. The bond she felt with Luke was no convenient little fairy tale, his need for her no mere excuse for endless lovemaking. Yet, in spite of that deep inner conviction, Joey was sometimes aware of a blank where the need to analyze and understand and make sense of a truth so irrational should have been. Luke filled that small emptiness so completely that acceptance came almost without struggle.

Acceptance should have been enough. Joey's happiness was real, more real than the phantoms of a previous life that sometimes haunted her dreams. But a new and strange restlessness came over her with the brutal cold of February, when Luke curtailed their walks and kept her confined to the cabin. The small gifts and enthusiastic loving continued, but Joey found herself stalking the cabin as if it were a cage, unable to shake the growing disquiet.

When Luke went for his daily runs, Joey began to walk the edges of the forest alone. She concealed her forays from Luke, knowing instinctively that he would forbid them if he knew; his protectiveness had almost begun to trouble her. She took pains to walk along previous tracks, using the new woodlore Luke had taught her to hide the evidence of her passage.

She made one concession to Luke's fierce concern for her safety; she always carried the rifle he had insisted she learn how to use.

It felt heavy and awkward and wrong in her hands. Luke never used it; she had never seen him hunt with a man-made weapon, and the touch of the rifle seemed almost a betrayal of what he was. Of what they *both* were.

But she carried it, and she walked alone in the winter silence. She watched the squirrels, rulers of an empty kingdom, chasing each other through their vigorous courtship rituals; she avoided the musky spoor of a wolverine and found the places where herds of moose had yarded up, stripping the foliage and packing the snow with their heavy tread.

And she found the tracks of wolves. She knew Luke's mark from among all the others, but she followed the lesser ones, drawn by the lure of that hidden part of herself.

It was on such a day that she discovered the tracks that did not belong. They blotted out the wolf spoor she had been following, blundering and awkward, human prints that violated the innocence of snow. There were many, a human pack's worth; they intersected the wolf prints and paced them ominously.

Joey rocked back on her heels where she had been kneeling in the sullied snow. She could smell them with her newfound senses, and the stench was disturbingly familiar. There should be no trespassers on Luke's land, especially at this time of year when even Nature forbade intrusion. The hair along the nape of her neck rose. She stood slowly, retrieving her rifle; closing her eyes, she breathed in the icy air, testing it. The men weren't close, but they had passed not long before. Her senses shouted a warning.

It was then, when all her inner awareness was tuned to the invaders, that it struck. She felt the stab of pain so powerfully that her body collapsed on itself, doubling over around a phantom injury that made her cry out. *Luke!*

She fell back against the tree, managing somehow to cling to the solid weight of the rifle. Her vision blurred, and for an instant her mind went black with shock. The report of a gunshot, and then another, slapped the air violently. Her senses reeled under the twin impacts of debilitating pain and the revelation that Luke was in terrible danger.

There was no time to assimilate any of it. Her mind screamed and battered at the frozen walls of her body. She could almost see him, floundering in deep drifts, his blood staining the snow. . . .

Joey drew in a deep, steadying breath and clutched the rifle as if it were her last grasp on sanity. She stared down at the human tracks and began to follow.

At first she walked, still dizzy with the repercussions of her mind-numbing awareness. But the urgency grew; she began to jog over the tracks, using them to break her path, new stabs of illusory pain making her stagger. For her they were not deadly, but for Luke . . . She forced her feet into the steady, mile-eating pace Luke had taught her. Her heart pounded as if it would force its way from her throat, marking rhythm in time to her sobbing breath and unvoiced cries.

The smell hit her like a wall. Forcing herself into utter stillness, Joey listened; she heard them then, gruff, angry human voices that taunted and argued, profaning the silence. She could not see them, not yet—but she knew they were there, beyond the next small rise of the forest. And Luke. She felt his pain and his desperation as if they were her own. The intensity of it made her close her eyes to gather her control and her courage.

Joey lifted the rifle and drifted forward, light as the gentle snowflakes that had begun to fall. The sound and scent of the men assaulted her, but their noise masked her approach so thoroughly that she breathed silent gratitude for their blatant disregard.

The last concealing screen of trees fanned across the top of the gentle rise. She pressed herself against the trunk of a grandfather fir, listening, forcing her heart to slow. Adrenaline made her legs tingle; with infinite care she rounded the tree and took in the tableau.

She knew the men at once. She recognized the blond ringleader and shuddered; they were the same roughnecks who had harassed her by the lake. Their attention now was turned to far less defenseless prey. Joey's heart nearly stopped.

He crouched at bay with his back to a copse of trees, huge and magnificent even as his blood burned steadily into the torn snow at his feet. His ears were laid flat to his skull, his eyes like chips of green ice; Joey stared at Luke and felt each wave of pain and fury as if it were her own. The men had fanned out in a half-circle with Luke at the center; they cursed and snarled at each other like a snapping pack of mangy dogs.

"Just shoot it and be done with it!" Joey knew the voice, though the man's hair was covered by a knit cap.

She pressed back into the tree and tried to still her trembling. The rifle was a leaden weight that burned through her gloves like frigid fire.

"If you hadn't 'a screwed up by missing the first time, it'd be dead already!" another familiar voice snarled.

"If you put more holes in it, the pelt won't be worth a damn," a third man complained.

"I don't give a damn about the pelt." The others fell silent at the fourth man's words. "I want this wolf dead, and as many others as we can find. That's what we came for."

Joey stared at the leader. He stood closest to Luke, a rifle tucked under his arm; she could smell his hatred and feel the vibrations of it without seeing his face. "Particularly this wolf," his rough voice growled. "So no more playing around."

As if in slow motion, Joey watched him shift his rifle and raise it to his shoulder.

"Hold it right there." She heard her own voice crack the sudden hush. Her feet carried her into the little clearing of their own accord, her rifle trained on the leader's head. "If any of you move, I'll kill you."

The stunned silence that followed echoed Joey's astonishment at the cold-blooded fury that had overwhelmed her. She walked among them without fear, and they fell back as if from some dire apparition. One of the men shifted; Joey froze and tightened her fingers on the trigger. "I mean it," she said icily. She watched the leader's eyes widen as he focused on her, saw him scan the faces of his companions.

Joey stopped a few feet from the leader and met his startled gaze. The chill rage that filled her had swept her mind clean of anything but the matter at hand; she stared into the man's vicious little eyes until he dropped them. "Put it down," she commanded as his hands tightened on his rifle. "Put it down *now*."

Again the man looked aside, swept his eyes over his friends in indecision. "You're outnumbered, little lady," he muttered ominously. "If you make one move . . ."

"If *you* make one move," Joey interrupted, "you won't be around to see what happens next." She took another step forward, so that the muzzle of her rifle was only inches from his chest. With a soft curse he dropped his weapon into the snow and slowly raised his arms.

"I put it down, see? Now why don't we talk this over, nice and friendly." His eyes slid sideways; his face was twisted into the mockery of a smile.

The growl warned her. Before one of the other men could slip up from behind, she had the muzzle of the rifle pressed into the skin at the base of the leader's neck. Her breath caught with suppressed violence. "You think I won't do it?" she said very softly. "Tell your friends to back off and put their weapons over there, behind those trees. Now."

She heard them begin to disperse even before the leader managed a half-strangled command. Some hesitated; she could hear the whisper of their feet on snow, the way they shuffled and muttered among themselves. But they complied. Only then, when they stood some distance away, bare-handed, did she let her gaze move past the man to Luke.

He had half-fallen into the deep bank, his eyes slitted with pain and weakness; blood had burned a black scar in the snow under him, and his right foreleg was unnaturally bent. Joey took it all in coldly and then met his eyes.

It was a shock that, at another time, might have broken her concentration. The message he sent to her was as clear as if he had spoken it aloud. *Go. Run. Leave me.* The inner words almost cracked the ice of her resolve. Then she broke the compulsion, beating it back with a message of her own, ignoring the desperate plea in his eyes.

Slowly she turned back to the man who waited under her rifle. His face was white except for two hot patches of red at the tops of his cheekbones: fury, she thought, and hatred and fear. Aimed at her. She could feel a frigid smile forming on her face. He could not meet her eyes.

"I'm going to let you go," she murmured. "I want you and your buddies to get off this land and never come back." She pressed the rifle into soft flesh for emphasis, and he choked on his strangled rage. The men muttered and stirred on the edges of her peripheral vision. "Now move—away from the guns." Shoving him, she held the rifle steady as he backed away. The men bunched, clumsy with emotion and herd instinct. She watched them dispassionately as they started away; their muttered threats floated back to her, growing louder and bolder as the distance increased. At last the noises faded, the clearing suddenly still. She waited until she was certain the men would not return and then dropped to her knees in the cold snow.

Luke was there, against her, solid and warm and alive. His breath came in heavy pants that plumed the air; Joey brushed at his shoulder with her hand, and it came away sticky with blood.

The pain surged through her again. "Luke!" she cried. Raking him with her gaze, she found the places where the lush gray pelt was matted with blood, the unmistakable sign of bullet wounds half-hidden in the fur. With a gasp of overwhelming fear, Joey tried to clear her mind. He was still breathing, still with her; he was strong enough to stay alive. He had to be.

With infinite gentleness Joey lifted the heavy head in her hands. "Luke, listen to me. Luke!" She gripped the fur to either side almost fiercely, willing him to hear her. "Look at me, Luke!"

He opened his eyes slowly. His tail thumped once against the snow, and a sound caught deep in his throat. Joey forced back tears. "Can you understand me, Luke?" His tail thumped again, and a sigh shuddered the massive body. Shutting her eyes tightly to impose control on her racing emotions, Joey considered her options.

"You're badly hurt, Luke," she said at last, hardening her resolve. "I can't help you here." She knew his weight was far more than she could hope to handle. Even his head dragged at her hands. "I need you to help me, Luke. You need to hang on." His tail thumped again, and his eyes locked on hers. The unspoken message there gave her courage. "Can you change? Can you help me get you back to the cabin?"

The despairing sound Luke made was answer enough. Another shudder racked his body. "All right," Joey said, breathing deeply. "You can't change. I can't carry you. That means going all the way into town for help, or finding some other way of getting you back to the cabin." The sound of her voice was harsh and brittle and practical. "Help me, Luke. What should I do?"

His head lifted from her hands. His eyes stared into hers with all the old familiar intensity, and knowledge came to her from some deep place beyond the reach of words.

The thing that flooded into her mind then almost made her lose her grip on Luke's fur; with deliberate care she lowered her hands to pillow his head in the snow.

"No," she whispered hoarsely. "No—I can't." Her body began to shiver in reaction, a glaze of denial blurring her vision. Luke lifted his head, slowly, painfully, to regard her. "I can't. . . ." Luke's head dropped back into the snow and his eyes closed as if in surrender.

Joey stared at Luke and felt as if her mind and heart were being torn apart bit by inevitable bit. With shaking hands she unzipped her parka and pulled her outer shirttail from under her sweater; she used her small knife to tear strips from it, enough to bandage his hurts. Her fingers were clumsy, her efforts painfully inadequate. The bullet wounds had almost stopped bleeding, but she bound them up as best she could and stroked his head while the resolve built within her and the weight of conviction settled into her bones.

She closed her eyes, feeling the blood rushing through her veins and arteries, the workings of muscle and sinew, the flow of cold air into her lungs. What passed through her mind then was nothing so clear as conscious thought. Raw need compelled her. To save Luke . . .

She looked down at him once more. "You told me once," she said softly, "that I had to hang on. Now I'm telling you." Bending down so close that her tears moistened the pale fur of his cheek, she clutched at his mane. "You said, 'I won't let you leave me,' remember? Well, it works both ways, Luke. It works both ways." She heard his shuddering sigh, saw his eyelids flicker without opening, and knew he heard her.

With grim haste Joey stripped away the parka and sweaters and shirts one by one, peeled off trousers and underclothes and boots until she stood naked in the cold. The snowflakes were like kisses on her skin; for a moment she felt nothing, and then the cold was gone. Utterly gone, as if she stood before a roaring fire. Her body went up like kindling in the heat, burst into flame and burned until the roar of the conflagration drowned out her cries of shock and pain.

When it was over, when the fire had settled again to embers, the world had shifted into an alien place. It bombarded her altered senses from every side. Instinct rescued her when her mind could not. She cried out to Luke a final time, hearing the thin wail of her voice, and began to run.

* * *

"Good God, Joey!" Allan Collier's voice came from a great distance as she fell into his arms. Medicinal smells assaulted her, filling her sensitive nostrils with their stink; she leaned heavily against the doctor as he pulled her in from the doorway. Her feet nearly gave out from under her, unable to accommodate the shift in balance from four legs to two. Collier was the only certainty in a world that spun and wheeled about her.

She was distantly aware of voices talking, exclaiming over her; she dropped into the chair Collier guided her to and tried to reorder her overloaded senses. Someone threw a blanket over her shivering body. The vinyl of the chair was icy cold under her bare rump; that, more than anything else, broke through. She blinked rapidly to clear her vision.

Collier was there, holding something hot and liquid up to her mouth. She sipped it, nearly choked at the taste, and managed to swallow; Collier made meaningless noises of approval and made her drink more. The heat of it stilled the helpless shivers. Blinking again, Joey felt the beginnings of focus and of returning sanity.

"Luke," she forced out at last. "Luke . . ." It was hard, nearly impossible to make the words come. She floundered desperately and flailed out with clumsy hands, pushing the blanket from her shoulders. With growing urgency she sought Collier's eyes as he moved around her to pull the blanket back up.

He stopped at last and crouched before her, taking her hands in his. They felt icy cold on her burning skin. "Tell me, Joey. As best you can." His voice was an anchor of calm reason.

"Luke," she gasped, the human words still thick and strange on her tongue. "Hurt. He's hurt."

"Where, Joey? Where has he been hurt?"

Bile rose in her throat as she forced her way around it. "Woods—his land. He can't move. Allan . . ."

For a moment his earnest blue eyes searched her face. She willed him to understand the urgency, to act, to run; he let go her hands and stood before she could scream at him in desperation. "Wait there, Joey, and rest. I'm going to go send the nurse in to look after you and go for help. If he can't move, I'll need someone to—"

"No!" Joey fought to keep hysteria from her voice. "No, no help. They shot him. He can't . . ." Somehow she made her tongue form the correct shape. "He's *wolf*."

Collier froze at the door, staring back at her. Understanding suffused his expression. "Good God," he murmured. There was a span of time in which Joey could see the thoughts moving behind his eyes, naked emotion as he reached the inevitable conclusion. "All right." He closed his eyes briefly and let out a deep breath. "Then it's up to you and me."

Relief washed over Joey. She hardly heard Collier as he spoke to someone outside the door, disappearing briefly to return with an armful of clothing. "Are you strong enough, Joey?" he said, searching her eyes. "Are you going to be able to help me find him and bring him back?"

Without answering, Joey stood up and cast the blanket from her shoulders. Collier looked away, his hand half-extended to help her as she caught her balance; she turned aside to tug on the borrowed clothing, embarrassment a meaningless burden for which she had no time. There was only one thing that mattered, one goal that carried her on shaking legs after Collier as he gathered up his equipment and led her out to the garage behind his office, firing off final instructions to his assistants and pursued by the puzzled questions of patients he had left in the waiting room.

Her inner vision was focused on Luke while Collier

pulled the Land Rover out into the thin, sluggish traffic of Main Street and headed out of town. *He* was alive; she knew that much, as she knew her heart would have stopped when his did. The dull ache of his pain throbbed along her nerves, and she welcomed it. It meant he was fighting. He was alive, and she drove the message home again and again, down the arteries of the new-made link in time to the beat of her blood, praying he would hear it. *Don't give up, Luke. I won't let you go.*

Chapter 19

Straightening up from his work, Allan Collier set aside the last of his instruments and stripped off his surgical gloves. Joey forced herself to rise, to leave Luke again where he lay on the folded blankets before the fire, and went to retrieve more hot water from the stove. Collier smiled up at her gratefully and wiped the instruments clean, sterilizing and packing them away carefully before blotting at his face with the cloth Joey provided.

"He'll be all right, Joey." The words descended like small miracles. Joey closed her eyes and spent several seconds walking on air. "You got me to him in time. His body was trying to heal itself, but he was too weak. He couldn't have made it without you." Joey felt his hand brush her cheek. "It took great courage to do what you did, Joey."

She opened her eyes slowly and stared at Luke, stitched up and bandaged, bullets extracted, his side rising and falling steadily. Her fingers stroked over the triangular space between his closed eyes. "I didn't want to do it, Allan," she whispered. "It was . . ." She closed her mouth on an inadequate description of something he could not hope to understand.

He smiled sadly, and his hand found hers. "Don't try to explain it, Joey. Luke tried once, and I'm afraid he wasn't very successful, either." His fingers squeezed gently. "But don't belittle what you did. You're a very brave young woman."

Freeing one hand to scrub at unshed tears, Joey managed a smile. "I don't feel very brave right now." She let the numbness of reaction settle over her. Soon enough the emptiness would fill with the new and terrible knowledge, harsher emotion rising to overwhelm relief and gratitude and joy. She wondered how she would be able to bear it.

"How did you learn about it, Joey?" Collier asked gently. "Did Luke explain—"

"What I was?" Joey finished, breaking free of the downward spiral of her thoughts. "Yes. He told me in Val Caché, or tried to. But I didn't remember that until much later."

"It must have come as quite a shock," Collier murmured sympathetically. He shook his head with a sigh. "I had guessed that Luke would never have acted— never have behaved as he did with you if there hadn't been some very solid reason behind it. Reason!" Barking a laugh, he met her startled gaze. "Reason isn't quite the word."

"No," Joey said softly. "Reason has nothing to do with it." There was a deep and awkward pause. "I didn't remember what he'd told me in Val Caché at first, but once Philippe came to visit and let it slip. At the time I didn't even question; it was as if I'd known it all along." The memory made her grimace. "I suppose I should be grateful for that. Luke didn't force me. He made it quite easy for me to accept it, and in the end, when I had no other choice, it simply happened."

"And was it so terrible, Joey?" Collier asked. There was such wistful sadness in his voice that she summoned up a smile, remembering why, for him, it was no idle question.

"Not terrible. Not that." Her vision darkened and blurred. "The terrible thing was waking up from a beautiful dream." Collier's eyes were locked on hers, intense with some unnamed emotion. "It was easy accepting what I was. It was easy living here with Luke, forgetting everything else. Too easy for me to guess anything was wrong." Slowly she closed her eyes against the black void that ached to swallow her. "Something happened to me after I changed, Allan," she whispered. "I learned more than how to be what he is. I woke up." She spaced the words deliberately, forcing them out. "When I knew he was safe and I'd done everything I could and the need was past, when I could think again, I realized—I found out—what he—what he . . ." The overpowering sense of loss engulfed her utterly; she dropped her head into her hands.

"Oh, Joey," Collier sighed. She heard him shift beside her. "I was afraid, when Luke told me you'd agreed to stay, when I spoke to you in Val Caché—I was afraid something wasn't right. Eventually, when it was too late, I guessed what it was."

Joey dragged her head up to look at him. His face was as grim as she had ever seen it. For the first time she noticed the deep hollows under his mild blue eyes. "You see, Joey, I've known Luke a very long time. I know what he fears, and what he's capable of. I tried to warn him. I didn't want to see either of you get hurt, but I failed to recognize what was coming."

Understanding came to Joey through a thick fog of confusion. "You know," she said in amazement.

"I know." A wry smile twisted his mobile mouth. "I know because it happened to me. And I should have seen it, been prepared for it." His eyes were suddenly very bright. "I should have known Luke was not rational in this—where you are concerned."

"What," Joey said slowly, "did he do to you?" She closed her eyes again, afraid to hear him confirm what she had realized in those terrible moments when her thoughts had cleared and she had known Luke was safe. When her awakened mind and Luke's weakness had broken the bonds of his will . . .

"He used his 'influence' on me. That's the phrase we coined for it, anyway." His voice was dry, almost pedantic. "He used to experiment with it as a boy, once he'd learned to change. When I found out about it, I tried to explain that it wasn't right—that his gifts should not be so misused. Eventually he found that out for himself, the hard way." Joey opened her eyes to see the lines of new pain etched into his weathered features. "I never really believed he'd used it on me. But then again, I never believed he'd find *you*, either."

"Influence." Joey mouthed the word almost silently, hardly hearing his final remark. "He made you forget?"

"It's nothing so simple as forgetting," Collier said heavily. "I don't know the limits of what he can do. I pray I never find out. But in my case, he simply didn't want me to reveal your whereabouts to anyone; as it happens, I didn't have any relatives to contact, but he knew I had doubts—about too many things. He arranged it so that any time I thought of you, my mind simply slid away from the thought, like oil on water. The image he put in my mind, when I thought of you, told me you where you should be, and if I managed to get beyond that image, I found myself believing that you'd been safely shipped off to the hospital and then back home. I never felt any need to speak to anyone about it." He blinked slowly. "Maggie asked me about you, once or twice. Each time I gave her some glib excuse without even realizing it."

Swallowing hard, Joey managed to keep her voice

remarkably even. "Yes. I think I understand." She drew in a deep breath and deliberately turned her back on Luke's sleeping form. "He must have found it pretty easy to do the same thing to me. I didn't even know it was possible. He walked right into my mind and took over."

Collier gazed at her until she felt compelled to meet his eyes. "I'm so sorry, Joey. I wish I'd had the sense to warn you when I first realized—when it became clear how irrational Luke was—but I didn't feel it was my right. . . ."

"You didn't know, Allan. Neither one of us was a match for him, were we?" The bitterness of her own words almost penetrated the depths of her despair. "He made me . . . not care about anything but the two of us in our own perfect little world. The past, the future—none of it seemed important." Tears spilled over. "I thought I was happy. I thought it was *real*. I believed . . ."

She reached blindly for Collier's hand, and he took hers between his palms. His kindly face was a mask of reflected pain. "It's not that simple, Joey. I wish I knew how to explain." Joey watched him search for words, his eyes dropping to Luke's still form with unutterable sadness. "There are many things even I don't know about Luke, and what he is. Even among his own people he's different. But I know"—his voice took on greater urgency as he looked back at her—"I *do* know he wouldn't hurt you, Joey, even in this."

"Even," she demanded hoarsely, "after what he did to you? Invaded your mind, took away your will?"

With a deep, shuddering breath, Collier nodded. "Even so. There is something you must understand, Joey. Whatever Luke did—whatever he felt driven to do—he couldn't steal your spirit or your intelligence. He couldn't give you what you didn't have within you. He couldn't force you to care, or to risk your sanity, perhaps even your life, to save his."

"Then how do I know what was real and what he did to me?" she cried, giving way to despair. "How can I possibly find the line between what I am and what he made me become?" The agony spilled over, and she let herself be pulled into Collier's embrace.

He was silent for a long moment. "There is only one answer to that question, Joey. Look within your heart." He barked a quiet laugh against her ear. "I know it's a terrible old cliché, but it's the only solution I've found when the world comes down around your ears." He pushed her away from him gently, tilting her chin up with his hand. "You have the strength, Joey, to discover your heart's truth. Take the time to find it. Give yourself that chance." Turning away before she could gather an answer, he busied himself with his bag, and his final words were little more than a whisper. "Give *him* that chance."

Joey stared blankly at his back. A chance. She turned her head and reached out to rest her palm on Luke's side, concentrating on the varied textures of his fur as it slid through her fingers; he stirred in his sleep and whimpered, a soft, sad sound dredged up from a troubling dream. Perhaps he had already guessed. She stroked him absently and wished, against all logic, that she might have gone on dreaming.

"Are you going to be all right, Joey?" Collier knelt beside her with a soft groan. "I don't like the idea of leaving you here alone."

She smiled weary reassurance. "I have the rifle, and Luke taught me how to run things around here. There's plenty of food, everything I need."

Collier touched her hand. "Do you want to come back with me?"

"I can't." It was becoming easier to speak as if nothing at all were wrong. "I can't leave him here alone." Her hand clenched in Luke's fur.

"Yes," the doctor acknowledged with a sigh. "I

greatly fear that Luke won't be up to changing back for several days—not until his body has had a chance to deal with his injuries. It might look a little strange for me to bring a wolf back to the office." He lifted one gray brow, and Joey felt herself returning his gentle grin.

Turning her hand to clasp his, Joey shook her head. "I suppose it's going to be difficult enough trying to explain a half-hysterical naked woman showing up on your doorstep in broad daylight." Heat rose to her face. "I wonder how many of them recognized me?"

"Don't give it any thought, Joey," Collier said gently, rising to his feet. Joey stood with him, still grasping his hand. "I hustled you into the office right away, and you'll find that I am exceptionally good at plausible explanations." He coughed dryly. "I've had a great deal of practice. And, incidentally"—his mouth straightened into a grim line—"I'll see that a report gets made to the authorities about trespassers and illegal hunting. It may not do any good, but my word is still worth something. When Luke's recovered, he may want to take stronger action."

Joey shook her head at the image of the kind of action Luke would most likely wish to take. It gave her a kind of grim satisfaction. Collier caught her look and flashed a wry, understanding smile.

As he turned for the door, Joey let go of his hand and hugged him hard, kissing his cheek. " Thanks," she whispered. "I owe you so much. . . ."

"No talk of owing, Joey," he said, pulling away to touch her chin. His eyes grew serious. "If you want to repay me, there is only one thing I ask of you. When the time comes to . . . decide . . . about your future, about what you are and what you want to be, follow this." He laid his hand over his heart. "Too much of *this*"—his finger lifted to his temple—"is not necessarily the way to understanding. Sometimes the true path to happiness doesn't follow the course of logic."

Joey dropped her eyes. "Sometimes it hurts too much," she whispered. "But I'll try."

"That's all I ask." He bent down to kiss her forehead and left her in the doorway where she watched him bring his truck to reluctant, sputtering life. He stopped once to wave, and Joey felt her throat tighten.

"Allan," she called hoarsely, "tell Maggie—tell her. . . ."

"I will," he called back over the rumble of the engine. "Take care, Joey."

The Land Rover's door snapped shut. Without quite seeing, Joey watched the vehicle bounce through the clearing and disappear among the trees. The utter loneliness welled up, flooding her soul and spilling from her eyes. She leaned her forehead against the doorframe and trembled there. "It hurts," she said softly. "God, how it hurts."

# Chapter 20

Just as Collier had predicted, Luke spent the next several days in wolf form, his body slowly mending, while Joey went mechanically through the motions of keeping the cabin warm, cooking meals, caring for Luke in a state of bleak and crushing emptiness. Luke was there and not there: the first day he slept through, twitching in the throes of dreams; the second he raised his head and spoke to her with his eyes, a mute question she did not know how to answer.

On the third day he staggered out into the snow and returned, limping, to lie panting before the fire, gazing and gazing at her until she turned away in despair. She did not want to look too deeply, fearing the things she might see: her own terrible vulnerability, the ignorant helplessness he had exploited.

In the cold, lonely days she went over it a hundred times in her mind—what she would say to him, how she would hurt him as he had hurt her. Used her. When he looked at her with his wolf's eyes, she wanted to scream out her rage and loss and sense of betrayal and beat him down with it, knowing he would be helpless to respond, helpless to act. . . .

But in the nights, she dreamed. She dreamed of Luke's touch and his slow-waking smile, the way his caresses made her burn. In the dreams it was always right at first, as it had been after Val Caché; a never-ending, glorious present without the burden of past and future. And then the dreams would change, and she would see his eyes and remember the moment when he had taken her mind as he had taken her body. *You won't leave me, Joey.* His voice grated, harsh and inhuman, over and over. His eyes dragged her down and ripped her away from the moorings of all she had known, all she had thought was real. Stole her away from herself, so that all she had left to hold on to was Luke.

"Luke!" She flailed out with her hands to push him away, and they slapped against flesh, solid contact that woke her from the dream with a start. He was warm, hard, human under her skin as she opened her eyes. The length of him was stretched out beside her on the sofa where she had slept each night, and he was most certainly no dream. Relief clouded her vision as she breathed him in and felt him with every inch of her body.

"Joelle," he said softly. She felt his hand come up to stroke her cheek and closed her eyes tightly against the gentle invasion of his gaze. "It was only a dream, Joey."

A shudder racked her, his gentle words a catalyst that shattered the brief and fragile moment of happiness. "Yes. Only a dream." She pushed against him, but he held her tightly, pulling her up as he shifted, stirring her hair with his warm breath.

"Joelle," he said again, caressing her name. "You feel so good." His hands laced through her hair, and he rubbed the strands of it against his face. "I thought I'd lost you."

Joey's heart lurched. "Lost me?" she said in a distant, tiny voice. Did he understand, truly, what he had done and what she had finally realized? . . .

"I thought I was dead," he murmured into her hair. "I would have been." He pulled his face away and caught hers between his hands, making her look up at him. "My brave Joey. You saved my life." Words seemed to fail him; Joey forced herself to meet his eyes and saw the suspicious brightness there. "Your courage astounds me."

She tried to shake her head, but he held her in his big hands and stroked the contours of her face with his fingers as if seeing it, feeling it, for the first time. His hard face was relaxed and vulnerable and alive, baring his need to her. Impossible to hate, impossible not to love. She tried to stop the trembling that betrayed her, weakened her resolve; the conflict started the useless tears yet again, and he bent down to catch them on his tongue.

It was too much. The wave broke over her and engulfed her utterly, and she lifted her mouth to his and took his kiss as hungrily as he offered it. "You're alive," she whispered against his hard, demanding lips.

The simple statement seemed to release all the tears at once. She was sobbing even as he kissed her mouth, her chin, her cheeks, her neck; he crushed her to him as if he would pull her inside himself. "You saved me, Joey," he breathed. "*You* saved me."

Emotion sparked between them, an electric current that shattered the icy walls about Joey's heart. She felt Luke—she *felt* him, felt *with* him, knew his joy and his overwhelming need for her. There were suddenly no barriers at all, their bodies nothing but husks to be cast aside. This was what she had known before when she had felt his pain; now it was blinding joy and wholeness so bright that it lit all the dark places of despair.

Joey leaned into Luke and drew in a deep breath as

they came down to earth again. The brightness faded, but it left its pattern behind her eyelids as if she had stared into the sun. The bond between them was still there. Inevitable, inexplicable, undeniable. She tucked her head under his chin and rested her hands on his chest as she traced the path of it in the matched rhythm of their heartbeats.

After a moment Luke set her back and caught her hands, kissing them one by one, such undisguised wonder in his face that Joey nearly lost herself in his eyes. She blinked fast and hard.

"Are you real, Joey?" Luke whispered, cupping her cheek in his hand. "Do you actually exist?" He accepted her evasion when she turned her face aside and pressed it into his shoulder. His arms closed around her again.

*Discover your heart's truth,* Collier had said. She closed her eyes so tightly that they flashed red sparks.

There was a silence then, so deep and profound that Joey followed it down, beyond the physical boundaries delineated by Luke's embrace, past the slow vibration of the emotional bond that tried to block her passage, deeper still into the very core of what she was.

Emptiness. It sucked at her, and she struggled to hold herself free of it. The core of her being was a black void. Above was the promise of light, Luke's strong hand reaching down to grasp hers and pull her up into brightness. Blinding brightness that was just as deadly, reducing her into a mere shade, a weak reflection of the man from which it came. Either direction was loss, terrible loss—the familiar aching loneliness of the void or loss of herself.

Luke had filled that void. He had not asked her if she wanted the brightness; he had simply filled her mind and soul with it so that no darkness remained. And in the absence of darkness, there was no contrast. No meaning. No truth. No self.

She only knew how hard her body was shaking

when Luke shifted her in his embrace and held her away. She stared into his eyes from behind dark shutters even his will would not penetrate. "Joey?" he questioned, his fingers tightening on her arms.

With deliberate care Joey pushed back the light that pulsed between them. She felt the bond constrict into a fragile cord, and Luke jerked; the muscles in his bare chest seemed to ripple under the tanned skin. The pupils of his pale eyes constricted with shock. It was as if she had struck him; she felt the blow rebound against her, just as she had felt his pain and joy. She rejected it and pushed again. The void came up to swallow her; the tiny, deadly kernel of ice that had formed in her heart when she had changed—when she had discovered his betrayal—grew hard with resolve.

She forced herself not to see the dazed and naked bewilderment on his face. "It's wrong, Luke," she said. Some small part of herself was stunned by the brittle coldness in her voice. Her arms slipped free of his nerveless fingers. "It's too late."

From a great distance she watched his expression change. Not quite grasping, not yet.

"Don't you understand, Luke? I know what you did." The locus of emptiness shifted within her; for the first time she gathered her anger, her fear, her outrage into a single hard knot and forced it outward, along the path of the fragile cord that linked them. There was a sudden, blazing shock when it struck him, and Joey reeled with the backlash.

He cried out, a harsh, astonished grunt of pain. His eyes were glazed with it as she stared into them.

"You think everything is fine, everything is completely under your control," she said softly. The broken waves of her distress slapped her and again, bringing tears to her eyes like physical blows. "You're wrong, Luke. When I changed—when I saved your life—I broke through. I broke your influence. I learned what you'd done to me."

Comprehension pierced the blank shock of Luke's gaze. "No," he gasped. Denial, and the first stirrings of reaction.

"Yes." Coldness began to melt in the heat of anger. Blazing, all-consuming rage. Fury that had banked its fire in loneliness and fear, fed by loss upon loss. "It must have been easy for you, when I didn't know what was coming. Easy and convenient—to make me forget everything but you." A voice not her own grated out a harsh, alien sound. "You made one small mistake, Luke. You underestimated me. You helped me break free by teaching me what I was."

The rage had a life of its own, and Joey could no more control it than she could slow her racing heart and the fierce need to make him realize his error. It overwhelmed her vision until all she could see were sparking embers in blackness. It blinded her to the sudden change in Luke, the moment when his astonishment gave way to cold resolve.

"Stop, Joey." The voice seemed as far away as her own, utterly emotionless. Joey tossed her head and ignored it.

"You lied to me. Violated me. Is that the only way you know how to form relationships, Luke? By taking over someone's mind? Not only mine but Allan's—yes, I know what you did to him, too, Luke. How you made him believe everything was all right . . ."

"Stop *now*, Joey." There was a sudden flash of pain, her own, as iron bands tightened on her upper arms.

"You wanted to suck me into yourself and make me lose everything I am. You're a coward, a damned, selfish . . ."

The wordless roar blotted out her words and blew them back, hard, shocking her into silence. She came back to herself as if she had been hit by a balled fist.

Luke was poised above her, his expression so savage that she retreated before it, the invulnerability of rage abandoning her all at once.

She teetered for an endless moment between ice and fire, between fear and defiance. There was still a tiny shred of sanity left in the maelstrom her mind had become, and she clung to it in desperation. Pain was another anchor; Luke's fingers bruised her arms with unleashed strength.

Then his eyes gripped hers. She knew when he tried to breach her defenses, and she found the strength to fight. She met his assault and repelled it, forced him back step by hard-won step, until she reached the place where she faced him on equal ground. Trembling there, she held the line between them until her body shook with exhaustion.

"No, Luke," she whispered, too weak to summon up any emotion at all. "It's too late for that."

His hands fell away. Inches apart, they regarded each other from opposite edges of a yawning chasm. A cold wind swirled up to scatter the ashes of Joey's heart.

In the absence of light or darkness, Joey stepped back from the verge. She had found a desolation beyond the void where nothing could touch her. Nothing.

"Why?" she said at last, meeting his alien eyes. "Why didn't you trust me?"

Slowly the harsh lines of his face altered, all the feral fury leeched away. She saw the hollows of exhaustion under his eyes; the bitter dregs of longing rose to choke her.

"Trust?" He curled his lip in a harsh smile. His glance raked her from behind a rampart of stony indifference, and he dropped back and away from her, rising to his feet. Firelight bathed his bare skin. Joey huddled deeply into the sofa and closed her eyes against him.

"My mother trusted my father," she heard him say, very softly. "She died because of it. Because he left her."

The words hung, heavy with bitterness, in the space that stretched between them.

"And you—you were afraid," Joey whispered, staring into the darkness behind her eyelids. "You couldn't risk giving me the right to choose."

"And what would you have chosen, Joey?" he asked. She heard the murmur of his footfalls as he paced before the fire.

She swallowed heavily. She had asked herself that question a hundred times, fearing the answer. "It was my choice to make. *My choice.*" The ashes of previous anger stirred. "You had no right. . . ."

"No right." He gave a harsh growl that might have been a laugh. "Do you remember when I tried to warn you, Joey? I knew what was happening between us. Once we bonded, there was no choice. No choice at all."

Forcing her eyes open, Joey felt the first lick of newborn flame. "Then this bond of yours wasn't enough, was it, Luke?"

She looked up until she found his eyes. "You couldn't trust me to stay with you of my own free will. You didn't really believe there was enough between us. The only way to keep me was to take my will away, even my memories. . . ." Something caught in her throat; she set her jaw and stared at him, clenching her fists until nails cut palms.

Luke met her eyes with such steady defiance that it took all her determination to meet it. His face was bleak in the shadows. "I didn't take your will, Joey," he said, utterly without inflection.

"What name do you give it then, this 'influence' of yours?" she flung at him. The flame of anger burned the words like kindling and rose higher.

He was cold, ice meeting her fire. "I didn't take your will," he repeated, eyes glittering. "I only made you forget your fears, and . . ."

"Forget?" She tossed her hair so that it whipped her face. "Forget everything but you. What's the difference, Luke?"

Their gazes locked. His pupils had expanded, leaving a narrow green-gold rim. "There was no compulsion," he said, too quietly. "I don't have that power." Suddenly he moved, advancing on her so quickly that she pressed back into the sofa and braced herself for attack. It didn't come.

"What you felt, Joey," he breathed, crouching before her, "was real."

"How do you know what I felt, Luke?" she said, trembling at his nearness. "Or could you read my mind as well as control it?"

For the first time she saw the icy calm of his expression flicker. His hands reached out and hovered inches from her arms where they clasped her knees. "I know you were happy, Joey." He challenged her with his eyes. "Can you deny that?"

Joey drew breath and choked on the denial she wanted to fling at him. Her vision blurred with the struggle between anger and honesty. She wanted to reject him, reject his quiet, cutting, deadly certainty. . . .

"The happiness you felt—*we* felt—was real," he whispered; his fingers brushed her wrists and left a trail of heat in their wake. There was nowhere left for Joey to retreat.

She threw up a wall of words. "And the dreams— did you give me those, too?" The memory of them made her treacherous body tremble. "Did you violate me that way so that I would come to your bed like those other women?"

He froze, all of his muscles going taut. The shock wave of his reaction reached her through the half-severed bond. "No," he said, his voice stunned. "No, I gave you no dreams."

His eyes flickered away at some inner vision. When

they came back to her, they were very bright. "I, too, had those dreams, Joey," he said slowly. "From the first time I met you." His fingers tightened on her wrists. "Those dreams came from within us, out of what we are."

Joey tried to drag her arms out of his grasp, to cover her ears and blot him out, but he held her too tightly. "Not by my choice," she cried. With every ounce of courage and anger she possessed, she held fast against him. "I wasn't allowed to choose—not any of this! I didn't want it. *I didn't want it!*"

The fragile cord that connected them knotted with pain that made her gasp. His hands slid up her shoulders. "It's because of what we are that it happened, Joey. The bond between us was forged in our blood—in your blood. It's not a matter of wanting. It's something far more powerful—"

"Are you saying," she said with sudden, bitter calm, "that it's all some sort of animal instinct, some kind of mating urge? Nothing more than that?"

He jerked back as if he had been struck. "No. More than that, Joey, much more than that. . . ."

"Then what is it?" she whispered hoarsely. "What is it, Luke?" Suddenly there were tears, and she tried to pull free again to scrub them from her face. She saw him through a haze of moisture, remembering how vulnerable she had made herself when she had believed all of it was real. She had told him the one thing she had been afraid to say ever since her parents had been torn from her life, given a part of herself she had never dared give to anyone. And none of it had been real.

She fought down the tears and forced them back and back until she had control again. Luke's hands dropped away from her shoulders; his eyes were strange with emotion that came to her in a knotted tangle of pain and longing.

"You're afraid," he said very slowly, as if at a revelation. "You're afraid because I made you feel too much."

His words sliced deep into her soul. He twisted the knife. "How long have you been afraid to feel anything, Joey?" he murmured, the heat of his body burning as he leaned closer. "Are you afraid to take the risk?"

Joey felt the shuddering start at the dark empty core of her being and radiate outward until her extremities vibrated with it. "You have no right," she whispered, "to talk to me of risk and fear. *You* have no right."

The cord stretched between them trembled, one fragile link in the void. "Joey," he groaned, and before she could prepare herself or think to resist him, he engulfed her in his arms, dragging her against him, pulling her from the sofa in one smooth and undeniable motion.

It was impossible to fight. Joey drew hard breaths into his shoulder as his hand cupped the back of her head and held it there. Her hands were trapped between them; she felt such utter helplessness that she knew herself on the edge of defeat. She knew she was on the verge of losing herself again, losing herself in him, and that one terrible fear prevented the final surrender he demanded.

She stiffened in his arms. "I have to go, Luke," she whispered.

His body went as rigid as hers, and she pulled free of him in the instant when the shock he felt slapped back at her through the constricted bond.

"No."

Drawing herself to her feet, she met his stare. He rose slowly to face her, his eyes bleakly fierce with threat.

"I won't let you go."

In that instant, when she knew words were no longer enough, she felt the uncertainty recede and something else gather to take its place, rising to the challenge in his eyes. Something dark and primitive, beyond the reach of human logic. Suddenly she understood what it was, grasped it, drew all the latent power together, shaped it into a weapon.

She struck before he was ready. He staggered under the force of it, white with shock; he almost swayed, almost grabbed her for support. Tasting the bitterness of her victory, Joey stepped back from his touch.

"You can't stop me," she said hoarsely. "I'm your match, Luke. You made me your match in every way."

Luke heard the challenge; she saw the acknowledgment in his eyes, felt his response through the roiling turmoil of emotions that persisted in the bond. Anger flared up to deflect her attack. Anger and pride beat against her will and drove it back until it was she who recoiled. Luke's hands shot out to catch her arms in a painful grip.

"Not quite, Joey," he growled. His eyes held hers mercilessly, no humanity in them at all. She fought him, hard, twisting to dislodge his mental and physical hold. Felt him slip, scrabble for control.

"Don't test me," he begged between clenched teeth. His body was poised on the edge of violence. He shook her with each word. *"I will not let you go."*

There was a sudden silence broken only by the twin rasps of their breathing. Deadlock. Neither one looked aside; neither one retreated. Pain and anger swirled and blazed between them.

"You can't watch me forever, Luke," Joey said softly, coldly. "You can't keep me prisoner." Somehow she freed herself from his grasp; Luke gripped empty air with fingers curled into claws. The very air vibrated with his tension and her own bitter resolve.

Joey gazed at him from behind a mask of remote and terrible calm. She felt as though her muscles were forever locked in ice, like the frozen world beyond the cabin walls. Cold. In frigid silence she held him back, perceiving the heat of his assault slide away where it could find no purchase. When she raged he could breach her defenses, but against this he was defenseless. Helpless.

She pushed deliberately into his weakness. "If I were to go now, out the door, what would you do to stop me?" The words were flat and almost indifferent. "Would we keep doing this until we both collapse with exhaustion or kill each other?"

Luke blinked, breaking the stare. Her victory. His wordless denial sparked like an electric current, briefly piercing her armor of ice. The thought of killing her, harming her, losing control, profoundly shocked him. The possibility of it made him tremble. For an instant Joey almost lost her grasp on the power that let her fight. His face—his face was nakedly vulnerable, so filled with yearning and desperation that she felt herself begin to shake in sympathy. And she felt what he felt: his rage, his fear, his need.

"You can't leave in the dead of winter." It was a last desperate argument; there was a flare of hope in Luke's eyes, and Joey fought to keep from closing hers. "It's too dangerous, too . . ."

"Have you forgotten, Luke?" she murmured with infinite sadness. "I'm like you."

And before she could weaken, before her will could falter and send her into his arms, before he made her forget everything once more, she turned her newfound power on him again and made him understand.

# Chapter 21

She was gone.

Luke came back to consciousness, awakening slowly to that terrible knowledge, feeling it to the core of his being even when bones and muscles were useless things beyond his control, when the world still trembled on the verge of oblivion.

*She had left him.* Her final words echoed in memory. Like him. She was like him.

Somehow he staggered from the sofa, lurched to his feet. His vision cleared, blurred again with the red haze behind his eyes. *She had left him.*

How much time had passed? How long had he lain here, insensible, after she had defeated him? His time sense was distorted, for it felt as if she had been gone for a lifetime. Luke felt a dull amazement that the twisted knot of his heart continued to beat.

The bond—the bond between them was there, almost vanished, strangled to a thin trickle of emotion that told him she was alive. No more.

He had faced total defeat only once in his life; nothing within his unawakened power had allowed him to save his mother when he had cried over her in Val Caché. She had gone beyond his reach forever. And now Joey—Joey had done the same, abandoning him to a slow fading death, half of his soul ripped away.

Everything had come crashing down, all the rightness that had been between them, the close and private world they had created, the happiness she refused to accept as real. She regarded it all as a delusion he had forced upon her.

And she had found the surest revenge. The curse that had killed his mother repeated itself, tragically and inevitably.

Luke wandered blindly across the room, vaguely aware of the late-afternoon sunlight streaming through the cabin window. The floor was icy under his bare feet. Her assault had left his mind dulled, the brilliant predator's edge worn down by despair. And yet, somewhere deep within himself, he found pride in her newfound strength, the way she had faced him, stood up to him. Defeated him. They were mated truly. Her stubborn pride and her fear of feeling—of losing herself and all the careful barriers she had built in a lifetime of loneliness—blinded her to that soul-deep understanding.

But that *he* understood it meant nothing. She had left him.

He moved about the cabin as his strength returned, touching every place she had touched. Her scent lingered, but it was many hours old, and the fires had been carefully extinguished.

An urgency came over him then, some half-forgotten instinct of self-preservation that sparked dormant anger. His muscles contracted, adrenaline charging his body like an electric current.

*No.* The denial came from the deepest part of him—

self, refusing acceptance, unable to endure defeat. A growl rumbled in his chest, nothing human in the sound.

It was not rationality that drove him as he flung himself into the kitchen and beyond into the bedroom; the drawers hung open, empty of her things. He found the chemise and held it to his face, drawing in the smell of her, letting the silk slide from his hands to the floor.

There was no note, no message. But the sculpture he had given her, its wooden head flung back in a mournful howl, lay on the bare dresser where she had left it for him to find.

The desperate anger returned, filling the void she had made in his heart, surging outward in a rush of primitive power. He felt his body shift; muscles knotted and screamed protest; through a savage haze he could see her eyes, steady, piercing, aching with echoed pain.

Her eyes guided him as he changed, hurling himself from the cabin at a dead run. He saw nothing, heard nothing, his mind shut off from all sensation; he knew where she was, where she had to be. There was still a chance to stop her. There was still some hope of living.

"It's all arranged."

Maggie sat down at the edge of the couch, studying Joey with anxious eyes. "There's a friend of mine who's heading out for East Fork first thing tomorrow morning. He'll be glad to take you along."

Staring at the shifting, meaningless images on the TV screen, Joey forced her eyes to turn, her head to nod in response. "I don't know how to thank you, Maggie. I only wish I could explain. . . ."

"Don't try. Not now." Maggie squeezed her shoulder. "You know we care about you, Joey, Allan and I. When he told me where you were, what had happened—I hoped, we both hoped, that it would work out for you."

For a long moment Joey was silent, searching for

words that had become no more than empty symbols. She remembered little of her flight from the cabin that morning; she had not changed, had been unable to surrender what remained of her humanity after she had left him. But she remembered her feet cracking the snow, icy winds unable to touch her, feeling a new strength in her body she had never known before, her dual nature granting the immunity to cold and weariness that Luke had always possessed.

She remembered the look on Maggie's face when she had turned up at the redhead's cottage: no shock, no real surprise. Only the same solicitous friendship, trying to make things right when the world had come crashing down.

And Luke—she could never forget Luke's face. She thought the pain of it would tear her apart.

Slowly Joey pushed the pain from her heart. It was done. There could be no going back.

"Allan," she said at last, clumsy with fatigue and grief. "Please tell Allan how much I—how grateful I am for all he's done. I'll write him when I can."

"Are you sure you don't want me to call him now? I know he'd come right over. . . ."

"No!" Joey clamped down on a surge of panic. "No, Maggie, please—I have reasons that I need to leave quietly, without any fuss. I hope you understand."

Maggie nodded sympathetically, but Joey ached at the deception. Impossible to tell Maggie that she didn't want Allan connected with her going. She could not risk driving a wedge between Luke and the man who had been his surrogate father. And his friend. Luke would need his friends, however much he denied the need for anyone.

Gentle fingers tightened on Joey's arm. "We wanted you to be happy."

Sudden moisture blurred the edges of Joey's vision.

"I was happy," she whispered, feeling the icy numbness settle into place. "For a while I *was* happy."

It was dark when he reached Lovell, and he loped into town oblivious of the risk. At the edge of an outlying street a woman saw him and froze, wide-eyed and smelling of fear; Luke dodged aside and melted into the shadows, clinging to them until he slid to a halt at the door to Collier's office.

The door was unlocked, and Luke's blow sent it crashing open, rebounding against the wall with a ringing crack. He bounded through the darkened waiting room and beyond into the short corridor. Collier was there as Luke had known he would be, quietly reading, no guilt in his face when he looked up to find Luke in the doorway to the study, shaking with exhaustion and rage.

"Where is she?" The words came thick and alien. Luke leaned into the wall and struggled to control the spasms that racked his overtaxed muscles. Collier closed the book that lay open in his lap; he leaned forward in the upholstered chair and met Luke's eyes. There was no fear in his gaze, nothing but a calm sadness that twisted in Luke's gut.

"Luke," he said softly, bending his long fingers over the ends of the armrests.

"Where is she, Allan?" Luke managed past the fist that seemed lodged in his throat. "Where is Joey?"

Collier's hands tightened, clenching into the soft leather of the chair until it dimpled under his fingers. "She hasn't been here, Luke," he murmured. "I haven't seen her."

Luke took a single menacing step away from the wall, his muscles bunching and shifting with the suppressed need to change. The beast was very close to the surface, far too close. "You're lying, Allan," he said. "You know where she is."

"I've never lied to you, Luke," Collier said. He stood up slowly, his gaze never dropping, and took a slow and careful step forward. His voice and movements were those of a man confronted by a dangerous and unpredictable animal, and Luke stood very still and trembled with the conflicts that seemed bent on tearing him apart.

"She left me," Luke admitted harshly, the words searing like acid. "You must know where she is. Tell me, Allan. Don't make me . . ." He shut his eyes, unable to voice the threat. The whisper of another careful footfall brushed the carpet under his feet.

"I know you won't hurt me, Luke," Collier said. Luke opened his eyes to find his old friend closer, too close, too old and fragile and earnest with his eyes full of trust and sympathy. "You won't do something that could destroy both of us, and her." Another step and his gentle doctor's hand was inches away from Luke's rigid arm, from his fingers curved into claws that could down Collier with a single casual blow.

"Where is she?" Luke rasped, pleading for release. "Please. Don't do this." His nerves and muscles spasmed again as Collier's cool palm closed over his fingers, bending the claw into a fist. There was no choice but to endure it in utter stillness or risk the destruction of all that he was. All that he loved.

"Luke." There was a terrible sadness in the word. "I was afraid—I was afraid this might happen. I prayed that it wouldn't."

From some fragile place of sanity deep within him Luke felt a bitter humor rising. "Don't lecture me now, Allan." He drew in a deep, shuddering breath and let it out again. "Don't . . . push . . . me."

The pressure of Collier's hand on his was steady. "No lectures, Luke. You're stronger than you believe, strong enough to know what is right. You always have been."

"No." The denial came without shame, numb certainty overwhelming the desperate fury. "You're wrong, Allan. My mother . . ."

"I loved your mother," Collier sighed. Luke felt him tremble. "But you are stronger." With a soft groan Luke tried to wrench his fist from Collier's grasp and failed. "Love can't be forced, Luke. Don't hurt her—and yourself—by trying to take what must be given."

With infinite care Luke took one step back, and then another, drawing Collier with him until they stood in the doorway. Night air drifted down the corridor, promising release. "I can't let her go," he whispered. "I can't."

"Give her time, Luke." He heard Collier's voice from some distant place, a world he was no longer a part of. "She came here to lay her past to rest, but you never gave her the chance to find her own future. Give her time to be true to herself."

There were no more words, no answer to give; the ability to speak had been taken from him as he stood shivering with the finality of his loss. It settled into his bones, paralyzing him, pulling him into an eternal darkness. And as he turned to give himself to the void, the dying thread of the bond burst into sudden and vibrant life.

*Joey.* He felt her as if she stood beside him, as if her blood coursed through his veins and her heart beat in time to his own. Collier had no chance to protest or question. Within a second Luke had flung himself out into the corridor and beyond, the night clothing his naked body in darkness. There was no time to think, no time to will the change. He followed the pull of the bond to where it led.

He found her bathed in moonlight, standing on the verge where the forest met the edge of town. Silver beams caught in the hair that cascaded over her shoulders; her head was flung back, an unvoiced cry shivering along the column of her neck.

She turned, as if sensing him, surely feeling him as he felt her, and he froze in place, Collier's words burned into his mind.

*Let her go.*

Her face was achingly beautiful, limned in the unearthly light, eyes catching the reflection of distant stars. The other half of his soul. His body screamed to move, go to her, take her back—but he stood behind a stand of trees and only watched her, drank in the sight of her, knowing it might be all he would have.

With a whisper of footfalls she began to move toward him, silent and graceful as a she-wolf. Luke trembled and felt the bond quiver with the wordless sound of his name. An abyss opened up at his feet, and he stepped aside; the beast within demanded victory, and he denied it. He rediscovered within himself something he had thought lost and vanished forever.

*Let her go.*

He melted back into the shadows before her eyes found him. As the moon rose over the forest, he ran, letting the bond unravel and disperse like mountain mist.

Survival. The wolves who ran beside him understood, and he took their strength and pulled it within himself. He would survive; he would learn to live with the loss and pain and sorrow. He would survive—and she would be free.

He clung one final, fragile moment to the feel of her and then let her go.

"Are you going to be all right?"

Maggie's eyes were very bright, her voice not quite steady; she held Joey's hand as if she would never let go.

The truck idled at the curb, shattering the dawn stillness. Morning should have been a time for beginnings, Joey thought sadly. This one brought only good-byes.

"Yes. I'll be fine." She managed a smile and brushed at her cheeks. "Thanks, Maggie. For everything."

"You're welcome." The redhead released her hand reluctantly. "Take care of yourself, kid." Maggie stepped back, her lower lip trembling, and as she turned away she collided with the lanky frame of Allan Collier.

"Maggie," he said softly, setting her back. His kind blue eyes sought Joey's over the mass of red curls.

"Joey. I'd heard you were leaving. I wanted to be sure to say good-bye."

There was no reproach in his voice, only a distant sorrow. Joey dropped her eyes. "I'm sorry I—didn't tell you. I didn't want . . ." Suddenly she met his gaze. "Is Luke—does he—"

With a quiet sigh he shook his head. "He isn't here, Joey." For a moment it seemed as if he would say more; Joey braced herself for questions that didn't come. When she searched his eyes, she saw understanding there—understanding that required no words or explanations. He stepped up to take her hand in his firm, warm clasp.

"Allan," Joey said softly. "What can I say—how can I thank you . . . ?"

"You can thank me by being happy, Joey." His smile was almost sad. "By being true to yourself." He reached up to cup her chin. "You're strong, Joey. Stronger than you know. Never be less than what you are."

Joey looked away, letting the tears fall unchecked. "I'll never forget you, Allan."

"Or I you, Joey." He began to move back, and she grabbed at him, pulling him into a fierce hug. His cheek was rough against her mouth as she kissed it. For a moment he held her just as tightly.

"Please," she whispered into his collar. "Don't leave him alone."

His hold loosened slowly, and he set her back to catch a single tear on the tip of his finger. "I won't, Joey," he said, so softly the words were little more than a sigh. "I love him, too."

"Are you ready to go, miss?" The rough, deep voice of the truck driver cut between them, severing the emotion before it could tear her apart. Collier's hands shifted as he helped her up the step, steadying her as she settled into the truck's patched seat.

"Good-bye, Joey," Collier said, his voice almost lost in the roar of the engine. "Take care." He smiled at her one last time and closed the door, stepping back from the truck. Joey rolled down the window and leaned against it, as if she could somehow memorize their faces, carry the clean mountain air in her lungs all the way home, take it all with her into lonely exile. She thrust her hand out as the truck pulled away, and Collier's fingers brushed hers; then he was receding, and Maggie's bright head was a splash of color just visible through a veil of tears.

She stared back until they left Main Street, rounding the gentle curve that led to the highway. The trees closed in on either side, and the twin cliffs that guarded Lovell from the rest of the world rose up against the brilliant morning sky. Joey leaned back in her seat and shut her eyes. He had not been there, but she felt him; even now she felt him watching her, and it wrenched at her soul like physical pain.

Her heart had become a dull, leaden weight in her chest when she heard the cry. She knew what it was before she turned, twisting her shoulders to look at the cliffs vanishing in the distance. It was just possible to see the silhouette balanced at the edge of the sheer drop: The wolf poised there for a moment of aching silence, flung back its head, and howled.

The lament of his cry twisted in her heart long after they had left Lovell far behind.

# Chapter 22

Joey stared at the blueprint rolled out on her desk, watching the neat lines and angles blur and shift. Spring sunlight shafted in the huge office window, patterned between the blinds like the bars of a prison.

She spread her hands to smooth the paper as if that might somehow resolve it into something that made sense; there was no reason, no logical reason that her eyes should refuse to see it for what it was, that her hands should move independently of her will to create fanciful embellishments that had no place in a world of strict function. Logic. Practicality . . .

"The client isn't happy with the design, Joey," Mr. Robinson said behind her, clearing his throat. She started, looking up without seeing, staring at a bland beige wall marked with a precise geometric pattern. "They want something much simpler, more . . . practical. Frankly, I don't understand why this wasn't clear to you before."

Joey's eyes fell to her fists where they clenched on

the tabletop. Paper crackled under her weight. It was wrong, all wrong. Everything.

"We hired you based on your excellent reputation for clean, functional designs," Robinson droned on at her back. "That's what the client wanted, and I don't understand why you're having such trouble coming up with it. This is an apartment building, not a cathedral."

Joey knew she should turn, face Robinson, defend herself. But there was no defense. He was right. The need to define the world with lines and angles, to close it into neat little boxes—slowly, inevitably, that need had drained away. For three months she had struggled to bring it back and be what she had been before. She had tried with all her strength to control the overwhelming desire to break free of those neat, tight little boxes and escape into chaos. The best she had managed was this: designs that satisfied no one. They were not hers, not any longer.

Now Robinson's voice pushed and pushed at the fragile calm she had somehow managed to maintain. Her fists clenched tighter, and her pulse began to beat in her ears. "You're going to have to resubmit, and you're going to have to do it fast. The client expects this design by the beginning of next week. Are you listening to me, Ms. Randall?"

Three months. It seemed like three years. Three months of trying to pick up the pieces of her life, searching for peace. Peace that should have been hers now that her parents had been laid to rest at last. Peace that wouldn't come. There was a gaping wound in her soul, a raw place that wouldn't heal. Where the bond had been was a sucking emptiness that seemed to take more of her every day, swallowing her, destroying even the bleak accommodation she had made with this life of lines and angles and walls and deceptive certainty.

There was no certainty. She had learned that at last. The needs could be denied and ignored, but they were there. When she suppressed them, they came out on paper to sabotage her best efforts to conform: ridiculous arches like the sweep of tree branches, patterns and color of rough bark and wolf's fur, great open spaces that echoed a brilliant mountain sky. All wrong. All part of another world.

And she had never said good-bye. . . .

"Ms. Randall." Robinson tapped her shoulder, not gently. "I didn't want it to come to this; frankly, you have a great deal of talent. But you're still on probation, and if you can't bring this up to snuff by Monday, I'm afraid we'll have to . . . reconsider your employment with the company."

Paper bunched under Joey's fingers. She could feel the hair rising along the nape of her neck; Robinson's hand dropped away the instant before she lost her rigid control. The words were on her lips, the inevitable words that would end it, when there was a firm knock at the office door.

"I'm sorry to disturb you, sir, Ms. Randall—but a package just arrived for you"—she nodded at Joey—"by Special Delivery. I need your signature on this." Robinson's secretary sniffed disapprovingly as Joey snatched the clipboard and scrawled her name. A moment later she accepted the small, neat package, hardly noticing when the secretary disappeared.

Robinson growled something under his breath. Joey ignored him, turning the package in her hands. No return address. A plain brown wrapper, something vaguely familiar about it . . . Inexplicably her heart lurched as she tore at the wrapping and tossed it on her desk, then pulled open the lid of the cardboard box.

The wooden wolf gazed up at her, its head flung back in a silent howl. For a moment she had to brace herself against the desk as the ground pitched and rolled under her feet. With shaking fingers she lifted the sculpture from its nest, cupping it in her hands and feeling the rough texture of it, smelling the forest from which it had come.

Her body began to tremble. She looked up and stared at the door, unable to move. The bars of the prison gave way. The void in her soul was suddenly filling, a flood of warmth and emotion washing through all the empty places he had left.

Perhaps—perhaps it was not too late. Not too late for endings. Or beginnings.

All at once it was as clear as mountain air. She turned to Mr. Robinson, whose mouth hung open on the first word of yet another lecture.

"You're right, Mr. Robinson," she said with a radiant smile. "I'm not good at practical little boxes any more. I quit."

The day was beautiful, as she had known it would be. All the world was brilliant with new life. Spring came late to the mountains; winter lingered long here and gave way grudgingly to the sun for a few brief months.

Joey drew in deep breaths of clean air, her feet guiding her effortlessly among the trees. She might never have been gone at all. The harmony she felt with this wild land, all she had learned of it and herself, brought a strange, abiding peace. In time—in time she might become as much a part of it as he was.

She walked along the edge of the lake and turned away to follow the course of one of the many streams swollen with snowmelt; the music of flowing water was everywhere, creeks and brooks and rivulets cutting eager new paths down from the mountainsides. She came to a halt at the edge of a small clear space among the trees, where the bond had led her.

They were gathered about the low slope of a hillside, five or six adult wolves sprawled on a bed of earth and old needles. And there were the pups; Joey felt a deep, spreading warmth at the sight of them where they tumbled and played just beyond the mouth of the den. A big dark gray she-wolf watched over them, her pricked ears attuned to every tiny growl and squeak.

He was among them, as she had known he would be.

Perhaps it was because of his preoccupation with the pups at his feet that he didn't sense her; she knew he had cut off the connection between them, even though she had felt the lingering touch of it in the long three months they had been apart. Or perhaps it was simply that she had learned, like a creature of the wilderness, how not to be seen or heard.

She watched in silence as he crouched among the pups who plunged at him with youthful, oblivious abandon. They were still small and clumsy, new to their world; blunt muzzles, round heads, and tiny flap ears bobbed and flashed at Luke's feet. He let them chew on his fingers and attack his knees, lost in a place where things were simple.

It was one of the wolves who sensed her first. The great head of the she-wolf lifted; she growled softly in warning.

Drowning in pups, he looked up. Joey saw him stiffen, then raise his head as if to scent the soft spring breeze. And then he turned his head, slowly, so slowly, as if he were afraid of what he would see.

"Luke," she whispered.

For an instant they were utterly still. The bond sputtered like a candle, flared and dimmed. Joey coaxed it to brighter flame, knowing it was Luke who feared to let it wake.

His eyes were fixed on hers, brilliant and unreadable. Joey drank in the sight of him, though she had never forgotten for an instant; she felt her heart begin to pound and watched the hard, closed planes of his face slowly alter.

"Joey."

Only one word, yet it held all the things she saw at last in his eyes: fear, yearning, need. Hope. And something else she didn't dare say, even to herself.

But he waited, waited while the wolves watched her like a jury prepared to pronounce their verdict. Twelve sets of eyes judged her solemnly. And she was the one to break the tableau, starting into the clearing on unsteady feet. The bond flickered hesitantly.

Luke rose to meet her, sloughing puppies with gentle hands. He took a step forward, and all at once the she-wolf surged to her feet and stood before him, stiff-legged, tail high. A low growl of warning vibrated in her throat.

It was enough to stop Joey halfway across the clearing, halfway to Luke, though her gaze never left his. The she-wolf growled again, more ominously; a slow, unexpected anger, anger that was almost pride, urged Joey to take another step.

"Look into her eyes," Luke said softly. "She knows you. Don't let her dominate you."

Joey forced herself to look away from his eyes to meet the she-wolf's lambent stare. Inexplicable feelings rose in Joey, instincts that made her bristle and brought an answering growl to the back of her throat. She let the instincts take over. She spoke to the wolf deep in her mind, without words.

Yellow eyes blinked, assessed, and, after an interminable moment, looked away. The she-wolf lowered her ears, turned her back, and drifted away to the far side of the clearing.

And then there was nothing between her and Luke, nothing at all.

She moved forward, one step and then another, until she was picking her way among round little bodies and felt the warmth of fur brushing against her legs. Her eyes flooded with inexplicable happiness as the pups growled ferociously and tumbled about her feet. They were warm and soft, dark fur like down, all savage innocence; they accepted her wholly.

"They're beautiful," Joey whispered.

"Yes," Luke agreed, though his eyes were only for her. "Yes."

A thousand emotions trembled between them, filling Joey's senses to overflowing. Words came from somewhere, from some other Joey who had the ability to speak.

"I've come back, Luke," she said. "I've come back to where I belong."

For an eternity he said nothing, only gazed at her with his heart in his eyes. "Joey," he said at last, as if he, too, had forgotten the use of human language.

She attempted to say what he could not. "I tried to stay away," she murmured. "Tried to convince myself that everything that happened here . . ." She shook her head. "It wasn't any good. I belong here. To this world."

Still he was silent, unmoving, unwilling to close that final distance between them. When she despaired of making him understand, he spoke very quietly. "With me, Joey?"

She smiled slowly, unable to answer and not needing to. The bond was opening, breaking free of its careful boundaries like a river in spring flood. Luke reached out across that last fragile distance and touched her. For a moment it was nothing more than the lightest brush of his fingers, and then he was pulling her into his arms, pressing his face into her hair. His voice was almost lost in it.

"Joelle," he breathed. "Joelle."

They might have been alone in the world, tasting, sensing, knowing nothing but each other. Joey felt his warm breath and heard the rapid beat of his heart under her cheek.

"I was afraid, Luke. Even after we found my parents,

I was afraid—of living, feeling again." Joey struggled to find explanations, but Luke already understood. The bond resonated with his acceptance.

"I was afraid too, Joelle. Afraid of living without you."

She tried to shake her head, but she felt herself pressing deeper, sinking against him as if she could become part of him. His big hands spread across her back.

"I was wrong, Joey. I hurt you because I was afraid." He pushed her back gently, lacing his fingers through her hair. "I thought I couldn't live without you, and I was wrong about that, too."

She looked away from his eyes, sudden fear stopping the question she so desperately needed to ask. Perhaps she had been wrong after all. She stiffened, trying to pull away, but he held her fast with gentle dominance.

"I *can* live without you, Joelle," he said with infinite tenderness. "But I don't want to."

The world seemed to lose focus as she felt his hands cup her face, drawing her up to look at him; his eyes were very bright. "I need you, Joey."

"Need isn't enough," she whispered, calling herself a fool, holding that last fragile barrier in place.

"I know." He sighed, and his hands trembled on her cheek. "It doesn't have to be." His eyes looked deep into hers. "I love you, Joelle."

In a sudden, vivid burst of light and heat the last barrier shattered, and the bond expanded to fill every last shadowed corner of her being, healing all wounds and erasing the scars in one brilliant instant. Before the fire could consume her, Luke's mouth found hers and drew the blaze into himself, until the incandescence faded and he was once again muscle and bone and firm flesh pressed against her.

"Luke," she said. "I love you." It was all that would come, and it was enough. His joy was hers, reverberating and rebounding between them until it filled her heart to overflowing.

When the world stopped spinning, she drew back from him reluctantly. Somewhere birds were singing, water flowed down from the mountains, wolf cubs tumbled at their feet, steady and changeless. It was she who had changed, whole at last within herself. Only one thing remained.

Luke drew her from the clearing, holding her tightly against him as he made his farewells to the wolves one by one. Even when his eyes turned away she felt him, and knew he felt her to the depths of his being. And as they drifted into the forest, hand in hand, Joey thought of that time when she had come to the mountains, so many months ago.

She stopped at the verge of open land that stretched before his cabin, breaking the peaceful quiet between them at last. The look of utter joy on his face made her catch her breath.

"Luke," she said softly, folding his big hands in hers, "There is one thing—I'd like to go back to the mountain, see my parents again."

Searching her eyes, he saw deep into her soul; a flood of memories blended with her love for him until there was no separation.

"They would have loved you, Luke," she whispered. "Maybe it's a little crazy, but I want to tell them everything that's happened. I know they'll give us their blessing. Will you come?"

She heard his silent answer as his mouth found hers.

Flowers caressed Joey's cheek and tangled in her silver-gold hair. Luke brushed them away and inhaled her warm scent, mingled with the rich earth and the last late-summer blossoms. He stretched out alongside her, resting his hand on her hip. He had never seen anything so beautiful.

She looked up at him through her dark lashes, a lazy smile of utter contentment curving her lips. It was too much of a temptation; he leaned over to kiss them, and she held him off with a laugh, her hands against his chest. Even so small a touch made his body quiver in response.

"I thought you said winter and early spring were the . . . dangerous times," she teased, holding him at bay. "You could have fooled me."

"Too much for you?" he asked with a grin. Before she could reply he shifted suddenly, dislodging her and carrying her up and over to sprawl across his chest. She gave a choked, half-protesting giggle and buried her face in his neck. Her lips were soft and deliciously warm. Luke closed his eyes and ran his hand from the strong curve of her back to the swell of her buttocks.

"I admit it," he sighed. "I can't control myself where you're concerned. I warned you to let me know if it ever got to be . . ."

"Overwhelming?" Joey moved her hips on his and lifted herself above him. Her hair drifted across his face. "I doubt anything you do could overwhelm me now."

Luke opened one eye and frowned up at her sternly. "Is that a challenge?" he growled. "I thought we'd gone beyond games of dominance, Joey."

Brushing her mouth across his jaw, she smiled. "Only because I know who's in charge." She bit the tip of his chin to emphasize her point, and he made a sound of mock anger and pulled her down, trapping her in his arms.

Her soft gasp became another kind of sound as she went slack, running her tongue along the rim of his ear. The heat of her breath made his heart pound and his blood rush to interesting places. He groaned softly, and Joey shifted her hips again in a tantalizing motion. "You don't make a very comfortable cushion," she complained into the hollow of his neck. "Much too lumpy."

He caught the flash of her grin before he caught her legs in his and tumbled her over so that she lay beneath him. He kept his weight on his arms and pushed her thighs apart with his knees. "But you make a very comfortable cushion, Joey," he purred, bending down to take one firm nipple in his mouth. She arched against him with a gasp. "So comfortable that it's very hard to leave." He caressed her other breast with his fingers and felt the bond throb with mutual desire.

"It is hard," she remarked, her moist female heat pressing against his arousal. "Hard enough, I think, to . . ."

It was entirely too much for Luke. He entered her in one smooth motion and felt her response, her legs coming up to pull him deeper. The bond flared into incandescence, linking their souls as their bodies were joined.

"I love you, Joelle," he murmured as he kissed her trembling eyelids. "That's why you'll always win."

When it was over, the fever of passion cooling in the late-afternoon breeze, Luke stroked back her damp hair and watched her face. No shadows darkened her gold-flecked brown eyes; no unanswered questions. The gold was brighter now, and he could drown in the swirling embers. He gathered her against him instead, holding her as tightly as he dared, listening to the sound of their heartbeats.

"This is where it started," she murmured, looping her arms over his. "I didn't know enough then to be afraid of the Big Bad Wolf."

Luke pressed his face into her hair. He could not control the sudden surge of pain through the bond, regret and fear that were still not entirely forgotten. Joey twisted in his arms with a sharp gasp. "Luke—I'm sorry. Bad joke." With the determined strength that always surprised him, she broke his hold and turned to face him, gripping his shoulders. When he met her eyes, she caught his face in her hands. "Listen to me, Luke. I love you." The words were a brilliant burst of joy that flooded the bond like a miracle. He grabbed her fiercely and kissed her until they both came up gasping.

"Don't ever leave me, Joelle," he whispered, tasting the tears on her cheeks.

"Never." They held each other as the sun began to lower, touching the mountains with a brilliant edge of gold. Joey shivered once, and Luke set her back to search her eyes.

"Are you cold?" He raised his head to scent the air. "It's late. We should be going back home." For an instant he closed his eyes. *Home.* For once in his life he understood what it meant.

Joey's touch made him open his eyes again. "Ordinarily, I'd like to stay here all night," she said softly. There was an odd little smile on her face. "After all, the night is our time." Luke grabbed her hand and kissed the palm. "But I'm going to be a little more cautious from now on. I'll even have to force myself to be practical."

There was an odd little lurch in the connection between them, and Luke held himself very still. His breath caught in his throat. "Joey!" he snapped. "What's wrong? You're not sick, or—"

Her laugh cut him short. "Oh, no. Nothing like that, Luke." Suddenly she was leaning against him, flinging her arms around his neck. "But it does look as if all your hard work and enthusiasm have paid off at last."

"Joey . . ."

She pulled away and took his hand in hers. "There are some kinds of blindness even a nice mental bond won't cure." With a firm motion she placed his hand on her belly. "Can't you feel it?"

Luke listened. And then he did feel it, as if the ground had opened up under his feet. He stared at Joey in astonishment until she laughed and kissed the astonishment away.

A lone howl rose up into the twilight, first one cry and then another, until there was a chorus of joy that filled all the world.

# About the Author

Susan Krinard graduated from the California College of Arts and Crafts with a BfA, and worked as an artist and free-lance illustrator before turning to writing. An admirer of both Romance and Fantasy, Susan enjoys combining these elements in her books. She also loves to get out into nature as frequently as possible. A native Californian, Susan lives in the San Francisco Bay Area with her French-Canadian husband, Serge, two dogs and a cat.

In Susan Krinard's next love story, coming in January 1995, the hero is a special kind of vampire. Instead of hungering for blood, Nicholas Gale feeds off dreams. His unsuspecting victims find their most secret fantasies played out in their nightly dreams. But with Diana Ransom, a San Francisco sleep disorder psychiatrist who is beautiful and all too mortal, Nicholas discovers that he is not immune to that human affliction called falling in love. . . .

What follows is an excerpt from this mesmerizing new romance.

Nicholas came back to Mama Soma's the night he returned to San Francisco.

He'd made the decision on the long flight back from New York; if Keely didn't turn up tonight, he'd break his usual rules and visit her at her apartment. Six weeks should be long enough; he'd waited a full two weeks after her opening before returning to San Francisco.

In all the time he'd known her, he'd always confined their friendship to neutral ground, here at Mama Soma's or similar places. That was his usual safeguard against dangerous intimacy—with those who benefited from his anonymous patronage as Keely had, and with those with whom he risked freindship.

His dreamers, those from whom he fed, never knew him at all except in dreams.

Nicholas paused on the steps that led down into the basement, standing on the threshold between cool, fresh night air and the smoke and heat of Mama Soma's.

The fanciful part of himself—the part he had almost suppressed, along with uncontrolled need and emotion—sometimes imagined that this descent was like a mortal's plunge into the subconscious at the onset of dreaming. Or perhaps, given the atmosphere of the place, a downfall into the netherworld that some said awaited humans after death.

Death and dreams were both beyond him. Nicholas shrugged off his useless fantasies and moved down the narrow stairs.

His usual table was empty this evening, the one set farthest back in the shadows, away from the small stage and the bar. He settled on the patched vinyl seat with a strange sense of homecoming and looked around the room. For once there was no blare of music to drown out the voices of the regulars. Nicholas listened idly to a poet at a nearby table reciting for a rapt audience of friends. Something very profound, no doubt. Love, or death.

His eyes wandered to the bar where Barb was serving beer and espresso, noting that sh'd shaved her head since the last time he'd been here. She was leaning over the scratched countertop, locked in conversation with another young woman. Someone Nicholas didn't remember seeing before. Someone who . . .

Nicholas froze. There was nothing outwardly remarkable about the woman; she dressed more conservatively than most of Mama Soma's regulars, but that was a minor distinction. Her short brown hair was neatly styled, her body slim and petite under the tailored trousers and blazer.

Nothing remakable at all, until he looked with his inner senses, those that enabled him to hunt what he must have to survive.

In the dim light her aura was almost blinding. For a moment he saw nothing of her except a silhouette, ringed by bands of brilliant color. His heart labored in his chest. Unexpected pain and longing gripped him, and he struggled to push it away.

He hadn't sensed an aura like that in over a century. The colors pulsed about the woman, violets and reds and golds, banded by white and blue. Barb literally paled by comparison, her own aura subdued and ordinary. Even Keely was nothing to this one.

Nicholas forced his eyes away from the woman and stared at his clenched fists. He could never forget the last time he had seen an aura so powerful, so desperately compelling.

Sarah.

His first instinct was to get up and walk away. If he stayed—deliberately Nicholas dulled his inner senses, until he could see only the surfaces that mortals perceived with their limited sight. He dared to look up then, just as Barb pointed in his direction and the woman turned around.

Too late. He knew then it was too late to rise and walk away. Clear blue eyes fixed on him unerringly, with the conviction of recognition. As if she knew. As if she were Sarah reborn.

He composed himself as she walked toward him, dispassionately noting her determined walk and the way her fists clenched at her sides. His gaze rose to her face. Not like Sarah's, not at all. This woman had a fierce set to her jaw that belied the delicacy of her oval face. Full lips were taut with emotion, and dark brows were drawn down over those direct, fearless eyes.

"You're Nicholas Gale?"

He hardly heard her. It was all he could do, in that moment when she drew so close, to lower his racing heartbeat and control the surge of hunger that overwhelmed him. He no longer needed to see her aura; he felt it, could touch the pulse of her life force without trying.

She leaned over the table, bracing her hands flat on the scarred surface. Nicholas stared at the soft hollow of her throat where her silk blouse openied in a vee, mesmerized by the pulse that fluttered under her translucent skin.

The sound she made was blunt and effective. Nicholas snapped his gaze back to hers. Her eyes flashed defiance, but her skin was very pale under the light makeup. Her lips parted slightly, and he could hear the soft sigh of her breath.

She was afraid. He knew nothing about this woman, but he knew she was afraid, and her fear vibrated through him as if it were his own.

"Nicholas Gale," she repeated, the barest hint of a tremor in her voice. "Is that your name?"

Nicholas felt his inner balance slip back into place as the old disciplines took hold of his body. The tension drained out of him; he leaned back in his chair and stretched his feet out under the table. He let his eyes rake over her, drawing on his nearly perfect memory to find some record of her face.

"Should I know you?" he countered softly.

The woman jerked, almost as if she hadn't expected him to answer. The frown deepened between her brows. Without a word she dropped into the opposite chair.

"I'll get right to the point," she said. Her voice was low and well-modulated; musical, Nicholas thought dispassionately, if it hadn't been for the way she tried to strip it of emotion.

"I'm looking for Keely Ames."

He sat up a little straighter in his chair, and for the first time Diana saw a flicker of emotion cross that impassively handsome face. She breathed in very deeply and released the breath as silently as she could. After a week of searching, she'd finally found the man she was looking for. She'd regonized him in an instant.

"Keely?" he echoed. He blinked, the first time she had noticed him do so; deep gold lashes swept down over eyes the color of dark jade. They had looked paler in the gallery, and his hair, in this dim light, was a more prosaic blond. But his remarkable, aristocratic good looks were rather overwhelming at this proximity.

Oh, yes, he was quite beautiful. Not so beautiful as to have lost his masculine edge; he had that in plenty, radiating outward from his seemingly relaxed body. A dancer's body, she thought, remembering the way he had moved with Keely on his arm. Lithe but strong, in a way his casual denim and leather couldn't conceal. The kind of man who would attract attention and expect it as his due.

She let herself meet his eyes, looking for the challenge she had seen in the gallery. Surely that had been her imagination; there was no mockery in his gaze now. In fact, the abandon with which he'd conducted himself in Keely's company was entirely absent.

The twitchy unease she'd felt when she'd seen him here in the coffeehouse was fading, leaving more confusing emotions in its wake. She could tell herself a million times that her interest in this man was limited to his connection to Keely, but somehow the explanation seemed dishonest. She remembered the way she had felt in the gallery, transported for an instant to an alternate reality where she was the woman in his arms, laughing and wild. . . .

Her eyes fell unwillingly to his lips. Strong, mobile lips, last seen kissing Keely with unbridled passion. Was it any wonder Keely had fallen . . .

Diana snapped herself out of her treacherous thoughts. She leaned forward, clasping her hands on the table top.

"Where is she?" she asked, schooling her voice to calm.

The man's eyes narrowed as he settled back into his seat. A fine network of tiny creases radiated outward from the corners of his eyes, and Diana wondered how old he was. Thirty? Surely not much older. Her own age.

"I don't know," he answered. His voice was deep and even and laced with vibrations like the purr of some great tawny cat. His simplest words held a note of refinement, the barest trace of an accent Diana couldn't place. He looked away, gestured to someone over Diana's shoulder. "Would you care for a cup of espresso, Miss . . . ?"

"Dr. Ransom," she supplied, watching him carefully.

He lifted one straight, golden brow. "The name sounds familiar." He paused with maddening nonchalance to order two cups of espresso from the leather-clad waitress and slowly turned his attention back to Diana. "Are you a friend of Keely's, Dr. Ransom?"

Diana struggled with the hostility and anger that suddenly threatened to overwhelm her necessary detachment. *Detachment?* a small voice mocked her. *You never had that where Keely was concerned.*

She forced her mouth into a cool smile. "Yes, Mr. Gale. I am Keely's friend. And right now I'm very concerned about her. I'd very much like to speak with her."

A trace of bemusement—feigned or otherwise—crossed Nicholas Gale's face. "I'd like to speak with her myself, Dr. Ransom. I haven't seen her in over a month."

The waitress appeared with the espressos, and Nicholas looked up with a smile that warmed his sculpted features like sunlight striking marble. He exchanged a soft word with the woman, and there was still a trace of the smile on his lips when he turned to Diana again.

"If you have come here looking for Keely, Dr. Ransom," he said, pushing one of the espressos toward her, "I can't tell you anything. I've been out of town for several weeks." He took a sip of his drink and glanced inquiringly at Diana. "I don't believe we've met before, though Keely may have mentioned your name. . . ." He shook his head, and a wave of golden hair tumbled over his forehead. "Is there a particular reason why you came to me?"

Reaching for her espresso, Diana concentrated on the slow and steady movement of her hand. What kind of game was he playing? Their eyes had met at the gallery a week ago, and it wasn't an overabundance of ego that made her believe he wouldn't have forgotten her so quickly. He claimed that he hadn't seen Keely in a month. . . .

"Mr. Gale," she said, feeling her control slip away. "Let me refresh your memory. I was at Keely's opening at Newbold's two weeks ago Sunday night. I saw you with her there, and I've been trying to locate her ever since. You weren't easy to find either, Mr. Gale. No one seemed to know your name or who you were. I came to this place because Keely mentioned it once or twice, and I—"

He did no more than lift his hand, but that single gesture stopped her words as if he had shouted. "I'm afraid you must have me confused with someone else, Dr. Ransom. I was in New York during Keely's opening."

She knew she was staring at him, dumbfounded at his barefaced lie. Confused with someone else? Not in a million years. And if she wasn't able to trust her own eyes and memory . . .

She wanted to lean forward over the table and stare him down, take him by his leather lapels and shake him. Irrational, irrational. Just like the feeling she'd had when she'd seen him take Keely in his arms and kiss her with passionate abandon.

"That's very interesting, Mr. Gale," she said at last. "Quite a number of people seem to remember seeing you with Keely recently."

Gale looked at her through half-lowered lids. "Not more recently than six weeks ago," he said. Diana thought she detected the trace of an edge to his voice. Abruptly he sat up again. Energy seemed to course through him, an almost visible thing. "Why are you looking for Keely, Dr. Ransom? Has something happened to her?"

Diana stood up so suddenly that she almost knocked over her chair. "If anyone knows, it's you, Mr. Gale. I don't know why you're playing this game, but I only want to talk to her. Or are you so insecure in your relationship that you have to keep her to yourself?"

She knew she had gone overboard, and she almost didn't care. The past weeks of growing worry and upwelling memory had done their work. All her attempts at objectivity were going right down the tubes, and the old emotions were coming back like furious, hungry ghosts.

Gale looked up at her. His face was expressionless, but she knew she had struck a nerve. "Ransom," he muttered. He looked away for a moment, and then back again. His green eyes were hard as crystal. "Diana Ransom. Keely has a relative—"

"Yes, Keely is my cousin. I've been looking for her ever since that day in the gallery, when she seemed to drop off the face fo the earth—"

*Easy, Diana,* she told herself. *Antagonism will get you nowhere.* Just because the same thing had happened to Clare before Adam had abandoned her, just before she'd taken her own life . . .

It wasn't difficult to pretend earnestness as she leaned over the table, using her position above him to reinforce her authority. She stared into Gale's eyes, searching for signs of recognition or guilt. "I only want to talk to her. She hasn't been living in her apartment, and I need to know where she is. Family business." She breathed in slowly. "I know your relationship with her is between the two of you, but I see no reason why you've had to hide her away from her family and friends—"

"I didn't, Dr. Ransom." He was on his feet before she realized it, his face inches from her own. She caught her breath, leaning more heavily on the table, unable to look away from his eyes.

"I didn't," he repeated quietly. "Keely and I are friends, but not in the way you're implying. I left town several weeks ago because she wanted our relationship to change."

His gaze held hers for another long moment and then snapped away. As if at a silent command, the shaven-headed barkeep wandered over to the table, looking curiously from Nicholas to Diana.

"You rang?" she said to Nicholas, flicking one of several earrings with a black-painted fingernail.

Nicholas sat down slowly, ignoring Diana. "Barb, when was the last time you saw me in Mama Soma's?"

The young woman rolled her eyes thoughtfully. "A few ago, I guess."

"And have you seen me anywhere else recently?"

"Well, as I told this lady here, once or twice as I was going home I saw you on the street with Keely. Haven't seen her here in a while, either."

Diana watched Gale's face. He was frowning now, a look of open puzzlement. "Are you certain it was me you saw her with, Barb?"

The woman wrinkled her nose and ran a hand over the smooth dome of her skull. "I don't know too many people who look like you, Nick," she said with a grin, "But it was kinda dark. . . ." she shrugged. "If it wasn't you, it had to be your twin." Someone called out behind her, and she winked at Nicholas. "Gotta run."

Nicholas muttered something and stared blankly at Diana. It was as if he looked right through her.

Diana gritted her teeth. She'd always considered herself a reasonably good judge of people—a very handy trait in her profession—but Nicholas Gale was an enigma. His bemusement seemed genuine. What possible reason could he have to deny his relationship with Keely, construct such an act to refute it, unless—

She had no chance to follow the wisp of thought. Nicholas leaned forward, and she found herself meeting his gaze, held fast by crystal-green eyes.

"Did Keely ever mention the name of the man she was seeing?"

His voice was low and even, but his words held all the intensity of a roar. She shook her head. "No. That was why it was so hard to find you, Mr. Gale. No one at the gallery had been introduced to you either—"

"Because it wasn't me," he said. "I've already told you, Dr. Ransom. I wasn't here."

Cold, sourceless fear raced up Diana's spine. She fought it with anger. "*Do* you have a twin, then, Mr. Gale?" she snapped.

Her words echoed in Nicholas's ears, rebounding and gaining power with each mocking repetition, carrying him away. *A twin, a twin, a twin . . .*

The woman faded from his sight as he withdrew into memory. Back to another time and place.

He had stopeed counting the years long ago, accepting the burden of guilt he would always carry. But he could never forget the day he had last seen that fallen angel's face.

*Adrian.*

Nicholas let the name settle into his mind. He hadn't spoken it, even inwardly, in all the time since he had condemned Adrian to eternal damnation.

It was the hell to which Nicholas had sent his treacherous brother. A hell with no hope of redemption. Adrian could not have returned from his terrible exile.

"*I don't know too many people who look like you, Nick.*"

Impossible. Nicholas felt a chill in his heart that worked it way through his body, draining his strength like a long fast. His instincts responded, bringing him back to himself and to the source of warmth and life so close at hand.

For a moment the woman across the table was no more than a jumble of colors and heat and flaring life force. Nicholas struggled to focus on her face, on her stubborn, intelligent eyes.

He said the first thing that came into his head. "Do you have a first name, Dr. Ransom?"

She blinked at him, caught off guard and resentful of it. "I don't see what that has to do with Keely or where she is, Mr. Gale. That's all I'm interested in at the moment. If you—"

"Then we're back to where we started, Dr. Ransom. As it happens, I share your concern for Keely." He lost his train of thought for a moment, looking at the woman with her brittle control and overwhelming aura. He could almost hear the singing of her life force in the three feet of space between them.

He nearly reached out to touch her. Just to see what she would feel like, if that psychic energy would flow into him with so simple a joining. It had happened like that with Sarah sometimes.

He stopped his hand halfway across the table and clenched it carefully. She had never seen him move. "Since you seem to require proof that I'm not hiding Keely in a closet somewhere, I'll give it to you." Withdrawing his hand, he reached into his inner jacket pocket. He set the card on the table between them.

She stared down at it. "Proof?" she echoed.

"This is the name of the friend I was staying with in New York over the past several weeks. He can vouch for me and direct you to others I did business with during that time."

The delicate skin of her neck shivered as she swallowed. Abruptly she snapped up the card and tucked it into the breast pocket of her blazer.

"What *is* your business, Mr. Gale?" she asked. The

antagonism in her voice had grown muted, and there was a flicker of uncertainty in her eyes.

"Whatever I can find," he said honestly. He smiled, and for a moment he let loose a tiny part of his hunter's power. "Keely would say I'm an artist, and I dabble in it. I don't have her skill. But my business and your first name don't have anything to do with Keely, do they?"

She stared at him and lifted a small hand to run her fingers through her short brown hair, effectively disordering the careful styling. That simple act affected Nicholas with unexpected power. He felt his groin tighten, a physical response he had learned to control and ignore long ago.

*When was the last time?* he asked himself. The last time he had lain with a woman, joined with her physically, taken some part of what he needed in the act of love?

Before he could blunt the thought his imagination slipped its bonds, conjuring up an image of the woman before him, her aura ablaze, naked and willing and fully conscious beneath him. Knowing what he was, giving and receiving without fear, as Sarah might have done before Adrian destroyed her. . . .

"Diana."

"What?" Reality ripped through Nicholas, dispelling the erotic, impossible vision.

"My first name is Diana," she murmured.

Her face was flushed, as if she had seen the lust in his eyes. She was an attractive woman. Mortal men would pursue her, even blind to her aura as they must be. Did she look at him and observe only another predictable male response to be dissected with an analyst's detachment?

His hungers were not so simple. He would have given the world to make them so.

"Diana," he repeated softly. "Huntress, and goddess of the moon."

She wet her lips. "It's getting late, Mr. Gale—"

"My first name is Nicholas."

"Nicholas," she echoed, as if by rote. "I'll be making a few more inquiries about Keely. If you were serious about being concerned for her—"

"I was."

Diana twisted around in her chair and lifted a small, neat purse. "Here," she said, slipping a card from a silver case. "This is where you can reach me if you should hear from her."

Nicholas took the card and examined the utilitarian printing. *Diana Ransom, Ph.D. Licensed Psychologist. Individual psychotherapy. Treatment of depression, anxiety, phobias and related sleep disorders.*

Sleep disorders. Nicholas almost smiled at the irony of it. He looked up at her. "If you need to talk to me again, I'm here most nights. Or you can leave a message with Barb or one of the regulars. They'll make sure it gets to me."

"Then you don't plan to leave town in the next few days?" she asked with a touch of her former hostility.

His gaze was stead. "No, Diana. I'll make a few inquiries of my own."

They stared at each other. *Diana.* Was she a child of the night, as her name implied? Did she dream vivid dreams that he could enter as he could never enter her body? Or was she part of the sane and solid world of daylight, oblivious to the untapped power that sang in her aura like a beacon in darkness?

She was the first to look away. Hitching the strap of her purse higher on her shoulder, she rose. "Then I'll be going." She hestitated, slanting a look back at him with narrowed blue eyes. "Perhaps we'll see each other again . . . Nicholas."

He watched her walk away.